OFF SCRIPT

OFF SCRIPT

Graham Hurley

SEVERN
HOUSE

First world edition published 2020
in Great Britain and the USA by
SEVERN HOUSE PUBLISHERS LTD of
Eardley House, 4 Uxbridge Street, London W8 7SY.
Trade paperback edition first published
in Great Britain and the USA 2021 by
Severn House, an imprint of Canongate Books Ltd,
14 High Street, Edinburgh EH1 1TE.

British Library Cataloguing in Publication Data
A CIP catalogue record for this title is available from the British Library.

ISBN-13: 978-0-7278-8979-9 (cased)
ISBN-13: 978-1-78029-688-3 (trade paper)
ISBN-13: 978-1-4483-0413-4 (e-book)

This is a work of fiction. Names, characters, places and incidents are
either the product of the author's imagination or are used fictitiously.
Except where actual historical events and characters are being described
for the storyline of this novel, all situations in this publication are
fictitious and any resemblance to actual persons, living or dead,
business establishments, events or locales is purely coincidental.

All Severn House titles are printed on acid-free paper.

Severn House Publishers support the Forest Stewardship Council™ [FSC™],
the leading international forest certification organisation.
All our titles that are printed on FSC certified paper carry the FSC logo.

Typeset by Palimpsest Book Production Ltd.,
Falkirk, Stirlingshire, Scotland.
Printed and bound in Great Britain by
TJ Books Limited, Padstow, Cornwall.

To Anneke and Phil
With love

Who scorns his own life is Lord of yours
—Seneca

ONE

This morning happens to be the moment when a bunch of scientists give us pictures of a black hole in space. I'm still in bed, gazing at my iPad, trying to make sense of the statistics. Fifty *million* light years away from Earth? A huge galactic plug hole, blacker than black, denser than dense, a cosmic beast ever hungry for yet more matter? Can any of this be true? Has the Event Horizon Telescope found the feral beast that will eat us all? Will the Royal Borough of Kensington and Chelsea be sending round an advice pamphlet?

Pavel, I think. He has a brain, a mindset, an imagination tailor-made for this new hooligan on the cosmic block. He'll know precisely why the image on my iPad is a tribute to Albert Einstein, how it sheds yet more light on the scary warping of something called space-time. The latter is the subject of one of the longer paragraphs in this morning's *Guardian* report and, even after the third reading, I'm none the wiser.

My eye keeps returning to the image of that black disc with its orange penumbra. Pavel is blind. How do I do this sinister presence full justice? How do I describe the latest reason for worrying ourselves to death? A curl of yellow brightens the orange. Half-close your eyes, I'll tell Pavel, and you might be looking at a brand-new emoticon. Think dense. Think black. Be *very* alarmed.

My phone rings moments later. This has to be Pavel checking in to tell me he's still alive. We still talk every morning and often during the day, rich conversations spiced with a variety of surprises. As I tried to explain to H recently, I truly love this man, partly because of the way he handles his situation but mostly because time at his bedside opens so many doors in my head. The word 'love' made H uneasy. I told him it was inadequate. If there was another word – stronger, fiercer – I'd use that instead. Try going blind in your early forties, I said. And then imagine being paralysed from the neck down. Yep. That surreal. Just like the black hole.

I'm wrong about the phone call. It's not Pavel at all but one of his two carers down in Exmouth where he lives. Felip Requena is a Catalan from Barcelona. He has one of the penthouse apartment's three bedrooms and is on hand throughout the night to attend to Pavel, should the need arise. His English is good but breaks down under pressure. Just now, I'm having trouble making any sense of his end of the conversation.

'Again, Felip. Is Pavel OK?'

'He's fine.'

'Then why the drama? And why are you whispering?'

'I don't want him to hear. I'm out on the balcony.'

This explains the mewing of gulls and the slap-slap of halyards on metal masts from the nearby dinghy park. I ask Felip what's happened.

'It's Carrie,' he says. 'She's not here. She won't come.'

'Is she ill?'

'I don't know.'

'Have you phoned her? Talked to her?'

'*Si.*'

'And?'

'Something's happened.'

'Like what?' I'm frowning now, the phone to my ear, the iPad abandoned, half out of the bed.

Felip says he doesn't know. I'm Breton by birth and grew up in France. Felip speaks a little French and when he's really challenged and thinks it might help, he summons the odd word or two.

'*Elle est choquée.*'

Choquée. Shocked. Something *has* happened.

'Why, Felip? Why is Carrie shocked?'

'She won't tell me. She won't say. Only you, she says.'

'Only me what?'

'She only tells you.'

'And Pavel?'

'I tell him she's got a cold.'

'And he believes you?'

'*Si. No. No se.*'

He doesn't know. This is awkward. It's been obvious for a while that Pavel has come to depend on Carrie. She's a local woman, gifted in all kinds of ways, and she spends an important part of every day at Pavel's bedside. I was lucky to find her and luckier still that all three of us – me, her, Pavel – so quickly became friends.

'You want me to come down? Talk to her?'

'*Si.*'

'When?'

'Now. Today.'

'So where is Carrie?'

'At home.' His voice is growing ever fainter, unlike the gulls. 'I said you could be here in a couple of hours.'

I cancel a lunch with a casting director and I'm on the road by half past nine. Holland Park to East Devon, on a good day, is a three-hour drive and I know every inch of the road, chiefly because my son, Malo, lives on his father's 300-acre estate in West Dorset. His father, by the way, is H. H stands for Hayden.

The way England becomes so green and empty beyond Stonehenge has always lifted my spirits and today – mid-April, sunny, cloudless – is no exception. As the road rises for the next hill, and then the hill after, it's easy to kid yourself that the folk who hoisted those immense blocks of stone knew a thing or two about eternity. Drive into one of those long sunsets on a summer's evening, and you'd never spare a thought for black holes.

Exmouth, as H recently told me, does what it says on the tin. I suspect it was meant as a throwaway comment but, as is so often the case, H was right. It's a low-rise traditional English seaside resort parked beside a sensational stretch of water where the wideness of the River Exe, itself a thing of exceptional beauty, flows into Lyme Bay. During the summer it has donkeys on the beach and armies of kids with buckets and spades. Whenever the wind blows, the view out to sea blossoms with kitesurfers. The town itself has an exceptionally slow heartbeat and appears to have turned its back on the rest of the UK. Nearly a lifetime ago, as a child, Pavel spent holidays here, which is why he's chosen to come back. He tells me he still has the happiest memories and, based on what I've seen of the place, I believe him.

Pavel is a scriptwriter by trade. By the time I met him in the flesh he'd already acquired a golden reputation for narrative reach and pitch-perfect dialogue. Both these phrases have become far too common among far too many critics to retain any real meaning, but the radio play he'd scripted with yours truly in mind spoke to me from the first page. Everything Pavel touches has a rightness, a distinctive authenticity, that give thesps like me the confidence to open the throttle and take a risk or two. That's not as common as you might think but *Going Solo* – the story of a woman who effectively becomes a fighter pilot – scored a decent audience and some glowing reviews. It also prompted an invitation from Pavel for lunch *à deux*. Which is where the trouble began.

Pavel Sieger, in keeping with someone who spends all his waking time making up stories, isn't Pavel Sieger at all. His real name is Paul Stukeley. Pavel, which happens to be the Slav cognate of Paul, is a doff of the scriptwriter's hat to the city he loves most in all the world. Prague is undoubtedly Pavel's real passion. It's also the place where he chose to go blind. Chose is his word, not mine. Blindness, he told me on our first date, runs in the family. Certain symptoms warn of its imminence. So, when the world began to slip out of focus he took a Ryanair flight to Prague, checked out his favourite view from the Charles Bridge, made himself comfortable in a darkened hotel room, and never laid eyes on the world again. It happened to be New Year's Day. When the summoned Czech doctor appeared at his bedside, Pavel asked whether it was still snowing. Snow, he told me later, is the enemy of darkness, along with sunshine, anything played by Paul Lewis, and the blessings of a listening ear. Since we met the latter has been my responsibility, and that, he told me only yesterday, makes him very happy.

To me, he should add Carrie. It's nearly lunchtime and I'm at journey's end in Exmouth, making my way to the curl of waterside land that houses the town's marina. Houses and apartment blocks in washed-out shades of yellows and blues line the basin, with its wooden pontoons and neatly moored lines of yachts, fishing smacks, and pricey runabouts. Anyone who still believes that England has emptied itself of serious money, squandered the lot on Brexit and one last foreign holiday, should come here. A year's rent on a single berth costs thousands; a third-floor apartment with a glimpse of the sea is squillions more. After the accident, when Pavel needed round-the-clock care, we listened carefully to where he said he wanted to live and a penthouse apartment out beyond the marina, on the very edge of the estuary, turned out to be the answer.

By this time, H was insisting on paying the bills. Typically, he handled the negotiations with the estate agents himself, keeping the details very close to his chest. To this day I don't know what it cost, but – with its three bedrooms, high-spec everything, plus an endless list of bespoke modifications – it has to be seven figures. The last time I asked, H waved the question away. 'Call it an investment,' he grunted. 'Call it whatever you fucking like. Just as long as the guy's enjoying the view.'

I'm looking at it now. There is, of course, no chance of Pavel ever enjoying any view, but H's rough humour points to a larger truth because my all-time favourite screenwriter sees through his ears, painting the inside of his head with soundscape after soundscape. Hence one of the early bills H paid was for the floor-to-ceiling glass doors in the room where Pavel sleeps. Everything he needs is voice-activated through a piece of clever software housed in a green plastic cube no bigger than a tea caddy, yet another expense, and it only needs a whispered command from Pavel's bed, or perhaps his wheelchair, for these fabulous doors to glide noiselessly open, parting the curtains on the world outside. Pavel calls this bedside device *Sesame*.

On my first visit down here, once H's team had settled him in, Pavel waited until dusk and then asked me to shut my eyes. It was low tide, he told me. The waders, oystercatchers and sundry other chancers would be feeding on the eel grass that carpets the mudflats in front of the apartment block. Just wait. And just listen.

I take direction easily. I shut my eyes and pretended to be Pavel. The software he uses can respond to a range of orders, depending on the user's mood. On this occasion he whispered *Sesame* at the bedside microphone and the moment the doors parted, the room – and my whole world – was full of the contented chuckles and mutterings of the starvelings on the roost tucking in. I might have been anywhere, any river, any stretch of seashore, and I'm guessing that was the point. God supplies the soundtrack and your memories fill in the rest. Then, minutes later, came a call I recognized, the liquid notes of a lone curlew, impossibly melancholic, and I was still trying to capture the feeling in a single word when Pavel spared me the effort.

'Schubert,' he whispered. 'Impromptu number three.'

'Paul Lewis?'

'Of course.'

He was right, as he usually is. And when I opened my eyes and saw the smile on his face, I realized that he'd probably spent most of his life rehearsing for moments like these. Paul Lewis, incidentally, is a concert pianist of genius with a presence and a face to match. Yet another debt I owe to Pavel.

Access to the apartment is naturally by a private lift. The stand of fresh flowers in the IKEA vase was one of Carrie's early ideas. Smell matters to Pavel, as well as sound, and she'd been nursing long enough to understand the way that the scent of a particular bloom can lift an entire day. As often as she can, Carrie takes Pavel out in his wheelchair and, judging by the latest offering, Pavel's current favourites are freesias. Lucky boy.

There's a safety door on the third floor with a security touch pad. I know the code but respect for Felip's feelings keep my hands by my side. Moments later, alerted to the lift's arrival, he's standing in front of me, framed by the view. He looks, to be frank, wrecked. Felip has never been friends with sunshine but just now, unshaven, balding and pale, he's a ghost of a man.

'Any word from Carrie?'

'No.'

'And Pavel?'

'He knows.'

'He knows what, Felip?'

'He knows something's wrong.'

This comes as no surprise. Pavel has an almost animal instinct for the imminence of any kind of disaster, big or small. He tells me you can hear it in the way people take an extra breath or two, in the hurry that danger imparts to what they're trying to say. In this respect, Felip would be an open book.

'So, have you told him? About Carrie?'

'I've said she's not well.'

'And?'

'You talk to him.' He gestured vaguely in the direction of Pavel's bedroom. 'See for yourself.'

Pavel occupies the biggest of the three bedrooms. The room has a sensational view across the estuary, with access to a balcony on sunny days, and there's plenty of space for Carrie to work around the hundreds of jobs, big and small, that come with looking after someone in Pavel's state.

Preparing the room for his arrival, I devoted lots of thought to trying to get it exactly right. He can't see, of course, and now he has no sensation in his fingertips, but I raided his house in Chiswick for a couple of his favourite oils, thickly rendered seascapes by his favourite *artiste*, in the belief that they might impart a slightly Zen sense of peace. Deep down I think this was more for my sake than his, a reminder of the old Pavel from the days when we were lovers, but the truth is that paralysis is no friend when it comes to home comforts. The room smells like a hospital ward – excretory notes laced with disinfectant – and always will.

Pavel has already sensed my arrival. He's middle-aged now, and it shows. He has a long, bony face, freshly shaved. His receding hair is beginning to grey and there are scabby marks of sun damage high on his temples. His thin arms lie inert on the whiteness of the sheet, his nails perfectly manicured, and as I step closer his head turns slowly on the pillow as if to inspect me.

'Carrie?' he whispers.

'Everything's fine.'

'You say.'

'I say.'

A tiny movement of his head invites me to sit down. The bed, which was probably the best investment of all, stirs a mix of envy and gratitude from its occupant. It has a special mattress and motors underneath that help ward off the dreaded bed sores and it has more life in it, more movement, than Pavel can ever hope for. In the middle of the night, when I stay over in the spare bedroom, you can hear it softly grumbling to itself. It must be like sleeping with an out-of-sorts insomniac.

I sometimes wonder what conversations with Pavel would be like if he was sighted, if I could see his eyes behind the tinted glasses, if I could feel *watched*. The fact that it wouldn't make the slightest difference is a tribute to his acuity, and to the way his other senses have managed to penetrate the darkness in which he lives.

Just now his head is tipped at a certain angle on the pillow. This means he's about to challenge me.

'She's dead.' The observation carries no hint of drama, or even regret. He simply wants a yes or no.

'She's not.'

'How do you know?'

'Felip talked to her just hours ago. She's upset for some reason.'

'And that's why you're here?'

'Yes.'

'You drove down specially?'

'Of course.' I pause, then ask how Carrie has been these last few days. She appears every day, except for most weekends, in line with the contract H negotiated. When I asked him whether any carer was really worth the money he was paying her, H told me a decent plasterer on a daily rate in my neck of the woods would trouser nearly as much. She's brightened him up, he grunted. And that's a fucking talent.

H is right. Carrie is beyond price, but Pavel still owes me an answer. Dependence isn't a word he has much time for but the fit between them has – to my delight – been near perfect.

'Felip is right,' he whispers gravely. 'She's been troubled.'

'About what?'

His head has moved again on the pillow. A tiny frown ghosts across his face. With such a meagre repertoire of gesture left to him, I recognize this for what it is. A plea for help.

'I don't know,' he says. 'But thank Christ you're here.'

TWO

I've never been to Carrie's place. Felip gives me directions to an address about a mile away. Isca Terrace turns out to be a neat row of houses that climbs a hill off one of the town's main roads. The terrace is interesting, well kept. Handsome bay windows. Bright paintwork. A cat or two, sprawled in the sunshine. These are the kind of properties that would earn top billing in the window of any estate agency. Nice.

Carrie lives at number seven. The basement, Felip told me with a cautionary look, not the whole house. Wooden steps lead down to a front door glazed in squares of pebbled glass. Unlike the rest of the terrace, it needs a little TLC. When I ring the bell, nothing happens. Carrie could, of course, be out, but Felip thought this would be unlikely and when I asked why, he simply shrugged, muttering something about bad things happening.

Bad things? I ring the bell again and this time I hear movement inside. Then comes a voice, low, wary, unsure of itself.

'Who is it?'

I recognize the voice at once but this isn't my Carrie, Pavel's Carrie, the thirty-something miracle-worker with brilliant references and a smile to match. Felip's right. Something very bad must have happened.

I tell her it's me. A shape appears behind the pebbled glass. The door opens an inch or two, just to make sure.

'It's me, Carrie. Can I come in?'

'Why?'

This isn't Carrie at all. While I've always been careful not to intrude in her private life, Carrie and I have always been easy with each other. Her sheer competence has never been an issue – she's been a trained nurse for more than ten years – but what I've always loved is her openness, her easy candour, and the sheer warmth of the spell she seems to cast, especially on the likes of Pavel. Pavel is world class at spotting life's fakes. And Carrie will never be one of those.

The door is open now and Carrie is already retreating down the hall. She's very good looking, not a curve out of place, and she's always held herself with that kind of effortless confidence you often find in Continental women. Nothing haughty. Nothing arrogant. Just a glad acknowledgement that her genes have been kind to her. Now, though, something has definitely changed. She's wearing a tatty old dressing gown several sizes too big, and she seems to have developed a slight stoop. One of life's bigger waves has taken her by surprise and it shows.

The basement flat is dark and cluttered. There are cardboard boxes everywhere, most of them half full. I've taken off my plimsolls at the front door and the hall carpet feels tacky beneath my bare feet.

Carrie is waiting for me in the kitchen diner at the back of the property. She perches herself on a stool beside the work surface and in the throw of light from the back window her face looks pale. Her eyes, a striking shade of green, are hidden behind a big pair of Ray-Bans.

'So, how's it going?'

'How's what going?'

'The windsurfing.' I gesture at the board propped against the brick wall in the back garden. 'Still putting all the guys to shame?'

My little jest fails to spark a smile. Windsurfing is big in Exmouth and the news that Carrie had been doing it for years explained – at least to me – a great deal about our new hire. H and I once spotted her out in the estuary when we were walking on the beach. In a stiffish wind, she had perfect balance, her body nearly horizontal as she carved a path through the slower mortals, urging yet more speed out of the huge sail before pirouetting at the end of the run and setting off again in a blur of effortless movement. A goddess, I remember thinking at the time, totally undaunted.

Just now, she's trying to avoid my gaze. Her head is down and she's picking at a nail. Would I like tea? Coffee? Something stronger? Is it too early to break open the Stolichnaya? Anything to defer a serious conversation. I take a long look at her. Never once, I remind myself, has she abandoned Pavel. Until now.

'So, what's happened?'

She shakes her head. She doesn't want to say. I ask the question again, tell her we're all worried, especially Pavel. At the mention of his name she says she's sorry, really sorry. She'll be back as soon as she can, probably tomorrow, in fact definitely tomorrow. The last person she wants to put out is Pavel.

'How is he?' At last she's looking at me.

'He's fine . . . but, like I say, he's worried. I know it's hard, Carrie, but maybe we can help here.'

'No.' Another shake of the head, more emphatic. 'This is down to me. I'll sort it. I promise.'

'Sort what?' I'm tempted to reach for her hand, give it a squeeze, but I don't.

'Nothing. It's nothing. I'm being silly.'

'About what? Are you ill?'

'No.'

'Are you sure?'

'Yes. That would be simple. I'm a nurse, remember.'

'So, what is it? Some kind of bad news? Some kind of shock? Stuff you don't want to talk about? Only I have to know, Carrie. It's important for all of us, especially Pavel.'

'Is that some kind of threat?' Her expression hardens.

'Not at all.' I shake my head at once and this time my hand closes over hers. 'We think the world of you, Carrie. That's why I'm here. I think maybe you need help.'

'And you're the one to give it?'

'Yes.'

'So how would that work?'

'Easy. I listen. I try to understand. If it's a question of money . . .'

'It's not money,' she says hotly. 'That's the last thing it is.'

'So, tell me. Trust me. Something's happened. Let's start there.' I give her hand a squeeze. 'Can you live with that?'

Behind the Ray-Bans, I sense that her eyes have closed. Her whole body has slumped on the stool and the dressing gown has come loose but she makes no effort to withdraw her hand to hide her nakedness. At length, she nods.

'OK,' she says. 'But you have to make me a promise.'

'Of course.'

'None of this goes any further. You don't tell a soul. Not H, not Pavel, not the police, no one. Yeah?'

I say yes to everything. Mention of the police has triggered a tiny alarm deep in my brain. There may be dimensions here I hadn't imagined.

'So, what happened?'

At last she takes the Ray-Bans off. Her eyes are open now, searching mine, wanting that final reassurance.

'You promise?'

'I do.'

'Really?'

'Yes.'

'OK.' She nods again. 'I was in bed.'

'When?'

'Last night. It was late, really late, half two in the morning. I keep the curtains closed at night. The room's very dark and normally I like that . . .' She pauses, suddenly uncertain.

'And?'

'This isn't pretty. In fact, it's horrible.'

'Go on.'

'I must have heard a noise. That's what woke me up.'

'Noise?'

'Someone in the room. A presence. A feeling. Someone there.' Her eyes are closed again. She's rocking gently on the stool, her arms folded, the way you might cradle a baby. 'There's a light beside the bed. I turned it on. He was young. That was the first thing I thought. So young. Curly hair. Chubby. Fat. A puppy. No chin. And eyes you wouldn't believe. Just staring down at me.'

'Age?'

'Young, like I said. Sixteen? I'm guessing but that's probably close.'

'What was he wearing?' I'm beginning to sound like a detective.

'Trackie bottoms, silver grey. Football top, blue. I'm clueless when it comes to teams, but I think there were two words on the front: King and Power.'

'Did he say anything?'

'Nothing. Not at first. That was the really creepy thing. The boy just stood there. No sign of movement. Not a flicker. He wasn't embarrassed. He wasn't aggressive. Nothing. Just that look. Those empty eyes.'

'So, what did you say? Do?'

'I told him to get out of my house. I told him he had no right to be there.'

'And?'

'He didn't say a word.'

'Were you frightened?'

'Of course. Maybe more shocked than frightened. Then I started wondering.'

'About what?'

'How he'd got in.'

'You asked him?'

'Of course.'

'And?'

'That's when it got really weird. He said he could get through any door. He said he could get into anyone's house, anyone's head. He didn't need a key. Doors. People. They were all the same. They just opened to him. Weird stuff, totally surreal. He had a slight lisp, too, which somehow made it worse. Then I asked his name and he just laughed. Braces on his teeth. Maybe younger than sixteen. I just don't know.'

'Had you seen him before?'

'What do you mean?'

'In the street, maybe? Following you around?'

'You mean stalking me?'

'Yes. There has to be some reason he chose you.'

'*Chose?*' This appears to be a new thought. Then Carrie shakes her head. 'No,' she says. 'I'd never seen him before.'

'So, what did he want?'

There's a long silence. The wind has got up and I can hear something metallic flapping in the back garden. Bang . . . bang . . . bang. Finally, Carrie stirs.

'I didn't know what he was after,' she says. 'Not to begin with. Then he got much closer to the bed, little tiny steps the way some people get into the water when they go swimming, and he dropped his pants. He said he wanted me to stroke it. He said he wanted to show me what he could do with it. I got angry then. I shouted. I told him to fuck off. I told him I'd call the police.'

'So he left?'

'No. He tried to masturbate, tried to get an erection, but nothing happened. I told him to put it away and get out of my house, but he refused. Then I made a big mistake.'

'Like what?'

'I laughed at him.'

'And?'

'He stopped playing around with himself. All the time he was just staring down at me, literally a couple of feet away. You know when you meet someone who's not all there? How this sixth sense tells you they're crazy? Out of tune? Off the radar? That's him. That's the way it was.'

'You think he was drunk?'

'No.'

'On something else?'

'I don't think so. He was just . . .' She shook her head. 'Different, absent, gone.'

Gone. The word lay between us for a second or two. Then Carrie seemed to gather herself on the stool. For a moment I thought the incident was over, but I was wrong.

'I got out of bed and asked him to leave again. Not asked, *told*. He didn't respond. His hand went back to his dick and this time he got a response.'

'Were you naked?' I nodded at the dressing gown.

'Yes.'

'Was that wise? Given the circumstances?'

'I don't know. Probably not. But I always sleep naked. By then I was really angry. Not scared, angry. My fucking flat. My fucking bedroom. He had no rights here, none. I wanted him out. I wanted him gone. I never wanted to see his pathetic little dick ever again.'

'You told him that?'

'Yes.'

'And?'

'He seemed to get the message – seemed, at any rate, to understand. I think I must have been playing the nurse by now. When I told him to pull his trackie bottoms back up, he did just that.'

'And he left?'

'No. And that's when he did frighten me. He was fully dressed then. As far as I could see he wasn't carrying any kind of weapon. Like I said, he wasn't pissed and he wasn't out of his head on anything else so I don't think he was going to hurt me, not physically. He took a step towards the door but then he stopped and turned around. He said he had something to tell me, something important, something he'd told the others.'

'Others?'

'Others. He said I was never to say anything about him to anyone else, ever. They were his exact words. Anyone else, ever.'

'Or?'

'Or he'd come back and kill me. Just like he'd killed the others.'

'Killed how?'

'With a knife.' She gestures vaguely towards her lap. 'The words he used were "rip you apart".'

'Shit.'

'Exactly.'

'And you believed him? *Believe* him?'

'I do. Of course, I do. Why? Because it fits in with everything else. And because I can't afford not to. I've told you already. The boy's off the planet. He's crazy. And crazy people can do anything. To anyone.'

THREE

It's nearly six o'clock. I've tried to tempt Carrie out for a drink but without success. I left her as I found her, draped in an oversized dressing gown and, judging by the expression on her face when we said our goodbyes, I suspect she was already regretting our conversation. Once again, when pressed, I said I'd respect her confidence. And once again, unprompted, she confirmed she'd be back on duty the following morning. 'Give my best to Pavel. Tell him I've had a touch of summer flu.'

Summer flu, or any other excuse, doesn't begin to cut it. Already, on the five-minute stroll to H's favourite seafront pub, I've started to examine passing strangers with new eyes. Are any of these people the right age? Are they wearing grey trackie bottoms? Do they have braces on their teeth? Are they lifelong fans of a leading football club in the East Midlands? The latter discovery took me exactly thirty-seven seconds on my mobile phone, searching the words King and Power. Might this be some kind of clue?

The pub has an upstairs balcony with views of the sea. A large gin and tonic has cleaned me out of small change but I'm grateful for the way it's begun to soften my worst fears. On the way out of Carrie's basement flat, I'd paused to take a good look at the door and sure enough the wood had been splintered around the frame where the tongue of the lock slips across. Carrie had seen it too, as if for the first time, but watching her carefully I suspect this was a small deception for my benefit. In her situation, once the boy had left, I'd be at the front door within seconds to check for damage and then double bolt it top and bottom. As it was, we agreed on a change of locks and remedial attention to the frame. Beware of madness, I said gently. Once frightened, twice shy.

Madness? The word itself is clue enough. It speaks of an entire life out of kilter, of volatility, of the unpredictable, and perhaps of serious violence. Anyone who can stand beside the bed of a complete stranger, having broken into their world uninvited and unannounced, is probably capable of anything. What the boy did was bad enough. What he may be capable of, and what he may have done already, is worth a serious conversation. But with whom?

Over a second gin, watching a lone windsurfer stitching back and forth between the beach and the offshore sandbank, I try and clarify the limits of my responsibility. My word pledged should end the argument. I've promised to respect Carrie's privacy and that should be that. But there are larger possibilities here, not least with regards to Carrie herself. What if the intruder makes a second appearance? What if he's become obsessed with her? With the memory of that naked body? And what if his next visit ends in serious violence? No one, least of all Carrie, would accuse this boy of ambiguity. He's threatened to kill her, as he's claimed to have killed others before. Shouldn't all this be put to some kind of test? Before Carrie – or some other complete stranger – pays an unimaginable price?

In situations like these, I always hanker after the opinion of others. At home in London I'd talk to my lovely neighbour Evelyn. She's recently returned her editing pencil to the jam jar after a lifetime in publishing, and those busy decades absorbed in other people's stories have made her wise as well as excellent company. Given the facts, suitably disguised, she'd know at once what to do and where – perhaps – to turn next. The dilemma posed by my last hour or so – whether to respect Carrie's privacy or risk the most horrific of tabloid headlines – would be meat and drink to her. But Evelyn, alas, is in Ireland just now, enjoying a late-spring visit to some sensational semi-tropical gardens near Killarney. The last thing she needs is a lengthy phone conversation about disembowelment.

I reach for the last of my gin and tonic. H is another possibility. My windsurfer, by now, is no more than a distant black speck beneath the crimson blade of his sail, but as he gets the next turn wrong and disappears in a tiny explosion of white spume, I recognize that H has no place in this story. I have a deep respect for his many talents. I've never met anyone else with more courage and less fear of real-life consequences. But these very talents are deeply problematic. H is a great believer in drawing the straightest of lines between any set of dots, and he'd doubtless have Carrie's young intruder in a chokehold within minutes. What might happen thereafter doesn't bear thinking about, a consequence almost as dire as the promise of evisceration. No, there has to be a better way. Something more subtle, kinder, less terminal.

When I get back to the penthouse apartment, I find Felip folded into his favourite armchair in the big lounge. He's heard the rumble of the approaching lift and he's plainly been waiting for me. When he asks me about Carrie – how is she? what's happened? – I dismiss his questions with a wave of my hand.

'Women of Carrie's age sometimes have problems down here.' I gesture lightly at my lower stomach. 'I've been through it myself. It can be bloody unpleasant.'

This is, of course, a lie. Carrie is far too young to have hit the menopausal reef but – a little drunk – I'm relying on Felip to buy the lie. He doesn't, of course, but at least I've kept my word.

'He wants to see you.' Felip nods towards Pavel's bedroom. 'Maybe you think up another story?'

Glad not to answer any more of Felip's questions, I step down the corridor and join Pavel in his bedroom. The sliding doors to the balcony are wide open and in a cloudless sky the sun has begun to sink over the soft green swell of the hills beyond the river. Pavel appears to be asleep and I tiptoe across the room to watch a gaggle of waders in search of mussels on the beach below. Then comes the faraway clatter of a train heading west on the distant bank. Trains have always excited me – the promise of numberless destinations – and it's still in view when Pavel whispers a command to his *Sesame* device. Moments later, a mechanism in the bed is lifting his upper body semi-erect. This is Pavel's wake-up call, not for his own benefit but for mine. He wants – needs – a conversation.

I ask him how he is. He says he's fine. To my surprise he doesn't even mention Carrie. Instead, he wants me to find a book she's been reading him.

'It's a diary,' he says. 'Ernst Jünger?'

I know about Ernst Jünger. He served as a German officer in both world wars and was a hero of my ex-husband, Berndt, whose scriptwriting and directorial talents nearly outstripped his many failings as a human being. Jünger was a novelist and philosopher, as well as a much-decorated warrior, and it was Berndt's ambition to put his wilder musings about war as a transcendental experience on the screen. I've no idea whether this ever happened but, drunk, Berndt never failed to raise a glass to the great man.

'*Storm of Steel*,' I mutter. 'My ex-husband used to read bits to me in bed.'

'Lucky you.' Pavel is smiling. 'I gather it's got a black and white photo on the cover.'

I find the book without difficulty and draw up a chair beside Pavel's bed. When he asks nicely, I also give him a kiss.

'You've been drinking,' he says at once.

'You're right.'

'Good. In fact, perfect. Carrie's been reading it at home. She's marked two entries. The first is eighth December 1941. Jünger is writing in Paris where he did a lot of translation work. It's the second paragraph you need. I thought of you at once.'

I do Pavel's bidding. The first paragraph sets the scene nicely. Winter in Paris. Curfew. Everything lifeless in the fog. Then comes the promised second paragraph. My eye floats from line to line, then I pause, astonished. One of Jünger's many tasks is evidently translating the farewell letters of Resistance hostages awaiting execution. And just now, these hostages are being held in Nantes.

'You remember that movie of mine?' I look up.

'Of course, I do. *The Hour of Our Passing.*' Pavel smiles. 'Maybe it was a mistake to peak so early, eh?'

'That's because you liked my body. Being a proper actress came later.'

The Hour of Our Passing was a film I made years ago on location in Nantes. It was a powerful script and I played the girlfriend of one of the Resistance figures condemned to death. A flashback sequence recalls an intimate moment Pavel has always treasured. He first saw the movie when he was still sighted and the image of yours truly, fully nude, riding the young *resistant* to an extravagant climax has stayed with him ever since. Blind, but before he was paralysed, Pavel mapped that same body with his fingertips and always swore that nothing had changed. Flattering. But sweet.

'You have the letters?' I ask.

'Alas, no. Try the twenty-ninth May, 1941. This time I want you to read the whole passage aloud.'

I leaf back eight months. The entry this time is much longer. When I ask Pavel how he found his way to the Jünger diaries he mentions a radio documentary he'd been listening to. And when I enquire whether he minds me taking a preliminary look at this second passage, he shakes his head.

'No problem,' he whispers. 'Enjoy.'

I bend to the text. Jünger has been summoned to witness the execution of a soldier sentenced to death for desertion. The condemned man and the shooting squad journey out to the depths of a forest. The officer in charge leads the way to a particular tree. It's an ash tree and its trunk has been splintered by previous executions. Two groups of bullet holes are visible, a higher one for the head and a lower one for the heart. Among the tree's exploded fibres are little groups of blowflies.

The detail here is chilling, and it gets worse. A truck appears with a military-issue coffin. The execution squad forms two ranks through which the condemned man must pass. The sentence of the military court is read aloud to him. Jünger records that the man doesn't seem to understand. His lips are moving as if he's trying to spell the words out. A tiny fly plays on his left cheek. When asked whether he wants a blindfold he makes no answer. The chaplain says yes on his behalf while guards tie him to the tree with white ropes. Then one of the guards pins a piece of red cardboard the size of a playing card on to his shirt over his heart.

The firing squad have taken up their positions. Against every instinct, Jünger forces himself to watch. On the command of the officer in charge, the soldiers fire. Five holes appear in the cardboard. The man's mouth opens and closes, as if registering surprise. Then his knees give out and the blood drains from his face. After a doctor confirms his death, his body is placed in the waiting coffin. As a postscript to this scene, Jünger remarks on the return of the fly which has settled once again on the cooling cheek of the dead man.

Enjoy? I ask Pavel whether he really wants me to read this piece aloud.

'Yes,' he whispers, 'I do.'

'But you just told me you've heard it before. When Carrie was here.'

'That's right. But twice won't hurt.'

'You think it's that good?'

'I think it's that important.'

I gaze down at him for a moment, at the bony face against the whiteness of the pillow, then do his bidding.

'Pretend this is an audition,' he suggests. 'Imagine you're trying to impress me.'

Bizarre. I turn the page back, take a moment to compose myself, and then begin to read. I deliberately keep my voice as flat as possible. A text like this, essentially reportorial, needs no additional colour. The facts, and the bareness of the language, speak for themselves. The soldier dead, I close the book.

'Well?' I say. 'Happy now?'

Pavel's eyes appear to be closed behind the tinted glasses. He answers my question with the faintest nod. Then, at last, he asks me about Carrie.

'She's fine,' I say lightly. 'She'll be back tomorrow.'

'But how did you find her? How was she?'

'Fine,' I say again. 'Just like always.'

'I don't believe you.'

'Care to tell me why?'

Pavel takes his time in mustering a reply. Finally, he clears his throat and, with some difficulty, tries to swallow. In Pavel's state, robbed of sensation and control, nothing is simple.

'*I have seen many people die . . .*' he says at last. '*But never at a predetermined moment.*'

This is a direct quote from Jünger's diary entry. Language, to Pavel, has always had an almost sacramental importance. He's written plays and film scripts that have won him a clutch of awards. The fact that this one phrase, word-perfect, has jumped out of Jünger's account should tell me a great deal. But what?

Pavel, typically, refuses to help. Finally, I think I get it.

'This is about Carrie?'

'Of course.'

'And she really read you this same piece?'

'She did.'

'And?'

'It made her cry.'

'*Cry?*'

'Yes.'

'Why?'

'That's a very good question.'

I nod. I'm staring down at him. In these situations, Pavel is very sparing with clues. He likes his audience, his readership, his fans, to do the real work. It was the same in his professional life, and it's exactly the same now. At first, I thought it was some kind of writerly affectation, a pleasing little quirk to spice up the attention he's always received, but now I know different. Pavel, like many writers, is a control freak.

'What has she been telling you?' I ask him.

'Nothing. She didn't have to. It was there in her tone of voice. In her presence.'

'And?'

'She's deeply troubled.'

'Because?'

'Because she thinks something bad is about to happen.'

'What kind of something?'

'I don't know.'

'Didn't you ask her?'

'Of course, I asked her. We're friends. Friends care for each other.'

'And?'

'Nothing. She wouldn't say. She's a strong woman. She's proud.'

'I agree. You're right. She's also beautiful. What else do you know about her?'

'Very little. With pride comes privacy. She keeps herself to herself.'

I nod. From what little I know about Carrie, this is all too credible. A previous marriage? A series of failed relationships? Even the possibility of a child? Aborted or otherwise? Any of these pieces might form a part of Carrie's jigsaw but neither of us appears to be any the wiser.

I open the book again. Something else has occurred to me. I find the phrase at once.

'*I have seen many people die,*' I murmur, '*but never at a predetermined moment.*' I look up. 'Was that when she started crying?'

'Yes.' Pavel is smiling again. 'Well done.'

'And yet you made her keep reading?'

'On the contrary.' The smile widens. 'Which is why I asked you to take over. She was unable to read the rest.'

'That bad?'

'I'm afraid so.'

FOUR

I stay over in the apartment that night, spending a couple of hours at Pavel's bedside. We talk a little more about Carrie, and how irreplaceable she's become, but when he tries to press me about any confidences she might have shared I insist that all is well. I know he doesn't believe me but there's always been an understanding between us, largely unspoken, that knows when to move the conversation on.

When he enquires about the small print of my own little life, I'm more than happy to oblige. My oncologist, for the time being, appears satisfied with the latest MRI scan. The shadowy remains of my brain tumour are still lurking, but my recent course of chemo has, for now, stopped any further growth. My agent, Rosa, has come up with a couple of decent offers and one in particular I really fancy.

'The big thing just now is dystopia,' I tell Pavel. 'Everything falling apart, lives torn apart, society in freefall. Is it Brexit? Donald Trump? Global warming? God knows. This is a four-parter for a French *chaine* and all I've got is a little cameo role, but I love it.'

The script calls for me to play the middle-aged mistress of a senior politician. The comely Vivienne has cheated death at the hands of a particularly vicious tumour and sees every reason to spend the rest of her life celebrating. This is, of course, a tad close to the facts of my own life but the writing is good, and the director is a woman I trust.

The working title for the series is *Terminale*. Pavel loves the idea.

'My little sunbeam,' he murmurs, 'on Planet Glum. Are you nude again?'

'Yes.'

'And that doesn't bother you?'

'Not in the slightest.'

This, too, pleases him no end. He tells me I'm as brave as Carrie and twice as beautiful. The latter compliment is pointless because he's never laid eyes on Carrie but courage like hers, on occasions, I could certainly do with. Before I leave him in peace, I tell him about yesterday's discovery of the black hole. Pavel is addicted to speech radio, especially Radio Four, and has already thought hard about what the black hole might look like. I play with the emoticon likeness for a while, a metaphor that sparks Pavel to reach even further.

'Maybe it's a punctuation mark,' he says. 'Semi-colon or full stop?'

'Full stop.' I'm thinking about the TV series. 'You're right. We're all doomed.'

Before I retire to the spare bedroom for the night, I have a brief chat with Felip. I suspect he might know more about Carrie than either Pavel or myself but he's very reluctant to open up. After we've agreed that she's great company and an accomplished cook, as well as being a nurse you'd trust at anyone's bedside, there doesn't seem to be anywhere else to take the conversation. Then, almost as an afterthought, he says he's been worried about her.

'Why?'

'Nervous.' He waves his hands, trying to conjure urgency into the word.

'In what way?'

'In here.' His thin hand closes over his chest. 'Bad.'

'Have you talked to her about it?'

'No. I try, but . . .' He shakes his head. 'No good.'

'You think it's something personal?'

'Sure. Of course.'

'So how long? Days? Weeks?'

'Yes.'

'Which?'

'Weeks. Since . . .' He frowns. 'Barca beat Real Madrid.'

'And when was that?'

'*Le deuxieme mars.*'

The second of March. Felip is football crazy. He's date-perfect on any game his beloved Barcelona has ever played and saves up match recordings to savour in the small hours while Pavel is asleep.

'You're telling me Carrie is a Real Madrid fan? Is that why she's been so upset?'

Felip is staring at me. At first, he thinks I'm serious, then he gets the joke.

'*Impossible,*' he says. 'No one that nice would ever support the Meringues.'

I sleep fitfully, one ear cocked for Pavel. A word to *Sesame* will be enough to summon help in the shape of Felip but the night passes without incident. As promised, Carrie appears promptly at nine in the morning with a tight smile and a bunch of freesias. The latter appears to be a peace offering or perhaps an apology for yesterday's absence and she's still arranging the flowers in a vase for Pavel's bedside when I down the rest of my coffee and leave.

Isca Terrace is a ten-minute walk away. It's much colder this morning, and I zip up my anorak against the bite of the wind. A white van is parked beside the hedge across the road from Carrie's basement flat and a glance down from pavement level reveals a guy in blue overalls working on the front door. A brand-new lock lies on a fold of cloth beside an array of tools and I can only assume that Carrie has taken my advice about sorting her security.

Isca Terrace trails down to a main road. I turn left at the bottom, and then left again, heading back up the hill to inspect the rear of the premises. A count of seven takes me to what I assume must be Carrie's place, but the back garden is walled and when I try the door to the street it's locked. Shards of glass have been embedded in what looks like a top dressing of fresh cement and I'm still pondering the implications of this when I pause for a coffee in the town centre. This, I keep telling myself, is really about Pavel. He's made it more than plain that Carrie has become important to him and for his sake, as well as hers, I have to make her feel safe.

A couple of minutes on my mobile gives me directions to the town's police station. It turns out to be a utilitarian sprawl of buildings dumped in the middle of what might once have been an attractive square. There's a scatter of vehicles in the car park, and blinds have been lowered in some of the upstairs windows against the glare of the morning sun, but it looks unloved and only partially occupied.

I linger for a while, trying to make up my mind what to do. Responsibility is a big word. Exmouth isn't small. Somewhere in this town, maybe sleeping rough, maybe tucked up on someone's sofa, is a young boy with serious problems. That he has the means, and the motivation, to break into a stranger's house in the middle of the night and appear in her bedroom is beyond doubt. Any woman, even Carrie, would have been terrified. Worse still, bluffing or otherwise, the intruder claimed to have killed.

This stuff happens. Only months ago, a guy in his twenties with what the media termed 'serious mental issues' murdered three pensioners in Exeter, barely a bus ride away. I happen to know because it made the national news. Three total strangers selected at random by a lunatic who should already have been locked up, both for his sake and for ours. Is Carrie's scary young visitor someone similar? Has he slipped through the net? And shouldn't I, a sort of witness, be doing something about it?

Still uncertain, I make my way back to the town centre. Outside the Co-op is a triangle of benches occupied by a noisy gaggle of rough sleepers. They're all on the young side of middle age. Two of them have dogs, artfully sprawled on a blanket beside an upturned cap. Elderly women ignore the mid-morning cans of White Lightning and add to the pile of coins inside the cap. From a distance, I watch this scene, wondering whether any of these men might know an overweight youth with a blue football top and a dental brace. Might a conversation be in order? Would money open a mouth or two? Once again, I'm uncertain. A walk along the beach, maybe. And a bit of a think.

*   *   *

I'm back at the penthouse by midday, still confused. Of Carrie, there's no sign. When I go in to see Pavel, he tells me that she's popped out for half an hour. Often, around noon, she drops into a local café to buy chips for Pavel's lunch. I check he's OK and set out to find the café. En route along the path that skirts the seaward side of the marina development I spot a figure hunched on the curl of sand beneath the wall. She's nursing a cup of coffee, her knees drawn up to her chin, staring out to sea. Carrie.

A ramp leads down to the tiny beach. It's obvious at once that I'm the last person Carrie wants to see. She looks up at me, shading her eyes. I squat beside her. She must have been crying because her cheeks are still wet with tears. I begin to go through it all again, how worried I am, how she needs help, how a situation like this has to be addressed. She has the grace to hear me out, but then shakes her head.

'I lied to you yesterday,' she says. 'None of that stuff ever happened.'

FIVE

What to do?

Mercifully, this very afternoon, I get a call from my only offspring, Malo. For seventeen years I assumed he was my ex-husband's son but then a DNA test proved that H was his real dad, the result of a drunken night aboard a super yacht in Antibes literally twenty-four hours before I laid eyes on Berndt, a discovery that has shaped all our lives ever since.

'How are you?'

Malo, it turns out, is badly hungover. He lives with his Colombian girlfriend, a woman he doesn't deserve. Her name is Clemenza and I pray daily that she'll never leave him. Last night, it seems, he'd fallen into bad company with a young Dutch anarchist and ended up at Clem's little mews cottage draining an entire bottle of *jenever*, which, as I know to my own cost, is Amsterdam's take on gin.

'And?'

'You don't want to know.'

'Clem?'

'She left us to it. I haven't seen her since. She may still be upstairs, but I doubt it.'

'So, where did you sleep?'

'It must have been the sofa. That's where I woke up.'

I find myself nodding. In my trade it becomes all too easy to picture a scene from a handful of clues. Clem, who never touches alcohol of any sort, would have left Malo and his new friend to it. Here's hoping she comes back.

'Dad says you're in Exmouth,' Malo says. 'You mind if I come down?'

'Why?'

'I just fancy a bit of time out, me-time, whatever. Is that woman still around? The windsurfer. Jackie? Gillie?'

'Carrie.'

'Yeah. Her. I thought she might teach me how to do it.'

'You mean windsurfing?'

'Yeah.'

'She's a carer, Malo. She looks after the sick and the helpless. Maybe that's where you should start.'

'Is that a yes, then? Spare bedroom? Proper food? I've got a couple of things to sort. How does tomorrow sound?'

My gaze has strayed to the window. The doors are open to the balcony and I'm watching a skein of geese in perfect formation heading for their roost across the river. In truth, having Malo here would be a complication I don't need just now but already it's too late to suggest he sobers up somewhere else. My darling boy has hung up.

I'm back at the police station by mid-afternoon. A slightly longer session on Google has given me a name. Inspector Geraghty is evidently Exmouth's lead cop. My lovely mum, a Bretonne to her fingertips, always insisted on going to the top of any organization when you have something important to say, but getting hold of Mr Geraghty isn't as simple as I'd anticipated. For one thing, the police station's front door is locked.

A small notice nearby advises me to phone a central number for help, or – in cases of extreme urgency – dial 999. Extreme urgency? I tap on the reinforced glass of the door. What I have in mind calls for an intimate conversation in the privacy of Inspector Geraghty's office. How on earth could I describe Carrie's situation to an anonymous voice on the phone?

I knock again, much louder. Beyond the door is a passage receding into the depths of the building. No sign of anyone. I knock a third time, then a fourth. Finally, a door opens, and a large woman makes her way towards me. She has a felt-tip pen in one hand and she's wearing what looks like a cardigan over a crisp white shirt. The cardigan must have been a long-ago Christmas present because the little motifs on the front turn out to be reindeers.

She opens the door, gestures towards the notice. 'You tried the phone?'

'I didn't.'

'Why on earth not?'

'Because it's personal. I need to talk to Inspector Geraghty. It's a private matter.'

She studies me for a moment. She has a full face, pleasing dimples, and the wildness of her hair – a blaze of auburn curls – badly needs a stiff brush. Clerical staff, I think. Not a police officer at all. Her eyes don't leave mine.

'Inspector Geraghty?' I gesture inside. 'Might he spare a moment or two?'

For the first time she smiles but I'm not sure she means it. She stands aside to let me in. We walk down the corridor to the still-open door. The office is under-furnished: a conference table, four chairs, two metal filing cabinets, and a poster on the wall urging women to report domestic violence. On the table is a recording machine and a foolscap pad full of jottings. The woman gestures at one of the spare chairs and settles heavily behind the pad, scribbling herself a note of some kind before looking up.

For the third time I enquire about Inspector Geraghty.

'That would be me,' she says.

'You're Inspector Geraghty?'

'Indeed. And you are . . .?'

I give her my name and I'm still doing my best to mumble an apology when she cuts me short.

'So how can I help you, Ms Andressen?'

In thespy parlance, I'm the goldfish in the tank, staring blankly out, mouth half open, eyes glazed. This has started badly and unless I get a grip it threatens to get a whole lot worse. I've managed to

make it across the drawbridge, I've avoided the boiling oil, but now
I have to justify my impatience with the house rules.

'I have a good friend.' I adjust my posture in the chair. 'And this
friend thinks she's about to be murdered.'

'Go on.'

'This is tricky. Maybe I shouldn't be here at all. It's really
difficult.'

'For you?'

'Yes. And for her.'

'She has a name, this friend of yours? Contact details?'

The felt-tip pen hovers over a fresh page in the pad. I do my best
to explain the situation. I've already broken a confidence, but my
friend is terrified and under the circumstances I don't blame her.

'Terrified how?'

This, of course, is the crux of the matter. If I want this woman's
help it has to be official. Otherwise, there may be no point in going
on. Nonetheless, the least I owe Carrie is a bid to keep the genie
in the bottle.

'Can I assume this conversation is private?'

'Meaning what?'

'That you keep it to yourself.'

'Of course not.'

'I mean just for the time being.'

'Why? I'm assuming you've come here in good faith. Your friend
needs help. Or maybe advice. So why don't you tell me what's
happened? Is that too big an ask?'

I'm staring at her. She's doing what a good cop should. She deals
in facts, in evidence. This is a police station, not a therapy centre.
And time – hers especially – is doubtless precious.

'So . . .' She's still waiting, pen poised.

I have a choice here. I can leave or stay. Leaving will resolve
nothing. Staying might, at the very least, offer Carrie a glimmer of
light. And so, I repeat her account, the story she told me yesterday,
more or less word for word. Waking up. Finding the youth beside
her bed. Watching him trying to masturbate. Doing her best to get
rid of him. And then, the real heart of it, the threats he made if she
breathed a word to anyone else.

Most of the story appears to have made little impact on my new
friend but the bit at the end, the denouement, has certainly won her
attention.

'He *said* that? Threatened to kill her?'

'Yes. And he also told her he'd done it before.'

'Killed people?'

'Killed people.'

She nods. So far, I've been very careful not to mention Carrie by name, but I sense that this ploy is rapidly running out of road. For Inspector Geraghty to be of any practical help, I need to trust her. Mercifully, she's already two steps ahead of me.

'Do you think this friend of yours would talk to us?'

'No. No chance. In fact, she'll probably deny the whole thing.'

'Why would she do that?'

'I've told you. Because she's terrified.'

'But what if she's making it all up? Have you thought of that?'

In truth, I haven't. I give it a moment's consideration, then shake my head.

'She hasn't,' I say. 'She's not that kind of woman. She's a qualified nurse. She's physically fit. She windsurfs. She's on top of it all.'

'Age?'

'Thirty-seven.' Her date of birth is on her contract of employment.

'Is she married?'

'Not to my knowledge.'

'In a relationship?'

'I don't know.'

'But she lives alone? Is that what you're telling me?'

'As far as I'm aware, yes.'

Question by question, the jigsaw that is Carrie is coming together. Sooner than I'd planned, I'll have to give her a name. But first Geraghty wants to know more about my own relationship with this woman.

'You told me earlier she's a good friend.'

'She is. Or I like to think so.'

'Then how come you know so little about her?'

It's a good question. I explain about Pavel, about the sheer weight of his medical needs, about the difficulties of finding someone like Carrie to look after him.

'You employ her?'

'I do.'

'Here? In Exmouth?'

'Yes.'

'Where, exactly?' I tell her Pavel has an address in the marina development.

'Which is what?'

I hesitate a moment, then shrug. Another little moment of surrender, I think.

'The block beside the slipway. Third floor. At the top.'

'The big penthouse apartment?'

'Yes.'

'Thank you.' The phrase carries no trace of irony, not the slightest indication that I'm making her life more complicated than it need be. I'm beginning to like this woman. She makes a note and then looks up. 'You said windsurfer.'

'I did.'

'Stripy sail? Red on white? Blonde? Middle-aged? Short-sleeved wetsuit?'

'Yes.' I try to hide my surprise. 'You know this woman already?'

'I do, yes. Everyone does, if you happen to be on the water.'

'You're telling me you windsurf, too?'

'Hardly. I keep a little runaround. When I get the time, I go fishing.' She offers me a thin smile, and then gestures at the notepad. 'I find it helps with the blood pressure.'

We return to Carrie's visitor. As best I can I offer a physical description. Young. Curly hair. Receding chin. Overweight. Braces on his teeth. Grey trackie bottoms and a distinctive football top.

'And mad, you say?'

'That's my friend's opinion. I've never met the boy.'

Geraghty looks up. Her patience, at last, is beginning to run out.

'Let's give her a name, shall we? This friend of yours?'

'Carrie.'

'Surname?'

'Tollman.'

'Thank you.' The name goes down on the pad, capital letters. 'Address?'

'Seven Isca Terrace. Basement flat.'

Another note. Then she asks me how the intruder got in. I describe the gouge marks in the wooden door frame and this morning's sighting of the guy fitting a new lock.

'Forced entry? Is that what I'm hearing?'

I agree that's what it sounds like. She nods, abandons the felt tip, and sits back in her chair.

'Here's the problem,' she says. 'Let's assume your friend hasn't made this up. Let's give her the benefit of the doubt. Let's agree she wakes up in the middle of the night with this disturbed young man standing beside her. There's only one witness. Her. Carrie. And if she won't talk to us, won't even admit it happened, then basically there's no way to progress the investigation.'

'You don't think it's worth trying to find the boy?' I nod at the note pad. 'On the basis of her description?'

'Of course. We'll keep our eyes open, make one or two enquiries, nothing too high profile, nothing to alarm him. But beyond that, there's very little we can do. Not until she chooses to make this thing official.'

'And you don't think he might be dangerous? That he might mean all this stuff about killing people?'

'We don't know. We can't tell. We have intel on the ground in town, officers who keep tabs on newcomers. It's April. The weather may perk up. Exmouth's a nice place, even if you have to sleep rough. We can ask around, make one or two enquiries, keep our eyes open.'

'And if you find him?'

'We can find a pretext to shake him down, do a light body search. That will give us a name and whatever else and it needn't involve your friend. But I'm afraid that's where it ends. Without hard evidence, without a statement from Carrie, our hands are tied.'

'But he may be mad,' I point out. 'He may do anything. To anyone. As I understand it, these people don't need a motive. They just kick off. Isn't that important?'

'Of course it is.' She's frowning now. 'Do you know how much police time is taken up with stuff like this? People with mental health issues? Forty per cent. *Forty*. Four Oh. That means my officers spend nearly half their paid time being social workers. And you know why? Because no one else will have anything to do with these people. Once we had specialist beds aplenty, qualified staff, places of safety. Those days have gone. Say we arrest someone who's kicked off in the street. It might be verbal abuse. It might go a whole lot further. We attend. We arrest the bloke. We sit him down, and we talk to him. Pretty quickly it turns out he isn't the full shilling. He doesn't fit in, he doesn't behave, because he doesn't know how to. He's not a criminal, he's a head case, and believe me there are hundreds of them, thousands of them. What do we do? We put

him in a cell for his own safety and then we start working the
phones. We're after a psychiatric bed. We need him properly
assessed. But unless he's done something really alarming, that kind
of provision just doesn't exist any more. So down goes the phone
and after a day or so chummy is back on the streets, as lost as
ever. Is he a threat to the public? We have no idea. Will he kill
someone one day? He might, but unless someone takes the time
and trouble to find out we have no option but to release him. Out
there. Into the wild. You think I'm making this up?' She shakes
her head, and then checks her watch. 'If only.'

This, I suspect, is my cue to leave. It's obvious that Carrie's story
has touched a sore point but it's equally clear that I am on my own,
and Carrie with me. I get to my feet. I want to thank her for her help
but under the circumstances the word 'help' sounds faintly surreal.

Geraghty ignores the proffered hand.

'Talk to your friend again.' She offers me a card. 'Suggest she
gives us a ring. Convince her that we don't bite. I'm afraid that's
the best I can do.'

At last she gets to her feet, pulling the cardigan a little tighter.
One of the windows doesn't quite fit properly and for the first time,
I realize how cold it is.

'Central heating's on the blink.' She follows me back to the front
entrance. 'But that's another story.'

SIX

Malo arrives that same evening. He knows the address
because he helped move Pavel in, and when I try and
find out exactly what's brought him down to see me, he
just shrugs. Clem's been a pain. He fancies a weekend away.
He's had enough of London. He wants a bit of sanity back in his
life.

None of this is remotely surprising. My son has a very developed
interest in his own well-being, something he may have picked up from
his years when he believed Berndt was his dad. H – his real father

– has done his best to knock him into shape, which is admirable, but a sizeable monthly allowance and a brand-new Audi convertible certainly haven't helped.

It's still barely eight and I've yet to eat, and when Malo announces that he's starving, I suggest a curry. Malo, who wants to laze in front of the TV, thinks I mean a take-out. I don't.

Ignoring his protests, we walk into town. There's an OK Bangladeshi restaurant on the main square and a glance through the window confirms that it's nearly empty. Perfect. Malo orders chicken jalfrezi, which also happens to be H's favourite dish. I settle for tarka dahl, rice, and a couple of veggie sides. While we wait for the food to arrive, I press him about Clem.

'Has she thrown you out again? Be honest.'

Malo says no but I sense he's lying. In these moods, denied his precious telly and probably still hungover, he has a sullenness that some women of his own age find wildly attractive. One of them has just walked in with, I assume, her boyfriend. She's insisted on a table that gives her a perfect view of my moody adolescent and they've already established eye contact.

Malo is blessed with coal-black curls and near-perfect cheek-bones. Lately he's taken to wearing a three-day growth of full-face beard and it suits him. With the right lighting and a good director, he could make a decent stab at a young Heathcliff. Period costume? Shirt ripped open to his navel? Thunderstorms rolling across the Yorkshire moors? Bring it on.

For a couple of minutes, he won't talk to me, but a second pint of Cobra perks him up. He wants to know about the windsurfing, and about Carrie. I tell him that she's really busy just now, her hands full with Pavel, but I have another idea.

'Like what?'

'Kitesurfing.'

'*Kite*surfing? But you told me she doesn't do kitesurfing.'

I tell him again that Carrie is otherwise engaged. Kitesurfing is becoming hotter by the day and this little town happens to be home to a world champion.

'This is a guy who doesn't care about gravity. He has one of those boards that rides high out of the water. A puff of wind, and he's airborne. Seeing is believing. The man belongs in a circus.'

'He does lessons?'

'Alas, no. Too busy. Too much in demand. But I've found another guy who's in the same league. Better still, he's French. Jean-Paul. You'll love him.'

'How much will he cost me?'

'You don't want to know.'

'But you're telling me he'd take me on? Teach me all this kite shit?'

'I am.'

My son, bless him, is an easy sell. After I'd left the police station, I'd spent half an hour or so in the town centre, watching the rough sleepers. Of Carrie's visitor there was no sign but a final exchange with Geraghty had stuck in my mind. These people are a little tribe of their own, she'd told me. Anyone new to the town, and they'd know about him within hours. The invitation was unspoken but it confirmed what I'd already assumed. If I really want to find this troubled youth, then here's where I might start. Watching one of the tribe hunched against the wind, rolling himself a thin doobie, I remembered another phrase of Geraghty's. *The wild*. Richly appropriate.

My next port of call was one of the town's kitesurfing shops. I'd heard of Jean-Paul through Carrie and the shop belongs to him. For quite a lot of money, he'd be very happy to offer my son one-to-one tuition plus a deal on a brand-new rig once he'd got the hang of it. This little arrangement, I point out to Malo, will be far from cheap, but he knows that nothing in life comes free and when I mention a tiny job I have in mind, he simply nods.

'Sure.' He grunts. 'Whatever.'

Whatever? Without mentioning Carrie, I describe a youth, probably in his mid-teens, maybe older, with a blue football top and braces on his teeth. He may be new to the town and Malo would be doing me a very big favour if he could track this person down.

'Why? What's he done?'

'Nothing. Yet.'

'So why do you want me to find him?'

'That doesn't matter. All I need is a name. Plus a clue to where I might be able to lay my hands on him.'

I mention the rough sleepers. For a can or two of industrial-strength cider, I'm sure they'd be happy to talk.

'You think this guy is homeless?'

'I've no idea. This isn't the biggest town in the world. It shouldn't take you long.'

'And the kite thing?'

'Starts the day after you find him.'

Malo nods. One of my son's few saving graces is an appetite for a challenge. He loves putting himself to the test, shaming anyone silly enough to doubt his awesome talents. H did just this a couple of years back, inviting him to organize a charity trip to the D-Day beaches and, to our delight, the results were spectacular.

The food arrives. Malo has kept half an eye on the girl at the neighbouring table and appears to have lost interest.

'She's a dog,' he says. 'Help yourself to jalfrezi.'

Next morning, to my intense satisfaction, I get up and wander into the lounge to find Malo already gone. He'd slept on the sofa, curled under a couple of blankets I'd found in a cupboard in Pavel's bedroom. Not only were the blankets neatly folded at one end of the sofa but the twenty pounds I'd left him for expenses was untouched. Better still, he'd written a note. I'd left one of the doors to the balcony half-open so he could doze off to what Pavel calls 'the music of the Exe'. In the middle of the night, according to the note, my son has risked frostbite by getting up and pulling the door shut. *Why don't those fucking birds go to sleep like the rest of us?* he'd written. I read the note to Pavel. He hasn't got much time for Malo, and it showed. *Tant pis*, I thought, brewing some fresh coffee and wondering how my son was getting on.

He didn't return until early evening. Carrie and I had spent the day quietly avoiding each other. I told her I was more than happy to keep an eye on Pavel, and that she was welcome to take the day off. Whether she did or not, I've no idea. Pavel and I passed an agreeable Saturday afternoon picking our way through more of Ernst Jünger's diary entries, and by the time Malo returned, Carrie had definitely gone.

'Well?'

Malo is excited. I can see it in his eyes. I'm waiting for details but my son knows exactly how to tease an audience.

'Anything to drink?' He's looking at the open kitchen door.

I fetch a couple of bottles from the fridge. Czech pilsner is Pavel's tipple of choice. A single mouthful of Urquell, he says, and he's back on the Charles Bridge, staring down at the water, wondering about the darkness to come. Since he went blind, Prague has remained his all-time favourite city, a source of dreams he insists on sharing the next day, either face to face or on the phone. The small print of these fantasies he's lifted from our nights together before he had the accident that paralysed him, but the settings – a series of improbable boudoirs in the depths of the old city – are a mystery.

I settle on the sofa. I want to know about rough sleepers.

'Amazing people.' Malo is drinking straight from the bottle. 'Loved them all.'

He canters through a list of street names: Bender, Stax, Angel, Zig Zag, Virgil, Killibegs. He'd come across them this morning in the Strand, as close as Exmouth gets to a town square. A group of them had settled on a bench and everyone had a can in his hand.

'They were happy to talk?'

'Not at first. I tried but they blanked me.'

'So, what did you do?'

'A couple of them had a chess set. It's a dodge to get people to part with money. They think it's a good look, playing chess.'

'At that time of day?'

'You'd be amazed. People on the way to the station. Old ladies walking their dogs. A couple of low-lifes playing *chess*? Brilliant.'

It was Berndt who got Malo into chess and there were a couple of years in his early teens when it became a real passion.

'You challenged them to a game?'

'We had a conversation.'

'About what?'

'The rules. They were clueless. They were just moving the pieces around the board, totally random.'

Totally random. This strikes me as a very serviceable metaphor for madness, for lives untethered, or perhaps for The Wild itself.

'So, what did they say? When you pointed all this out?'

'They laughed. They thought it was really funny. One bloke, Stax, is really bright. *It's marketing, man . . .*' Malo is an excellent mimic. *'It's got fuck all to do with any rules. You want money, you look serious, you're sitting cross-legged beside the board, you're studying the play, you move a pawn or two, you make a mistake, you shake your head. You're clever, you're educated, but you've fallen on hard times. Pity's the name of the game. And you know why? Because pity, done right, opens purses. And purses give you money. And money buys you stuff.* This is kosher, Mum. This

is the way he talks. It's brilliant, fucking awesome. I told the guy
he should be writing books or doing stand-up and you know what?
He told me to get a life.'

It turns out that Malo stayed with this little group for most of
the morning, drifting around the town centre from favourite site to
favourite site, pausing from time to time to lift a quid or two from
a bunch of regulars.

'You wouldn't believe how much money they make. Chess does
it for some of the punters, but the real earner is the dogs. Some of
the old ladies have almost adopted them. If it isn't money, they turn
up with a tin or two of Pal and a sandwich from the Co-op for the
owner. It's all first names. Stax even has a bank account. Can you
believe that?'

This seems to me to be rather heart-warming. What's harder to
imagine is quite where Malo fitted in. Trophy guest? Snooper from
the revenue? Born-again Christian?

'I was the entertainment.' He grins. 'They spent most of the time
taking the piss. They thought I was some kind of journalist at first,
after a story, and I was OK with that, but Stax didn't buy it at all.
Not that it mattered.'

This is developing into a travelogue. My son has ventured into
the wild and returned with unimaginable goodies. Where most of
them doss at night; how bacon and cheese – easy to sell on the
estates – are the items of choice when you fancy a spot of shop-
lifting; why Bargain Booze and Iceland are must-visit destinations
as soon as you've begged enough for another evening's oblivion;
how, on a Friday, a two-line text can summon the dealer from
Exeter with his little bags of reliable gear. Glimpse by glimpse,
Malo is burrowing deeper into the netherworld of this sleepy little
town.

Thanks to my son's own flirtation with drug dealing, all too
recently, I happen to know quite a lot about lives lived in the shadows.
But just now I'm more concerned with a youth with a football top
and a talent for housebreaking.

'Any luck? With our young friend?'

Malo is halfway through a story about a recent small-hours
incident in the Shoe Zone shop doorway when he breaks off.

'You were right, Mum. They know him. They call him Moonie.'

'You met him?'

'No. I tried, but I couldn't find him. Stax says he's been in town around a month. Started off kipping in one of those shelters on the seafront. Since then he's moved on, but no one seems to know where.'

'What else did they say?'

'They all agreed he was crazy. Not off his head. Not pissed. Not out of it. Just crazy.'

'Mad?'

'Yeah, full-on Tune.'

'Tune?'

'Loony. Stax says having a conversation with the guy is impossible. He says it's in the eyes. He looks at you, but he doesn't look at you. The word he used was "creepy". As in creeps you out.'

'Not part of the tribe, then?'

'No way. These people look out for each other. They bicker all the time, just like kids, but basically they're all signed up for the same thing. Indoors scares the shit out of them. Having a roof over their heads means responsibility, bills, people knocking at the door. Better to spend the night with each other in some shop doorway, and then move on. You're right. It's a tribal thing. They've formed a circle and the rest of us are on the outside looking in.'

'This is you speaking?' I'm impressed.

'Stax. The man's wasted as a dosser. Not that he'd ever admit it.'

I nod in agreement. My bid to disentangle my son from some very heavy drug dealers led me to a similar conclusion. Out in the darkness, out in the wild, lurk good things as well as bad.

'And Moonie?'

'I've got a list of places to check. It'll be dark by nine, so we'll start then.' He drains the last of the Urquell and then shoots me a grin. 'Another? While we're waiting?'

'We?'

'Yeah. I thought you might come, too.'

We set out after supper. Pavel has thrown up a couple of times for no obvious reason and I'm reluctant to leave him, but Felip is in charge and says there won't be a problem. Pavel, he says carefully, suffers from bad nerves. He gets upset easily and that's when what's left of his body gives him away. When I press him further, wondering what might have triggered this latest bout of vomiting, he won't say but his eyes slide sideways towards Malo and I think I understand. Men, as I know to my own cost, are hopelessly territorial. Pavel can't stand the thought of another male in my life, even if this one happens to be my son.

Distant church clocks are tolling ten o'clock as Malo and I make our way along the seafront. A thin drizzle is drifting seawards in the throw of light from the lamp posts on the promenade and I can hear the rasp of surf from the darkness at the foot of the beach.

'Where first?'

'The Land Train.'

I've seen the Exmouth Land Train, a deeply retro amusement for the benefit of visiting tourists. During the day, it clank-clanks around the town picking up and setting down, while at night it's put to bed beside a garage at the back of a car park near the lifeboat station. Malo, sensibly, has laid hands on a torch. An area of flattish turf behind the garage is a favoured dossing spot. Here we find discarded rectangles of flattened cardboard boxes but no bodies, least of all Moonie.

Malo's flashlight lingers on a couple of discarded syringes beside the cardboard. Stax, he tells me, refers to these as 'electric blankets'. All the comforts of a good night's sleep, he says, without the hassle of plugging the fucking thing in. I follow the logic but what really grabs my attention is the stencilled warning on the damp cardboard. Extreme Caution, it reads: Battery Acid.

Next stop is a patch of woodland and undergrowth on a feature called Orcombe Point. During the summer, especially, this is a favoured dormitory for the town's homeless, but the cold and now the rain must have put them off. We find a couple of festival tents badly in need of TLC, and a scatter of empty tinnies, but nothing else. To my surprise, Malo isn't the least bit downhearted.

'Town,' he says briskly.

En route back along the seafront we check every shelter, just in case, but all but one are empty. The latter happens to be the last. A youngish woman has just been servicing a much older man. Malo appears to know her.

'Moonie?' he enquires.

'Exeter, my lovely.' She's folding a ten-pound note into her ample cleavage while her client zips up. 'He hates this fucking weather.'

The news that Moonie has sought shelter elsewhere brings our search to an end. Exeter, Malo explains, has a handful of hostels where street people can kip. Most of them prefer to take their chances in the open air here in Exmouth but Moonie appears to be the exception. Tomorrow, Malo promises, he'll come up with a list of these hostels and either he or I will pay them a visit. Meanwhile there's a pub he's heard about that doesn't shut its doors until midnight. He checks his watch, and then shoots me one of his melting smiles before offering me his arm.

'Shall we?'

SEVEN

The pub Malo suggests, the Venture Inn, is packed. It's Saturday, open-mic night, and a small stage in one corner of the cavernous bar has been spot-lit. Threadbare gold lamé curtains supply a backdrop and just a *soupçon* of showbiz. Tables press against the stage and recede into the semi-darkness.

The last act, featuring a thin, heavily tattooed elfin figure in her late twenties, is just finishing to a storm of applause and the landlord is already lining up repeat orders as drinkers get to their feet and head for the bar. The singer milks the applause and does the phony thank-you thing, her right hand pressed to her heart. This is all lovely but on the evidence of the last thirty seconds, there's only one problem. She can't sing.

A beered-up stranger has just appeared from nowhere. He stands in front of me, his half-empty glass tipped at an alarming angle.

'Aretha Franklin? Don't you love her?'

As it happens, I do. The woman with the tatts has just been treating us to her take on 'A Natural Woman'. This, to be frank, comes as a bit of a surprise. Aretha had girth, body, soul, and a voice. No disrespect, but the woman with the tatts, aside from the scary purple hair, has none of those assets.

Drunks are often very intuitive. My new friend can read my mind.

'Not impressed?'

'I can't really say. We've only just arrived.'

'We?'

'My son and I.' I nod towards the bar. With commendable guile and both elbows, Malo has jumped the queue and acquired a pint of something fizzy plus a large glass of red. He joins us in time to head off a rant by the drunk about the last act. Claudine appears to be a town favourite. He says she hogs the stage on most of the open-air raves in one of the town's parks. She's flat as a pancake and can't hold a tune to save her life. Expecting something very different, I can only agree.

'*Salut.*' I raise my glass. 'Here's to Aretha.'

The drunk won't leave me alone. Malo, bless him, shoots me a glance but I shake my head. Let's hear the man out.

'You really like her?'

'I love her.'

'You want to hear the real thing?'

'I thought she was dead.'

'Sure. But it might be your lucky night. My pleasure.'

He gives me a full-on grin and then turns to make his way to a nearby table. The house lights are up now and I've got a feeling that one of the four men sitting round the table has been watching me. He's got to be a year or two beyond middle age. He's physically big, broad-chested, but unlike most of the men in this bar he's carrying not an ounce of fat. He's wearing a scuffed leather jacket that I like on sight. Add the white T-shirt, the baggy jeans, and the tiny nod of acknowledgement, and I'm undeniably impressed. Strong face. Good eyes, deeply set. Broken nose. Acceptable buzz cut.

My drunk pauses beside him, bends to his ear, and starts a conversation. I know it involves yours truly because the guy at the table doesn't take his eyes off me. At length, he checks his watch and nods. I haven't a clue what happens next but it's a tribute to first impressions that I can't wait to find out.

'Mum?' Malo gives me the wine. When he enquires whether the drunk is a problem, I shake my head.

'Absolutely not.'

'What does that mean?'

'I've no idea. *Salut* . . . and thank you.'

The wine is foul. Thin? Sour? *Imbuvable?* There isn't an adjective in the world that would do it justice. Malo, solicitous to a fault, offers to get me something else. I shake my head. The wine goes with the venue, and with the last act. I'm more interested in the man at the table.

He finishes what looks like a glass of Guinness and gets to his feet. A woman beside the stage appears to be the guardian of the open mic. They have a brief conversation before the woman nods, stands on her tiptoes, and kisses him on the mouth. *Marché conclu,* I think. Deal done.

Mr Leather Jacket has found my face at the back of the room. Another nod. For me. Then, again from nowhere, the drunk is back with us. I've misjudged this man. Maybe he isn't as pissed as he looks. Or maybe he's simply a gentleman. Either way he's returned to impart a single piece of information.

'You'll be wanting a name,' he says. 'We all call him Deko.'

I nod. In any other circumstances I might blush but tonight, here and now, I don't care. Malo has been a dream. We're on the way to finding young Mr Moonie. Time to celebrate.

The house lights dim again. The sight of Deko, spotlit, at the mic sparks a roar of approval. He takes his time, waiting for the room to settle. 'Over the Rainbow' isn't an Aretha original but she's given it the full soul treatment and to me it's become a favourite. When things got very bad between me and my ex-husband, I'd wait until he'd stormed out and slammed the door before clearing up the shards of broken glass and sponging the wine stains out of the sofa. Only then would I find the track I wanted on my precious vinyl. Aretha Franklin's voice, the space she made for me to hide and recover, offered both solace and the strength to carry on.

Singing it here, unaccompanied, a teary, plaintive, beautiful song in front of a bar full of drunken men, is a very brave move indeed, but from the opening bars, this man absolutely has it nailed. His pitch, his control, the texture of his voice, the way he never has to strain for the high notes, sweeps me away. Half-close my eyes and he could be Van Morrison on a wet night in Belfast. Yep, that good.

This time, the moment he brings the song to an end, the applause is richly earned. Even Malo is whooping, and when Deko steps off the stage and makes his way towards us, my son is the first to congratulate him.

'Glastonbury,' he says. 'The Pyramid Stage. I'll book you in.'

'You're very kind, my friend. Do they pay, by any chance?'

'Trillions.' This from me. 'Squillions. And you're not even drunk.'

'How do you know?' He's smiling now.

'I don't. My son's always first to the bar. What would you like?'

I'm rarely this bold but surviving a brain tumour teaches you a number of lessons, and the most important is to trust your instincts.

As if by magic, Deko has found a table at the back. This is far from private, but Malo has the tact to leave us to it. He's still watching from the bar, making sure I'm OK, but he's sensed that something special may be happening. My lovely, lovely boy.

He arrives with a Guinness for Deko, and a white wine for me. The wine, he admits at once, is a punt but nothing could be worse than the red. Deko is looking up at him.

'Your mother?' He nods in my direction.

'Yeah.'

'An actress, right? Movies?'

'Yeah.'

'The last one I saw was *Arpeggio*.' He's talking to me now. 'Superb.'

Malo beats a discreet retreat. For once, I can't think of anything coherent to say. This man has a physical presence that is close to overwhelming. Everything about him – the way he sits at the table, the way he holds my gaze – oozes confidence. This man, I know for certain, has led a life or two. And it shows.

Hands have always fascinated me. I choose to believe they can tell you a great deal and Deko's hands are a perfect example. They're big, well cared for, trimmed nails, no rings, but they're working hands as well, with a hint of callous when he spreads one or other to make a point or reach for his drink. Even more telling is a tattoo on the inside of his left wrist. It's hard to tell in this light but it looks like a plant of some sort.

He spots my interest at once and pulls up his sleeve.

'You want a proper look?' For the first time, I detect just a hint of a foreign accent. German? Scandinavian? I don't know.

I take his wrist in my hand. On the upper side, an interesting down of faintly ginger hair. On the softer white flesh beneath his thumb, the tattoo.

'What is it?'

'A peanut bush. In Holland, we call it *pinda*.'

'You're Dutch?'

'I am.'

'Living here?'

'Of course. You make it sound like a sin. Or maybe a mistake. It's neither. It's my home. And it makes me very happy.'

He has the courtesy, or maybe the intelligence, to turn the spotlight back on me. He wants to know about *Arpeggio*, about what it's like to make movies like this, about translating the deadness of words on paper into something living, something seemingly real, something that will keep a bunch of strangers rooted to their seats, something that might even change a life or two. Very few people in this world have a talent for listening, but Deko is very, very good at it. Not only does he listen but the kind of comments he slips in tell me he absolutely understands what I'm trying to say. This, too, is amazingly rare, and by the time Malo drifts back to the table I feel that I know this man.

Malo plainly thinks it's time to go, and Deko is the first to get to his feet. Already, I've told him about Pavel, a true god when it comes to movie scripts, and I've told him he's welcome any time if he fancies a bedside chat. A smile and a nod have confirmed his interest but to my faint disappointment he doesn't press me for an address or even a mobile number.

'Exmouth's a funny place,' he says before extending a hand. 'Enjoy.'

I watch him making his way back to his friends. En route, he pauses to chat to a number of others. There's lots of physical contact which seems unforced, both with men and women, and I like that. Something tells me this man has the gifts of a politician, or perhaps a priest, as well as a soul singer, and it's only when Malo takes me by the arm that I consent to head for the door.

Out in the street, it's still raining. We're fifty metres down the road before Malo brings me to a halt.

'So what the fuck was all that about?' he asks.

I grin at him. I don't have an answer but for once it doesn't seem to matter.

'I've no idea,' I tell him. 'Does that make any sense?'

EIGHT

Next day, which happens to be a Sunday, I'm in Exeter by eight o'clock in the morning. Malo went online when we got back from the pub and has given me a list of city hostels. Just after dawn, when I creep into the lounge, he's fast asleep on the sofa and I don't have the heart to wake him up. Logic tells me I have a better chance of getting to Moonie if I arrive early and I'm very happy to get in my car and do this thing by myself.

The first two hostels are a disappointment. Neither St Julian's House nor St Petroc's have ever laid eyes on a sixteen-year-old in the blue football top with braces on his teeth. *Good luck. Try elsewhere*. On my third attempt, thankfully, I get a result.

St Christoph's lies in a busy road between the city centre and the football stadium. It's a converted chapel, maybe Presbyterian, with a fuggy smell of unwashed bodies and a faint hint of joss sticks. A half-open door takes me into a communal dining room where half a dozen men of indeterminate age are watching TV over bowls of cereal. No one appears to be in charge but from what I can gather from the oldest of the men around the table, the hostel is better than most and last night – yes – they had space in the main dormitory for a young man wearing a blue football top with braces on his teeth.

When I ask for a name, the man says he hasn't a clue. 'Never seen him before in my life. Kept his head down. Read a book most of the evening. Didn't say a word to anyone. Wasn't interested in this morning's breakfast. Gone by half seven.'

'Was he wearing trackie bottoms by any chance?'

'Yeah. They all do, the kids.'

'What colour?'

'Grey.'

I nod. The law of probability tells me this has to be Moonie. At this point, blue smoke begins to curl upwards from a toaster on a trolley by the door. The smell of burning sparks no interest at the battered refectory table. All eyes are on the *Sara Cox Show* where a reporter against a desert background is trying to explain how to sew suicide vests.

I get to my feet, but a woman has appeared to deal with the toaster. She's wearing a saffron-orange shift over black jeans. She looks like a refugee from an ashram and is barefoot on the wooden parquet floor. Her nails are painted black and she sports an assortment of silver toe rings. For a moment I assume that she, too, has stayed the night. Wrong.

She unplugs the toaster and upends it over a tray, trying not to burn her fingers.

'Bloody thing,' she says. 'One day it'll be the death of us.'

No one stirs around the table. When I offer to help, she shakes her head. She wants to know who I am, how I got in. Light Irish accent.

'I walked through the front door.'

'Did you phone earlier? Make an appointment or anything?'

'No.'

She nods. She wants to continue our conversation somewhere a little more private. Seconds later, I find myself in a cluttered office with sunshine flooding in through the broken slats of the venetian blind. Tins of red kidney beans spill out of a cardboard box on top of the desk. The woman shuts the door, then turns to face me.

'And you are?'

I give her my name, which she writes down. When I try to explain my interest in one of her clients, she wants to know more. My description of Moonie sparks a nod of recognition.

'So why your interest in this boy?'

I shake my head. I tell her it's personal.

'Everything's personal. Especially with the kind of people we deal with.'

'You've got a name for him? Maybe contact details?'

'Of course. We book everyone in. Am I going to tell you any of this stuff? No way. The least we can give these people is a little respect. Rule one: we never share data.'

I nod. Common sense tells me I should have expected this, but it still comes as a disappointment.

'What was he like? Do you mind me asking?'

'I've no idea. I only saw him briefly this morning before he left. My shift starts at seven. He'd gone by half past.'

'Did he say where he was going?'

'No. And even if he did, I wouldn't tell you. Like I said, the least we can give our clients is a little respect.'

Clients? Sweet. I'm looking at her. I'm trying very hard to make friends with her. Just one tiny clue, for Christ's sake, just one tiny fragment of this boy's life that might take me a step or two further.

'You really have a name?'

'Of course, we have. Maybe it was his real name, maybe it wasn't. Either way it's his business and briefly ours. But that's where it ends. These people are often damaged.' She taps her head. 'Up here.'

'And you think that might apply to him?'

'It applies to most of them.'

'But to him as well?'

'I've no idea. I've told you. The boy's a stranger. He comes. He goes. End of story.'

'Did he look . . .' I shrug. 'Troubled?'

The woman studies me a moment, biting her lip. I sense this conversation is seconds away from ending and I'm right.

'You're a relative, yeah?' she says at last.

'Yes.' I'm easy with the lie.

'His mother?'

'No.'

'OK.' She looks at the window for a moment, weighing some inner decision, then her eyes are back on me.

'He looked knackered. The boy needs a proper night's sleep. I think he might have been going to the railway station. I'm afraid that's all you get.'

Google Maps take me to Exeter Central. By now it's 8.40 a.m. I park my car on the forecourt and run down the stairs. The station is deserted except for a middle-aged man in a green uniform sweeping one of the platforms. When I ask him about a young guy maybe waiting for a train, he nods at once.

'The only one here.' He gestures at a nearby bench. 'Waited nearly an hour.'

Blue top? Grey bottoms? Braces on his teeth? He ticks every box.

'You talked to him?'

'Yeah. He wanted the Exmouth train. I told him that a bus might be quicker but he wasn't interested.'

'So, how was he? How did he seem to you?'

'OK. No trouble. Some Sundays the kids are still pissed. He wasn't. Shame you weren't here a bit earlier. You could have talked to him yourself.'

The 08.34 has only just gone. The journey, it seems, takes about half an hour. Moments later, I'm walking down the platform, trying to get Malo on my phone. When he finally picks up, he sounds groggy.

'Mum . . . what is this?'

I tell him he needs to get down to the station. Moonie's on the train back from Exeter. He could meet him at the station, introduce himself, start a conversation, or maybe just follow him. This is our first real sighting.

I can hear movement in the background. Then Malo says Carrie has just arrived. She's got a car. She could drop him down.

'No,' I say at once. 'Don't do that. Don't even mention it.'

'Why not?'

'Just don't. I'll explain later. Phone for a taxi. I'll pay.'

Malo grunts something I don't catch and rings off. I'm left holding the phone, staring down the tracks into the far distance, trying to imagine this boy on the train. The last thing I need is Malo telling Carrie that I've betrayed her confidence.

I hurry back to my car, wondering whether there's any way I might beat the train back, but the needle on the fuel gauge is hovering on empty and I know I need petrol. Better to leave it to Malo. The rain has stopped overnight, and sunshine brightens the empty street outside the station. Fumbling for my keys, I have a sudden flashback to last night in the pub. Persistence, I tell myself, has delivered a result. I went to all three hostels. I stayed the course. And I managed to squeeze the tiniest clue from the barefoot warder at St Christoph's. Deko would definitely be impressed.

It's nearly half past nine before I'm back in Exmouth. The road into the town passes the railway station. Malo is sitting on a bench, studying his iPhone. I park in a lay-by and cross the road. For a moment, he's totally oblivious to my presence. Then he looks up, shading his eyes against the sun.

'He wasn't on the train,' he says. 'You must have got it wrong.'

The M&S food hall beside the station is open. I buy two coffees and we find a bench beside the nearby estuary. When Malo demands to know what's so special about this Moonie, why he shouldn't mention him to Carrie, I try and fend him off. It's personal, I say. She's really upset about something.

'You mean him?'

'Yes.'

'Why?'

This, of course, is the crux. What do I tell him? How much can I trust this son of mine? It's already obvious that some limp evasion, or even an outright lie, won't do. He wants the truth, and if he doesn't get it then all bets are off. This is his phrase, not mine, but the implications are very clear. Either I tell him why this boy matters, or I'm on my own.

In the end I tell myself I have no choice. For Carrie's sake, as well as mine, Malo has to know.

'He broke into her house the other night,' I mutter. 'And threatened to kill her.'

'Shit.'

'Exactly.'

'So why didn't she go to the police?'

'She's too frightened. It was even an effort to tell me. I pressed and pressed and had to promise I wouldn't breathe a word. Does that make any sense now?'

Malo nods. After the handful of passengers had got off, he'd checked the train to make sure it was really empty. Then he'd got hold of a timetable.

'Eight stations,' he says, 'between Exeter and here.'

We debate the possibilities. Neither of us really knows the area. Digby & Sowton? Topsham? Lympstone? Moonie could be anywhere.

'You want me to hang on?' He nods back towards the station. 'Check out the later trains just in case?'

It's a generous offer, totally out of keeping with what I know about my son, but I shake my head. If anyone's going to spend the morning at Exmouth station it'll be me. But then Malo comes up with another idea.

'You should go to the police,' he says. 'They have CCTV on trains now. And on station platforms. There'll be pictures, video. All you need is the time of the train.'

'The 08.34,' I tell him. 'It's written on my heart.'

'Do it, then. Tell them everything.'

I'm staring at him. For the time being, my conversation with Inspector Geraghty remains a secret, but getting hold of the CCTV is a good idea. Then Malo and I will at least know what Moonie looks like.

'Carrie won't talk to the police. That's part of the problem. She wants no one to know. Absolutely no one.'

'Doesn't matter. Front up. Tell the Filth what's gone down. If you won't do it, I will.'

The Filth. Very H. I pat Malo on the thigh.

'Tomorrow,' I tell him. 'No one works on a Sunday.'

Back at the apartment, Malo treats Carrie with what feels like genuine respect. This appears to confuse her. She doesn't know my son well and what little she's seen has probably confirmed her initial impressions: that my boy is too callow, too spoiled, and too selfish to merit serious attention. Now, after he's organized an impromptu breakfast for all of us, he wants to sit her down and talk kitesurfing. At first, she says she's too busy seeing to Pavel. Only when I insist on taking over next door does she accept a bacon sandwich and join Malo on the sofa.

Pavel is in a very bad mood. He has a sixth sense about dramas developing beyond closed doors and it's a tribute to this instinct of his that he's very rarely wrong. A good screenplay, he once told me, is only real life compressed, thought hard about, and then squeezed like an orange. The clues to his trade are all around us. All you have to do is listen.

'So, what's going on?' he whispers. 'And why won't anyone tell me?'

This is a difficult question, and I fudge it as best I can. Malo has decided to stay for a bit, I tell him. He's got very excited about learning to kitesurf and Carrie is doing her best to help him out. I'm in the process of telling him what little I know about Jean-Paul, soon to be Malo's instructor, when Pavel orders *Sesame* to raise him up in bed.

'They're *à deux*,' he says. 'You know that, don't you?'

'Who?'

'This Jean-Paul. And Carrie. She's been mad about him for weeks. She's even trying to learn French. I've given her a phrase or two. I'm surprised she hasn't told you.'

So am I. I abandon Pavel's catheter and make myself comfortable at his bedside. The scrape of the chair on the lino puts a smile on his face. It means a proper conversation.

'Tell me more,' I say.

'I'm not sure there is much more. He's married, of course. Kids, too. Two of them. That probably gives it an extra piquancy. I gather they meet at her place.'

'She tells you all this?'

'She does, and you know why? There's doing it, being part of it, taking that risk, and then there's celebrating it. To celebrate it, you have to talk about it, boast about it, share it. Think value added. Think whatever you like. In the telling, second time round, a love affair is often even sweeter. That's why women have girlfriends, sounding boards, people they trust. Maybe that's my role here. I'm no threat to anyone. I'm parcelled up like a turkey. I'm totally in Carrie's hands. She controls every moment of my waking day. I'm part of her life now, and it suits us both very nicely indeed.'

I love Pavel in these moods, one phrase, one thought, sparking another. *In the telling, second time round, a love affair is often even sweeter.* I close the distance between us. I put my lips close to his ear.

'So, who did you talk to about us?'

Another smile. Nothing pleases Pavel more than the cut and thrust of a real conversation.

'No one. I didn't have to. If I talked to anyone, I talked to myself. That's what writers do.'

'Because they don't need anyone else?'

'Because they're fascinated with their own company. You know that already. You don't have to ask. That's why I'm still alive.' He nods down at the faint shape of his body, inert beneath the crisp white sheet. 'Not kicking, alas, but alive. You must have worked that out, too. Must have.'

'But why would I bother?' I say softly. 'What's in it for me?'

'This. This conversation. You know what happened when I got that bloody dive wrong? Wrong end of the pool? Wrong time of night? Pissed out of my head? Away with the fairies? You know what happened when I couldn't feel my feet, my legs, my arms, anything? Time stopped. God took the deepest breath. Decided whether he could spare the time to have someone come along in the middle of the night and fish me out. As it happened, they did. Because what really interested God was what might happen later. Whether I'd pay him back, settle my debts, try and conjure something from the wreckage. Which sort of brings us full circle. You? Me? Here? This conversation? I love you for listening. Believe me, worthwhile is too small a word.'

'I almost believe you.'

'You should. Because it's true.'

I nod. He can't see the film of tears in my eyes. I kiss him softly on the forehead. In another life, before the small-hours accident in that hotel pool, we'd have made love, stayed in bed for the rest of the day, snacked on nibbles from the fridge, shared a couple of bottles of whatever came to hand from Pavel's cellar. But now, overwhelmed by a sudden gust of bewilderment and maybe antici-pation, all I can think of is that big face across the pub table. Deko.

NINE

I insist that Carrie takes the rest of the day off. In return, after their chat on the sofa, she says she's more than happy to drive Malo down to the kitesurfing shop to talk to Jean-Paul. With Felip still asleep, I make Pavel a pancake for lunch and fill it with his favourite mix of camembert spiked with chopped spring onions. He turns out to be less than hungry, so we split the pancake between us while he recounts some of Carrie's stories from the nursing home.

This is a rambling property in one of the roads that trail back from the seafront, a warren of corridors and assorted rooms where Carrie held the post of matron, physio, counsellor, and occasional cook before she answered our ad in the local paper. Carrie is the first to concede that the name – Second Wind – was wildly optimistic but Pavel says she enjoyed her time there, though parts of the place were falling apart, and the economics of the business were a joke. Most of the twenty or so residents came on local authority contracts and as time went by there was barely enough money to feed them and keep them warm.

According to Pavel, she made good friends in the home. Many of these residents lived in the twilight between sanity and full-on dementia and Carrie developed an admiration for the various ways they managed to cope. One of them, a widow in her late eighties, had recently lost her husband. Her son and her daughter-in-law paid regular visits to take her out for supper in a local pub. Often they had kids in tow. The old lady's name was Peggy. By now she was getting through a bottle of red vermouth a day, a habit that insulated her against thinking too hard about the past. She loved the trips to the pub, but vermouth costs a fortune across the counter and it was Carrie who came up with the solution. The first double, said Pavel, would be paid for. The rest would come from a new bottle hidden in a bag under the table. Safe in her wheelchair, as cheerful as ever, Peggy always returned in one piece with the same song on her lips. 'Wish me luck as you wave me goodbye'. Word-perfect, without the faintest slur.

It's a nice story and Pavel recounts it beautifully. He admires resilience, grace under pressure, and the fact that Peggy had retreated into dementia by pretending that everything was better than fine simply adds to his admiration for this woman. Pavel has never let the truth ruin a good story, just as Carrie had no time for the stony-faced army of health and safety inspectors who occasionally descended on Second Wind. Once, she told Pavel, an unannounced visit unearthed a stash of empty bottles awaiting disposal in the back yard. Accused of violating every care rule in the book, she insisted that she'd emptied every single one of them herself. Grace under pressure, again. And a round of applause from Pavel.

I want to know whether she's happy working with us. Pavel says yes. H has been very generous with her contract and our money has apparently settled a number of troubling debts.

'What else do you know about her?'

'Not much. I don't think she was ever married, no kids that she ever talks about, but I gather she was in a relationship for a while.'

'Recently? Before Jean-Paul?'

'Yes. It didn't work out in the end and I think that upset her, but she's never given me any details. I gather she's got a place of her own in town now, the love nest where she trysts with her new *beau*.'

I say nothing. What little I saw of Carrie's basement flat was faintly depressing: the unpacked cardboard boxes, the stale air, the lack of natural light. Would this gloomy cave really be somewhere you'd try and nurture a new relationship?

Either way, it doesn't matter. Pavel settles down for his afternoon nap, and Carrie and Malo are back before he wakes up. Not only has Carrie managed to conjure a huge discount on a series of kite-surfing lessons, but she's found a rig at the back of the shop that has only been used a couple of times and would be perfect for Malo. Better still, my son has taken his first steps towards getting afloat under Carrie's tuition.

'It was low tide, yeah? We flew the kite on the beach without a board. Body harness, helmet, the lot. You can't believe how powerful these rigs are. Bit of wind and it's hard not to take off. Brilliant.'

Carrie, ever the diplomat, confirms that Malo is a natural. Next week, once he's less busy in the shop, Jean-Paul has promised to get him on a board in the water. In a couple of days, with luck, he should be outside our window, mastering the basics in tidal shallows the locals call the Duck Pond. Malo nods. He says he can't wait and, looking at his face, I believe him. With Carrie still in the room, he adds a tactful caveat.

'But don't think I've forgotten, Mum.'

'About?'

'Our little deal.'

That evening, I insist that all of us – including Pavel – eat together around the table in the big lounge. We all think it's a fine idea. Carrie volunteers to do the cooking while Malo and I sort out Pavel. Felip has taken the train to see a friend in Exeter and will be back by nine-ish.

I've given Pavel an all-over wash earlier, so it only remains to get him out of bed and into his wheelchair. Thanks to Carrie's tuition, I mastered this manoeuvre in Pavel's early days. Malo has never helped before and I talk him through the basics: park the hoist beside the bed, slide the reinforced seat under Pavel's skinny bum, raise him into the sitting position, gather up the webbing straps and attach to the waiting hook, then hit the button and let the electrics do the rest. Then comes an urgent whirring from the motor and Pavel begins to part company with the bed.

He always insists he loves this routine. He calls it levitation, part magic, part miracle, but I'm watching him carefully and the expression on his face suggests he's far from happy. He's dangling in mid-air, his pale arms limp, his legs hanging down, his head floppy. This may have to do with the presence of Malo, who's readying the wheelchair for touchdown, but I have another theory that the bed itself has become his cave, the one place on planet earth where he feels safe. Thanks to *Sesame* he has at least the illusion of control. He can listen to whatever he wants, summon help, control the room temperature, play emperor in his own tiny kingdom. Now, a parcel of skin and bone, he's entirely in our hands.

Malo has control of the hoist, a little hand-held panel of buttons, and apart from a rather heavy landing which Pavel, of course, can't feel, he does a fine job. We're in the process of disconnecting him from the hoist when Pavel asks me to take him out on to the balcony. I tell him it's cold outside. It's still sunny, just, but the wind has gone around to the north-west, blasting across the water.

'That's what I want,' he whispers. 'The wind in my face. The taste of the estuary.'

We don't get Pavel out of bed as often as we should. A minute or two of fresh air is the least we owe him. Pavel tells *Sesame* to open the balcony doors, and they do his bidding. The temperature in the bedroom is a carefully controlled twenty degrees Celsius but instantly we can feel the difference. We can hear it, too, that keening note, the voice of the wind that Pavel also adores.

'You're sure about this?'

'I am.' His head is sunk on his chest, and when he mutters something else I have to bend and ask him to say it again. 'Just you. You and me.' He manages to raise his head. 'Please?'

I push the wheelchair towards the open doors and out on to the balcony. In the early days before the move, H and I toyed with getting an electric wheelchair, but it was Carrie who pointed out that Pavel could never control it. They're beasts, she said. And they weigh a ton. She was right. The one we finally bought is made of lightweight aluminium and there's not much left of Pavel when it comes to weight.

We're on the far edge of the balcony now, beside the stainless-steel railing. The see-through glass panels give Pavel a little protection from the wind but his head is back, his mouth wide open, his tongue out, sipping at the freshness of the air, and I realize that this is our private moment, him and me and the view beyond.

'Tell me,' he says. 'Describe it.'

I do my best. Cloud shadows racing across the distant hills. The worm of a train on the farther bank. A yacht making its way upriver. A flurry of dunlin foraging above the tide line. The chatter of a pair of terns, darting swallow-like across the wind. A lone curlew, head down, feeding on the gleaming mudflats.

'I can hear it.' Pavel is smiling now.

'The curlew?'

'The train. Where is it going? Is it full? Empty? Can they see us? Are they *happy*?'

The train has to be at least a mile away. I haven't a clue where it's going but that doesn't seem to matter. In these moods, Pavel delights in letting his imagination off the hook. He thinks my little worm might be going down the coast. To Plymouth, maybe. Or perhaps Istanbul. The latter seems unlikely, but it doesn't matter in the least.

As a student, Pavel tells me, he'd jumped a series of trains heading east from Vienna, hopscotching across the Balkan badlands, flat broke but deeply content, always one step ahead of ticket inspectors,

most of them enormous women who never took prisoners. He'd
survived on bread rolls pilfered from the restaurant car, and the
kindness of strangers. A soldier had given him plum brandy, cup
after cup, while a priest had done his best to school him in elemen-
tary Bulgarian. Only on the Turkish border at three in the morning
had this wild adventure threatened to come unstuck. Passengers
queued on the platform for passport control. Without buying a visa,
there was no chance of getting back on the train. And Pavel had no
money.

'So, what happened?'

'My priest paid. He told me it was a gift from God.'

All this, of course, is probably a fiction, a tribute to the richness
of Pavel's imagination. As it happens, he loves a drink, but I've
often marvelled at the way his natural playfulness, his sheer delight
in knocking up a story or two, has exactly the same effect. It juices
him. It sets him free. The world – his world – becomes suddenly
real again.

Now, he's wanting to know more about the view. I'm starting to
worry about him getting cold but then it occurs to me that he can't
feel a thing anyway and so I search high and low for more fuel to
toss on the giant bonfire that is Pavel's brain.

'I can see an old boy out on the cockle sands. I think he's digging
for bait. There are kids around, too. And dogs.' I lean out over the
railings, peering down. Then I freeze. Immediately below the apartment block is a walkway open to the public and standing there is
someone I've been thinking about for most of the day. He looks
like he's just stepped off a building site. He's wearing a pair of
faded blue overalls, scabbed with plaster and white paint.

Deko.

We maintain eye contact for a second or two, then he blows me
a kiss. Startled, I feel a sudden warmth flooding into my face. From
three floors down, there's no way he can see this, but it doesn't
matter in the slightest because already, without even knowing it,
I've blown him a kiss back. Deko nods, grins, and turns away. Pavel
must have heard my tiny gasp – surprise, delight – because he wants
to know what's going on.

'Just a friend,' I tell him lightly.

The meal, despite my best efforts, turns out to be a bit of a trial.
Pavel, after a spoonful or two of Carrie's tomato soup, decides he's

not hungry. Malo is plainly bored. For the main course, Carrie has made a chicken risotto with a big side salad but between us we eat barely half of it. I do my best to revive my son's passion for kite-surfing but even Carrie seems to have given up on the conversation. Before we've even made a start on the cheesecake, Pavel says he's had enough. Too much excitement, he murmurs. Time for an early night. *Over the rainbow*, I think glumly, trying to cheer myself up.

This time it falls to Carrie and me to get Pavel back into bed. Carrie is world-class with the hoist and within minutes I'm tucking Pavel in. It's starting to get dark outside and before I give Carrie a hand with the washing-up, I ask Pavel whether he wants me to close the curtains.

'You've never asked me that before,' he says. 'What difference would it make?'

'It might keep the heat in.'

'Of course. Silly me.'

Pavel has rapier skills when it comes to irony. Decades of penning dialogue that most actors would die for have taught him exactly where to place the nuance in a sentence. *Silly me* means he thinks I'm lying.

'You think there's some other reason?'

'I'm wondering, that's all.'

'Wondering about what?'

'About what happened out there. About who he was.'

'He?'

'He.'

'You think I'm covering something up?' My laughter sounds hopelessly *faux*. 'By closing the curtains?'

'I'm asking you a question. That's all.'

I'm looking down at his face on the pillow. He has a tiny smear of tomato on his chin and I wet a finger to remove it.

'Well . . .?' he says.

'What makes you think it was a man? Can't I meet women down here?'

'Of course you could. But it wasn't that kind of reaction. If we're lucky, life can take us by surprise.'

'And I'm lucky?'

'Yes, you are. We make our luck, of course, so maybe that doesn't quite work.' He pauses for a moment, then moistens his lips. 'You want to tell me about him?'

'No.'

'Is this shyness I'm hearing? Or guilt?'

'Neither.' I see no point in lying. 'I met this guy last night. I spent ten minutes in his company. Maybe fifteen. That's it. That's as far as it got.'

Pavel nods. Then he turns his head away on the pillow. 'That's bad,' he murmurs. 'Much worse than I thought.'

TEN

I sleep badly. I've always marvelled at Pavel's intuition. Even when blindness was his only handicap, he had an uncanny knack of teasing the truth from the barest handful of clues, most of them auditory. He used his ears the way a truffle hound relies on his nose, and all too often he feasted on the proceeds.

Scriptwriters trade in the smallest print of people's lives, building a cage of circumstance around a handful of characters, and often relying on an audience to do the heavy lifting thereafter. I suspect this must sharpen your appetite for those odd little ways we all betray our inner feelings and as long as Pavel could keep all this plunder at arm's length, safely dead on the page, then so much the better. But out there on the balcony, my little giveaway gasp was evidently a dagger to his heart, and now is the first time I've realized how much he still wants to control every particle of my life.

He, too, has a bad night, as Felip confirms over my first cup of coffee the next day. Twice he'd had to go into the bedroom to comfort him, and on both occasions he'd found Pavel in tears. Pavel likes Felip, trusts him, and normally there are no secrets between them. But last night, pressed to explain why he was so upset, Pavel had simply turned his head to the bedroom wall.

'I think he hurts.' Felip pats his chest. 'In here.'

That may well be true. Guilt is something I thought I'd left in the wreckage of my marriage to Berndt. Guilt at never calling out the grosser dishonesties. Guilt at not being firm enough with Malo.

Guilt at mistaking money and a degree of celebrity with the simpler comforts of a proper life for all of us at home. But now is different, because any kind of surrender to Pavel's very special form of emotional blackmail is out of the question. When it was physically possible, for all too brief a time, Pavel and I were lovers. What sparked so gloriously in conversation after conversation worked equally well in bed. Blindness had taught Pavel to map the world through his fingertips and that, believe me, can take a girl to some very special places.

Those days and nights, alas, have now gone. Pavel is still the closest of friends and – I hope – an ally, but paralysis has left both him and us in limbo. We can still kiss. He can still, just, chase my tongue around my mouth. But these little gestures, kind and intimate though they might be, have a limited currency of which Pavel is only too aware. He, above all, understands the urgency of other needs and just now, I suspect, he's fearing the worst. He can still make me laugh. His wilder stories still entrance me. But the worlds he mapped for me in bed are now beyond him, and that – in a phrase he'd recognize at once – is fucking sad.

A full house has emptied the fridge. Carrie gives me a shopping list and despatches me to town. I suspect that she and Jean-Paul might have been doing some mapping of their own overnight, though God knows when or how, because she's brighter than I've seen her for days. 'Get something nice for lunch,' she says. 'And don't forget the ciabatta.'

On the way into town I make a minor detour to steal a look at the nursing home where Carrie used to work. The stories she's told Pavel have whetted my curiosity. If we're to believe the gloomier predictions about the breakdown of family life, then we're all destined to end our days in the hands of strangers.

Second Wind, at first glance, is on its knees. The grey stucco render is in a terrible state, whole shards missing, cracks everywhere. The windowsills on the ground floor have begun to rot and one of them supports a thriving growth of something that looks like moss. Inside, it must be even worse because the waste skip in the tiny triangle of front garden is piled high with sodden mattresses, broken furniture and stained washbasins. Taking a closer look, I get the impression of a whole generation of oldies laid to rest. God forbid I ever end up here.

'Morning . . .'

The voice comes from somewhere above me. I step back on the pavement, peering up. A sash window on the first floor is wide open and I'm looking at that same pair of faded blue overalls.

'Deko.' I'm trying to keep the excitement out of my voice. 'This is becoming a habit.'

'Lucky me. I've got the coffee on. If you've got a sense of humour, you might fancy a look round.'

I agree at once. The front door is open and I'm already in the hall by the time I hear boots clumping down the bare wooden stairs. The air is thick with dust and the place smells of damp. I can't be sure but there appears to be no one else here.

Deko halts at the bottom of the stairs. In a bid to tear my eyes away I do my best to affect an unruffled interest in my surroundings. Anaglypta wallpaper and one of those hand-embroidered sayings, poorly framed, hanging at an angle. I cock my head, trying to decipher it.

For God so loved the world, it reads, *that he gave his only Son, that whoever believes in Him should not perish but have eternal life.*

'Do me a favour?' Deko is laughing. 'It's yours. No charge.'

He leads the way through to the back of the property. The kitchen, smaller than I'd expected, is still intact but clearly ripe for demolition. I'm trying to remember how many residents this place held. How would you feed twenty souls from a narrow little space like this? And where would you hide the red vermouth?

Deko is filling a new-looking electric kettle. A cafetière and a bag of coffee stands beside it. Strength five. Perfect.

'This is just you?' I gesture back towards the chaos behind me.

'For now, yes.'

'I hope they're paying you well.'

'They don't have to. It's mine.'

'It belongs to you? You're telling me you *bought* the place?'

'Yes.'

'Why?'

'Is that a serious question?'

'Yes.'

'Because it was very cheap. And because I can do something with it. Vision, thank God, is a dirty word in this country.' He nods upwards. 'Give me six months and I'll be looking at twenty-two rooms. New basins in all of them. Showers and cooking facilities down the corridor. New boiler for the central heating. Can't fail.'

'And then what?'

'Four hundred quid a month each. Five hundred if you want it furnished. Do the maths. A hundred and thirty-four grand a year. More if you take the furnished option. The refurb's a pain but nothing lasts for ever. You take sugar?'

We drink the coffee, which is excellent, perched on a pair of wooden stools in the concrete bareness of the back yard. The rear of the property, if anything, is worse than the front. One or two of the downpipes are visibly leaking where the old iron joints have rusted away and there are damp stains under some of the windows. What I still can't understand is how one man can possibly sort all this out.

'I'm not hearing the question.' His big hand envelops the mug. 'Which bit of impossible do you want me to explain?'

'Electrics? Plumbing? Carpentry? Plastering? You know all this stuff?'

'I do, yes. But I guess that makes me lucky.'

As a kid, he explained, he'd always hated school. He and his mum had been living in Den Haag. A school mistress herself, she'd kept him on a very tight rein. At the earliest opportunity, at the age of fifteen, he'd taken the bus to Rotterdam and gone to sea.

'And your dad? Your father?'

'He'd disappeared.'

'Where?'

'It doesn't matter. Basically, it was me and my mother. I was a big boy. Going away was best for both of us. If the relationship is shit, there's only so much you can take.'

'What are you telling me?'

'I'm telling you she was better off without me. A quieter life? Definitely. A safer life? Yeah, maybe that too. Once she told me I'd be the death of her. I guess that made her wise. At sea, I calmed down because you have to. I also became a much nicer human being. I was working for nothing on this little coaster. They fed me and they kept me warm and they taught me how to chip rust and paint the upper works. I was good at it. Very good. Then one night we were in Algiers with some cargo or other and we went ashore and the skipper, a lovely man, got in a row with a couple of Arabs. It was going badly for him, but I knew how to fight. I got him out of that bar more or less in one piece and I found a local doctor the next day to treat him on board. The skipper started paying me the following

week and from then on I was part of the family. It's a tiny crew on
these little boats. Skipper, first mate, engineer, couple of ABs, and a
cook. Just the six of us.'

'ABs?'

'Able seamen. Lowest of the low. Blokes like me. On a boat
like that you really get to know people. Looking back, I was in
deep shit as a kid. The *Anneke* was the best thing that ever happened
to me.'

'That was the name of the boat? The *Anneke*?'

'Yeah. Three thousand tons deadweight and paintwork you
wouldn't believe. I stayed with that crew for the next couple of
years and it taught me everything. At sea, you're on your own. And
so you have to pick up stuff from the blokes around you. Plumbing?
Hydraulics? Carpentry? How best to sweep the hold after you've
just offloaded a cargo of fish meal? The fish meal, believe me, is a
joke. It's a great fertilizer, farmers love it, but the stuff's evil and
even after you've got rid of it you stink for days afterwards. Try
impressing the women in a foreign port when you've just arrived
with tons of ground-up leftovers from the Faroe Isles.' He shook
his head and drained the mug. 'Not easy.'

I'm deeply impressed by this man and I'm guessing it shows.
He has Pavel's command of language, not just the words but the
little tricks that dramatists and actors use to make the ebb and flow
of a story irresistible. This can't be easy for a foreigner, but what
makes his company so compelling is the ease with which he's slipped
back into those years that took him away from home.

'Is Deko your real name?'

'No. My parents christened me Rolf.'

'So why Deko?'

'Think about it. Those first months at sea? Me with my little
chisel and my hammer and my brush. Chip, chip, chip. Then on
with the paint. Two coats and a third for the God of Mistakes. Are
you close, yet?'

I'm not. Then I get it.

'Painter? Decorator? Deko?'

'*Ja*. And it's stuck to me ever since. A nickname's like a medal.
I wear it with pride. Deko? *Parfait*.'

'You speak French, too?'

'*Oui*.'

'*Couramment?*'

'*Oui.*'

'*Et en plus?*'

'*Allemand. Italien. Espagnol. Un peu de Russe.*'

I'm counting them all up. The man performing major surgery on this half-dead property speaks no less than seven languages. Remarkable. I try to imagine him thirty years ago, voyaging from port to port, sponging up all that knowledge, preparing himself for whatever next adventure lay beyond the horizon.

'You had favourite ports?'

'Of course. Tangiers was good, as long as you could handle yourself. Marseille, the same. Casablanca? Unforgettable. Santander, ultra-posh. But remember you're only there for a couple of days because time is always money. So, on you go.'

'And a favourite? You had a favourite?'

'Yes.' He's on his feet now, checking his watch. 'Here. In Exmouth. You're free tonight? You want an idea for a movie? Only there's lots, lots more.'

Of course I'm free tonight. And tomorrow night. In fact, given the mood I'm in, I'm probably free forever if it stays as good as this. Deko names a restaurant I've never heard of and asks me to be there by half seven. I tell him I'm sure it'll be a pleasure, and he smiles and says he'll do his best. Then, without the slightest pressure, I find myself out in the street watching him at the upstairs window, tossing yet another broken chair into the skip.

En route to the Co-op in the town centre I'm trying to find the flaws in what I've just been hearing. It's not that I want to disbelieve him, that I have any intention of waking up from the sweetness of this dream, but it all feels so perfect, so seamless, as if he's told the stories a thousand times before. One puzzle is his mention of Exmouth. Where on earth a little place like this finds room for the *Anneke*? Then I picture today's marina and remember Pavel's own stories of the way that corner of the town used to be. Commercial docks, he said, and a nearby *bidonville* that was the playground of every child's dream. *Bidonville* is French for shantytown. Tonight, I think. Tonight, I'll find out more.

I do the shopping and return to the apartment. I've bought a couple of tubs of crabmeat from the fishmonger for lunch and while Carrie whips up a salad, I find Geraghty's card and try to give her a ring.

She's not picking up, so I leave my number and ask her for another ten minutes of her time. She phones back when we're minutes away from finishing the meal. I step out on to the balcony, close the door, and begin to explain about yesterday's excursion to the Exeter hostels when she cuts me short.

'This is about our young friend, am I right?'

'It is, yes.'

'Be at the police station by two. Someone will be looking out for you.'

She hangs up without another word. There's a new note in her voice that I haven't heard before and it's several seconds before I realize what it is. She's worried, which means she's beginning to take me – or perhaps Moonie – seriously.

I'm five minutes early at the police station. The wind has dropped and there's a hint of warmth in the spring sunshine. Approaching the front door, I'm aware of a stir of movement behind one of the adjacent office windows. Moments later, a youngish woman with a nice smile is letting me in.

'Ms Andressen?'

I nod.

'This way, please.'

I follow her upstairs. This door has Inspector Geraghty's name on it. She's sitting behind a cluttered desk, eating a Pot Noodle with a plastic fork. She waves me into the empty chair on the other side of her desk and asks me whether I fancy a cup of tea. When I decline, she nods.

'Right answer,' she says briskly. 'We're low on milk.'

I explain about my visit to Exeter. Carrie's intruder had spent the night in St Christoph's hostel but had bailed out before I got there.

Geraghty abandons the last of the Pot Noodle and scribbles herself a note.

'They had a name?'

'They did but they wouldn't give it to me. Maybe it would be different if you asked. The street people call him Moonie.'

'You've talked to them?'

'My son has.'

'Good. He's right. We've had a couple of conversations as well. You were wise to come to us in the first place. I'm grateful.'

'So what did they tell you? The street people?'

'They said he's crazy. Not active crazy. Not barking mad. But quietly crazy, like you're looking into the middle of his head and there's nothing there. That's a direct quote, by the way. We've got a very good PCSO on the ground and that's one of the bits of intel she came back with. She says they're all a bit mystified by him. One or two of them hear voices but not the way he does. Mystified might be a touch weak. Maybe frightened would be closer to the mark.'

'You mean he's violent?'

'Not like you might expect. She asked exactly the same question down in the town this morning. One of the street people is called Stax. He's the sharpest tool in the box.'

'I know about Stax.'

'From your son?'

'Yes.'

'And?'

'He thinks he's way too clever to be poor.'

'He's not poor, not in his own head, but that's not the point. He thinks we're looking at trouble and after last night, he might be right.'

Last night?

When I press her for details, she consults a typed report on her desk. 'This morning,' she says, 'force control room received three separate calls from Isca Terrace. You know this street?'

'I do.'

'May I ask why?'

'Carrie lives there. Basement flat. Number seven.'

'Ah . . .' Her eyes return to the report. 'That makes sense. Number nine, number ten, and number four.'

'So, what happened?'

'All of them reported an intruder during the night. There's rear access. Not everyone keeps their gates locked.'

'And?'

'In every case nothing was stolen except items from the washing line. The last address had movement-activated floodlights. Nothing missing.'

'And the first two houses?'

'Underwear from the washing line. Bras and panties.' A thin smile. 'Neighbours talk to each other. Our young man may be sending a message.'

I nod. When Carrie hears about this, as she undoubtedly will, we might just be having another conversation. On the other hand, she might be able to persuade Jean-Paul to abandon his family and move in. Either way, the news will do nothing for her peace of mind.

I tell Geraghty about Moonie taking the train back to Exmouth. My son, I explain, was lying in wait at the station but Moonie never showed. Geraghty needs no prompting. She understands at once. Requests for CCTV footage are apparently routed through force head-quarters. She'll have it in hand within minutes.

'You've got the time of the train?'

'I have.'

Another note. I can sense she's impressed. We seem to have stepped out of whatever relationship we had before and she's studying me with what I can only describe as interest.

'Weren't you in a movie once?' she says. 'With Liam Neeson?'

'I was.' I return her smile. 'And it ended very badly.'

Minutes later, she's escorting me back to the front door. She wants to know whether I've convinced Carrie to pick up the phone and give her a ring and when I tell her I haven't even asked, Geraghty looks briefly perplexed.

'Why on earth not?' she asks.

'I made Carrie a promise I'd talk to no one. She seems sure I'll keep my word. That's important to me.'

'I'm sure it is.' Geraghty pats me on the arm, an almost motherly gesture. 'Good luck with that.'

ELEVEN

Deko has asked me to meet him at a pub called The Beach. From there, he says, we'll make our way to the restaurant. I'm clueless about eating out in Exmouth and have no idea what to expect. I'm half-minded to consult Carrie but decide that this latest development in my private life is best kept to myself. I don't even tell Malo about tonight's adventure. When he asks where

I'm going, I tell him I'm off to the cinema for one of those live feed evenings. *Measure for Measure* from the RSC? My son would pay good money to avoid it.

What to wear for my date is an interesting dilemma. I'm being hosted by a man who spends his working days in hand-to-hand combat with a semi-derelict building. I'd love him to turn up the way he was dressed in the pub, especially the leather jacket. That's the man who took my eye and it's pointless dressing up for anyone else. And so I walk into The Beach in a pair of olive green culottes and a favourite top which shows more of what my mum calls my *embonpoint* than might be wise.

Hesitating by the door, I spot Deko at once. He's standing at the bar, deep in conversation with an overweight woman in a Hawaiian shirt probably visible from the moon. She can see me at the door and she touches Deko on the arm. He shoots me a nod, kisses the woman lightly on the cheek, and collects a pile of clothing from a nearby stool. That leather jacket again. Wonderful.

We step outside and he hands me a heavily padded yellow anorak and suggests I try it on for size.

'Are we expecting rain?' There isn't a cloud in the sky.

He smiles but doesn't answer. It's a minute's walk to the marina basin. Access to the pontoons is via a locked gate protected by a keypad. He taps in a number and the gate swings open. Gazing briefly down at the neat lines of moored boats, I begin to get the picture. Not a restaurant at all but a trip on the water.

The anorak fits beautifully and I'm still wondering why when we come to a halt beside a sizeable RIB. I count the seats. There are seven.

'This is yours?'

'No. But I have a key.'

For a big man he moves with the grace of a dancer. He steps off the pontoon and into the RIB, and then turns to extend a hand. Moments later, the boat is moving beneath my feet as he fires up the engine before returning to the pontoon to cast off. The final line is attached to the bow and it's my job to sort it out when he's back aboard.

'Ready?'

'Waiting for you, skipper.'

I slip the line, coil it at my feet as we reverse neatly out. Deko is standing at the wheel. He nods at the seat beside him and moments later we're burbling softly seawards. At the dock entrance, the tide is full, not a stir of current, and Deko eases the throttle forward, skirting the dozens of moored yachts we can see from Pavel's penthouse. To his immense credit, he doesn't play the Alpha male at the wheel – no punch in the back from a surge of acceleration – but simply lets the RIB pick up speed.

It seems to find its own way from buoy to buoy. When Deko asks, I admit this is the first time I've been out on the Exe and the news seems to please him. We're heading upriver now, past another line of moored yachts, and he slows to point out one in particular. It looks brand new. It's broader than the rest and radiates what I can only describe as a sense of purpose.

'State of the art,' Deko says. We're moving at walking speed. 'Total beast. Eats any other yacht alive. Cleans up on Tuesday and Thursday evenings. This RIB belongs to the bloke who owns it.'

'He's a friend of yours?'

'Yes. Anyone who tells you there isn't money in fancy hotels is lying.'

Deko, it turns out, is a member of the local sailing club. They race twice a week and Deko's friend usually wins. As we pick up speed again, he tallies the moored yachts one by one, not by their owners' names but how they made their money. Retired solicitor. Financial advisor. Eye surgeon. Big name in rental vans. University don. Commercial pilot. Jobbing stockbroker. Finally, we slow again. Ahead, untroubled by the beginnings of the outgoing tide, is a luminous confection in wood, and rope, and carefully gathered canvas. It has two masts and a sturdiness that would put you in the best of moods ahead of any voyage. But this sturdiness, this sense of self-confidence, is softened by something close to grace. As the light begins to die, its reflection shimmers on the water. Beautiful.

'And this one? Judge? Brain surgeon?'

'Pirate.' He grins. 'Me.'

'This is *yours*?'

'It is. Every nail. Every plank. Every last spoonful of varnish. If you want the full story, it's called a Breton Thonier. That means it's a real boat.'

A Breton Thonier. Somewhere deep in my childhood I've seen a boat exactly like this. I'm still trying to remember where when Deko eases the RIB alongside and then asks me to take the bow line and make it fast to a cleat on the deck. I haven't a clue what any of this stuff means but I get the broad picture. The wooden hull

towers above me. Standing on tiptoe, I can just loop our line around
the cleat.

'Nicely done.' Deko is securing another line at the stern. As if
by magic, we're riding alongside a rope ladder with wooden steps.
I make my way carefully towards it as Deko shuts down the outboard
motor. Then I pause. A wooden plaque is set into the base of
the main mast of this fabulous craft and it frames the single word
that must be its name: *Amen*.

I scale the ladder, glad I settled for wearing a pair of plimsolls,
and wait on deck for Deko to join me. At last I've remembered
where I've been on a boat like this before. My mum had an aunt
who lived in a fishing port in southern Brittany. Tante Beatrice was
very old and always wore black. She had a round face, wet eyes,
big red hands, and white whiskers that sprouted from her chin. We
were all slightly frightened of her, my mum included, but just
occasionally – always in summer – we'd go and stay.

'Douarnenez,' I announce.

'What?' Deko is checking my bow line.

'Douarnenez. That's where I've seen boats like these before.'

'You know Brittany?'

'I grew up there. The best part of me is Breton, thanks to my
mum.'

Deko steps towards me. He clearly doesn't believe a word.

'You were *born* in Brittany?'

'I was. A long time ago. Never press a lady about dates but it's
true. Perros-Guirec on the north coast. Douarnenez is south, beyond
Brest. That's where boats like this come from.'

'I know. That's where I bought it. Douarnenez . . .' He shakes
his head. 'Amazing.'

We stand together for a moment.

'Tell me you live aboard.' I gesture out at the gleaming spaces
of the river. 'Who'd want to wake up to any other view?'

He doesn't answer me but produces a key. The long plank deck
is flush, a working space, I assume, in the days when a boat like
this would be out fishing. The clue here is Thonier. *Thon* means
'tuna' in French.

I follow Deko back towards the stern. The sight of the big, spoked
steering wheel unlocks another memory. A couple of years ago, H
and Malo organized an Armistice Day expedition to the D-Day
beaches to raise funds for injured veterans. They hired an ancient

Brixham trawler called *Persephone* and we took half a dozen paying guests across the Channel. A storm on the passage back nearly killed us all but standing here, feeling the slow stir of the river beneath my feet, moments from that expedition come flooding back.

Deko wants me to take a look below. Wooden steps lead down from the deck.

'Help yourself,' he says. 'See what you think.'

There's an element of pride in the invitation, impossible to miss. The steps lead down to a space I recognize as the doghouse, a working space full of charts and navigational gear, then – after yet more steps – a saloon. Everything is familiar from *Persephone*, but everything is on a smaller scale. Instead of the big circular table that sat more than a dozen of us, there's a neat rectangle of what looks like polished oak with seats for six. Instead of a sizeable galley, a more intimate space. I'm still staring at the table when Deko joins me. It's set for two places. A tall vase offers an explosion of purple lilies. Beside it, an uncorked bottle of Côtes du Rhône. Judging by the cutlery, I should be expecting a three-course dinner, and the entrée has already been plated: fish fillets in a nest of onion rings garnished with fresh coriander and thinly sliced tomato.

'You like herring?'

'I love herring.'

'Thank Christ for that.'

'You did all this?'

'Chrissy. A friend of mine. You might have seen her in the pub. She was out here this afternoon. Everything we'll eat is down to her.'

I settle at the table while Deko uncorks a bottle of white wine from a fridge in the galley. Framed black and white prints show this glorious boat earning her living.

'Why *Amen*?'

'It's Breton. It means "the rock". *Ar men*. I thought you'd know that.'

I nod. Of course, I think. The Ar Men lighthouse, featured on every Breton calendar ever printed, battered by centuries of wild Atlantic storms.

'You really bought her in Douarnenez?'

'I did. I'd been looking for a while. Buy the wrong boat and you can kiss goodbye to years of your life.'

'A bit like nursing homes?'

'*Touché.*' He fills his own glass. 'The home will be an investment, an earner. This is a love affair.'

I nod. I say I understand completely. We touch glasses. The wine is ice cold, exactly the way I like it. A crisp Chablis. *Promettant*, as my mum would say. Deeply promising.

We start on the herring fillets. The depth of the cure takes me back to the earliest years of my marriage to Berndt, when we'd fly to Stockholm to spend the odd weekend with his parents. They practically lived on herrings, which became a bit of an issue with Berndt, but these are truly special.

'Your friend made the cure?'

'I did.'

'You're very clever, Mr Deko.' I glance up. 'Tell me about peanuts.'

'You mean my dad? Java? The years out east? All that?' I nod. It's a tribute to his intuition that Deko knows exactly what I'm after. 'It's the old story,' he says. 'The French empire? The Spanish empire? What the Brits got up to before the locals – the Indians and the Africans – chased them out? You must have heard it all before.'

'Try me.'

'OK.' He shrugs, forks a curl of herring into his mouth and reaches for his glass. His dad, he says, had been a farmer in Java with a plantation inland from the coast. He'd grown sugar cane to supplement his fields of nutmeg and black pepper and had been experimenting with tobacco in the years immediately after the Japanese occupation.

'He was happy out there?'

'Very. It didn't make him rich but he loved the people. One of them, a local woman, became a kind of wife. They were together for years and years. In fact, she ended up breaking his heart.'

Her name, she said, was Raya. When I ask whether they ever had children, Deko shakes his head. He can't be sure, but he thinks not. Either way, when life after independence became impossible for the ever-shrinking remnants of the Dutch settler community, she refused to accompany him back to Holland. Everything she'd heard about life in Northern Europe – the cold, the wet, the food – told her to stay among her own people. And so, when Deko's father finally returned to the Netherlands, he found himself alone.

'Money was never a problem,' Deko says. 'The problem was

Raya. And you know why? Because she was right. Holland was shit. And Dutch women, especially my mother, turned out to be even worse.'

His father, Deko says, married on the rebound. He met this up-and-coming teacher, good looking, ambitious, full of plans for their joint future, and on the basis of a couple of months together they became husband and wife.

'That was in the late Fifties. They postponed a family because my mum was so ambitious but then I came along and ruined it all. Actually, that's not fair on me because I think he hated her by then, hated her coldness, and I'm not sure I blame him.'

'So, what happened?'

'He went off. Just left us. I was eight at the time and I always assumed he'd gone back out east because when he drank too much that's all he ever talked about, but later I found out what really happened.'

'And?'

'He threw himself under a train. It was winter, at night, in the rain, and I expect he was pissed again. The details don't really matter but I'm guessing there were good reasons for drawing the line. My mother had to identify his remains but never bothered to tell me.'

'So how did you find out?'

'My father had a brother. He knew.'

'And you were how old? When you found out?'

'Fifteen.'

'Shit.'

I extend a hand across the table. Deko ignores it. The past, he says, makes us what we are. He studies me for a long moment, then laughs softly and apologizes for the cliché.

'So, you ran off to sea to get away from your mother?'

'Of course.'

'And it worked?'

'It did.'

We eat the rest of the fish in silence. You'd never feel sorry for a man like this because he seems so comfortable in his own skin, but sometimes that kind of self-assurance can hide deeper wounds. I'm still wondering whether to probe a little further when he collects our empty plates and heads for the galley.

The main course is a lamb tagine, a favourite of Chrissy's. Deko suggests I pour us a glass of Côtes du Rhône while he dishes out. The boat has begun to move beneath us as the tide sluices out.

'I love your hair,' he says. 'Do you mind a compliment?'

'Not at all.'

'So, what happened?'

'Is it that obvious?'

'Yes. In a good way.'

Three courses of chemo took most of my hair away. By now, it's grown back, a downy blondish fuzz that I keep cropped short.

'I had a tumour. Still have, as a matter of fact.'

'Where?'

'Up here.' I touch my forehead above my right eye. 'I'm told most of it's gone and of course I'd like to believe it but . . .' I muster a shrug. 'Nothing's forever, is it?'

Deko ignores my question. He wants to know whether I'm still under the consultant, and when I say yes, he wants to know more about the chemo. I tell him the truth. I tell him that nothing in this world prepares you for the experience of lying on a hospital bed in the knowledge that the stuff slowly dripping into your arm is setting out to attack every cell in your body. You feel spiritless. You feel dead. Things that used to have some logic, like words on a page or a script, mean nothing. You can't concentrate. You can barely think. You're in limbo.

'A friend who'd been through exactly the same thing once told me it's the chemical equivalent of being burned at the stake. Except it happens very slowly. It sounds dramatic but, in a way, I have to say she's right. I never want to go through that again. Ever.'

'And on the brighter side?'

'I'm here.' I smile. 'And the tagine is delicious. In fact, every-thing's delicious. You're spoiling me and if you want the truth, I love it.'

Deko follows the main course with a simple fruit salad, laced with Cointreau. I've had more than enough of tumour talk and I press him for more tales from his seafaring days. In particular, I want to know about the impact Exmouth made in those early days.

'It was the scruffiest place. I loved it. We all did. There was barely room enough to con the ship in through the dock entrance, a couple of feet clearance either side. That meant only the little ships, the skinny coasters, could make it. You'd tie up and the dockers would swarm all over you. Sometimes we'd arrive with a cargo of timber, and every last piece was hand-carried off. They had pads on their shoulders, those guys, and in summer it gets hot in the hold. Timber weighs a ton, but they were on piecework and that was their job. We kept everything neat and tidy and in the evening we'd go ashore. The pub where we met this evening – the Beach? That was the centre of everything. The landlord would change money for us, guilders for pounds sterling. The dockers would play three-card brag all night and bet their next day's wages. Afterwards we'd go back to the ship with some of the locals and party. We had Advocaat, brandy, jenever. Wild times.'

'And?' I sense a story here.

'I fell in love, of course. A local girl. She was a bit older than me and she lived in a shack on Shelly Beach. She was lovely. She had a little girl, sweet, really cute, and I wanted to be that little girl's dad. You know how old I was? Seventeen. They'd just started paying me after the fight in Algiers and I blew my first six months' wages on two diamond ear studs, one for her, one for me. I bought them in Antwerp, cost me a fortune. I was writing to this girl, telling her how great we were going to be together, and it worked fine for a couple of visits, but then we were away for a while, mainly down in the Mediterranean, and by the time I got back to Exmouth, she'd gone.'

'*Gone?* Just like that?'

'Yeah. It shouldn't have been a surprise, really. I hadn't heard from her for weeks, maybe months. The friend she lived with told me the little girl's real dad reappeared and took the pair of them up country. End of.'

'And you?'

'Heartbroken.'

'Worse than chemo?'

'Definitely.'

I can't tell whether he's joking but somehow it doesn't matter. The story fits the jigsaw I'm putting together: the son as passionate as the father, and both burdened with relationships that didn't work out. When needs must, I tell myself, you cut your losses and start again. Just like myself and Berndt.

This time he takes my hand, strokes it, then lifts it to his lips and kisses it softly.

'You like jenever?'

'Once.' I pull a face. 'Never again.'

'I don't believe you. Woman of the world? Film star? All those movies? All those exotic locations?'

He shakes his head and rummages in a cupboard before producing a bottle and holding it up against the gently swinging light suspended over the table. The bottle appears to be nearly empty.

'Enough for a taste,' he says. 'See what you think.'

Jenever is Dutch gin. You drink it neat. It turns out to be oilier than I remembered, and almost immediately potent.

'If you're trying to get me drunk,' I tell him, 'there's no need.'

He smiles, and once again we clink glasses. The last of the jenever seems to be warming all those half-forgotten corners deep inside me, and I find myself reflecting on the obvious contrast with chemo. Then, I felt poisoned. Now, totally relaxed, I'm ready for anything.

We sit in silence for a minute or two, listening to the birdlife beyond the portholes. Then comes the rumble of an approaching train, much louder than I'm used to, before the darkness once again belongs to the chuckling waders and a lone curlew.

I'm trying to work out how many berths this boat must have, and whether any of them are doubles, when Deko finally gets to his feet. He stretches those enormous arms, then checks his watch.

'Nearly eleven,' he says. 'Time to get you back.'

TWELVE

Angry? Disappointed? Sad? It's next morning, and I still can't make up my mind. Then, for whatever reason, I think of that depthless picture in last week's *Guardian,* the black hole just fifty million light years away, and I realize that we know nothing, should expect nothing, and that whatever happens next is probably another riff on one of God's cosmic jokes.

Malo brings me tea in bed, which – believe me – is a first.

'How was the movie?'

'It was a play.'

'And?'

'Underwhelming. I was expecting more.'

'From Shakespeare?'

'From the production. Anticipation is everything. To be honest, if you're really interested, it never delivered. *Tant pis*. Maybe next time.'

We have this conversation with the door open. Pavel's bedroom is next to mine. His door is also ajar because Felip is busying around and, later in the morning, it turns out that he's heard every word.

'So, where did it go wrong?' he enquires. '*Measure for Measure*?'

At once, I'm struggling. Pavel keeps up with the reviewers. If there's a radio recording of the RSC production, he's probably heard it.

'It lost its way,' I tell him. 'I know it's a play about darkness, but you have to shed at least a little light.'

'Of course. I agree.' When he asks about a nearly famous actor who was playing Lucio, I shrug. I badly want to talk about something else.

'He was OK,' I mutter. 'The direction didn't help.'

'I'm sure that would have been true. Alas, he's been down with a broken leg since the week before last.' Pavel's eyes are closed behind his tinted glasses. 'So, where did you really go last night?'

I stare down at him, then I quietly close the door before returning to his bedside. My memories of last night are still confused, hours of conversation, increasingly intimate, followed by an abrupt and bewildering denouement. We swapped mobile numbers on the pontoon back at the marina but we barely kissed goodbye and I haven't a clue where this thing is headed next. All I know for sure is that Pavel has no role in what may or may not happen.

'What I do with my life is my business,' I point out, 'not yours.'

'Has it occurred to you that I may have a stake in all this?'

Stake? I pull up a chair and sit down. Time for a sort out.

'You're very precious to me,' I tell him. 'And that means that you matter to all of us . . . H, Malo, Carrie. We're family. We look after each other. And you're part of that. We brought you down here because we need to know you're happy, as well as safe. You've told me a great deal about the way this place used to be and in that head of yours I expect very little has changed. As it happens, last night, I was with someone who also lived through those years. The pair of you were lucky. You saw the best of the place.'

'He said that?'

'He? Maybe I was with a woman. Maybe I was with lots of people.'

'No.' Pavel shakes his head. 'You were with a man. The same man you saw from the balcony. Don't bother to deny it. You wouldn't have lied to that son of yours otherwise.'

It's a tribute to Pavel's plotting talents that he should have squeezed the truth from such meagre clues, but that's not the point because I'm very, very angry. *That son of yours*, that single phrase, has given him away. Anyone else with trousers in my life is a threat: Malo, my mystery date, and any other rogue male who happens along. Only H, oddly enough, is spared Pavel's scorn. Maybe because he's paying the bills.

'This conversation is over.' I get to my feet. 'We'll talk again later, but in the meantime, I suggest you ask yourself what you really want from me. Does that make sense? Or am I being unduly harsh?'

The text arrives shortly before midday. It comes from Geraghty's phone and it wants to know whether I might be up for yet another visit to the police station. Early afternoon, once again, would be ideal. This suggests developments in the hunt for Moonie and I'm only too happy to agree. Judging by the expression on Carrie's face, Pavel is starting to take his mood out on her and the atmosphere in the penthouse apartment is becoming oppressive.

This time, there's no sign of a snatched lunch on Geraghty's desk. She clears a space among the mountain of paperwork and angles the screen of her PC towards me. A couple of keystrokes conjure a series of CCTV sequences acquired from Great Western Railways. The colour and definition are perfect. A figure sits alone in an otherwise empty carriage. He's wearing a camo anorak but there are glimpses of the giveaway blue football top beneath. His jeans are nicely cut, a surprise because I'd been expecting trackie bottoms, and his white Adidas trainers look brand new. A rucksack lies on the adjacent seat and is probably large enough to contain his entire life.

'No sign of a sleeping bag.' This from Geraghty. 'Which tells us that he may not be sleeping rough.'

I nod. I can't take my eyes off this boy's face. Carrie was right. He's slightly overweight. The curly hair and the dimpled cheeks give him a slightly cherubic look. I've seen faces like this on the walls of Italian churches. He looks like a fallen angel.

The footage jump-cuts from station to station and Geraghty tallies them all. Moonie has the window seat. A book lies open on his lap, but he seems more interested in the view and what strikes me with some force is his stillness. He never moves, never shifts his weight on the seat, never plays with his hands, never succumbs to the normal repertoire of fidgets. In quarter profile, he might be a figure made of stone.

At last, the train still moving, he gets up and shoulders the ruck-sack. His passage out of the train brings him very close to the camera. The lens has a distorting effect as he heads for the door, but I swear he glances upwards as he leaves the carriage.

Geraghty agrees he's probably aware of the CCTV. We've cut to the camera on the station platform. Once again, there's nobody else around. The train is on the move again and Moonie pauses to watch it leave before heading into a car park. After that, he's gone.

'Lympstone,' Geraghty grunts. 'Last station before the end of the line.'

'Are there more cameras? In the village?'

'Sadly not.' She nods at the screen. 'We need to know whether you recognize this boy. Have you seen him in the street? In a shop, maybe?'

'No.' I shake my head.

She has prints from the footage, shots of Moonie making his way out of the train. Full-face, I'm struck more than ever by his seeming innocence. Never would you associate someone like this with Carrie's account of the moment she woke up to find him at her bedside. Housebreaker? Wanker? Self-confessed serial killer? Not a chance.

Geraghty is watching me carefully. She wants me to take one of these prints and show it to Carrie.

'I can't do that. She'll want to know where it came from.'

'Of course she will. And maybe now's the time you ought to tell her. Believe it or not, we're here to help.'

'You think the boy's a danger?'

'We think he might be but without evidence that he's actually done something, our hands are tied.'

I nod. I'm thinking of Carrie.

'You need a statement from her?'

'Of course. And confirmation that this is the person in question. In the meantime, now we have an ID, we'll try to find him. Stealing knickers from washing lines isn't homicide but you look for a pattern in cases like this. The rough sleepers have a nose for trouble. That's what you need to survive on the streets. And you're right, they think this young man is unhinged.'

'You'll show them the photo?'

'Of course.'

I leave the police station with a set of prints in an envelope, having agreed to talk to Carrie again. Out in the sunshine, I'm wondering how best to handle her when my mobile begins to ring. I glance at caller ID. Deko. For just a moment or two I'm tempted to ignore the call, to play Madame Cool and leave him dangling, but then my finger – with a mind of its own – swipes to the right and I'm listening to Aretha Franklin's own take on 'A Natural Woman'.

I shake my head. My feet are tap-tapping on the pavement and I'm starting to sway with the sheer force of the performance. Then the music dips and Deko takes over.

'The Kennedy Center Honors, 2015.' He sounds amused. 'Check it out on YouTube. Obama's there, too, with Michelle and other showboats. Grossly over the top but the tune's as good as ever.'

Kennedy Center, I think. 2015. But Deko hasn't finished. When he asks whether I've got time for a coffee I say yes.

'The Beacon,' he says. 'Come in round the back. You'll find it behind the big church. Look for a red door.'

Then he's gone.

I've heard about the Beacon before. Pavel has mentioned it. According to him, this is an ancient terrace of Regency houses where the great post-revolutionary shaggers left their cast-offs. The abandoned Lady Nelson lived at one address, Byron's forlorn wife at another. The Beacon, warned Pavel, served as a terrible warning about the alleged sanctity of the marriage vows. Admiral or poet, you dumped your baggage and moved on.

The big church Deko mentioned is visible from most parts of the town. En route, still clutching the envelope with the shots of Moonie, I wonder whether to start showing them around. *Have you seen this man? Do you know he's crazy?* But then I realize I still need Carrie to make a proper ID. The knowledge that, at the very least, she's found herself a lover is some comfort. Jean-Paul, fingers crossed, might be able to make her see sense.

The rear of the Beacon isn't pretty. The terrace straddles the crest

of a hill, property after property, each a study in red brick and
Victorian pipework. These houses aren't small, four stories at least,
but the longer I pause to study them, the more the terrace begins
to grow on me: the uneven jumble of roof lines, the hint of shadowed courtyards behind high walls, the explosions of wisteria and
honeysuckle softening the bare brick.

Many of these properties seem to have been sub-divided into
flats, and neglect has settled on some of them, but somebody –
Deko? – has obviously spent money on the one with the red door.
I'm still gazing up at the Georgian windows, thinking how handsome
they are, when the door opens and I'm suddenly looking at Deko.

'I saw you coming up the street,' he says.

He stands aside to let me in. I find myself in a smallish garden
designed around an area of slabs that serves as a parking space.
Deko evidently drives an old Land Rover, dents in the bodywork,
caked mud on the tyres, a ladder lashed to the roof rack.

'You like it?'

'I love it. It's a leather jacket on wheels.'

'I meant the garden. Flowers bewilder me.'

The garden, I assure him, is wonderful. The back door that leads
into the house is open and we step inside. It's obvious at once that
this property is a very different proposition to the shell of the
nursing home I saw yesterday. Wherever I look, there's evidence
of careful restoration: the wood stripped back and sanded on the
endless flights of stairs, newly plastered walls in subtle shades of
grey, rich bursts of sunlight pouring in through stained-glass panels
on each landing. This, it occurs to me, is the work of the same
hands, the same sensibility, that transformed a worn-out Breton
Thonier into *Amen*.

'You live here?'

'I do. For the time being.'

'It's amazing. Truly incredible.'

'You mean the view?'

'Everything.'

We've reached what Deko assures me is the top of the house. In
contrast to the floors below, the entire floor is open plan. Huge doors
fold back to access a balconette that spans the width of the
property.

'Help yourself.' Deko opens one of the doors and steps back. 'Enjoy.'

I'm more than happy to do his bidding. Out in the sunshine, the view seems to stretch forever. To the left, the long curl of the beach. Ahead, the open sea, improbably turquoise under the blue of the sky, framed by the long grey arm of a distant bay. And, best of all, the mouth of the river that gave birth to this town.

From Pavel's penthouse the view is pretty special, but it's nothing compared to what the Beacon has to offer. With the detachment of height comes a deeply wonderful sense of omnipotence. This must be like finding yourself on the bridge of a ship, I think. The view, the options, are limitless. From here, in my head, I could haul up the anchor and voyage anywhere. I step back inside. Twice in twenty-four hours this man has taken my breath away.

There's a modest kitchenette in one corner. Deko's pouring fresh coffee from a cafetière and when he asks whether I'd fancy a crois-sant I just nod. There are bookshelves everywhere and the room has been artfully designed to offer intimate little corners where you might sink into a chair under an occasional light and read. A big sofa has been positioned to take full advantage of the view and I settle into one corner, studying the art on the walls. The sheer range of this man's taste reminds me slightly of Pavel, the same mix of watercolours, oils, and a scatter of black and white photographs. The theme is obvious, the ocean and its choice of a thousand landfalls.

'You paint as well?'

'No. The photos are mine but the rest I collect. You're looking at half a lifetime afloat. Chrissy thinks I'll come back as a dolphin.'

I smile. It's a nice image.

'You're telling me your days at sea are over?'

'Far from it. That's why I did the boat up. From here I can be on the Brittany coast in less than a day.'

'Wonderful.'

'You mean it? You'd fancy a trip across?'

'I would, yes.'

'*Aucun problème*. I'll sort it.'

'In *Amen*?'

'Of course.'

I'm grinning. So easy, I think. So natural. So – dare I say it – *us*. I reach for the coffee. I don't bother asking whether this restoration is all his own work because I know what the answer will be, but I'm still intrigued to find out more.

'This is one of the projects? This house?'

'It is. I've started a company called Grace and Favour. The deal is finding old properties with amazing views. Spend your time looking, and they needn't be that expensive. Then you do them up to a proper spec, think carefully about each floor, and create a different kind of retirement home. This place is a good example. Every floor will be self-contained. I'll sort full-time help, someone to keep a gentle eye on things.'

'You mean a matron?'

'More a friend. Medically qualified, of course, but someone you'd enjoy having around. There when you need her. Invisible when you don't.'

'This person will live in?'

'Nearby. But always accessible. The key is letting people believe they're secure, as well as happy. Think an intimate version of McCarthy and Stone. A view like this and you'd age very happily.'

'Sounds perfect. How old do you have to be?'

Deko wisely ignores my little joke. He's rummaging in a cupboard, looking for some marmalade for the croissants. In the meantime, I get up and study the view again. A lone kitesurfer is riding one of Jean-Paul's high-tech boards. The sea is flat calm, the wind steady, and he carves a perfect line across the water. I find myself telling Deko about my son's first steps into this world, and how lucky we've been to find Jean-Paul.

'We?'

'Myself and Malo. Pavel has a carer called Carrie. She does everything for him. She's close to Jean-Paul and that worked for us, believe me.'

'She scored you a deal?'

'She did. I've never asked how that worked but she seems a happy girl.'

'Pleased to hear it.' He's found the marmalade. 'I'll show you downstairs after coffee. I need some inspiration myself.'

I leave the Beacon mid-afternoon. After what I've seen of the work waiting for him in the retirement home, I'm surprised that Deko has time for in-depth discussions about colour schemes and the merits of certain shades of washed-out greeny-greys. The standard of the finish on every floor exactly meets the clientele he seems to have in mind when the building is ready for occupancy. When I gently press him about the money these people might be paying, he says it's complicated. What he has in mind is a leasehold purchase they can sell back at any time, plus a monthly service charge to take care of the all-important medical support. That leaves me guessing about the actual figure.

'Pretend I'm seventy-five,' I suggest. 'I'm white, respectable, I might just have been widowed or I might not, I've got perfect manners, and I've just sold the family acres. What am I parting with?'

The question makes him laugh. My client profile, he says, is spot on. No DHSS. No arsonists. No one with a taste for Led Zeppelin. The greyer the pound the better.

'So how much?'

'On today's market?' He shrugs. 'Three fifty for the leasehold. Plus a couple of hundred a month for peace of mind.'

'You mean aspirins?'

'I mean anything from company to shopping to low-level medical support. If it comes to bed baths and trips along the front in a wheelchair, we'd have to reassess. This is a trial run. I can't complete until I've sorted the other place out but there might be a case for taking this to market first and then using the proceeds to hire some help and give the other place a kick up the arse. That's not as easy as it looks. Finding the right guys can be a nightmare.'

'You've got backers?'

'I have.'

'Are they patient?'

'Always.' He laughs again. 'If this place works, I've got a list of other properties. Budleigh Salterton. Ottery St Mary. A couple of those little villages around Dartmoor. Anywhere with low blood pressure and a view. This country's dying on its feet. It's getting older, and fatter, and more frightened. Believe me, you can make money out of that.'

'Really?' The way he puts this proposition gives me a moment's pause. He's clearly thought all this through, and I don't quarrel with any of his conclusions, but there's a hint of steel, a ruthlessness, that doesn't quite go with Aretha Franklin and exquisitely cured herring fillets. 'So what will you put on your tombstone?' I ask him. 'Apart from your name?'

'My *tombstone*? What sort of question is that?'

'I want to know how you view yourself. Builder? Sailor? Businessman? Everyone's got a label. What's yours?'

He nods, seeming to understand, and gives the question some thought. Then the big hands shepherd me towards the final flight of steps that lead to the basement. Only in the back garden, shaded now, does he give me an answer.

'Chancer.' He stoops to kiss me. 'Happy now?'

THIRTEEN

C hancer? Perfect. This is the world where Deko belongs. The world of risks, and effort, and never losing your nerve. The world where you back your own instincts, your own judgement, weather the hard times, and never lose a night's sleep. Chancer, I think. How come I've been lucky enough to meet a man like this?

Carrie is on the phone when I get back to the apartment. I wait for her to finish and then join her on the balcony. She sees the envelope in my hand, and I sense she knows what's coming. The first of the CCTV prints shows Moonie sitting alone in the carriage. She gives it a cursory glance and then moves on to the other one. This time she looks at it properly, shaking her head before turning away.

'Where did you get these?'

'Look at me, Carrie.'

'I asked you a question.'

'The police. Because I worry about you. And so do they.'

'You told me you'd keep it a secret.' She turns to face me at last. 'You promised. You gave me your word. Otherwise I'd never have told you.'

'About him?' I gesture at the print.

'Yes.'

'It *is* him?'

'Yes. And you know what happens now? When he comes for me? You know what he'll do? You remember what he said to me? That night? In my own fucking *bedroom*?'

I blink. Carrie never swears.

'You can sleep here,' I say at once, 'until they find him. You can have my room. It's the least I can do.'

'That's not the point. I trusted you. And now look what's happened.'

I take a step closer to her, try and give her a hug, but she fends me off. I've betrayed her. Worse still, I've opened the door to all kinds of nightmares.

'This is unreal,' she says. 'I can't get that night out of my head. Things like that aren't supposed to happen, not in a little town like this, not to someone like me. Don't tell me it'll all be OK. Don't tell me I'll get over it. I don't want to hear any of that shit. One day it may happen to you and then you'll understand. Everything you've ever taken for granted, *everything*, it's just gone. I can't sleep properly. I can't get that face, those eyes, out of my mind. Then you turn up with pictures like these and suddenly it's all much, much worse.'

'We'll take care of you,' I tell her again. 'But first you have to go to the police. I've got to know the woman in charge. Her name's Geraghty. She's good. She wants to find him but first you have to give her a statement. Otherwise she can do nothing.'

'No.' She shakes her head. 'No way.'

She's crying now, her back to me again, her hands clutching the railing. She blows her nose between her fingers, then shakes them over the drop. Finally she turns to face me. Her face is like stone, pale, expressionless.

'I'll have to leave town,' she mutters. 'Find somewhere else to live, some place he'll never find me.'

At this point, my phone begins to ring. I ignore it.

'And Pavel?' I'm staring at her.

'You'll have to make other arrangements, look after him yourself, whatever it takes. You should have kept your word, thought it through, not go running off to the police.'

'You really think that was an option? After what you told me?' I mention the thefts of underwear from gardens on her street. I somehow assumed that she must have got word of these creepy visits but – once again – it seems I'm wrong.

'When did this happen?' She's horrified.

'A couple of nights ago.'

'It's him. It has to be. It's so fucking obvious. He's sending me a message, isn't he? He'll be leaving dead animals on my doorstep next. He'll take a knife to them first, do horrible things to them. If he can get them through my letterbox, he probably will. The boy's sick. He needs help.'

'Exactly. And that's what the police are for. You have to talk to them, Carrie. Before he really kicks off.'

She studies me for a long moment. For the first time I notice the reddening around her fingernails where she's been picking them. I have Geraghty's card in my jeans pocket. I fetch it out and give it to her.

'Call her, Carrie. Please. We care about you. We really do.'

'You know nothing about me,' she says hotly. 'Nothing.'

In a number of ways, that's probably true. There are whole areas of Carrie's private life she's kept to herself, but just now that's of absolutely no relevance.

'Make the call,' I say again. 'Just do it.'

'You had no right.' She shakes her head.

'I had every right. Let's get this thing sorted.' I pause. 'Yeah? We agree?'

She doesn't make the call, not that afternoon, not later. After she's left the apartment, handing over to Felip, I try and sort out the implications for all of us in my mind. If she really does leave town, then Pavel's care will fall to me until I can find a replacement. A trillion agencies deal in all kinds of care but I know Pavel far too well to have any confidence in an easy fix.

Pavel, once we'd installed him in the apartment, insisted on auditions when it came to hiring someone to look after him and we were in double figures before Carrie turned up and won his full approval. Do I really want to go through all that again? An endless succession of strange faces at the door? Women, and occasionally men, without the faintest idea of what it needs to put a smile on Pavel's face?

At this point, Malo turns up. He's been out on the Duck Pond with Jean-Paul, trying to master the basics of getting the huge kite to take him in the right direction. This was way more difficult than he'd ever expected, and he was glad I hadn't picked up when he'd finally managed it, phoning me to witness a second attempt.

'I was hopeless,' he said. 'I blew it completely.'

I tell him it doesn't matter. Tomorrow, or maybe the next day, he'll get it together.

'Here, take a look.' I show him the CCTV prints.

'Cool.' He's grinning. 'Peng.'

'Peng' is a term of approval in Malo's world. The shot on the station platform wins special attention.

'Look at his eyes,' he says. 'There's no one at home, no one there.'

'He got off at Lympstone,' I tell him. 'I thought the police might make enquiries, you know, house to house, but I'm not sure they've got the time. At least they know what he looks like now. We live in hope.'

For a moment, I toy with telling him about Carrie, how upset she is, but the very mention of her name sparks another grin.

'They're at it,' he says.

'Who?'

'Carrie and Jean-Paul. He thinks she's the dog's bollocks. I bet he can't get enough of her.'

'And Mrs Jean-Paul?'

'I didn't ask. He's forty-something, for Christ's sake. You think he doesn't know how to handle this kind of shit?'

'Sweet thought,' I tell him. 'All I care about is Carrie. She needs looking after. I've no idea how she'll fit into his life, but I hope he recognizes a woman in trouble when he sees one.'

That evening passes in near silence. Malo recognizes tension when it surrounds him, a legacy of what Berndt and I mistook for parent-hood, and after a glum supper I'm relieved when he slumps on the sofa and switches on the TV. He flicks through the channels like any other adolescent, giving each programme a couple of seconds to make its case, then he digs his Xbox out of his rucksack and starts to play Grand Theft Auto. I retire to the silence of my bedroom, glad of my own company. I know I owe Pavel a conversation, and I know as well that he'll blame me for not showing up, but just now I can't face it. In Malo's parlance, it's been a truly shit few hours. Enough.

FOURTEEN

I must have been exhausted because I don't wake up until gone nine. Carrie is standing at my bedside. She's holding out my phone, which I must have left in the lounge.

'For you,' she says tonelessly, turning on her heel and leaving the room.

'We've got him.' It's Geraghty. 'Picked him up at the station at quarter past seven.'

One of her officers, she says, had left a set of CCTV photos with the station staff. Moonie is now in the custody suite in an Exeter police station, awaiting his first interview.

'So what's he said so far?'

'Nothing. We're still waiting for the duty solicitor to turn up.'

'You've got a name?'

'He calls himself Montague. Foster Montague.'

'Calls himself?'

'We searched him but found no ID.'

'Nothing at all?'

'Nothing. No credit cards. No correspondence. No bills. My guess is he's too young for a driving licence. So, Foster Montague it has to be. Oddly enough, we found the name scribbled inside one of the books he had. The book looks second hand. He probably got it at a charity shop and lifted the name.'

'He gave you an address?'

'No. He said he couldn't remember.'

'So, what else did you find?'

'Very little. The boy needs a good wash, and a visit to a laundrette wouldn't do any harm.'

'No women's underwear?' I'm trying to hide my disappointment.

'I'm afraid not, and when we asked him about the thefts, he denied all knowledge.' She pauses to fire a question at someone nearby. Then she's back on the phone. 'You talked to Carrie?'

'I did. Has she called you?'

'No. She's there now?'

'Yes.'

'Then try again. Be forceful. Point out how important we get her onside. We'll hold the interview until we hear from you.'

The phone goes dead and I lie back for a moment or two, my eyes closed, listening to the beat of my heart. Foster Montague. Moonie. No address. No background. Nothing. *Rien. Nada.* I try to imagine him in the custody suite, probably alone, waiting to see what happens next. At length, I force myself to get up. In the bathroom, when I look in the mirror, I barely recognize the face that is staring back at me. Gaunt is too kind a word. As the scales confirm, I'm definitely paying the price for ratting on Carrie. I've lost six pounds in as many days. In any other circumstances, I'd view that as a triumph.

Showered and dressed, back in jeans and a T-shirt, I fiddle in the kitchen, waiting for Carrie to emerge from Pavel's bedroom. To my relief, it seems we're back on speaking terms.

I tell her about Moonie. The news that the police have found him appears to alarm her.

'They've arrested him?'

'That isn't clear. They certainly want to talk to him.'

'About what?'

'I'm guessing the theft of the underwear.'

'Not me?'

'I don't think so. Not yet.'

'What does that mean?'

For the umpteenth time, I try and explain. A statement, plus a positive ID, would – I'm assuming – lead to a formal charge. Breaking into someone's house in the middle of the night and threatening to kill them, even these days, isn't something the law takes lightly.

'So, what would they do? If I gave them what they want?'

'I'm guessing they'd want an explanation.'

'From the boy?'

'Of course.'

'He'll deny it. He's bound to. He'll say it never happened. His word against mine. No other witnesses.'

'Then they'll dig around.' I'm trying to put her mind at rest. 'Look into his past. Make enquiries elsewhere. Find out what else he's been up to.' I'm making this stuff up and Carrie knows it.

'You really think that?'

'Of course. That's what the police are for.'

'And if it goes to court? If the police can make some kind of case? What then? Say he's got a good lawyer. Says he hears voices in his head. Says it's not his fault. Where would all that take us?'

'They'll lock him up. Section him. Put him away.' I shrug. 'Whatever.'

'But he'll come out in the end, won't he? And then he'll come looking. It happens all the time. Domestic abuse. Take all those battered women. The husbands get a slap on the wrist, told to stay away. Some of them even go inside for a couple of months. But doing time like that means nothing when you're lying in bed,

listening for noises, listening for those footsteps down the hall. No.'
She shakes her head. 'I'm sorry, but no. I won't phone your police
friend. And I'm definitely not making a statement.'

I try a little harder, try getting angry, but Carrie refuses to budge.
This is her life we're talking about, her peace of mind, and both
are precious. Thank you, but no.

I relay the news to Geraghty, who appears to be at the Exeter
police station. She tells me the duty solicitor has arrived and is in
an office downstairs, talking to her new client. The detective consta-
bles assigned to the case will need to make a start on the first
interview very shortly. Am I sure Carrie won't attend?

'Sadly, I am,' I say. 'I tried, and I failed.'

I listen out for my mobile for the rest of the morning, half-expecting
an update from Geraghty. When it doesn't ring, I'm not sure whether
this is good news or not. Finally, mid-afternoon, I get a call.

'We've had to release him,' Geraghty says. 'He's back in the wild.'

At first I assume she's joking, but it turns out she's not. Pressed
on the underwear thefts, Moonie continued to deny everything,
and in the absence of hard evidence the interview team were helpless. Asked to account for a lack of address, he simply shrugged
and refused to comment. Earlier, he'd given his age as eighteen,
which was a relief because otherwise Geraghty would have had to
lay hands on someone she calls an Appropriate Adult, but now she's
inclined to doubt even this.

'We think he's younger,' she says.

'What about his past? Stuff he's been up to? Previous
convictions?'

'We checked our databases. Nothing.'

'What name did you use?'

'The only one we've got. Foster Montague.'

'No wonder, then.'

'You're right,' Geraghty seems to agree. 'It's a mess.'

So far, I've been conducting this conversation in the lounge,
standing by the window, staring out at the view, but suddenly I'm
aware of Carrie in the room. She must have ghosted in without a
sound. I shoot her a look and step out on to the balcony, sliding
the door closed behind me. Geraghty, thank God, is still on the line.

'He's mad,' I say. 'He has to be.'

'That may be the case, but it doesn't help us. Under the Mental

Health Act we can hang on to him for seventy-two hours and keep him in a place of safety pending an assessment, but we've got a problem with cell availability and the mental health folk are in denial. No time. No beds. Nothing. To be frank, I can't afford to have officers babysitting this boy for the next three days. It's just not going to happen. Not on the basis of the available evidence. The duty seems to think he's harmless.'

'Duty?'

'His solicitor. That doesn't make life any easier for us but that's not her job. Like I say, we live in a world of diminishing choices.'

'Which is why you released him?'

'Why we had to, yes.'

I'm peering back into the lounge. Carrie seems to have gone.

'Surveillance?' I murmur. 'Can't you keep tabs on him?'

'You're kidding.' My suggestion draws a mirthless laugh from Geraghty. 'We'd be talking a team of fourteen. If he was a terrorist, it might be different. Someone like this boy, any surveillance bid from me would be turned down flat.'

'But he told Carrie he'd killed people. And he threatened to kill her, too.'

'Fantasy, Enora. I'm sorry. We've done what we can.'

This is the first time Geraghty's used my Christian name. I thank her for her efforts and ask whether she considers the case closed.

'There is no case,' she says. 'But if it helps at all, we bought him a ticket and put him on a train. The ticket will take him to London. Let's hope that's where he stays.'

The line goes dead. I slip my mobile back into the pocket of my jeans. It's high tide and two figures are knee deep in the Duck Pond, sorting out a tangle of lines on a big scarlet kite. One of them is definitely Malo. The other one must be Jean-Paul. I watch them for a moment. Finally, Malo gives the control bar a hefty tug and the kite blooms like a flower in the wind. Seconds later, he's hopped on the board and headed upriver. I hear the faintest whoop of triumph before the door slides open behind me, and Carrie appears.

'They've let him go?' Her voice is flat.

'They have. He's gone to London. It's over, Carrie. He never killed anyone. The boy's a fantasist. You'll never see him again.'

She looks at me for a long moment, then she spots the lone figure standing in the Duck Pond, waiting for my clever son to come back.

'That's JP.' She's talking to herself. And smiling.

FIFTEEN

Next morning, I'm up early, feeling infinitely better, determined to put the past week behind me. A text from Deko suggesting a leisurely Good Friday cruise down the coast is full of promise and he even adds a thought or two about what we might be eating. Scallops, a big salad, fresh ciabatta? A couple more bottles of Chablis? *Parfait*, I text back. *Marché conclu.*

Deal done. Malo's still asleep on the sofa, doubtless dreaming about big red kite sails, and I busy around in the kitchen, brewing coffee for Pavel, waiting for Carrie to arrive. The news that Moonie had left town definitely lifted her spirits yesterday and she even lingered for an hour or so last night to help with a celebratory bottle of Rioja. The bottle nearly empty, she had the grace to apologize for, in her words, being such a pain, but – as she was the first to point out – her conscience was clear as far as Moonie was concerned. She hadn't breathed a word to the police and so there was no way her visitor could possibly connect her to his brief stay in custody.

By half past ten, she still hasn't turned up. So far, I've resisted the temptation to give her a ring, thinking she might have slept in or be nursing a hangover, but with Pavel beginning to get fractious I try to raise her on my mobile. Nothing. I try again. She doesn't pick up. This is a pain. I've made a late-morning appointment with a hairdresser Carrie herself has recommended, ahead of my date, and I don't want to miss it. By now, Malo is at least semi-conscious. I tell him to keep an eye on Pavel until I get back and set out for Carrie's place.

The moment I get there, I know something has happened. The front door at the foot of her steps is an inch or so open. I stare down at it, debating what to do. When I phone her number again, I can hear her distinctive ring tone – the opening bars of a Billie Eilish song – but again she doesn't pick up. Slowly, step by step, I make my way down to the door. The sight of fresh damage in the wood around the lock freezes my blood. *Dear God, no. Please, please, don't let this thing happen again.*

At this point I should phone the police, I know I should, but I've left Geraghty's card in the apartment and I can't bear the thought of going through the whole story again. And so I push very lightly on the door, watching it swing slowly open.

'Carrie?' I step inside, fearful now. No reply. I call her name a second time but all I can hear is the slow drip-drip from a leaking tap and the low burble of a passing car. Is now the time to beat a retreat? To spare myself whatever might lie behind one of these closed doors? I shake my head. She's out somewhere, I tell myself. Maybe she's with Jean-Paul, snatching a precious half-hour over a coffee. Maybe she's in the Co-op, caught in a queue, laden with goodies for the weekend. Maybe she went out and forgot to close the door. Anything but what, deep down, I'm beginning to dread.

Opening the first door reveals a sitting room, airless, sparsely furnished, unused. Next door is a bathroom, no windows, an abandoned towel on the curling lino tiles, everything jigsawed together. A worm of Colgate on a blue toothbrush catches my eye. It's propped on the handbasin, readied for use, but for some reason it never got as far as Carrie's mouth. By now I'm uncomfortably aware that I might be trespassing on a crime scene, but something inside still tells me I owe Carrie a duty of care. Whatever lies behind that third door falls to me. My responsibility. My call. The kitchen, which I saw last time I was here, is at the back of the property. This has to be her bedroom.

I hesitate a moment. My heart is thumping, and I have a strange tightness in my throat. I do my best to steady myself, then I push down on the handle and ease the door open. It's dark in the bedroom, the curtains pulled tight against the sunshine outside, and for a moment or two I can make no sense of the shape on the bed. Then my eyes adjust, and I realize that I'm looking at Carrie.

She's sprawled on her side, one knee up, a semi-foetal pose. Her eyes are wide open in the blankness of her face. Naked, she's lying in a drying pool of what must be her own blood. It's everywhere, over the sheets, the duvet, the pillows, the wallpaper, everywhere.

I take a tiny step forward, as if I could help somehow. Whatever happened, she must have put up a fight because her hands and lower arms are criss-crossed with what look like knife wounds. I'm sure every crime scene has a story to tell, and I've read far too many scripts to think otherwise, but this one is truly horrible. Below her breasts, Carrie's lovely body has been ripped apart.

I call 999 from the pavement at the top of the stairs. Within seconds, I'm talking to a woman who doesn't register the slightest surprise when I give her a bare summary of what I've just seen. A friend of mine. Dead in her own property. Attacked with a knife. Blood everywhere. The woman takes my details and a careful note of Carrie's address. She checks to make sure I'm OK and asks me to stay where I am until help arrives. Minutes later, I can hear the distant howl of what I assume is a police siren, but when the vehicle turns the corner at the bottom of the street it turns out to be an ambulance. It pulls to a halt beside me. The driver is out first. When I gesture down towards the basement flat and tell him it's a bit late for resus, he shakes his head.

'It's you, love. You're sure you're all right?'

I protest that I'm fine. Shocked? Yes. Upset? Just a bit. But still standing. Another siren announces the arrival of a marked police car. Geraghty is sitting beside the driver. She joins me on the pavement. By now, I'm in tears. What must have happened down there has finally hit me. Carrie on her own. Carrie waking up to hear those same footsteps down the hall. Carrie on one elbow, watching the door creak open. Carrie fighting for her young life.

Geraghty has her arms round me. She's swaying gently, just the way my mum would when I was a child. The paramedic has produced a fistful of tissues. These people, I think vaguely, couldn't be kinder but none of that matters because Carrie, our Carrie, my Carrie, J-P's Carrie, is still down there. Dead.

I've managed to tell Geraghty enough for her to seal the house off. The uniformed officer disappears down the street to investigate the rear of the property while Geraghty uses her personal radio to summon CID and forensics. In this mad flurry of activity we exchange glances a couple of times. If only things had been different, if only we'd taken more notice, if only we'd taken Moonie at his word, this needn't have happened. Geraghty's fault. My fault. Maybe even Carrie's fault. A life tossed needlessly away.

More vehicles attend, men and women in uniforms, men in suits. The street is now sealed at both ends and neighbours have appeared to have a gawp. This, I think numbly, is beginning to look like a film set and I wonder what Pavel would have made of it, when he still had eyes to see. Geraghty has despatched a PCSO to brief the neighbours and encourage them back indoors. Very soon, I suspect detectives will be knocking at every one of these addresses and I'm still wondering about the trail of clues Moonie must have left when Geraghty is back at my side.

'You'll need support,' she says. 'Who shall we phone?'

It's a good question. The obvious answer is Malo. He's definitely kith and kin, but I need someone to keep an eye on Pavel, and in any case, I don't want him seeing me in this state.

'There's a guy called Deko. He's a good friend. He's in my contacts under D.' I give Geraghty my mobile. 'What happens next?'

'We take you back to the station. We'll need to take a full statement. You're OK with that?' There's something in her voice I haven't picked up before and I don't much like it.

'You're telling me I'm a suspect?'

'I'm telling you nothing. Until we know exactly what's happened, we keep an open mind. You've had a terrible shock. Relax. I'll run you up myself.'

We drive to the police station. Geraghty parks round the back and escorts me to a rear entrance. The place is buzzing, office doors opening and closing, footsteps on the stairs, officers hurrying past with phones pressed to their ears.

Geraghty finds me a chair in her office and lifts the phone to summon a younger woman to look after me. The woman arrives with tea minutes later, but I notice that Geraghty, who must be more than busy, won't leave me unattended. Do these people think I might do a runner? Have I really become the victim of cinema's oldest cliché? That whoever discovers the body automatically becomes the prime suspect? I park the thought for later. Pavel again. He'd have lots to say.

Deko appears at the door half an hour later. He enfolds me in a long hug, for which I'm more than grateful, and he has the tact to resist asking me exactly what happened. All I want is to be held, to be comforted. Conversation, just now, is beyond me. All I can think of is that hideous basement flat, and the darkness in Carrie's bedroom. No one, least of all her, should die in circumstances like that.

At length, I summon just enough strength to offer Deko an apology.

'What for?'

'You're a busy man. You don't need all this in your life.'

He shakes his head. He kisses me softly on the head. My mum, again. Exactly the right response.

I'm thinking about H when a detective arrives and asks for a private word with Deko. He nods, gives my hand a squeeze, and joins the detective in the corridor outside. H, I realize, has to know about all this as soon as possible. I'm finding it very hard to think straight, to be practical, but the fact is that Pavel will need someone to replace Carrie. We've still got Felip but he can't possibly cope 24/7 and although Malo and I can fill in during the day, there has to be a more permanent solution.

The office door opens and Deko is back at my side.

'They want to interview you,' he says. 'I'm guessing here, but it might take a while. Do you want me to stay?'

I just look at him and he knows there's only one answer.

'Of course.' He stoops to kiss me again. 'I'll be around just as soon as you need me.'

I accompany the detective downstairs to the same office where I first met Geraghty. Another detective, a woman, is already sitting at the table. She gets to her feet and introduces herself as DS Williams. She's tall and watchful. Lovely hair, cut short, urchin style, softening the gauntness of her face.

'Do you mind if we record this?' She nods at the machine beside her notepad. At the top of the pad, in careful capital letters, she's written my name.

I tell her I'm fine with the machine. Anything I can do to help. Anything. Williams, as I expected, wants me to describe exactly what happened at the flat: where I'd been before, why I came looking for Carrie, what I found in her bedroom. When she asks whether I'd noticed anything out of place, anything that seemed odd, I mention the toothpaste in the bathroom. This earns a nod of approval.

'Good.' She makes a note, the faintest smile on her face. 'You should be doing our job.'

Next, she wants to know about my earlier visit when I managed to coax Carrie to tell me about Moonie. She must have been briefed by Geraghty already, but she insists on every single detail: what time he turned up, how he appeared to have got in, what happened in the bedroom, and – crucially – what he said before he left.

'He threatened to kill her,' I say. 'Exactly the way he'd killed before.'

'Which was?'

'Disembowelment.' I gesture down at my lap. 'Which proves he's a man of his word.'

'You think he did it? Is that what you're telling me?'

'I think he's mad, crazy. It may be the same thing.'

Williams holds my gaze for a moment or two, then scribbles herself another note. So far, to my disappointment, we've yet to discuss the woeful lack of psychiatric provision for lunatics like Moonie.

'We need to know about Carrie.' It's the DC this time. 'What can you tell us?'

'I'm not sure I understand the question. She's dead. The boy Moonie came back and killed her. Stabbed her. Tore her innards out. Just the way he promised. Like I just said, a man of his word.'

I pause. The two of them have exchanged glances. There's a slightly uncomfortable silence before the DS takes up the running again.

'Her private life? Carrie. How well did you know her?'

I shake my head. This line of questioning, at least to me, is beyond surreal. Somewhere out there, in the wild, an adolescent is still running around. He'll probably be covered in blood. He'll have poor Carrie's DNA all over him. He might fancy disembowelling some other poor woman. Why do we need to discuss Carrie's private life?

Williams seems to understand exactly the way I'm feeling. She's patience on legs, but she can be stern when she needs to be.

'You're a material witness, Ms Andressen. You're doing your best to help us and believe me, we appreciate that. In return, you should understand where we're coming from. Time is of the essence. We need to know as much as we can, as quickly as we can, and it needs to be information we can trust.'

'About Carrie?'

'At this point in the investigation, yes. So, let me put the question again. How well did you know her?'

'I was her employer,' I say woodenly. 'And, I hope, her friend.'

'She confided in you?'

'She told me what she wanted to tell me. As far as her work was concerned, she was brilliant, utterly brilliant.'

I tell them about Pavel, the sheer complexity of his needs, how intelligent he is, how intuitive, and how difficult he can be.

'Carrie coped with all that. His physical demands are never-ending, a challenge in themselves. Patients like him are always one nursing mistake away from a bed sore. Bed sores can become ulcers, and ulcers can kill. Pavel has never had even the beginnings of a bed sore under Carrie. But that's not the point. He needs handling, he needs stimulation, he needs a listening ear, and she supplied all that, too.'

'You're telling us they were close?'

'Very.'

'Might he have become a confidant?'

'Yes.'

The DC is writing all this down. When I pause for breath, his head comes up.

'Where would we interview him?' he asks. 'Would here be appropriate?'

'Absolutely not. You'd have to come to the apartment.'

I give him the address. He makes another note. Williams hasn't finished.

'You said you were a friend. With respect to Carrie.'

'I did.'

'Was she in a relationship of any kind?'

'Long term, I don't know. She never mentioned anyone and to be honest I never asked. These things can be tricky.'

'Any children that you know of?'

'No.'

'And more recently? Was there anyone special in her life?'

I hesitate. I have to be careful here. These people are painstaking. They're clever. They'll doubtless be talking to others as they cast their net wider and wider. The last thing I want is the spotlight returning to yours truly because I've been less than honest. I was the one, after all, urging Carrie to go to the police in the first place.

'There's a guy I know she was keen on,' I say.

I give them Jean-Paul's name and tell them where to find him.

'They were close?'

'I think so. Jean-Paul's married. That must have made things difficult.'

Another exchange of glances. My heart sinks. Have I just given them another suspect? Another motive? Christ, I hope not.

'How long has this relationship been going on? To your knowledge?'

'Not long.'

'And does he have children? This . . .' She glances down at her pad. 'Jean-Paul.'

'Yes. Two, as far as I know.'

Another note. I sit back and fold my arms, trying not to imagine the tap-tap on Jean-Paul's door and his wife's realization that her marriage might not be everything she'd imagined. Maybe they were in trouble already. Maybe it took someone like Carrie to administer the last rites.

Williams asks whether there's anything else I need to tell them about Carrie, and when I shake my head she thanks me for what she calls 'my candour'. To my relief, the interview appears to be over. Williams says she knows it's difficult for me and she mentions an organization that offers post-trauma support and therapy for witnesses in my situation. I tell her I'm grateful for the offer, and when the DC asks when it might be convenient to pay Pavel a visit, I give him my number and suggest he gives me a ring tomorrow.

Williams is on her feet now. She wants me to accompany her downstairs. She's made arrangements for me to be fingerprinted and DNA-swabbed.

'Why?' I'm staring up at her.

'You were the first into that crime scene. Our guys will be crawling all over it and they'll need to be able to ID prints and DNA that you'll have left on various surfaces. Don't worry, Ms Andressen. This is strictly for purposes of elimination.'

I think I follow the logic. Downstairs, a youngish man with a beard greets me with a smile. Williams makes a phone call while he takes a print of each of my fingers and then swabs the inside of my mouth.

'Happy?' Williams has finished her call.

'Yes, Skip.' He's readying my swab for despatch.

Williams shepherds me towards the building's main entrance. Before she says goodbye, she tells me that the investigation into Carrie's death will be run by something she calls the MIR at force headquarters in Exeter.

'MIR?'

'Major Incident Room. We throw a lot of resource at crimes like these. The duty Detective Superintendent will be putting a squad together as we speak. There'll be a post-mortem, of course, and that may open one or two doors. My guess is that the SIO will probably want to have you interviewed again by one of his own team.'

'SIO?'

'Senior Investigating Officer.'

'To tell him what?'

She studies me for a moment, and then puts a hand on my arm.

'You've been through the mill, Ms Andressen. Shock's a funny thing. Lots may come back to you over the next day or two, you'll be amazed. We'll be passing on your details to the MIR. I suspect it'll be one of their detectives who comes to talk to . . .' She frowns. 'Pavel?'

I nod. In truth, I'm past caring. Then, as if by magic, Deko appears from nowhere, the leather jacket hooked over his shoulder.

'May I?' He has his other arm round me and he's looking at Williams.

'Of course. And you are?'

'A friend of Enora's.'

'Pleased to meet you, Mr . . .?'

'Miedema. It's Dutch.'

'Pleased to meet you, Mr Miedema.' She gives us both a card and scribbles a mobile number on the back of each. 'Any time, day or night.'

We exchange rather stiff handshakes, and then leave. Out in the sunshine, Deko gives me another long hug.

'I'm here to take care of you,' he says. 'No ifs, no buts. Deal?'

I nod. 'Deal,' I mutter wearily. '*Marché conclu.*'

SIXTEEN

When Deko asks me where I want to go, I tell him I'd like him to drive me back to his house on the Beacon. I need to draw breath before I face Malo and Pavel, and I have to talk to H.

'Who's H? Do you mind me asking?'

'Not at all. He's my son's real dad. In another life I had a one-night stand on a yacht in Antibes. H poured margaritas down my throat and Malo happened nine months later. For the next seventeen years we were all convinced that my husband Berndt was the father but mercifully that turned out not to be true. I owe those margaritas a very big debt. And so does my son.'

Talking like this does me good. For at least a minute, I haven't thought about Carrie. Then we're suddenly driving past the end of her street, with Deko slowing for the traffic. The street is still sealed at both ends, and I stare numbly at the blue and white tape stirring in the wind. Police Line – Do Not Cross. A van is parked outside Carrie's basement flat with the back doors open, and a masked figure in a grey, one-piece suit is standing on the pavement, making notes on a clipboard.

'You live with H?' Deko asks.

I know what he's doing here. He's trying to take my mind off it. Anything, I tell myself. Anything to swamp the memory of that ruined body on the bed. He asks the question again, lovely man, and I force myself to answer.

'No. He'd like me to, but I don't. H made a lot of money. He did well for himself – better than well.'

'So, where did the money come from?'

The bluntness of the question takes me by surprise but just now I don't have the energy to lie. Besides, I trust this man.

'He was big in drugs.' I shrug. 'Back in the day.'

'Cocaine?'

'Of course.'

'He handled the importation?'

'He handled everything. That's the kind of guy he is. With H you get what you see. That's not as common as you might think.'

The fact that I've been so candid appears to earn Deko's respect. We park up and he lets me into the house. I know my way round by now and when he asks me what I want, I settle for coffee and half an hour of privacy.

I climb the stairs to the top of the house. The view is as breathtaking as ever but so much has happened over the last few hours that it barely registers. I collapse on the big sofa and fight the urge to cry again. H, I think. He needs to know about all this.

The moment he picks up the phone, I sense it's going to be a difficult conversation. Since Brexit turned sour, H has had designs on eighty-five acres of a neighbour's land, plus the handful of sheep he runs. He thinks – knows – that hard times are coming, and the yeoman peasant in him, never far from the surface, wants to be prepared for the moment when it dawns on everyone that they've been conned and it all – in his phrase – turns to rat shit. I have many reservations about Malo's real dad – his impetuosity, his taste in antique furniture, his language – but I'd never question his commitment to his new family. Drunk, H promises to protect us all to the death, if necessary, and I have no reason to disbelieve him. He is a good man. We're lucky to be part of his little gang.

'The fucker won't bite.' He's talking about the fields he's after. 'I've raised him twice. Ten grand an acre? That's way over the top and he knows it. I'll go another grand and a half. After that, he's on his own.'

'Maybe he doesn't want to sell. Have you thought of that?'

'Everyone's got a price. That's what money's for. He's just a greedy bastard. I shouldn't even be talking to him. Next time you're over we'll have a leg of lamb. And I won't be buying it at the fucking butchers.'

H never fails to make me laugh. Even now, after everything that's happened, he can put a smile on my face.

'Something's happened.' I need to change the subject.

'Like what?' H's voice has hardened. Like most rich men, he hates surprises.

I tell him about Carrie, the whole story, beginning to end. Getting it all out in one go makes me cry again. H has limited patience in any conversation but to his immense credit he doesn't once interrupt me.

'Shit,' he grunts when I've finished. 'I loved that girl. I'm really sorry. When do you want me down? Tonight? Tomorrow? You name it.'

'Tomorrow would be good.' I'm on my feet now, blowing my nose on a fold of kitchen roll.

'Tomorrow it is. What about the boy? How has he taken it?'

'He doesn't know yet. I've got that pleasure to come. You'll be glad to know he's into kitesurfing. Carrie scored him a fifty per cent discount on the lessons and the kit.'

'Good girl. Bless her. Where are you now?'

'With a friend.'

'She looking after you?'

'Yes.'

'Laters, then. Yeah? Take care, babe. Pecker up, eh?'

The line goes dead and I linger by the window for a moment.

'Laters' is an expression H has lifted from his son. All his life, I suspect, H has been a magpie, nicking anything that catches his attention and bedding it seamlessly into the cheerful chaos of his own life. Roast leg of lamb, I think. An unwitting gift from the neighbour who refuses to say yes.

I find Deko one floor down. The rooms below the top of the house have retained their original dimensions – high ceilings, big sash windows, handsome spaces designed for a civilized life. This one appears to serve, at least for now, as an office.

Deko is sitting at a big antique desk, studying what I recognize as a tax demand. He wants to know whether I feel the need for a drink.

'I do,' I admit.

'Jenever?'

'Perfect.'

While he fetches a bottle from a cabinet in the corner of the room, I steal a look at the figure on the bottom of the HMRC form. This is indeed a demand for unpaid tax. £84,598.03? Christ.

Deko is back with the bottle. He splashes generous measures into a couple of mugs.

'No glasses?' I enquire lightly.

'They're upstairs. Sometimes in life you have to slum it. A toast?'

'Of course.'

'Your call.'

'To Carrie.' I say at once. 'God rest her soul.'

I'm back at the penthouse by six o'clock. Felip has taken over from Malo, who seems to have disappeared.

'On the water.' Felip's thin hands shape an imaginary sail. I go to the window and check on the estuary. My boy's red sail is a speck in the distance. Progress, indeed.

Felip wants to know what's wrong with Carrie. The jenever has made me bolder, more direct. When I tell him she's dead, Felip just stares at me, uncomprehending.

'*Que?*' He says at last.

'Dead. *Morte.*'

'*Muerte?*'

'*Si.*'

He shakes his head, takes a tiny step backward as if to fend off this terrible news. Like all of us, he thought the world of Carrie.

I start to explain the circumstances, but I don't think he's listening, so I get him to sit down. I pour him a glass of whisky from the bottle that Carrie kept for H's occasional visit. Felip shakes his head. He doesn't drink.

'It might help,' I insist. 'Just a little sip?'

He turns his head away, then he's on his feet again. He's heard enough. He leaves the room and moments later I hear the slam of his bedroom door.

Pavel's heard it, too. He can activate a speaker in the lounge when he needs to talk to us. He wants – demands – to know what's going on. He sounds wheezy.

I join him in his bedroom. I pull up a chair and settle at his bedside and tell him that Carrie is dead. Pavel isn't Felip. The face on the pillow remains totally impassive. All he wants to know is how and when. I do my best to explain. This isn't easy because I know that Pavel will want every last detail, and I'm right.

'Damage around the door?'

'Yes.'

'What kind of damage?'

'Like someone had taken a screwdriver to it, or maybe a chisel. Trying to get at the lock. Trying to force it.'

'And you say the door was open?'

'Yes. Just an inch.'

Pavel nods. So far I've never told him about the earlier visit to Carrie's flat but I realize that now might be the time. The police will probably be at his bedside tomorrow and they're bound to mention it.

'Carrie had an intruder a week ago,' I say carefully. 'The night before I came down.'

'When she didn't turn up?'

'Yes.'

'You told Felip she had menstrual problems.'

'Yes.'

'And you told me she was fine.'

'Yes.'

'Both lies.'

'Yes.'

'Why?'

'Because she was scared. In fact, the poor girl was terrified. This man, this boy, was promising to kill her if she breathed a word to anyone. The street people call him Moonie. They think he's crazy, mad. You take that kind of threat seriously. You have to.'

'She never went to the police?'

'No.' I swallow hard. 'But I did.'

I swear those eyes behind the tinted glasses are looking straight through me. He knows everything, I tell myself. Absolutely everything. The truth seeps into him, an almost chemical process. No matter how hard I might try, he calls out every lie.

Now he wants to know when the police detained Moonie. I explain about yesterday's arrest, and the interviews at the custody centre.

'They had nothing from Carrie,' I tell him. 'And nothing else, either. They had to let him go.'

'And you think he came back? And killed her?'

'Of course he did.'

'Because he was blaming her for the arrest?'

'Yes. She didn't need to make a statement. In that head of his it had to be her, had to be. He'd promised to disembowel her.'

'And that's what happened?'

'Yes.'

'You're sure about that? You saw it yourself?'

This is becoming worse than uncomfortable. The last place I want to revisit is that fuggy little bedroom behind the closed curtains.

'Describe it.'

'*What?*'

'Describe what you saw in there.'

I want to say no. I want to get up and leave the room and close the door behind me. I'm all too aware of Pavel's appetite – need – for detail, for the smallest print of this hideous tableau. That's the way he must have worked since his sight failed him, and his world was plunged into darkness. In some ways the adjustments he's made have been truly remarkable, but in others he seems to have thickened that same darkness.

'She was lying on her side.' I've closed my eyes. 'One leg was drawn up as if to protect herself.' I offer more details. Her body beneath the rib cage, especially.

'And her head? Her face?'

'Her eyes were open.'

'Mouth?'

'Open, as well, just a little.'

'You think she was taken by surprise?'

'I've no idea but she must have fought. There were cuts on both hands, arms too.'

'Blood?'

'Everywhere.'

Pavel nods. Then a tiny frown comes and goes, ghosting over his face.

'You're telling me her stomach was slashed open?'

'Yes.'

'These are deep wounds?'

'Very. That's where most of the blood must have come from.'

'What could you see? Inside?'

This is a question too far. I'm aware of myself physically recoiling at the bedside. Enough.

'It was dark,' I say. 'And I didn't stay.'

'Did you touch her?'

'*Touch her?* Why would I do that?'

'To make sure she was dead.'

I shake my head in disbelief and try to spell it out again. The poor bloody woman has been savagely attacked, probably hours ago. Most of her blood is all over the sheets and half her guts are spilling out.

'So, you did see.'

'See what?'

'Her guts.'

'Yes, yes I did. It was an impression, intestines, loops of the stuff . . .'

'Viscera.'

'Yes, viscera, much better. No way would anyone survive that. All I could do was leave. And make the call.'

'Nine-nine-nine.'

'Of course.'

Pavel nods. At last he has the tact to pressure me no further. Maybe that's an act of charity. More likely he's acquired enough grist for his private mill. Over the hours to come he'll lie back, imagining Carrie's final minutes, fighting Moonie, fighting madness, and then, once he's happy he truly has the measure of that grotesque finale, he'll start to widen the focus to ask the questions that really matter. Why would this man-child ever do such a thing? And how come he was still free to walk our streets?

At this point, I hear the rumble of the lift. Moments later, footsteps approach the open bedroom door. I look up to find Malo staring in at us. He's wearing a pair of shorts and a T-shirt, and his Nike runners are soaking wet.

For a second or two, neither of us says a word. Then he beckons me into the hall. I ignore Pavel. I'm glad to be out of that room. The door shut, I follow Malo into the lounge. I've made a start on breaking the news about Carrie, but I can tell he's not listening. Something else must have happened, I think, and it turns out I'm right.

'I've just come back from the Duck Pond,' he says. 'Jean-Paul's been doing a session down there tonight, maybe half a dozen of us.'

'And?'

'The police turned up.' He gestures out at the view. 'And took him away.'

SEVENTEEN

It happens to be Good Friday. Here's hoping.

H turns up at midday. After less than five minutes in the apartment, he badly wants to take Malo and myself out to lunch but neither of us are remotely hungry.

Felip is down the hall, sorting out Pavel. H shuts the door. As I suspected, the offer of lunch has nothing to do with appetite.

'This place is a fucking morgue,' he says. 'You need to be out of here.'

'Dad . . .' Even Malo is shocked. The news about Carrie has hit him badly and I think it's the first time he's lost someone who mattered to him. We sat up together until late last night but even the remains of H's Scotch didn't really reach him. Thanks to his conversations with the street people, he probably knows more about Moonie than any of us, but he simply doesn't understand how anyone, no matter how crazy, could ever have done such a thing.

In the end, as always, H prevails. There's a restaurant beside the bridge in the marina, and mercifully it's only half full. H commandeers a table at the back and calls for the menu. Everyone else might have had breakfast but he, very definitely, hasn't.

'So, what are we going to do?'

I assume he's talking about what happens next to Carrie. I'm in the process of explaining that there'll be a post-mortem, and then – presumably – a funeral, but we know very little about her immediate family. Who do we phone? Who do we comfort?

H dismisses both questions. He wants to know about Pavel. The apartment, he says, is a major investment. How do we lay hands on a new Carrie?

This time, Malo has had enough. He's used to H's habit of cutting to the chase, of dismissing anything that might be mere sentiment, but this is different.

'The woman deserves respect, Dad.' He's ignoring the offer of a menu. 'Fucking get used to it.'

H isn't used to having his wrist slapped, least of all by a nineteen-year-old. I'm about to push for a ceasefire in all our interests when H leans across and places his big hand over his son's wrist.

'I'm sorry, son,' he mutters. 'You're right, I'm out of order. Steak or fish?' He nods at the surrounding diners, busily tucking in. 'Hard to make a fucking decision, eh?'

Malo goes for the fish. I settle for a small bowl of mussels in a white wine sauce.

'Steak.' H looks up at the waitress to complete the order. 'With fries.'

We eat in silence. Our armed truce isn't helped by the fact that most of the other people in the restaurant appear to be talking about yesterday's murder. Already, it's featured on national newscasts, both TV and radio, and when Malo checked this morning on some of the newspaper websites, the bare bones of the story were there too. Carrie Tollman has yet to be named, which I assume reflects difficulties getting in touch with her next of kin, but there are hints that a serial killer may be at large. Tomorrow, I suspect, we'll all wake up to shots of Moonie sitting in the train, or perhaps his photo from the custody suite. *Have you seen this man? Approach with great care.*

I've already levelled with both Malo and H about the story I managed to winkle out of Carrie more than a week ago. For H, who's always regarded the police as Filth, the news that they couldn't do anything about this lunatic comes as no surprise.

'Dickheads,' he says briskly. 'Dickheads then, and dickheads now. Never knew their arse from their elbow. In my game that did us no end of favours, but it wouldn't have helped poor Carrie.'

Thanks to Inspector Geraghty, I now know a great deal more about the lack of provision for people like Moonie, but neither H nor Malo are in the mood to listen. When I point out that they tried to keep the boy in custody, pending a psychiatric bed that didn't exist, or a psychiatric assessment that no one was prepared to offer, they ignore me. Carrie's story, they both appear to believe, writes itself.

'In her own fucking interests,' grunts H, 'the Filth should have paid her a visit, got a statement, taken DNA samples, lifted finger-prints, all that bollocks. Then they could have something to chuck at the boy when they finally laid hands on him. He'd be inside now,' he tells me, 'banged up on some fucking remand wing. As it is, once the facts come out, half the women in the country will be going to bed scared fucking witless. We've lost it, totally lost it. I hate to say it, but you heard it here first.'

This, once again, is less than fair.

'If it's anyone's fault, it's mine,' I say. 'I should have been firmer with her. I should have marched her there myself.'

'Bollocks. You did everything you could. Once they knew, they should have been round there like a shot. That's what happens in real life. Sod the fucking rules. The woman's terrified of reprisals? Respect her privacy? Brilliant. Except the bloke delivered, didn't he? And now she's gone.'

H, of course, has a point. We trail back from the restaurant, only too aware that we haven't even discussed a replacement for Carrie. For the next couple of hours, H and I draw up a list of care agen-cies and begin to call them. We've done laps around this same circuit before and the response is wearingly familiar.

We're naturally keen to detail the degree of nursing attention that Pavel requires, and the truth is that most of the agencies are reluctant to take on the responsibility. By the end of the afternoon, we're looking at a single name: Ndeye. According to the agency, she's Senegalese by birth but has been in the UK for the last twenty years. Her English, we're assured, is perfect, she's a treasure in all kinds of ways, and better still she has recent clinical experience in a spinal injuries unit outside Salisbury.

I phone the agency back at just gone five and enquire how quickly she could make herself available for interview. The woman says she'll check. Minutes later, she calls back.

'Ndeye lives in Exeter,' she says. 'It's rush hour. Fingers crossed she'll be with you by six.'

I confirm our address. Surprised and relieved, I'm about to hang up when H signals from across the room.

How much? he mouths, rubbing two fingers together.

I put the question, realizing that we've yet to discuss money, and back comes the reply.

'Forty-five pounds an hour?' I'm not sure I've heard properly. 'Have I got that right?'

I have. H rolls his eyes but has the grace not to be difficult. Moments after I hang up, Malo is back with us. H gives him a look.

'It's nursing for you, son. Nearly four hundred quid a day? Money for fucking nothing.'

Hardly. Ndeye appears less than an hour later. She's much younger than I've been expecting, and H perks up when I walk her into the lounge. She's a big woman, with a wide face and dazzling teeth in a huge smile. Her English is indeed perfect, and we've already established that she also speaks French, which has to be her mother tongue. Her voice, husky, would be perfect in a number of roles I could name, and I'm still thinking a young Aretha Franklin when she apologizes to H for being out of uniform. This, it appears, is her day off. The call from the agency has caught her by surprise.

H is shaking his head. He can't take his eyes off the blaze of colour that is her dress. Yellows and greens and splashes of red tumble from the swell of her breasts, and I warm to the way she's so artfully disguised the body beneath. She may be on the plump side, but I somehow doubt it. As does H.

'Don't worry about any uniform,' he says. 'You look wonderful.'

She acknowledges the compliment with a tiny nod, a delicate gesture from a big woman, and we sit her down while I tally the must-do checks on which Pavel's very survival depends. None of this appears to daunt her in the least and my heart leaps when she suggests that she and Pavel ought to take the measure of each other.

'Life is a market,' she says. 'Your friend has very particular needs. Try before you buy.'

H, I can tell already, is thoroughly smitten.

'Someone taught you that?' he asks. 'Try before you buy?'

'My mum. Back in Dakar.'

'Great. Bang on. Wise woman.'

At this point, I ask Ndeye why she bailed out of the Spinal Unit in Salisbury. If it's personal, I say, she has every right not to answer my question.

She studies me a moment. She's been emphatic in turning down the offer of a coffee or something harder, but I get the impression that she likes us.

'Personal?' she muses. 'Sure, you could say that. I had a flat share in the town centre. We were a minute away from that bench where it all happened. Russians. Nerve gas. Who needs any of that in their lives?'

H is laughing. Another perfect answer.

'Take the lady through.' He nods towards the door. 'Your Pavel's in for a treat.'

Pavel, of course, is denied the sight of Ndeye. We step into his bedroom and at first he doesn't even know she's there. The bedside chair is exactly where I'd left it earlier and I gesture for Ndeye to take a seat. She does so without making a sound. Only the faintest twitch of a nostril and a tiny adjustment of his head on the pillow suggests that Pavel might be aware of the presence of someone new in his life. A strange scent. Slightly sweet.

'Where have you been?'

I ignore the question. I tell him I want to introduce Ndeye.

'Who?'

'Ndeye. She may be helping us out for a while.'

'Good.' He nods. 'Excellent.'

Ndeye is gazing down at him. The fact that she takes her time, that she has no fear of silence, is a very good sign. Finally, she stirs.

'Your breathing OK in there?' She's picked up on Pavel's wheezing at once. Another tick in another box.

'Fifteen cigars a day.' Pavel is smiling now. 'I know I shouldn't.'

'You lie.'

'I do. It's an occupational hazard. I've lied all my life.'

'So why the wheezing?'

'It's the bloody weather. I've never liked snow.'

'Another fantasy.'

'You're right. You want the truth? Most of me hasn't worked for a while, and what's left has to run to keep up. Those little knots of muscle in my throat? They get a little tired from time to time. I know it's a bit late, but they offer their apologies.'

'Accepted, Mr Pavel. Tell them to have the rest of the day off. See if that does the trick.'

Pavel is delighted. I can see it in his face. He loves slightly surreal dialogue like this and over the last year or so I've noticed that he uses it to put passing strangers to the test. Most fail, because they're slow off the mark as well as slightly frightened, but this woman is already fluent in Pavel-speak.

'One last favour,' he says. 'Then I'll stand the guys down. You mind?'

'Not at all.'

'I have a tiny itch on my cheek, my right cheek, level – I think – with the middle of my nose. Might you oblige me?'

'Of course.'

Ndeye extends her forefinger and a perfectly shaped nail settles on the paleness of Pavel's cheek.

'Down,' he murmurs.

The nail, a deep, rich shade of red I can only describe as labial, tracks very slowly towards the corner of his mouth.

'Now, up again.'

Ndeye hesitates a moment, teasing him, then the nail does his bidding. This is bonding with a very special twist, I think. Any woman of my age should know a thing or two about seduction, but I've never seen anything as artful, and as effective, as this. In a movie script, especially one of Pavel's, this scene would end with him lifting his hand and finding hers. Alas, that's never going to happen, and Ndeye knows it.

'Tomorrow,' she says. 'We have a deal?'

Pavel nods, and then sighs.

'We do,' he whispers.

EIGHTEEN

After Ndeye's departure, H and I conference around Pavel's bed. All three of us agree that Ndeye seems – on the face of it – to be a perfect replacement for poor Carrie, and I make the call to the agency. We're very happy to offer her a month's contract, I say. After that, if the arrangement's in good shape, we could be looking at something more permanent. The woman at the agency is delighted, as is Pavel. When I tell him she's Senegalese by birth, it appears to come as no surprise.

'French blood in her veins,' he says. 'I can feel it, smell it. *Bonne nouvelle, quoi?*'

Good news? We all hope so. The last two days have left me with a feeling of profound exhaustion. The shock of finding Carrie in her basement flat has gone, but – like the child I doubtless am – I want to be comforted, talked to, held. In this respect, I tell myself, I'm lucky because the two key men in my life, my son and his father, are both within touching distance.

We're all back in the lounge and I'm about to suggest a very large drink when it occurs to me that H wants to leave. He keeps checking his watch. It appears he has an important meeting back at Flixcombe Manor, something he can't afford to duck. This, of course, is a fiction. H gets profoundly unhappy in the presence of grief, or even need. I've never quite understood why, and once or twice in what passes for our relationship there have been exceptions to the rule, but this isn't one of them. He needs to be back on the road. Pronto.

Malo nods. He, too, doesn't fancy an evening with his fraught mother. He's been on the phone to Clemmie. She knows how upset he is about Carrie and she wants him back in London where she can look after him.

'Fine,' I say numbly. 'Best be off, then.'

Minutes later, after the briefest pecks on the cheek, they've both gone. I pour myself a large glass of Sancerre and take it out on the balcony. Thin sunshine bathes the gleaming spaces of the estuary and despite everyone's expectation that this first bank holiday of the year will be semi-tropical, it's cold enough to warrant a thick sweater. I linger on the edge of the view for a moment or two, somehow expecting Malo's kite to appear, but of course there's no sign of him among the dozens of novices trying to master their unruly rigs. Malo, like his father, has fled the scene. Neither, I realize, can I see Jean-Paul.

This troubles me. I was the one who gave the police his name. It was my fault they detained him – doubtless politely – down there by the Duck Pond. What did they ask him? How did he account for all the stolen hours he'd shared with Carrie? Did they demand an alibi for the night she lost her life? Was he tucked up with his wife at the family home? And – most important of all – how could he possibly explain their interest in him?

These are questions to which I have no answers and I find myself once again at Pavel's bedside, partly because – aside from Felip – he's the only person left to talk to, but mostly because he's so consistently able to unpick the knottier tangles in my life.

I find him listening to something hopelessly plaintive. The swell of an orchestra behind a solo violin fills the room. I stand in the open doorway for a moment, wondering whether this is the time to break the spell, but a whispered command to *Sesame* lowers the volume.

'Dvořák,' Pavel says. 'Romance for violin. Tanja Sonc. The orchestra is Slovenian. These people understand the Bohemian soul.'

This, I know, is my cue to join him. I slip into Ndeye's chair and kiss him softly on the forehead.

'You're upset,' he says. Statement, not question.

'Of course.'

'H?'

'Gone.'

'Malo?'

'Gone.'

'Not good.' He closes his eyes, shakes his head. 'Dvořák may help.'

It does, a little. Towards the end of the piece I start to well up again, glad that blindness has spared Pavel the sight of me in tears. Finally, the music comes to an end and we sit in silence. I'm back in the darkness of Carrie's bedroom. However hard I try, the image of her body sprawled on the bed won't leave me.

'I told the police about Jean-Paul,' I say at last. 'I had to.'

'And?'

'They've taken him in for questioning.'

'About Carrie?'

'I assume so.'

Pavel nods. He seems deep in thought. Finally, he turns his head towards me.

'She told me that his marriage was over.'

'Jean-Paul's?'

'Of course.'

'Did you believe her?'

'I believed she believed him. That's not the same as saying it was true.'

'You think Jean-Paul might have been lying?'

'Men will do anything to get what they want, what they think they need, what is rightfully theirs. A broken marriage suited Carrie. And it probably eased her conscience. Jean-Paul would have known that.'

I nod. I need to know more.

'So how long was all this going on?'

'Since Christmas. They'd danced at a party together. They'd known each other for a while and Carrie said she'd always fancied him but after that they started meeting. All they needed was a flat, and she had one.'

I sit back on the chair. All of this is news to me. Not for a moment had I suspected anything.

'You once told me she was troubled,' I say softly. 'Troubled about what? About what was left of the marriage? About whatever guilt she might have felt? And how come she was talking to you about all this?'

'Because I'm safe. Because I don't get out much. And because she thought I'd understand.'

'And did you?'

'Yes.'

'She asked for advice?'

'Of course.'

'About calling it off?'

'Not at all.'

'What, then?'

Pavel takes his time. One of his own film scripts would, at this point, call for a chord or two of anticipatory music and some tell-tale body language. Being Pavel, all he can manage is a turn of the head on the pillow.

'By last week, she was ten weeks pregnant,' he mutters. 'She didn't know whether to have an abortion or not.'

This is a bombshell. Carrie pregnant? Already, I'm trying to think it through. The police will know already from the post-mortem. Hence, I'm assuming, their eagerness to lay their hands on Jean-Paul. Thanks to me, Malo's favourite kite instructor has become the putative father of Carrie's child. All they need to prove the link is a DNA test. I know about DNA tests. That's how we finally established that H, and not Berndt, was Malo's natural father.

'You're shocked?' This from Pavel.

'I am.'

'Don't be. Jean-Paul didn't kill Carrie.'

'But he has a motive, doesn't he? And isn't that supposed to matter?'

'Of course. And the police will work it through. It won't be pleasant for Jean-Paul, to say nothing of his wife and kids, but people are always more resilient than you think.'

If this little *aperçu* is meant to comfort me, it fails completely. I ask Pavel how he can be so sure of himself. I know that writers adore playing God. I know that control freakery is embedded deep in their genes. But sometimes life doesn't quite obey the script and now might just be the perfect example.

'You're telling me Jean-Paul had nothing to do with Carrie's death?'

'I am.'

'So, does that take us back to Moonie?'

'It may.'

'*May?*'

'Yes.' Pavel permits himself a tiny smile. 'We live in the world of the subjunctive, Enora. *May. Might.* Dismiss the notion of possibility and we rob life of its richness. Carrie, oddly enough, understood that at once. Which makes her passing all the more regrettable.'

Enora. I can't remember the last time Pavel called me by my Christian name. It has a formality that chills me to the bone. This man has been my friend, and then my lover. Now, very suddenly, he seems remote and slightly forbidding. Especially in his choice of language.

'Regrettable' is probably worse. It isn't a word I'd use in any context, least of all the maiming of someone we both regarded as a close friend. Pavel has always used language with a reverence and precision I've hugely admired. He thinks in paragraphs. Every word, every phrase, is carefully chosen, then sifted and weighed to carry the meaning he intends, measured to the last ounce. Sometimes his sheer intelligence, diamond-bright, has astonished me and – spell-bound – I've been only too happy to become part of his life.

Now, for whatever reason, his tone has changed. In some strange way I'm still struggling to define, he seems to have become my keeper. By rationing information, he's playing with me. Worse still, he wants me – needs me – to understand that.

'So, what happens next?' I manage at last. 'Are you ever going to tell me?'

He doesn't. Instead, he pleads exhaustion. One way and another, it's been a tiring day. He'd appreciate a little peace, and perhaps some more Dvořák. I leave him to it, closing the door behind me. Now all three men in my life, doubtless for their own good reasons, have saddled up and headed for the hills.

I stand alone in the lounge for several minutes, aware of Pavel listening to music next door. We have a baby-alarm device wireless linked to a microphone in his bedroom and I've switched it on. My knowledge of classical music isn't all it should be but even I know this isn't Dvořák. Instead, Pavel is listening to Beethoven and within seconds I recognize the opening movement of the Eroica Symphony.

Back in the days before the accident in which Pavel broke his neck, he was living in a lovely house in Chiswick. That's where we started sleeping together, and the memory of those nights I still treasure. We'd make love to a variety of music, usually classical, and for moments that deserved special celebration, Pavel always chose the Eroica. It was, he said, the music of the Gods.

Gods? I turn off the baby alarm and slump on the sofa. Five minutes with my eyes closed tell me that I – like H and Malo – have to get out of this place. Felip can deal with Pavel. I fetch out my mobile and find the number I want.

Deko, thank God, is at home.

'Of course,' he says at once. 'Come over.'

NINETEEN

The Beacon is a ten-minute walk away. I knock at the front door and take half a step back. A sash window on the second floor is an inch or two open and I think I can hear the roar of a sizeable crowd. Seconds later, the door opens and Deko is inviting me in. He's watching football thanks to Eurosport, and something exciting is about to happen in Amsterdam.

Does this come as a surprise? Not really. On reflection, as I follow him upstairs, the blokiness that I've always associated with football – crowded pubs, spilled pints, intense focus, wild abandon – absolutely goes with the battered leather jacket and the baggy jeans.

The room at the front on the second floor is where he watches TV. The set is perched on a card table in the bay window and the two unmatched chairs may have come from the tip, or perhaps the nursing home. Apart from this, the room is definitely a work in progress: bare floorboards, recently sanded, and daubs of tester paint on the walls. Deko has a colour sense that is anything but blokey – interesting shades of olive green and what I can only describe as swamp yellow – and already, back watching the action on the tiny TV, he's noted my interest.

'Anaglypta wallpaper,' he says. 'Nightmare to get off.'

I smile. Already I've noticed a tiny whisker of cream paper in one corner of the room. Unable to help myself, I carefully remove it, feeling the indentations of thick paper between my fingertips.

'I don't understand how you make time for all this,' I tell him. 'The nursing home? All that work? How do you do it?'

'I get help from time to time.' He nods at the spare chair. 'Help yourself. Drink?'

I say yes and settle for wine. He's so obviously absorbed by the game that I volunteer to find a bottle myself. He thinks that's a great idea.

'Upstairs in the office,' he grunts. 'Drinks cabinet in the corner.'

'And you?'

'I'll have the same . . .' He glances across. 'You OK?'

'Never better.'

In a curious way, I mean it. There's something very normal about this man. More and more, I'm intrigued by the life he seems to have made for himself, and I love his lack of drama. He must know what I'm going through, how hard it must be to cope, and yet he resists the temptation to feel my pain. Modern relationships, for whatever reason, seem to be sustained by extravagant displays of empathy. Maybe it has to do with reality TV, hour after hour of oddballs banged up together until one of them loses it. Or maybe grief itself has become a race to the bottom, a competition to see who chokes first. Either way it's a huge relief to find someone sitting in an empty room watching football. Sanity, I think.

The bottom of the drinks cabinet offers an assortment of wines, most of them red. I select a Macon my mum happens to like and look around for a corkscrew. Deko's desk is littered with paperwork and I can't resist a peek. Most of this stuff turns out to be invoices, and none of them appear to have been paid. Garage bills. Demands from building suppliers to settle his account. A £389 invoice, again unpaid, from a skip-hire company. Of the HMRC tax demand I'd seen earlier there's no sign but I'm starting to get the picture. No wonder he's doing all the work himself, I think. The last thing he can afford is the luxury of paying someone else.

I'm still at the desk when I hear a voice behind me. It's Deko.

'Take a look at this.' I can hear the roar of the crowd from downstairs. 'The Hunter just scored. Amazing goal. You need to see the replay.'

I follow him downstairs with the still-corked bottle. Me snooping around his desk doesn't seem to have registered. All that matters is the game. Ajax are already one-nil up. Huntelaar, Deko tells me, is on fire but this second goal is a peach.

Huntelaar is evidently an attacker, and Deko points him out: tall, deep-set eyes, scary haircut. He dances towards the enemy goal, beating one player after another, tempts the goalie towards him with a lift of his right leg, then slides the ball into the bottom left-hand corner of the net. While the crowd erupt, we see the goal again from a different angle, and then a third. I'm no expert on football but Deko is right. This man belongs in a corps de ballet. He has perfect balance. He defies the laws of gravity. He moves like a ghost, or maybe an assassin.

'Well . . .?' Deko wants a reaction.

'Perfect,' I tell him. 'Albright in *Giselle*. The women in the audience would wet themselves.'

He shoots me a look and then tells me I'll find a corkscrew in the kitchen in the basement. Glasses, too. I leave Deko back in his chair, eager for the game to re-start, and go downstairs. The kitchen, like much else in the house, has been stripped back to bare walls. New units and a huge fridge are still boxed and for the time being Deko seems to be relying on a camping stove, with a couple of saucepans and a single frying pan. A slotted wooden block contains a collection of kitchen knives of various sizes. I recognize the make at once, a Japanese company famed for the exquisite sharpness of their blades. I have a collection myself and they're perfect for making sushi. The biggest of the knives is missing but I use a smaller one to peel back the foil on top of the bottle. A corkscrew and a couple of glasses lie on the draining board in the new sink.

Back upstairs, I find Deko distraught. Excelsior, the other team, have come back with a goal of their own, thanks to a slender, unshaven *metisse* my mother would love.

'Mounir El Hamdaoui.' Deko shakes his head. 'Rotterdam boy. Plays for Morocco.'

Once again, we watch the replays while I uncork the bottle. This time, the goal is unspectacular.

'Huntelaar's on a hat trick,' Deko tells me. 'This lot have got it coming to them.'

I pour the wine and pass him the bottle. There's a remote on the floor beside his chair and he picks it up and freezes the action as soon as he sees the next close-up of Huntelaar.

'You don't want to watch any more?'

'It's a recording. The game happened last week.'

'You're telling me you know the score already?'

'Of course. Six–two.' He nods at the figure frozen on the screen. 'And he did get that hat trick.'

We raise our glasses to The Hunter. Van Gaal, Deko tells me, thinks there's no better player in the world when it comes to close control in the penalty area. I've no idea who Van Gaal might be, but I can imagine the audience at Sadler's Wells on their feet.

I'm still curious to know what satisfaction Deko gets from watching a game like this when he already knows the score. Where's the tension? Where's the surprise?

He dismisses both questions. It's not about the result, he says, it's about the team. They've just beaten Juventus in the quarter finals of the Champions League. Next, in the semi, they're meeting Spurs. He needs to know they're ready, properly prepared. The first leg will be at Spurs' new stadium at the end of the month.

'And?'

'The boys are on fire,' he says. 'All of them. The thirtieth is a Tuesday. I'll be taking the boat to France the previous week, staying over a couple of days, back in time to catch the game. Fancy it?'

This invitation, so natural, so casual, is a real tonic. It tells me that there really will be a life after what's happened to Carrie, something I'd begun to doubt.

'You want company?'

'Yeah, and I want crew, too. I can sail the boat alone, no problem, but two of us will make it a lot more fun.'

Fun. Normally I distrust the word but not now.

'Where are you going? Exactly?'

'Guess.'

I gaze at him for a long moment. I haven't a clue.

'You're telling me I should know?'

'I am.' He smiles. 'Breton Thoniers? *Amen*'s spiritual home?'

'You mean Douarnenez?'

'I do. Think you might be able to cope?'

I nod. Since he showed me his boat out on the estuary, memories of the fishing port have come flooding back.

'There's a cliff walk through the trees to an amazing beach,' I tell him. 'We used to take that path as kids. I can still smell the resin from the pines. At low tide, that beach goes on forever. We could go there. I could take you.'

I grin, cupping my wine glass in both hands the way a child might, comforted by the memories.

Deko still has the remote. He thumbs a button at the top and The Hunter fades to black.

'No more football?'

'No.' He shakes his head. 'I think maybe we need to talk.'

'Here?'

'Your call.'

'And we can take the bottle?'

'Of course we can. I'm afraid you don't get much more than a bed and a view but I'm thinking that might not be a problem.' He gets to his feet, extending his spare hand. 'Am I right?'

He is. The bedroom is at the rear of the property and we make love as dusk steals in from the east. Deko has left the curtains wide open and afterwards, when I leave him briefly to step into the en suite, the dark outline of the church looms above us. Deko has made me very happy and for that, in ways I find hard to describe, I'm deeply grateful.

Back in bed, I tell Deko the truth: that I'd wanted him from the moment I laid eyes on him.

'So, what else do I owe Aretha?'

'Nothing. You hadn't sung a note.'

'That sounds like a line from a movie.'

'Then you're watching the wrong films, Mr Rainbow Man.' I run a fingertip through the light auburn curls on the broadness of his chest. 'There's something else I need to tell you, too. You can blame my mum for this.'

'Always say thank you?'

'Exactly. Not just a stud. Not just the Rainbow Man. But someone who took the right kind of care of me.'

'Took?'

'Takes.' I'm delighted by his acuteness, and by the change of tense.

I start to tell him about Pavel, how he has the same talent for mind-reading, and maybe for one or two other things.

'You fucked him, too?'

'I made love to him. There's a difference.'

'So, what happened? How come he's paralysed?'

I start to tell him about the accident that broke his neck, the small-hours dive into the wrong end of a swimming pool at an Orkney hotel.

'He'd been diving on the wreck in Scapa Flow,' I explain. 'He'd come up with this movie idea and German TV wanted to film him underwater. A blind man? Mapping the remains of a long-dead battleship through his fingertips? That's his phrase, not mine. Pavel loved the dives. He said it set him free. Made him weightless. They all got drunk that night and Pavel couldn't get enough of the water so he found his way to the pool at three in the morning. Rule one: never dive in the shallow end.'

'He broke his neck?'

'He did. There was CCTV in the pool, monitored from the front desk, and that made him lucky because they managed to fish him out before he drowned. You know about any of this stuff?'

'Yeah. We had a guy on the crew once. He fell off the gangplank in Rotterdam and broke his neck. Booze again. Very similar. Last time I saw him was in a nursing home in Antwerp. Won't ever get out of his wheelchair, poor bastard.'

'Pavel's got a high break, C-three and C-four.' I touch the back of Deko's neck. 'Any higher and he'd be dead. As it is, he can turn his head. He can chew and swallow. He can talk, hear, smell. He has feeling on his face and around his neck but that's about it. Nothing else works. No feeling, no control. The inside of his head is where it all happens, but that's always been his story so *plus ça change . . .*'

'The more things change?'

'Exactly. The more things change, the more they stay the same. Pavel's a one-off. I've never met anyone like him. In my business you need people with vision, people prepared to take a risk or two, people with that little chip of ice deep inside them. Pavel's always had that. He's a magpie. He thieves bits of other people's lives and turns them into something special on the page. I had a lovely part in one of his BBC radio plays when I was still too wobbly to go back on set. That's how we met.'

'And now?'

'Now we all look after him.'

'I meant the movie sets. You're still in the game? Still doing it?'

Good question. The fact is, I haven't done a proper film for nearly a year. I'd like to blame this career break on a lack of scripts but that wouldn't be strictly true.

'I'm a jobbing thesp,' I say defensively. 'When the call comes, I'll report for duty, but lately . . . I don't know . . .'

'Lost your appetite?'

'Lost something.'

I gaze at him a moment, and then we kiss. I can taste cigars on the smoothness of his tongue. He rolls on to his back and lets his head settle on the pillow. I hang over him.

'You look a bit like Pavel,' I tell him, 'with your eyes closed like that.'

'There's a difference,' he murmurs. 'Try me.'

I do. The second time is slower, more gentle, less urgent. Afterwards, I slip off him and lie enfolded by one giant arm. For minutes on end we say nothing. Then I prop myself up on one elbow, looking down at the big face on the pillow.

'Why do you owe so much money? Do you mind me asking?'

At first, I think he might be asleep, then one eye opens.

'Why the question?' My snooping doesn't seem to bother him in the least.

'I'm curious,' I say. 'Maybe that's something I've picked up from Pavel. All those invoices on your desk. The tax demand. I know I shouldn't have been looking but we must be talking six figures.'

'Easily. Does that upset you?'

'Not at all, but if I had debts like that it would frighten me witless. So either you're a great actor . . .'

'Or?'

'That's my question. There must be something I'm missing.'

'Like what?'

'I've no idea. Are you expecting some huge windfall? A legacy, maybe? Is there someone rich in your family?'

'Christ, no. My dad's gone. You know that. I told you. He died without a guilder to his name. My mother remarried recently and her new guy hasn't worked for more than a year. She always took in the strays, cats mostly.' He pulls a face, and then shakes his head. 'So, no. No magic fairy. And no money tree.'

'Just the debts.'

'Yeah.'

'Unsettled.'

'Yeah.'

'Until?'

'Until I can pay them. How does next month sound? Would that make me respectable again?'

We're very close, just inches away. I can feel the warmth of his breath on my face. Just now, I'm doing a Pavel, trying to pinpoint the key word in that little speech.

'Respectable?' I murmur. 'Is that something that should matter to me?'

Deko has a smile I can only describe as winning. It creeps over his face like an incoming tide. Laugh lines around his eyes. A hint of crooked teeth in his smile.

'*Respectable?*' He pulls me even closer. 'Christ, I hope not.'

TWENTY

I spend the night at the Beacon. Next morning, by the time I make my way back through the town, the police tapes at both ends of Carrie's street have gone, and everything appears to be back to normal. I linger for a moment, wanting to believe nothing ever happened, that it was all some kind of dream, but then a passer-by pauses outside Carrie's place and peers down at her basement flat. Bad news lingers, I think. Like the worst of smells.

Back at the apartment, Ndeye has already arrived. On her first day of work, she's wearing a uniform in a subdued shade of deep blue. After last night's explosion of colours, this comes as a mild disappointment, though nothing can lower the sheer voltage of her smile.

'Ms Andressen.' She kisses me on both cheeks, the way us French do.

'Enora,' I tell her.

We both go in to see Pavel. Felip is sponging his chin after feeding him breakfast. I glance down at the bowl. Porridge again, with a dusting of brown sugar.

Pavel is fractious. In the privacy of the kitchen, Felip tells me he's been at his bedside most of the night.

'Why?'

'He won't say. He won't tell me. The only question he asked, I couldn't answer.'

'Like?'

'Like where were you? I told him you were away for the night. Malo, I tell him. His father, Mr H. All of you together some place.' He hesitates a moment, searching my face. 'No?'

'Yes.' I put my hand on Felip's skinny wrist. 'These are difficult times, Felip. All of us need to talk, to be with each other. Pavel will surely understand that.'

'You think so?'

'I know so. He and I will have the conversation . . .' I summon a tight smile. 'Later.'

I brew fresh coffee and warm croissants in the microwave. Next door, in the lounge, I can hear Ndeye busy with the Hoover. She's singing a Paul Simon classic, 'Mrs Robinson', and in the lower registers her voice gives the song a slightly sinister heft I've never been aware of before.

I take her a cup of coffee, and some for Pavel in his special mug. Exhausted, Felip has retired to bed. Back in the lounge, I wait for Ndeye to finish before turning on the TV and settling on the sofa. Moments later, I'm watching the local news. Resorts around the south-west are reporting brisk business as the Easter weekend unfolds. A brief item on a National Trust property in deepest Cornwall reveals terrace after terrace engulfed in daffodils. Then, all too suddenly, I'm looking at a familiar face. Moonie.

As the camera slowly tightens on the image – the receding chin, the cherubic locks of hair, the scarlet flecks of acne – the voiceover tells us that this is a person of interest in connection with the recent murder of a woman in Exmouth. 'Person of interest' is a phrase I might have used myself barely a week ago when I first went to the police. If only they'd headed him off earlier, I think. If only I'd been more insistent – tougher – with Carrie. Then, with the same abruptness, there's a new face on the screen, a forecaster from the Met Office, and I'm being warned to brace myself for an altogether different order of risk. Torrential rain, moving east. Better tomorrow.

Mid-morning, my mobile begins to ring. I don't recognize the number.

'Ms Andressen? DS Williams. We met at the police station a couple of days ago.'

I nod. I say I remember her. She says she wants to pay Mr Stukeley a visit with a colleague from Operation *Mandolin*.

'Operation what?'

'*Mandolin*. Regarding the murder of Carrie.'

I say I understand. Mr Stukeley is Pavel. I tell her there shouldn't be a problem. All I have to do is check with him and then phone her back and agree a time.

'That won't be necessary, Ms Andressen. We're outside now. And it's pouring with rain.'

I go through to the hall and check on the video screen. DS Williams wasn't joking. She and a male figure I don't recognize are hunched beneath what little protection the entrance awning provides. Williams's umbrella has just blown inside out and she's fighting to control it.

'Third floor.' I still have the phone pressed to my ear, and I buzz her in. 'Lift's right in front of you.'

I've already mentioned the possibility of a CID visit to Pavel but it seems he's forgotten.

'Now, you mean?' He sounds alarmed. 'Here?'

'Yes.'

'Why so little warning?'

'I've no idea.'

'Then you must be here, too. Appropriate adult is the phrase these people use. It normally applies to children but I'm just as helpless. Do your best. See what they say.'

I meet Williams and her colleague as they step out of the lift. They're both soaked.

'DI Sanderson.' Williams is still trying to get her umbrella back into shape.

Sanderson extends a wet hand. He's older than Williams. What little hair he has is razored to the bareness of his scalp and he's wearing a suit that is a size too small. I rustle up a towel and offer tea or coffee. When I mention Pavel's request, it's obvious that they'd prefer to talk to him alone.

'That might not be possible,' I say. 'He can be very stubborn sometimes, even difficult.'

'He has something to hide? Your Mr Stukeley?'

'Absolutely not, but the very idea of strangers sometimes upsets him. It would be a kindness if I was there.'

'And if you're not?'

'He may say no.'

The detectives confer briefly in the hall while I retire to the kitchen. By the time I reappear with the coffee, they've decided that my presence at Pavel's bedside will, after all, be permissible.

They follow me into Pavel's bedroom, their eyes drawn immediately to the view. The wind is blasting up the estuary and the water is pocked with sizeable waves. The curtain of rain parts for a moment, offering a brief glimpse of the hills beyond the far bank, then we're back with umpteen shades of grey.

'Grim.' This from Williams. 'Must be lovely when the sun shines.'

I arrange chairs around the bed, side by side so Pavel doesn't have to turn his head to catch a question. In the event, though, I needn't have bothered because he's lying on his back, the shape of his thin body barely visible beneath the single sheet and cellular blanket. His lips are pressed tightly together, giving him the look of a sulky child, and what little colour the sun has recently put on his face appears to have gone. He looks paler than ever. Not a good sign.

Williams explains where this interview fits in *Mandolin*'s ongoing enquiries, and asks whether Pavel has any objection to her using a tape recorder. When Pavel says no, she produces a tiny machine, announces the date, the time, and Pavel's real name. Her understanding is that Mr Stukeley was especially friendly with the victim. True?

'Carrie.' Pavel's voice is a whisper. 'Her name was Carrie.'

'Of course. Carrie. You got to know her well?'

'Very well.'

'You saw her every day?'

'Yes, and every night. Sometimes we went out dancing.'

Williams and the DI exchange glances. I'm tempted to tell Pavel to behave but on second thoughts I say nothing. If he wants to make enemies of these people, so be it.

'My apologies.' Pavel's voice is a little stronger. 'I'm afraid this is all a bit distressing. Under the circumstances, I hope you'll pardon my little joke. The answer is yes. I think the word is friends. We were friends, good friends.'

'So, you trusted each other? Would that have been the case?'

'Of course.'

'Confided in each other?'

'Always. It became a habit. And perhaps a consolation.'

A thin dribble of saliva is tracking down Pavel's chin. I mop it up with a pad of cotton wool. A tiny nod tells me that Pavel thinks that he and I are in this thing together. Complicity? I'm not sure.

Williams has sensed it too, and I make a mental note not to underestimate this woman. She wants to know whether, in Pavel's view, Carrie had any problems in her life.

He nods at once. 'Jean-Paul,' he says. 'Falling in love isn't as simple as people often assume. The man may be a delight, every-thing may be beyond wonderful, but he's married, and he has children. I'm assuming you know all that.'

Thanks to me, of course they do. Williams confirms that the post-mortem report has arrived. According to the pathologist, Carrie was ten weeks pregnant.

'Did you know that, Mr Stukeley?'

'I did, yes.'

'She told you? Carrie?'

'Yes. You've taken DNA from him? From Jean-Paul?'

'I'm afraid that's not something we're at liberty to discuss.'

'But you did, of course you did, and that little swab will have top priority. The last time I wrote a crime series, the going rate for twenty-four-hour turnaround was eighteen hundred pounds. I imagine that's probably gone up by now but in circumstances like these, speed trumps everything. So, did you get a positive? Nodding, I'm afraid, won't do. Just a yes or a no will be sufficient.'

Thanks, once again, to me, Williams knows that Pavel is blind. I'm still trying to work out whether the hint of a smile on her face indicates a degree of admiration for Pavel's chutzpah when the DI takes up the running. He makes no mention of a DNA match. Instead, he wants to know how close Carrie really was to this boyfriend of hers.

'He was her lover.' There's a note of reprimand in Pavel's voice. 'Boyfriend is a frivolous term.'

The DI says nothing. Neither does Williams. Finally, it falls to me to ask Pavel whether he's had enough.

'By no means.' He sounds irritated. 'The least I can do is try and honour the poor girl's memory. I know it's an unfortunate turn of phrase, but if she was here now, if she heard Jean-Paul referred to as her "boyfriend", she'd die. What I'm guessing you really want to know is how close they were. As I say, they were lovers. They were enchanted by each other. They'd found themselves in a very special place and it was a joy to hear it. Boyfriend, the very idea, belongs in TV soaps. A little respect, please. Is that too much to ask?'

I'm gazing down at Pavel, full of admiration. He's seized this interview by the throat and he won't let it go. His terms, no others. Even yesterday's wheeze seems to have gone. It's obviously the DI's job to tease some kind of evidential value from these exchanges with Pavel. He has a pad open on his lap but so far, he's scribbled no more than a couple of lines.

'In love, then?' He's looking at Pavel. 'Is that the way we're hearing it?'

'It's the way I heard it, certainly. But Carrie was a good girl, a decent person, and the circumstances distressed her.'

'You mean the fact that he was married?'

'Of course. And kids as well, in fact, *especially* kids. That changes everything. You can't fall in love with an entire family, no matter how hard you try.'

'Tense, then? Troubled? How would you describe her?'

'The latter. Troubled.'

'And from his point of view? Jean-Paul?'

'I gather he felt the same.'

'Rock and a hard place? Your lover or your wife?'

'Your lover or your family. That isn't quite the same thing.'

The DI nods, and at last makes another note. It falls to Williams to take up the running.

'Did Jean-Paul know that Carrie was pregnant?'

'I've no idea.'

'You'd have asked her, surely.'

'I did, yes.'

'And?'

For the first time, Pavel seems to have lost his place in the script. He's taking his time. The frown could mean anything.

'The night before she died . . .' he says at last.

'Yes?'

'I suspect she was going to tell him.'

'Suspect?'

'Knew.'

'So, what did she say?'

'This isn't simple.' The frown has deepened. 'I'm afraid you'll need to be patient.'

'We have lots of time, Mr Stukeley. Just tell us what you know.'

There's a long silence. The rain is still drumming on the window and I can hear the halyards dancing against the metal masts in the nearby dinghy park.

Finally, Pavel appears to be ready. 'They used to meet in the early evenings,' he says, 'as soon as Carrie was finished with me. As you might imagine, I remember that last conversation very well. There's a passage in a book we'd been reading together. Ernst Jünger's wartime diaries. Do you know them, by any chance?'

Another exchange of glances between the two detectives, this time totally blank. In case they think Pavel's making this up, I direct their attention to the book, still visible on Pavel's bedside table.

'And?' This from the DI.

'Jünger is in Paris. In many respects, he's a tortured man. As a writer, he understands what a lethal proposition the truth can be. In wartime, under enemy occupation, it can get you killed. We were discussing that proposition, Carrie and I, when she began to cry. That's when I finally realized what must be going on in that lovely head of hers. There's just so much any human being can take, and in this case Jean-Paul was worrying her to death.'

I wince at Pavel's choice of phrase. Williams wants to know why Carrie was so concerned about Jean-Paul.

'Because she'd lied to him.'

'How? In what way?'

'She'd told him she was taking the pill.'

'And?'

'She wasn't.'

'He didn't know that?'

'No.'

'So why did she lie to him in the first place?'

'Why does anyone do anything?' Pavel asks. 'How can we ever be sure about anyone else?'

This is a deeply philosophical question. Once again, the DI's pen doesn't move.

'You said "lethal" just now,' he says carefully. 'You were pointing out what a lethal proposition the truth can be. What, exactly, does "lethal" mean, Mr Stukeley? In a situation like this?'

Pavel is well aware of the trap he's just set himself. Indeed, knowing him the way I do, I suspect that this, too, may be deliberate.

'The truth can kill any relationship. That was Jünger's insight in the diaries. He wrote about the gambles we take, the tricks we play with the truth, and he wrote about loss. The last thing Carrie wanted to lose was Jean-Paul, what they'd made together, the place they'd found for themselves.'

Neither the DI nor Williams are quite sure what to make of this. Finally, it's Williams who asks the obvious question.

'Did she ever talk about having an abortion?'

'Yes, often.'

'And?'

'She hated the very idea. Carrie was a spiritual person. What they'd made together was sacred. She'd never cast it aside. Never hurt it. That's what she believed, and if you want the truth, I suspect Ernst Jünger would have agreed with her. Does that shed any light on the matter? I do hope so.'

At this point I can tell that Pavel regards the interview as over. He's tolerated the presence of these strangers in his room, in what passes for his life, for long enough, and now he says he's very tired. Tired of making these journeys back to the conversations with Carrie, tired of fretting about the way she must have felt that final evening, tired of trying to cope with her absence. He hopes they can squeeze something helpful from what he's shared with them.

'So good luck,' he murmurs. 'And *bon voyage*. Fingers crossed, the rain may stop one day.'

Neither of the detectives knows quite what to say and it falls to me, as Appropriate Adult, to suggest that they fold their tents and beat a tactful retreat. Mr Stukeley, I tell them, is unused to pressures like these and it's my responsibility to make sure he comes to no more harm.

Instinctively, I sense they both want to stay. I've no idea what else they think Pavel might be able to tell them but when Williams looks at me and raises an enquiring eyebrow, I shake my head. The interview is well and truly over.

They both get to their feet. I'm about to offer them the loan of an umbrella but the DI can't take his eyes off Pavel.

'Mr Stukeley? Can you hear me?'

'He can,' I say. 'One last question. Then I'm afraid that's it.'

'Of course.' The DI makes sure the recorder is still running. Then he bends to the bed, his mouth to Pavel's ear. 'Is there anything else you'd like to tell us, Mr Stukeley? Anything else Carrie might have shared with you? Just nod or shake your head. Either will be perfectly acceptable. We can always come back later. We just need to bottom out this thing.'

Pavel's head lies unmoving on the pillow. The DI asks exactly the same question a second time. Finally, Pavel tries to swallow a yawn before asking for an ice cube. The ice cube comes wrapped in a layer of muslin. We use it to moisten the dryness of his mouth. Pavel opens his lips to let me in. Then I step back again.

'Interesting question.' Pavel's voice has sunk to a whisper again. 'But I'm afraid the answer is no.'

Outside, in the hall, I summon the lift. When I ask how the investigation is going, neither Williams nor the DI is prepared to give me a proper answer. Early days. Multiple lines of enquiry. Persons of interest. Certain forensic issues. None of this takes me any further but when the lift arrives, and the door opens, Williams asks about my own availability. The SIO, she says, has asked her to organize another interview in slightly greater depth. Might this afternoon be convenient? At Exmouth police station?

For a split second I toy with saying no. I've had more than enough of these people's company, of trying to work out how much they know, and how much they don't, of trying to figure out where

Operation *Mandolin* might lead them next, but then I remember Carrie, and the debts we all owe her, and I say yes.

The DI has his foot wedged against the lift door. Williams extends a hand in farewell and steps past him. Then something else occurs to me.

'You made an appeal on TV this morning.' I nod towards the lounge. 'It was Moonie's face you used. Does that mean he's your prime suspect?'

'We'd value a conversation, certainly.' The DI offers me a thin smile. 'It's been a pleasure, Ms Andressen. And thank you for the coffee.'

The lift door closes, and they've gone. Back in Pavel's bedroom I linger for a moment or two. For the life of me, I can't work out whether he's faked the sudden exhaustion.

He has. His head turns slowly on the pillow. He wants me to kiss him. He says it's the least I owe him.

'For what?'

'For bringing that charade to a close.' He's smiling up at me. 'Why does anyone do anything?' he whispers again. 'How can we ever be sure about anyone else?'

TWENTY-ONE

An hour or so later, I'm in the lounge having a sandwich lunch and catching up on my emails. One of them is from Evelyn, my lovely neighbour back in Holland Park. She's just returned from a week in Southern Ireland and she's insisting on taking me out to lunch. She has photos of a particular garden which has exceeded her wildest expectations. Acres of plantings, she writes. And an ornamental lake to die for. When am I back?

Good question. I check my watch. I'm not due at the police station until three and I'm in the process of tapping out a longish reply when I hear what I can only describe as a commotion next door in Pavel's room. Moments later, Ndeye's face appears around the door.

'*Venez.*' I can hear the panic in her voice. '*Urgence.*'

Some kind of emergency? Has Pavel somehow fallen out of bed? I get to my feet and hurry next door. To my relief, Pavel seems intact, the same face on the same pillow, but then I take a closer look, aware of Ndeye beside me.

'*Une attaque.*' She taps her head. A stroke.

'How do you know?'

'I was reading to him. We were talking about Paris. Then he suddenly stopped as if there was something in his throat, and his eyes went, and he started to choke. I've seen it before. A horrible noise. An animal noise. From way down here.' She pats her chest.

'Is he breathing?'

'Just. Not much, but just.'

'Pulse?'

'Very light. Here.' She has Pavel's hand. I take it, trying to find the slightest flutter on the inside of his wrist. She's right. He's barely alive.

I phone 999 on my mobile and ask for an ambulance. I give my name and the address and postcode of the apartment. Then comes a change of voice and I'm talking to a man with a to-do checklist. An ambulance will be with us as soon as possible, he assures me. In the meantime, it will help to make the patient as comfortable as possible. Are his or her airways clear? Am I familiar with the recovery position? Has he or she been eating recently?

'He,' I say helplessly. 'He's a he.'

'Has he complained of pains anywhere?'

'He's paralysed.'

'Are his eyes open?'

'He's blind.'

'Can he hear you?'

'I don't think so. Not so far. I'll try again.'

The phone still pressed to my ear, I kneel beside Pavel. 'Can you hear me? It's OK. It's Enora. Just move your head, open your eyes, any bloody thing.' I glance up at Ndeye. She's staring at Pavel the way you might look at a ghost, disbelief spiked with something close to fear. I try again, and then a third time, my lips to Pavel's ear.

Nothing. Not the slightest hint of a reaction.

'Is he still breathing?' asks the voice on the phone.

'Just.'

'Do you have access to a defib?'

'No.'

'CPR?'

I look at Ndeye again.

'Cardio resus?' I mime the actions with my hand. Mercifully, she nods.

I pass on the good news to the voice on my phone. Should we get Pavel out of bed? Lie him on the floor? Try and work on him?

'He's in bed already?'

'Yes. At nursing height.'

'Perfect. Start with light pressure. Keep his pulse going. If it fails completely, ramp it up to max. And you are . . .?'

I give him my name. He already has the address for the ambulance. He says he'll keep the line open in case I need any more help.

'Paralysed *and* blind? Have I got that right?'

'You have.'

'Good luck, Ms Andressen. The paramedics will take over as soon as they arrive.'

'Thank you.'

Ndeye has already exposed Pavel's upper body. Now she's standing over him, her arms out straight, applying little jolts of pressure to his pitifully thin chest. After a minute or so, his breathing seems to pick up and watching him fight like this I feel a fierce gust of what I can only describe as pride. *Hang in there. Do it. Don't let the darkness steal you away.*

The ambulance is with us minutes later. I hear the wail of the siren first. By now I've left Ndeye with Pavel and I've gone out in the rain to intercept the paramedics. They park on the hardstanding behind the apartment block. One of them grabs a resus bag and follows me into the building. The other slides a wheeled stretcher out of the back of the ambulance and follows. The lift, mercifully, is still open. The three of us ascend to the top floor while I do my best to explain what awaits them. Male. Mid-fifties. Blind. Paralysed after a C3 break. And now, it seems, felled by a stroke.

The older of the two paramedics hasn't taken his eyes off me. As the lift whispers to a halt, he reaches out and gives my shoulder a little squeeze.

'Excuse my French,' he mutters. 'But shit happens.'

I follow them into the apartment. Ndeye is still at Pavel's bedside.

She's stopped the CPR and for a moment I fear the worst but then I catch the smile on her face.

'His breathing is much stronger,' she says. 'His pulse is good, too.'

The paramedics circle the bed and try to get a response from Pavel. Sheer willpower may have dragged him back from the brink but he's clearly in no mood for conversation. Ndeye has already removed Pavel's glasses. Now the older paramedic gently parts his eyelid and shines a light into his eyeball.

I want to ask what he expects to find in there, but I don't. He shakes his head, checks his watch and looks across at his colleague.

'Wonford,' he says. 'ETA fifteen minutes. Query TIA.'

The younger paramedic has a radio. He transmits the details, then helps transfer Pavel on to the stretcher.

'You're taking him to hospital?'

'Wonford, my lovely. You want to come?'

I say yes at once and follow them out to the lift, leaving Ndeye to clear up. Only when we leave the block, with me doing my best to shield Pavel's face from the rain, do I realize that I've left my mobile in the apartment. My helpful friend from ambulance control, I think, may still be on the open line. Bless him.

Wonford is the main site for the Royal Devon and Exeter Hospital, a sprawl of buildings to the south of the city. We roar through every red light en route from Exmouth and seem to spend most of the journey on the wrong side of the road. Pavel is breathing oxygen now and I'm perched beside him, bracing myself against the tighter corners, trying to offer some kind of physical comfort. His flesh is cold to the touch and I can feel the bones in his hand beneath my fingertips. I'm used to the deadness below his neck but now is somehow different. *Please God, don't let him go.*

The A&E unit is at the rear of the hospital. The paramedics ease the laden stretcher carefully out of the back of the ambulance and wheel him into the fast-track channel reserved for acute emergencies. Pavel is still breathing but his face behind the oxygen mask is the colour of thin, grey parchment. I'm still walking beside the stretcher, still holding his hand, when a nurse in blue scrubs intercepts me. I give her my name and she steers me into a side cubicle and takes Pavel's details. The news that he's blind as well as paralysed produces just a hint of surprise.

'Remarkable.' She clips her pen back in her pocket. 'Are you the lead carer?'

'In some ways, yes.'

'His wife, perhaps?'

'No.'

'Partner?'

'No. Just a good friend.'

The moment she leaves me in the cubicle, promising to return when she has any news, I feel an overwhelming sensation of self-disgust. A good friend? Is that all I am? After everything Pavel and I have been through? Before he had the accident, and afterwards? I shake my head and do my best to settle in the moulded plastic chair, my head tipped back against the tiled wall, my eyes closed.

Sudden crises like this, unannounced, unfathomable, can shake you to the core. I had a similar feeling when my consultant confirmed that my brain tumour, that little knot of rogue cells, might well kill me. You follow the prognosis, and nod, and try to be brave, but your normal defences are useless. You can make no sense of anything. Maybe I should be talking to H, I think. Or perhaps Malo. But I know deep down that even if I had a phone, I'd never make the calls. The paramedic was right. There's nothing to be said. Shit happens. Deal with it.

A little later, the nurse returns. She says that Pavel is undergoing a series of tests and will certainly be staying in the hospital for a while. His condition appears to have stabilized and his vital signs are remarkably good. When I ask whether he's back with us – whether he's talking, listening, being difficult – she shakes her head. The word she uses is 'coma', which I find a bit chilling. Is this something temporary? Or will he grow out of it?

I apologize at once for the latter phrase. My own brain, I tell her, keeps letting me down. She smiles and tells me where to find a cup of tea. It comes from a machine but it's not too bad. In the meantime, she'll try and persuade the registrar to come and have a word with me. She's about to leave the cubicle when, all too late, I remember my appointment at the police station. I have no watch, no mobile, nothing.

'Do you have the time, by any chance?'

The nurse checks her watch. Nearly half past three. I close my eyes and rock slowly back and forth on the chair. I must look a picture because the nurse squats beside me.

'Everything OK?'

I start to explain about my mobile and about an appointment I've missed, but when she offers to make a call on my behalf I shake my head.

'It doesn't matter,' I tell her. 'Everything will have to wait.'

It's gone six when I finally get the first proper news about Pavel. At first I assume the slight figure who's just slipped into the cubicle and closed the curtain behind him is the registrar but he turns out to be the A&E duty consultant.

'You look far too young,' I tell him. 'And that's a compliment.'

He has a sheepish smile, which is nice, and what's also unusual is the way he tries to soften bad news. I've met dozens of medical luminaries over the last couple of years, most of them oncologists, and some of them have an occasionally brutal habit of offering unvarnished truths. Not this infant.

'Your friend will be a challenge, whatever happens,' he says. 'We've taken a good look at him and we don't think he's going to die. He's still unconscious at the moment but there's every chance that he may come round within the next twenty-four hours or so. That's not a promise, but we think it's very likely. What's also more than possible is what little he may have left. In my experience, episodes are very unpredictable. They'll know more on the Stroke Unit and I'd feel more comfortable if you had a longer conversation with them.'

I thank him for his tact, and I tell him I understand his reluctance to go any further. The phrase that haunts me is 'what little he may have left'.

'Will he be able to talk?'

'Possibly not.'

'Hear anything?'

'That, too, may have been compromised.'

Compromised? I shut my eyes again, determined not to cry. My poor bloody man. Paralysed. Blind. Mute. And maybe even deaf. Why would God waste a minute, a second, keeping him alive? Why would anyone?

I feel a hand on my shoulder, the lightest touch.

'It may not be as bad as you fear,' he says. 'Let's hope your friend makes a full recovery.'

*   *   *

A full recovery? I'm sitting on the top deck of the bus, going back to the penthouse. Pavel will never make a full recovery because most of him is dead already. Then I remember those precious moments at his bedside when we're discussing a favourite movie, or the dream script he's still hoping to write, or the madness of the Brexiteers, or any of the countless other moments in our time together that spark laughter and a sense of kinship I can only describe as unique. Pavel and I have been marching in lockstep for the best part of a couple of years. We've always agreed that the world is going mad, clinically insane, and that there's precious little that either of us can do about it except compare notes and watch out for each other. That, in a way, is loving the man and now, I tell myself, is not the time to stop. I want him, need him, back. With whatever the medics have been able to salvage.

It's a five-minute walk from the bus stop to the marina. Mercifully the rain has stopped. I skirt the tidal basin and pause on the walkway at the foot of the apartment block. Rags of cloud are racing across the distant swell of the Haldon Hills and the sunset, in a phrase Pavel would have used, promises to be operatic. I linger a moment longer, watching a lone curlew pecking at the mud flats, and then take the lift up to the apartment.

Ndeye, it seems, has gone. Felip meets me as the lift door slides open. He's desperate for news of Pavel and I tell him as much as I can. He wants, very badly, to know that Pavel will come back mended and I do my best to tell him that this happy outcome is more than possible. Then, almost as an afterthought, he nods towards the lounge.

'A friend of yours,' he says. 'Mr Deko?'

TWENTY-TWO

Pavel has gone. I've no desire to spend the night in the apartment without him, and so I'm very happy to accompany Deko back to the Beacon. He says that Felip has told him about Pavel's stroke, and when he puts his arms round me and gives me a long hug, I'm deeply grateful.

'This is becoming a habit,' I tell him. 'You're good at this. I'm running out of friends, but you could start a business.' When he wants to know whether that's some kind of joke, I can only nod. 'In very bad taste,' I admit. 'All you have to do is forgive me.'

We leave the apartment. En route back to the Beacon, Deko suggests a detour to a pub called the Grapevine. When I ask why, he says there's someone I ought to meet.

Ought?

I've never been in the Grapevine. It lies just off the town's main square and according to Carrie it has been vastly improved in recent years and has become the must-visit pub for monied drinkers with a passion for craft ales. She gave me the impression that it attracts a certain demographic – youngish hipsters drawn from the professional classes – and on first sight it seems she's right. Early evening, three guys are joshing at the bar, while a quartet of women at a nearby table are doing serious damage to a couple of bottles of Sauvignon nesting in buckets of ice.

Deko is making for a table by the window where a lone drinker with a glass of something fizzy at his elbow is reading yesterday's house copy of *The Times*.

'Boysie.' Deko stands aside and gestures in my direction. 'Enora.'

Boysie must be younger than Deko, but not much. He's wearing a pair of pink chinos and an exquisitely ironed open white shirt. He's heavily tanned and the lick of hair falling over his forehead appears to be genuinely blond. The third nail on his left hand is painted an eye-catching scarlet and when his head turns towards me, I glimpse a silver ear stud in the shape of a dove.

A man like this, I think at once, belongs in one of those sultry period movies set in the White Highlands. Without even opening his mouth, he exudes a slightly louche arrogance. Colonial Kenya before the locals took over? Perfect.

He gets to his feet. The handshake is warm, immediately intimate, and the moment we all sit down, I sense that these two – Deko and Boysie – are brothers-in-arms. They must also be Grapevine regulars because drinks arrive at the table without anyone appearing to have ordered. A beer for Deko, a glass of Merlot for me.

'They make this stuff in a microbrewery round the back.' Deko raises his pale ale. 'Here's to crime.'

The pair of them pick up the threads of some recent conversation, and I gladly tune out. I'm trying to imagine the Stroke Unit where

Pavel must be lying by now. How will the nurses cope with his many other needs? Might he be showing signs of life by now? Is there any chance he might even recognize me when I roll up tomorrow morning? I sit back in the spill of late sunshine through the window, toying with my glass, telling myself there's absolutely nothing – for the time being – I can do. My precious Pavel is in good hands. *Just relax.*

Impossible. I realize Boysie is studying me with some interest. Deko's big hand settles briefly on my arm.

'You owe this man a thank you,' he says.

'For what?'

'For that ride the other night. Out to the boat.'

I nod. Dinner *à deux* aboard *Amen* seems a lifetime ago.

'That was your speedboat? The one in the marina?' I'm looking at Boysie.

'We call it a RIB, but yes. My pleasure. Any time, eh?'

Deko tells him to behave, and then turns back to me. Boysie, he says, is a man on a mission. Lately, local opportunities for fine dining have brightened no end. A newly opened hotel down by the river offers Michelin-standard cuisine. Topsham is awash with top-end eateries. But Boysie, bless him, is determined to raise the bar even higher.

I'm not quite following this. Is the figure across the table some kind of super chef?

'Christ, no.' Boysie has an infectious laugh. 'Money buys all that. I just provide the setting.'

'You mean a restaurant?'

'A hotel.'

'Here? In Exmouth?'

'Up towards the Common. The place goes way back. Once it was a rectory. Then a manor house. Now we're talking seventeen rooms, a decent menu, six acres of woodland, and views across the river you won't believe.'

'And a casino.' It's Deko's turn to laugh. 'For Exmouth's high rollers.'

Boysie gets to his feet and checks his watch before telling Deko to drink up.

'We're off?' I've barely touched my wine.

'Afraid so.' Boysie shoots me that same smile. 'In our game, seeing is believing.'

He has a big Audi parked outside the pub. We leave Exmouth at some speed, making our way through a maze of country lanes that climb away from the river valley. Acres of trees finally part to offer a pair of impressive wrought-iron gates, with glimpses of a drive beyond. Inlaid on a huge chunk of granite beside the gates is the name of our destination: Hotel Zuma.

'Zuma?' I ask.

Boysie is driving. I can see his eyes in the rear-view mirror.

'It's a theme thing, a branding thing. Ask Deko. It was his idea.'

Deko is riding in the back beside me. He says it has to do with Africa, with a long-ago expedition to find the source of the River Niger. All the real clues, he says, are in the wellness spa. If I can contain my curiosity, Boysie might give me the tour.

By now I've realized that this little expedition is Deko's way of trying to get my mind off everything else that has gone so catastrophically wrong in my life. Felip has told him about Pavel, and so he's summoned Boysie to the pub with instructions to cheer me up. And so here we are, rolling to a stop in front of an exquisite confection in warm brick, and mullioned windows, held together by webs of wisteria and ancient vine.

'Come.' Boysie is holding the door open for me.

I get out and follow him towards the entrance. I must have been in hundreds of hotels in my life, mainly on location, but never anywhere quite like this. There's none of the showy bling and bravura that some hoteliers use to bludgeon their clientele. *Au contraire*, the scale is unabashedly domestic. I might have stepped into someone's house. It radiates a sense of comfort, of quiet elegance, of people at ease with each other. That this homely space may once have been a rectory comes as no surprise: the scatter of rugs on the polished wooden floorboards, the deeply upholstered armchairs, begging you to take a seat, the low occasional tables with their folded newspapers and piles of magazines, the leaded windows, with glimpses of a lawn and flowerbeds beyond, the smiling waitress delivering a tray of drinks to newly arrived guests. Half-close my eyes, and I could be at Flixcombe Manor, H's pile in West Dorset, and believe me, that's a compliment.

'Spa, Boysie?'

My host leads the way to what must have been a recent extension to the property. I'm half-expecting a more contemporary space, better suited for a thermal suite or two, and a plunge pool, and somewhere you might enjoy a whole-body massage, but once again

I'm wrong. The spa is deeply intimate, scored for clever lighting, mosaic tiles, and the kind of bony Arab music that teases your nerve ends. It has a souk-like feel. It reminds me of shadowed parlours I've seen and loved in Tangiers and Istanbul, and the walls are hung with beautifully framed pen and ink washes, all – I suspect – the work of the same hand.

I take a closer look. The face that dominates two of these little masterpieces belongs to a woman. She stands erect, full-breasted, in front of a jaw-dropping landscape that has to be African. There's a wild extravagance in this setting, a surrender to the towering mountains and billowing clouds beyond the nearby river, and the expression on the woman's face warns the artist that nothing but his best efforts on the canvas will do.

'The mighty widow Zuma,' Boysie whispers. 'It's 1825. We send four men to West Africa to find out what happens to the River Niger. They end up deep inland where they happen across the widow Zuma. This is the daughter of an Arab trader. She has a thousand slaves she rents as prostitutes. She's also desperate to marry a white man. The leader of the expedition is a naval officer called Clapperton. He tells his servant, Lander, to do the business. Lander isn't keen and in any case the widow Zuma has decided on Clapperton. Our hero is horrified and demands a military escort out of town. Already, two of the expedition have died of fever. Clapperton succumbs, too, which leaves his servant, Lander, to bring back this little tale. Deko thinks the widow Zuma was wellness on legs and suspects she's still alive. You like her? Our mighty Zuma?'

I take a closer look, amused by Boysie's playful romp through this episode of our colonial history, and ask what his guests make of a setting like this.

'You want the truth? Some don't get it. They've come for the lotions, the exfoliations, all the other nonsense, and they don't see the point. But others love it, and they're the guests who will keep coming back.'

'And you've really got a casino?'

'We have. It's smaller than most. Deko calls it "intimate". But when I tell you it does the business, you'll know what I mean. I'd show you round but we've got the decorators in. We tried to theme it around Lieutenant Clapperton, but serious gamblers have no interest in history and absolutely no sense of fucking humour, so we gave up. Faux wooden panels and drinks on the house. Never fails.'

I steal a glance at Deko. He's clearly heard all this stuff before, but I tell him it's refreshing to find something so different when it comes to hotels. Boysie says he's hungry and insists on a snack. The snack turns out to be a table laid for three in the Hotel Zuma's dining room. Guests finishing their supper eye us as we sit down. Boysie doesn't bother with a menu. Instead, he enquires what – in a perfect world – I'd like to eat. The kitchen, he says, is at my disposal. Anything.

This, too, is novel. Never have I been faced with unlimited choice. To my surprise, I realize I'm hungry.

'Anything,' Boysie says again. 'Just name it. We have free-range pork, if you're interested. The pigs live up in the woods there.' He waves a hand towards the window. 'Eat their weight in acorns, mushrooms, anything. We pen them in and leave them to it, and from time to time we grab the fattest and pop him down to the slaughterhouse. Delicious. And fun, too. Eh, Deko?'

I shake my head. The image of Boysie and Deko chasing some poor animal to his death does nothing for me, but I've realized something else about this relationship that I should have nailed earlier.

'Sea bass?'

'Of course. Chef does a twist on apple butter. It's dark and a little spicy with a hint of liquorice. It comes from Jersey. Just like him.'

I say that sounds perfect. New potatoes? Fresh spinach from the garden? Yes, please.

Boysie summons a waitress and orders a bottle of Chablis, then turns back to me. 'Don't think any of this is for free.' That smile again. 'We have a proposition.'

It's nearly midnight by the time Deko summons a taxi and we ride back to Exmouth. It turns out that he and Boysie have been putting their heads together over the last couple of days. Thanks to Brexit and the general glumness of things, advance bookings for Hotel Zuma are beginning to flag and they're looking – in Boysie's phrase – for clever ways of keeping the bank at arm's length. Deko had mentioned some of the movies I'd done, some of the people I'd met, some of the stories I might be willing to share, and Boysie is now wondering about a themed weekend with yours truly in the chair, and a programme of suitable movies to go with it.

This is very similar to the idea that H had to brighten our passage to the D-Day beaches on *Persephone*. At first, to be frank, I doubted whether anyone would part with serious money just to hear little me, but in the event it worked. Not only that but I was quietly flattered by the interest and intelligence that our paying guests brought to the feast. A couple of these people – middle-aged, bookish, serious – knew more about my career than I did, and when Boysie told me to sleep on the proposition and give him a ring in the morning, I shook my head.

'I love what you've done with this place,' I told him. 'The widow Zuma would never leave.'

'And the sea bass?'

'Exquisite.'

We parted as friends. Now, driving down into Exmouth, Deko asks me what I made of him.

'He's in love with you,' I say. 'Head-over-heels, totally smitten, probably has been for years. It's a compliment. He's a nice man.'

'You're right. He is.'

'And you?'

'I think he's great. We've been through a lot. We make each other laugh.'

'That's not my question.'

'I know it isn't.'

'Well . . .?'

Deko shakes his head. If anything, he seems amused. For a minute or so we drive on in silence. Then he has the tact to ask me where I want to sleep. Four hours ago, I couldn't wait to get out of the apartment. Now, thanks to a very agreeable evening, I've changed my mind.

'Drop me at Pavel's place,' I tell him. 'It's nothing personal. I just need to get my head back together. You don't mind?'

'Not at all.'

The taxi drops me at the marina. I blow Deko a kiss through the back window and head for the apartment. The lights on the third floor are still on, and I know Felip will be waiting up for me.

I'm right. I make a pot of coffee and we sit in the lounge for the best part of an hour, talking about Pavel. Felip's admiration for his charge occasionally verged on hero-worship, and it comes as no surprise when he tells me that he spent half the evening at the hospital, trying to make sure Pavel was getting the nursing he deserved. The fact that they wouldn't let him anywhere near the Stroke Unit didn't upset him in the least.

'He's a clever man.' He taps his head. 'He'll know I was around. He'll sense it. I couldn't let him down. I had to be there. Even in a different building.'

On the page, this sounds a bit wacky, but I know exactly what he means. People in comas may not be as lost as we imagine. Hearing, they say, is always the last sense to go and after Felip has drained his mug and said goodnight, I steal into Pavel's room.

Ndeye must have tidied up before she left because there are fresh sheets on the bed, and even a single rose in a vase on the chest of drawers where we keep all the items Pavel's care demands. I spend a minute or two just gazing at that rose. As a down payment on Pavel's future, maybe all our futures, I find this little gesture deeply touching. Then I remember what I'd come for.

The Ernst Jünger diaries are still on Pavel's bedside table. I carry the book back to the lounge and curl up on the sofa. I know that Carrie marked particular passages and I want to find an entry that might spark Pavel back to life. Tomorrow, I think, I can take the book to the hospital and read it to him. He might or might not hear me. Either way, throwing a lifeline like this is the very least I can do.

I begin to thumb through the book, page after page as the months, and then years, spool by. Guided by Carrie's marks, lines pencilled lightly beside the text, I pause and read. Jünger reflecting on Proust: the gloves, the fingernails, the noises off, the ever-closed windows, his occasional visits to the local slaughterhouse. Might this touch a nerve deep in Pavel's brain?

Then, eight months on, I find another entry, simpler this time. Jünger is in Paris. It's late September, 1942, and the push into Russia has begun to run out of steam. Beset by doubts, Jünger remembers a day he once spent climbing a mountain in the Canary Islands. He feels the spray of a heavy, warm rain and he pauses to study a fennel plant. The passage, beautifully written, has earned a double mark from Carrie, and thus – presumably – from Pavel. Tomorrow, I think, I will buy fennel before I get on the bus. The scent, and the words to go with it. Two doors into whatever Pavel has left.

I glance at my watch. Nearly two in the morning. I leaf quickly through to the end of the book and then I pause. Beside one of the final entries, in Carrie's loopy handwriting, is a telephone number. I stare at it, then reach for a pen and a scrap of paper to jot it down.

Tomorrow, I think.

TWENTY-THREE

To the hospital, again.

It's Easter Sunday and I'm heading for a ten o'clock bus. The town centre is dead except for an untidy huddle of street people on a bench near the war memorial. I'd like to think they're talking about Moonie, but they're not. Yesterday's weather was clearly a nightmare. The oldest among them, a skeletal figure with wild eyes and a greasy-looking tangle of beard, got soaked to the skin. The rain had stopped by dusk but it was an evil night, the wind from the north, freeze your nuts off. I give them what small change I can muster and run for the bus.

There's not much traffic on the road, and I sit on the top deck, listening to Carrie's Walkman. I found it a couple of days after her death, lying on a shelf in Pavel's bedroom. It's got Bluetooth, no wires, and the little buds sit nicely in my ears. Strictly speaking, I should be giving this back to whoever is responsible for sorting out her affairs, but we still have no idea who that person might be, and in the meantime, I've been curious to know what kind of music she listened to. It's definitely classical, scored for a full orchestra, and the slower passages carry an edge of sadness or maybe regret. Pavel, I suspect, would have recommended the piece and the more I listen, the more I like it.

The Stroke Unit at the hospital is upstairs on the second floor. An orderly directs me to the nursing station where I enquire where I might find Mr Stukeley. The fact that they don't know him as Pavel adds to the strangeness of this place. It's quiet up here, like a movie without a soundtrack, and most of the patients appear to be asleep. There are flowers everywhere, and I'm admiring a spectacular bunch of dwarf daffodils when a male nurse appears. He's wearing a nose ring and he has the stub of a pencil tucked behind his ear.

'Mr Stukeley?' I enquire again.

He nods and leads the way to a side room. Pavel is lying in the single bed and I hesitate for a moment in the doorway. It's warm in the unit and the single sheet is folded neatly below his chin. His head lies at the centre of the pillow. The absence of his usual glasses gives his bony face a special vulnerability I've never seen before. His eyes are open, staring up at the ceiling, and his lips are slightly parted. There's absolutely no sign of life, no movement, nothing. He might have been laid out for inspection, an object of curiosity for anyone with more than a passing interest.

'How is he?'

'Poorly, I'm afraid, but still with us. Can I fetch you a chair?'

I nod, stepping into the room. As I approach the bed, I'm half-expecting Pavel to acknowledge my presence but I tell myself that things are bad with him, that he's fighting demons in that vast head of his, that he must conserve what little energy he has.

The nurse returns with a chair and asks me whether I'd like a cup of tea. I sense he wants to know more about this new arrival, and I'm right.

'You know Mr Stukeley well?'

'Pavel. His name's Pavel. And the answer's yes.'

I tell him a little about Pavel: the scripts he's written, the awards he's won, the name he's made for himself.

'You're telling me he's famous?'

'Yes. Not big-name famous. Not up-there-with-the-stars famous. Not that. But well known, certainly.' I name a couple of TV series authored by Pavel. The nurse hasn't heard of either of them.

'I'm afraid I don't watch much telly,' he says. 'You take sugar?'

I settle in the chair beside Pavel, gazing at the emptiness of his face. A blank sheet of paper, I think, after a lifetime of furious typing. If I bring my cheek very close to his mouth, I can feel the faintest warmth when he breathes, but his flesh is cold to the touch. I stroke his hand for a moment or two longer and then delve in my bag. I've brought the book, the Ernst Jünger diaries, but only now do I remember about the fennel. I should have gone to the farm shop in the town centre. *Tant pis.*

I start with an entry from early spring, 1942. Jünger has had a visit from an old friend, back from the Eastern Front. This man happens to be a Prussian aristocrat and has witnessed death on a scale unimaginable before the First World War. The trenches were bad enough, but out on the limitless horizons of the steppe, whole armies are grinding each other to pieces like some surreal bone mill,

and Jünger finds himself listening to his friend's longing for
something he calls 'the old death'. I've positioned my chair very close
to the bed. I'm leaning towards the pillow, my mouth very close to
Pavel's ear, the book open on my lap, and I don't hear the nurse
when he returns. He's staring down at me, the cup and saucer in
his hand.

'The old death?' he asks. 'What are you trying to do to the poor
man?'

This turns reading into a health and safety issue and I'm in the
process of trying to explain Pavel's admiration for these diaries
when an alarm sounds out in the ward. The nurse mumbles an
apology and leaves. Moments later, consulting my list of page
numbers, I try another entry.

Nothing happens. For the next hour or so, using Carrie's markings as a guide, I hopscotch through the middle years of the war,
hoping against hope that Pavel will follow me. All it needs, I tell
myself, is a line, or an image, or a sentiment that will reignite all
the loose fragments of memory that litter his subconscious. And
once that happens, the Pavel I've known and loved might surface
again.

I'm beginning to run out of marked passages when another
figure appears at the door. He's an older man, lean, balding. He's
abandoned his jacket and his sleeves are rolled up.

'Miles Kennaway.' He extends a hand. 'I'm the consultant here.
I gather you and Mr Stukeley were friends.'

Were? The choice of tense is slightly alarming, but to his credit
Mr Kennaway apologizes at once. Mr Stukeley is undoubtedly on
the upper reaches of the scale when it comes to nursing challenges,
but he thinks he has a fighting chance.

'Of what?'

'Of regaining consciousness. In the world of strokes, we talk
about a gross insult to the brain. At first, we thought he'd had a
TIA, which is a junior version, but it's turned out rather more serious
than that. An MRI scan will tell us more.'

I know a great deal about MRI scans but now isn't the time to
own up. This is about Pavel, not me.

'What makes you so sure he'll come round?'

'Sure isn't a word I'd use, but age is on his side. The rest of his
body is obviously compromised, and being blind doesn't help, but
his vascular system should be in working order. Assuming we can

tempt him back, we'll put him on blood thinners for the rest of his life and keep our fingers crossed. You'd be amazed how resilient the human body can be.'

In any other set of circumstances, this would be another cue for a more personal conversation, but once again I resist the temptation. The consultant has spotted the book. He knows about Ernst Jünger. He's even read *Storm of Steel*.

I explain my attempt to coax just a flicker of recognition from the face on the pillow.

'And?'

'Nothing.'

'Shame. No harm in trying, though, eh?' He's about to leave the room, when he pauses. 'I've seen you before, I know I have.'

He's seen one of my movies, I think. Or maybe he remembers my photo alongside some review or other. This happens more often than you might think, and it always puts a smile on my face. Never believe any thesps who pretend not to be in love with the limelight. They lie.

'*The Hour of Our Passing*. Am I right?'

'You are. It was a very long time ago. Which says a lot about your memory.'

He offers his hand again. This time his touch is warmer.

'I'd just met the woman who became my wife,' he says. 'It was our first date. How could I forget it?'

We look at each other for a moment and the silence is in danger of getting awkward when I remember Carrie's Walkman.

'Do you listen to classical music, by any chance?'

'All the time.'

'Would you mind?'

I dig out the little player and the ear buds and ask him for a clue about what I've been listening to. He fits the buds and presses the Play button. Seconds later, he starts to nod.

'Hector Berlioz,' he says. '"Harold in Italy". Wonderful stuff.'

Without going into details, I explain about Carrie. 'The Berlioz might have come from Pavel. He loves music like this.' I'm looking at the figure in the bed. 'Would you mind if I tried it on him?'

'Not at all.'

The consultant slips the buds into Pavel's ears, and then cues the music again. Because we're so close, we can just pick up the violins in the higher registers. For a long minute, nothing happens, then – unmistakably – the faintest smile appears on Pavel's face. Nothing else. No movement. Just the smile. Hector Berlioz has knocked on Pavel's door, I think, and Pavel is struggling down the hall to open it.

I glance up at the consultant. He, too, is smiling.

'Remarkable,' he says.

TWENTY-FOUR

The call from DS Williams finds me still in the Stroke Unit. It's early afternoon by now and I'm demolishing a tuna baguette at Pavel's bedside.

'Ms Andressen?' Williams sounds far from happy. 'We've been trying to find you.'

I explain about Pavel, about leaving my mobile at the penthouse, about the dash to the hospital, and now about the Stroke Unit. This clearly gives her pause for thought.

'That's unfortunate. Might our visit . . .?' She leaves the thought unvoiced and when I hasten to tell her that there are probably a thousand reasons for Pavel's poor brain to seize up, she sounds relieved.

'So how is he now?'

'Still unconscious, I'm afraid. He raised our hopes earlier but not for long.'

'What's the prognosis?'

'His consultant won't commit but I still get the feeling there's a chance he may come round.'

'And then what?'

'Nobody knows. He may be able to talk, and his hearing might be OK but nothing's certain.'

'I see.'

During the silence that follows I sense the presence of the elephant in the room. Will Pavel end up as a vegetable? Beyond reach? Nobody knows.

Finally, Williams is back on the line. Operation *Mandolin* is moving forward. The need for another meet has become pressing. A police car could pick me up at the hospital and take me back to be interviewed in Exmouth. On the other hand, the interview could take place at Heavitree police station in the city itself. My choice.

'Heavitree,' I say lightly. 'And then you can bring me back here.'

I wait for the police car in the road outside the hospital, waving at the uniformed driver as he signals to turn into the hospital site. The drive to the police station at Heavitree takes a couple of minutes. Williams is waiting for me in the custody centre and I wonder for a moment whether I'm to be processed once again. A photo to go with my earlier prints and DNA? Mercifully not.

The interview is to take place in a small, airless room that reminds me a little of the space that Pavel is currently occupying. Sitting behind the table is the DI who came to the penthouse in yesterday's downpour. He gets to his feet the moment I step in and says he's sorry to hear about Mr Stukeley. It seems Operation *Mandolin* was contemplating a second interview with him as well.

'That might not be possible,' I tell him.

'So I understand.'

The interview gets underway: the same notepad, the same recording machine, the same hint of weariness on the faces across the table. The investigation, says the DI, has been concentrating on the victim, Carrie. Specialists attached to the enquiry team have been analysing her phone records, her emails, her Facebook page, and the contents of the hard drive on her laptop.

'I want to take you back to last September,' the DI says, 'when you first interviewed her for the job looking after Mr Stukeley.'

I nod. Early autumn, I think, and my first real taste of Exmouth.

'That was a bit of a nightmare,' I say. 'We'd found the apartment and had some work done but finding the right person for Pavel wasn't easy. We'd put the word round where we could, talked to various care agencies, even advertised in a couple of retirement magazines. Pavel, of course, was the key. He didn't like any of them.'

'And Carrie?'

'He loved her, I'd like to say on first sight, but that would be unkind. Let's just say he thoroughly approved. And that, to be frank, came as a bit of a relief. Time was moving on. We all had lives to lead.'

'Loved her? What exactly do you mean?'

'I mean he took to her, trusted her. In a situation like Pavel's, it has to be an instinctive thing. He liked the sound of her voice. He liked how relaxed she was, how easy she was to have around, we all did. And she made him laugh, too.'

'She told jokes?'

'She was quick. She was witty. The pair of them shared the same sense of humour. Given the time they'd be spending together, that was going to be important. We needed a companion, a friend, as well as a carer. It was obvious from the moment they met that Carrie could be all those things. That made us lucky. To be frank, we were getting desperate.'

'She came with references?'

'Of course.'

'And you checked them?'

'We checked it.'

'There was only one?'

'Yes. It came from the owner of the nursing home where she'd been matron. The place had been forced to close, no fault of Carrie's. There's a problem now with local authority funding. There simply isn't enough.'

'You met the owner? You talked to him?'

'We corresponded. He'd gone back to Scotland.'

'And what did he say?'

'He confirmed everything he'd already written about her. How trustworthy she was. How conscientious. How good she'd been with the residents. How she'd managed to keep the place going way past its sell-by date.'

'That was the phrase he used?'

'Yes. We already knew we'd found the right person for Pavel and here was the proof that we were right. I remember H bought champagne on the strength of that letter. We were celebrating.'

'H?'

'My son's father.'

The DI writes himself a note. Then he looks up.

'Did you ever ask to see a birth certificate for Carrie? Or a driving licence? Or any other form of ID?'

'No, I don't think we did.' I'm frowning. I'm trying to remember. 'Why?'

'Because her name wasn't Carrie Tollman at all. It was Amy.'

'Really? And her surname?'

'Phelps.'

Amy Phelps? I'm finding this hard to believe.

'When did this happen?'

'She did it by deed poll. Her application was dated the thirteenth of July. She never told you?'

'Never. As far as we were concerned, she was Carrie Tollman. She had a bank account in that name. That's how we paid her. BACS. Straight into the account. Carrie Tollman. The first of every month.' I shake my head. I can't begin to understand any of this.

'So why would she have changed her name?'

'That's a question we'd like to ask you. And Mr Stukeley, of course.' The DI's pen is readied over his pad. 'Any ideas?'

'None.'

'You think Mr Stukeley might have known?'

They're both looking at me, both waiting. I hold their gaze.

'I've no idea,' I say finally. 'Maybe one day you might be able to ask him.'

Williams lifts an eyebrow, says nothing. I can almost taste their disappointment, their frustration. I'd like to help them – I'd be only too happy to solve this riddle – but the fact is that I can't. Pavel may well know. It would be completely in character for him to have become the keeper of Carrie's secrets. But even if he comes back from the brink, from this chilling half-death, there's every chance that he won't be able to speak, or to move, or to even hear.

The DI has produced a list of names. He wants to move the interview on.

'We've checked people Carrie was in touch with. One of them is obviously Jean-Paul. You knew about him?'

'Only recently.'

'They were talking and texting since Christmas. She never mentioned it?'

'I live in London,' I point out. 'I never saw much of her. We put her in place. I was talking to Pavel, of course, and I got the impression that it was working out very nicely between them. That's all I needed to know. I wasn't concerned about her private life.'

The DI nods, and then gives me a couple of other names, both of them female. Jodie? Cara? I shrug, shake my head. Never heard of them. Finally, another name, a man this time.

'Miedema? Rolf Miedema?'

I hesitate. The way I'm staring at him must give the game away.

He repeats the name a third time, then adds – almost as an after-thought – a nickname. Deko.

'You know him, Ms Andressen?'

'I do, yes.'

'Might I ask how?'

'I met him one night. It was very recently. We were in a pub.'

'And?'

'We've become friends . . .' I shrug. 'Sort of.'

Another note on the DI's pad. Williams is watching me carefully.

'He came to the police station,' she says. 'The day you found the body.'

'Carrie. She has a name. I found Carrie.'

'Yes. I apologize.' She pauses, then sits back from the table. 'Did he ever mention her?'

'You mean Carrie?'

'Yes.'

'No, never. Was he supposed to? Did he know her well? What are we talking about here? You're telling me they were in touch all the time? Is that it?'

'Not at all. Just a handful of calls.'

'When?'

Williams and the DI exchange glances. Neither of them will tell me. Then, far later than I should have done, I get the link.

'Deko bought that same nursing home,' I tell them. 'The one where Carrie was the matron. Maybe it was a business thing. I've no idea.'

Business thing. I realize I'm searching for some kind of excuse, rationale, and I hate being on the defensive like this. Deko has done nothing, and neither have I.

'That afternoon at the police station.' Williams hasn't finished. 'I got the impression you were glad to have him there. Would I be right?'

'Of course. Pretend you're me. I've just found someone I was close to ripped to pieces. I think the word might be shock. Deko was there for me. He gave me what I needed. He took care of things. If it's any of your business, I was grateful.'

'And now?'

'He's still taking care of things. And yes . . .' I offer them both an icy smile. 'I'm still grateful.'

TWENTY-FIVE

The interview lasts for another hour or so. Between them, Williams and the DI trawl endlessly up and down the last few months of Carrie's life, pressing for every detail I can remember from the few conversations we had on the phone, and from what more I might have gleaned from Pavel. On one level, their persistence is impressive. The closed book that turns out to be Carrie is obviously where Operation *Mandolin* begins and ends, but the longer I spend in this cell of a room, the more I realize that I never knew Carrie at all.

As promised, Williams arranges for me to be taken back to the hospital. Sitting in the same marked car, glad to be out of the custody centre, I'm only too aware that the police and I are beginning to be an item. Only last year, thanks to my wayward son, I spent hours and hours at the hands of another pair of detectives, that time in Bridport, up the coast. On that occasion, I was under arrest in connection with the death of a young junkie, and the experience was deeply unsettling.

I had the services of a solicitor I both liked and admired, and thanks to his candour, I knew that the Crown Court and a lengthy prison sentence might await me if all went wrong. Looking back, it was beyond surreal, but in a way this experience is equally troubling. Both Williams and the DI have made it clear that I am a witness, not a suspect, but as we creep ever deeper into the events of the last few months, I'm becoming more and more aware that nothing is quite what it seemed. How come Carrie hid her pregnancy for so long? And why on earth did she change her name?

Pavel, God help us, is probably the key to all this. In his writerly way, he's always been mean with information, rationing it out spoonful by spoonful, hint by hint, making any story a rich source of guesswork. This, of course, is what writers do and I get it completely. Indeed, I owe my own career, my own success, to the imagination and penmanship of a small army of Pavels. But if scripts are one thing, real life is quite another.

Back in the Stroke Unit, I once again close the door and pull up a chair. Absolutely nothing has changed since I left this room – the same wide-open eyes staring up at the ceiling, the same faint whisper of breath from the half-opened lips – but this time I'm determined to be firm with him. I'm his mother, his keeper, his conscience. I've had more than enough of his little games.

'This has to stop,' I tell him. 'You have to help me here. It matters, Pavel. That lovely girl is dead, and I think you know why. Just a clue or two? Is that too much to ask?'

Nothing.

Is he faking? Is this so-called stroke just another piece of theatre? Neatly conceived, artfully delivered, wholly made up? Is he lurking in that head of his? Aware of me at his bedside, desperate for some tiny scrap of information, totally under his control? Worse still, was his blindness another fiction? Another piece of fakery? Another plot twist? Has he been watching us all this past year and a half, in perfect focus, with 20/20 vision, making his little mental notes, taking the measure of us while all the time we thought he lived in darkness?

Mad, I think. Not him, but me. This, in a phrase that might well have come from Pavel himself in happier times, is not going well.

I'm back in the apartment by early evening. To be frank, I'm sick of being at the mercy of events. Time, I think, to regain a little control.

I find the phone number Carrie scribbled in the margins of the Jünger diaries and settle on the sofa with my mobile. Felip is out for the night, staying with a friend in Exeter, and I have the apartment to myself. When I ring the number, I get a recorded message. It's a woman's voice. She sounds rough, worn out, exhausted. She's busy at the moment but she'll phone back when she can. I play the message again. I'm good with accents and I recognize this one. West Country, I think. Maybe Bristol.

I wonder about pouring myself a glass of wine. The irony, of course, is that once again I'm in the hands of someone else. She'll phone when she wants to. Her call, not mine.

In the end I don't have to make a decision about the wine because my phone rings barely a minute later. It's the same voice, the same number. Sensibly, she wants to know who I am.

'My name is Andressen,' I tell her.

'What do you want?'

I should have been anticipating this question, but for whatever reason, I haven't. The way I'm feeling just now, putting a voice to a scribbled phone number is a major triumph.

As far as Carrie is concerned, I don't know where to start. Thankfully, she spares me the effort.

'Is this about Jason? Because if it is you can fuck off. Just get out of my face, right?'

'Who's Jason?'

'My son. Don't think you're the first. People are sick out there. He's all over the papers, the telly, everywhere. It's none of your business. It's none of anyone's fucking business. Do you understand what I'm saying? *Do* you?'

She's very angry and something is starting to occur to me.

'Your son's in the papers?'

'Of course he is. Horrible picture. Just look at him. Would he ever have done something like that? *Would* he?'

That emphasis again. Incredulity. Disbelief. Rage.

'How old is your son?' I'm trying very hard not to sound like a police officer.

'Seventeen. What's that to you?'

'He lives with you?'

'He's away. He's been away for ever. What is this? Who are you? A kick, is it? You're getting a kick from all this?'

At last I explain exactly who I am, who Carrie was, where we live, what happened. This takes quite a long time. She doesn't interrupt once.

'Hello? Are you still there?'

Silence. I curse under my breath. I should have broken this account up, exactly the way Pavel would have written it. I should have turned a monologue into a conversation. I've lost her. She's gone.

Wrong.

'That name of yours again?'

'Andressen. Call me Enora.'

'Ignora?'

'Enora.' Me laughing seems to break the ice. 'And yours?' I ask.

'My what?'

'Name?'

'Karen. Karen-Ann.'

'Pretty.'

'Pretty shit, is what I think. What kind of name is Karen-Ann?'

I tell her again that it's a lovely name. By now it's dawned on me that this number must have come from Jason. Or Foster Montague. Or Moonie. Or whatever the courts finally decide to call him. He probably gave the number to Carrie. Which means that her account of what happened the first time might be – a generous word – incomplete.

'Did Carrie call you recently? Do you mind me asking?'

'I don't know no Carrie. Never. This is the woman who died?'

'Yes.'

'The woman Jason's supposed to have done in?'

'Yes.'

'Never. Why would she call me? Why would she bother?'

'Because your son might have wanted her to. Don't ask me why.'

'No. Never happened. I don't know no Carrie. I told you.'

'And Jason himself? Have you heard from him?'

'You mean my Jason? That boy of mine?'

'Yes.'

'No, love. He's another fucking stranger in my life.' I can hear cigarettes in her bark of mirthless laughter.

At this point, I play my Malo card. It's a shameless thing to do but I very badly want to meet this woman.

'I've got a son,' I tell her. 'And I know all about strangers. You bring them up. You think you've got the measure of them. You spoil them rotten. You think they might even have time for you. And then one day they leave, just like that, pack a bag, steal your money, and go.'

'That happened to you?'

'It did. His name's Malo. And he went to live with his dad who happened to be Swedish. I didn't see him for what felt like forever. It's better now but, believe me, I know how it feels.'

There's a longish silence and I try and picture this woman at the other end of the line. Is she sitting down? Might she be smoking? Is she alone?

'Won't ever be better with Jason,' she says at last. 'That boy's a head case, poor fucking lamb.'

Poor fucking lamb. There's a rough poignancy in this phrase that makes me physically shiver. Could he really have stepped into that bedroom? Done something so terrible?

'We have to meet,' I say. 'I'm sorry, but we do. You'll say no and I don't blame you but believe me it'll be for the best.'

'*Meet?*'

'Yes.'

'Why?'

'To talk. To talk like this. Compare notes. If all else fails, we could get drunk.'

That laugh again, warmer this time. Then another long silence.

'I live in Weston,' she says. 'You know Weston-super-Mare?'

'No. But I'll find it.'

'A little place over a betting shop.' She gives me an address. 'When? When's all this supposed to happen?'

'You mean us meeting?'

'Yeah.'

'Tomorrow,' I say. 'I'll be with you by ten.'

'*Tomorrow?*' This time the laughter is unfeigned. 'Fuck me.'

TWENTY-SIX

Next morning, I'm on the M5 by half past seven. It's Easter Monday but the traffic is surprisingly light. In my head I've anticipated a couple of hours to get to Weston, but I'm parked up on the seafront by nine o'clock. A big wheel throws a long shadow over the promenade and the pier, a glorious confection in rusting Victorian iron, seems to stretch for ever. In a couple of hours, I'm guessing that this beach will be packed but for now all I can see are clouds of gulls and three solitary figures, all of them walking dogs.

One of the dogs is delinquent. It bounds away over the wet sand, chasing anything that moves, ignoring its owner's attempts to bring it to heel. The owner happens to be a man. He's oldish, a bit stooped, unsteady on his feet, and watching him shake his head, plunge his hands in the pockets of his beige anorak and turn away, I think I know exactly how he feels. Life is ungovernable, beyond control. In the end, it probably wears you down, but just now – thanks to making last night's phone call – I have an opportunity to steal a brief advantage. *Carpe diem*, I tell myself. *Seize the moment.*

The betting shop is a street or two inland from the seafront. The premises next door, once a hardware store, are boarded up. On the other side is a charity shop for something called the Mare & Foal Sanctuary. The pub across the road, offering a breakfast for £3.40, is doing brisk business. A drift of takeout boxes from the Turkish eatery down the road fills the gutter.

The betting shop has yet to open. A door beside the bannered window – *Put a Smile on Your Face!* – is marked 17a. This is Karen's address. The plastic doorbell has been untidily taped to the brickwork. I give it a press and step back.

I can't hear footsteps descending the stairs inside. I'm about to ring again, when suddenly the door opens. Last night's voice on the phone has led me to expect someone bigger, broader, and possibly a little younger. Instead, I'm looking at a thin woman marooned in her fifties. She's wearing a nylon housecoat and fluffy slippers. I can see patches of white scalp through her greying hair and she sports a small tattoo on the side of her neck, the way an item might be marked down in a sale. *Love*, it says. Just that.

'You the lady on the phone?' I nod, and extend a hand, which she ignores. 'Upstairs,' she says. 'First on the right.'

I wait for her to double-lock the front door, then climb the stairs. The place smells of cheap air freshener. I should have brought flowers, I think. Anything to brighten this place up.

The first door on the right opens into a room at the front of the property. It's not a small space but it's wildly over-furnished and it takes me a moment or two to disentangle the various elements: a two-seat sofa, faux G Plan, badly stained, an armchair with sagging upholstery, evidently home for Karen's cat, a two-leaf table, piled high with saucepans, mugs, plates, an electric kettle, plus a cleared space for the kind of portable TV you never see any more. A chunky kitchen dresser, built on a grander scale, occupies half an entire wall, and at the back of the room, approached by a path through years of accumulated debris, is a single bed.

'Cosy,' I say.

'Yeah? You like it? I go halves on the bathroom with the old guy next door. He never washes so it's mine, really.'

'And cooking?' I'm looking at the saucepans.

'There's a place out the back next to the bathroom. The landlord calls it a kitchenette, which has to be a joke. Cheap, though. No one in this town would complain at the rent.'

I nod. I can't help remembering Deko ripping the guts out of the nursing home. Twenty-two versions of a room like this, I think. Barely a fingerhold on what we used to call life.

I'm standing at the window. I can feel a draught where the sash doesn't fit properly, and there are crusts of white bread on the sill.

'You feed the birds?'

'Try to. The bloody gulls take most of it. None of the little ones stand a chance.'

I nod. I'm watching an elderly couple emerge from the pub across the road. Their arms are linked together. They look poor but they've made an effort with the way they've turned themselves out, and I'm still wondering how long they've been saving up for this bank holiday breakfast when Karen offers me a cup of coffee. I'm about to say no but it's too late. She's already pouring hot water on to the granules of Kenco.

'Mind if I sit here?' I'm looking at the cat.

'Help yourself.' She shoos it away. I take a sip of the coffee, and then put it carefully on the carpet by the chair leg.

'You've been here long?'

'Seven years. Best part of. It grows on you after a while and you know why? I'm the only person on earth who knows where everything is. Someone like you, you maybe wouldn't think that matters. But it does. Because it's mine.'

I nod. The room is warm and airless, and Karen has taken off her housecoat. I've deliberately dressed down for this occasion but I can't compete with charity shop jeans, way too big, and a scarlet football top someone probably left on a park bench. Like mother, like son, I think.

I ask about Jason. When did she last see him?

'Christmas.' She doesn't seem to mind the directness of my question. 'He's still got friends here, places he can doss down. He paid a visit on Christmas Day, brought me a bar of chocolate.'

'How was he?'

'Pissed. Those mates of his thieve from Bargain Basement. You ever want cheap vodka, I'll give you their address.'

'Was it good to see him?'

'It's always good to see him. His dad used to say that everyone needed something to do in life. What I do is forgive. He's always led me a dance, Jason, but in the end I'm the only mum he's got.

That's why I said yes to you coming. That boy of yours? Whatever his name is?'

'Malo?'

'Yeah, him. Kids are a handful, especially these days. Being a mum to him, being kind to him, is all I can afford and of course he knows that, the little tyke.'

I'm looking at a photo taped to the top edge of the TV screen. The colours have faded badly but I think I recognize the pier behind the bloated, sun-reddened face. The man looks even older than Karen, but the warmth of the smile explains everything. No wonder she prefers it to watching TV.

'That's my Bradley.' She's noticed my interest. 'In happier days.'

'Jason's dad?' The weak chin, I think. And the natural curls in the receding hair.

'Yeah. We was never married, never got round to it, but he was a good man. Know what I mean? Watches out for you? Does his best for you? That was Brad. I loved that man.' Her fingers, heavily tobacco-stained, find the tattoo beneath her ear.

I want to know more. Again, she seems to be almost expecting this torrent of questions. Maybe it's come as a relief, a total stranger stepping briefly into your life and appearing to take an interest. I doubt she gets many visitors.

'He was in the army, Brad, in the Paras. That's where I first met him. I was on a night out in Bristol and he was there with his mates. It was the end of the Nineties. We was all young, stupid. He was a good-looking bloke then, especially for his age. He had a mouth on him, but that never mattered, not then, and not afterwards.'

'So how old was he? When you met?'

'Thirty-five. Never looked it. Married, of course. Kids.'

'And?'

'We got it on. He used to come down here, to Weston. I had a proper flat then, ground floor in a lovely old house. He'd stay over, push off in the morning.'

'He was still in the army?'

'No. He told me he was working in security and I believed him. Turned out it wasn't true. He wasn't working in anything and that wife of his, cow that she was, threw him out in the end.'

'Because of you?'

'Dunno. Don't care. Because of any fucking thing. You love someone, you don't ask too many questions. Brad says he wants to live with me down here in that little flat of mine? No problem. Jason loved him too. Right from the start.'

'Jason was his son?' I'm getting lost.

'Yeah, big time. Bingo, that first night. Treble twenty. Brad was mad for the darts.'

'You're telling me you fell pregnant? The night you met?'

'Yeah. Four in the morning in the back of a minicab. Brad paid the driver extra to take a walk so we could shag. We were in a right old state. Happiest night of my life.'

She's smiling at the memory, staring at the photo. I'm less pushy now, knowing that I've breached the dam, knowing that the rest of the story will trickle out, and it does. How she found out that Brad had never managed to hold down a job after leaving the army. How he'd been getting by on the whack of money they gave him after a medical discharge. And how that money, in the end, had all gone.

'Medical discharge?'

'Hurt bad. Up here.' She taps her head. 'Brad was at Goose Green. And he was still fighting the fucking Argies twenty years later.'

'But you still supported him?'

'Of course I did. That was one of the reasons *why* I supported him. He was my man, my Brad. He always told me them Paras was the making of him but he was wrong, poor lamb. The army was the breaking of him. He'd seen stuff no one should ever see. And believe me, that never goes away.' Another tap on the head.

At the time, she said, she was working for a cable TV company, selling subscriptions house to house. She had all the right skills. She made a point of working the estates and on the doorstep, she says, people trusted her. She was ordinary, no airs, no graces. And she made them laugh.

'Decent commission in them days. Some weeks, especially in the summer, I'd be taking home four, five hundred quid. It's funny, hot weather. People lighten up. They'll take a risk or two, see no point not to. Sign on the bottom line and you've probably got them for life, but they never seemed bothered.'

'And Jason?'

'He was at school. He was always slow, never the full shilling, but he was a lovely, lovely boy. He worshipped Brad, as he should, and the truth is we had a good life, all of us, yeah . . .' She nods, turning away. 'Until we didn't.'

'So, what happened?'

She looks down at her hands, shaking her head, and for a moment I think I've lost her, but then she's back with me. Set out on a story like this, I think, and there's no way you're not going to finish it.

'I used to give Brad a load of money for the housekeeping every week, the food, all the bills, council tax, everything. He was mum really, or maybe mum and dad together, looking after Jason, doing the laundry, tidying up, keeping things together, making life sweet for us. That was another reason I loved the man. He was so fucking *good* at everything. Stuff round the flat, anything going wrong, he'd just sort it. The army probably taught him that . . .' She frowns, picking at the yellowing remains of what looks like a burn on her wrist. Then her head comes up again. 'It was just before Christmas. We started getting demands, shitty letters about unpaid bills, I couldn't understand it. Then suddenly Brad isn't going to Sainsbury's any more and we're all sitting round the table eating this crap old bird he's got from somewhere and that's when I had it out with him.'

'On Christmas Day?'

'Yeah. I'd found more of the bills. They went way back. He'd been hiding them. So, there we are, and Jason wants us to pull the crackers and tell the jokes and put on the funny hats, but I wasn't having it. I wanted the truth. I was still making good money, still giving him a fortune every week, but all we had to show for it were all these bloody debts.'

'Was he drinking it?'

'A bit of it. But that was OK. I never met a squaddie who didn't like a drink. No, that wasn't it.'

'So, where did it go?'

She holds my gaze for a long moment and then nods at the floor. At first, I can make no sense of the gesture. Then I remember the premises downstairs, and the banner in the window. *Put a Smile on Your Face!* As if.

'He was betting?'

'Every day. At first, he said it was the horses. Then it was anything, anything that might change his luck, bring him that big win that would magic everything. Problem is it never really happened, and even when he won, he'd never put it in his pocket, he'd just put another bet on, and then another, and another. Then, like he needed it, they brought in these fixed-odds betting machines. You want to lose four hundred quid in half an hour? My entire week's commission? No problem. Easy. Piece of piss.'

'And all this at Christmas? Around the table?'

'Yeah. I'd sent Jason to his bedroom to play with his toys. I was really, really angry. Not just about the money. That was bad enough, but Brad had lied to us, and not just to me but to Jason, too. No money for school trips. No money for anything, not even a pair of shoes. Brad was pathetic, just admitted it all. That night I threatened to throw him out, and you know something? I meant it. I'd have done it. And he knew that.'

Next morning, she says, she went off to work as usual. You'd never miss a Boxing Day. People were in a good mood. They'd sign up to anything.

'And Bradley?'

'He was quiet. There was a bit of an atmosphere before I left but at least I'd got it off my chest. Next thing I know it's afternoon and I'm coming out of a place on one of the Nailsea estates and a policewoman is walking towards me. She asks my name and takes me to one side and it's one of those moments when you know something terrible has happened. At first, I thought it was Jason, but I was wrong.'

'Bradley?'

'Yeah. They were both at home. Jason had been watching TV and when he went to find his dad he wasn't there. He looked in all the rooms, in the bit of garden we had round the back, but he couldn't find him.'

'So, where was he?'

'We had a shared entrance in that house, like a kind of hall. All the meters and everything were in the cupboard under the stairs. It was a big cupboard, tall, lots of space, nothing in it except the meters. The door was open, and Jason took a look.'

I'm staring at her. I've lived in a world of stories all my life and I think I know what's coming next.

'Bradley?' I murmur.

'Yes.' She nods. 'He'd hung himself. I saw the shots they took, the police shots. His tongue was out, and his head was at a funny angle. He'd used the cord from my dressing gown. And Jason was the one who found him.'

'Christ.' I shake my head. 'So how old was Jason?'

'Nine.' Karen is picking at her wrist again. 'Just.'

TWENTY-SEVEN

I don't leave Weston until early afternoon. After everything Karen has told me, I know I owe her a story of my own and I'm determined to share it with her. I tell her about the worst times with Malo, nights when he'd hide away in our apartment when fights with Berndt got out of hand, whole weeks when he'd disappear into the badlands of west London without a trace, just fifteen years old, turning his back on everything – school, home, us, the lot. And then I describe the morning when he walked out of the apartment a final time, a year older, and used his father's credit card to buy himself a ticket to Stockholm. There, I tell Karen, he began a new life with his dad, and his dad's latest bimbo. That was the morning my life hit the buffers. Failed mother. Hopeless wife. Totally useless.

'And then?'

'And then I got cancer.' I touch my own head. 'Up here. Bits of it are still there, as a matter of fact, though they say it might not kill me. A good friend once told me that life is full of the smaller mercies, and he's right. Sometimes it's enough just to be here, to have survived.'

The friend, of course, was Pavel, but I've said far too much already. When Karen isn't looking, I check my purse. I've got seventy pounds in notes and I tuck them under a mug on the table because I know she'll refuse the money if I offer it. This woman has pride, as well as a great deal of resilience, and I sense we may have become friends. I certainly hope so. Before I leave, I ask about Jason's surname.

'Macreadie,' she says. 'After his dad.'

'And is that yours, too?'

'No. Like I said, we was never married.'

I hold her gaze for a moment, and then I give her a hug. Under the football shirt, she's skin and bone.

'Come back if you want to,' she says. 'I'm sorry about the coffee.'

*   *   *

On the way back to Exmouth, I take a detour off the motorway. I need, as my son would say, to decompress, to take stock, to re-run the last four hours and understand what it's taught me. I also need to check on Pavel.

I make the call from the garden of a pub in some nameless village in the depths of Somerset. When I get through to a nurse in the Stroke Unit, the news is far better than I'd expected. Pavel, it seems, is showing signs of life. My heart leaps.

'He's conscious. Just. And we think he might be hungry.'

'Think? What did he tell you?'

'Nothing. He can't speak. Not yet, anyway.'

I nod. Not such great news.

'Can he hear?'

'We don't know.'

'You think he might?'

'It's possible.'

'Then tell him Enora loves him. And give him a big kiss. You'll do that? You promise?'

The nurse is male, the guy I met yesterday. He says I'm the talk of the unit. He's been on to Amazon already. A DVD of *The Hour of Our Passing* is on its way.

'Apparently there's a sequence towards the end worth watching,' he says. 'According to Mr Kennaway.'

Kennaway is the consultant I met yesterday.

'I was much younger then.' I'm laughing. 'Just remember that.'

I fetch a cappuccino from the pub and return to the garden. I have a loose-leaf pad in my bag, and I prop it on my knee, enjoying the thin bank holiday sunshine. Karen has a mobile but nothing else – no laptop, no PC, no email address – and if I want to keep in touch with her, then it has to be by post. The notion of words on paper, as it happens, is perfect. Lots of crossings-out, lots of time to think. I can type it up later and pop it in the post. Think 17a. Above the betting shop.

Jason. He was still at primary school when he found his dad under the stairs and from that day on, according to Karen, he was a different boy. She said she did her best, and I believe her. She sat him down and tried to explain how difficult life must have been for his dad, what happened at Goose Green, what that kind of stuff does to you, to the insides of you, how brave he was to keep it all a secret, locked away, never discussed. When Jason asked about doctors, and getting better, Karen said it was hard, because soldiers were supposed to be the tough guys, but talking to this son of hers, hours and hours in his bedroom beside photographs of his precious dad, she knew that nothing was getting through.

'He became someone else,' she told me. 'He became someone I didn't know any more.'

I scribble the phrase down. *Someone you don't know any more.* Maybe the same applies to Carrie, I think. To Pavel. And to anyone else whom life trips up and then abandons. First some kind of trauma, then the splintered remains of the person you thought you were. Has it happened to me? Did Berndt, and then my tussle with the Grim Reaper, turn me into someone else? Take a hard look in the mirror, I think. And see what you find.

I shake my head. This is about Karen, and about Jason, not me. The aftermath of Bradley's death hit Karen hard. When a reporter knocked at her door, she sent him packing. When the Coroner's officer requested an interview, she had a panic attack. At the inquest, an hour and a half she'll never forget, she wept. Real women, she said, never cry in public. But she did. Buckets and buckets of tears. Horrible.

Her life fell apart. Selling cable TV contracts was out of the question: she could barely sign her own name. The debts kept mounting, new demands through the post every day, and after a visit to the Citizen's Advice Bureau she decided to file for bankruptcy. Thanks to Bradley, she didn't have a penny to her name. The car had gone. Her savings account was empty. Her landlord, previously sympathetic, had lost patience. By Easter, she and Jason were living in a boarding house in the back streets of the town that was a safety net for Social Services. Two beds in a cupboard of a room, junkies for near-neighbours, cereal for breakfast, and whatever she could afford on her weekly benefits for the microwave at night.

At this point, she got a handwritten note, forwarded from the flat she'd shared with Bradley. She had trouble reading it, but it turned out to come from the manager of the betting shop where Bradley had spent most of her earnings. He had two rooms upstairs and she and her son could have one of them. It wasn't much but it would be hers for as long as she wanted it. More to the point, she wouldn't have to pay a penny.

'No one's a saint in this life,' she told me. 'But that man came close. He felt guilty, of course. He should have stopped Brad, he should have reported him, barred him, whatever, but he didn't. In a way I don't blame him. Everyone has to make a living. But the thing that got to me was the offer of that room. Me and Jason did the sums. With child benefit, and housing benefit, and whatever work I could find, we could start all over. Jason was about to go to big school. Losing Brad like that still hurt but I thought we might get over it.'

Wrong. Jason, rather earlier than Malo, went off the rails. He began to obsess about the Falklands War. He read everything he could lay his hands on about the battle for Goose Green. When Karen had saved enough for a second-hand laptop, he watched videos, played war games, locked himself away in a little bubble of grief, and violence, and loss. He had no friends. He was at first clueless about girls and then said he hated them. What mattered was his dad.

Karen was finding this hard to take. The precious room above the betting shop became, she said, a kind of prison cell. Every time she tried to talk to her son, or even look at him, she thought of his father. Jason, she said, was out of reach, banged up with himself, lost. Like his dad, he might as well have been dead.

Jason left on his fourteenth birthday. At first Karen thought he might still be in town. She walked the streets, checked on his favourite haunts, talked to kids his own age who might know where he'd gone. None of the kids knew, and neither did any of them much care. One of them said Jason was a weirdo, a numpty, and Karen told him to wash his mouth out.

At his school, the staff were more helpful. One of the teachers, a youngish man who taught science, said he wasn't surprised. He'd made the time to have a couple of conversations with Jason. The boy had been flagged for special attention after Karen had told the head of school about Bradley's death, and the science teacher, who'd had experience in this field, recognized that Jason had turned his back on the world. He doesn't concentrate, doesn't see the point, he'd told Karen. He might as well not be here.

Karen went to the police. They had a procedure for missing persons, especially anyone young and vulnerable. The word 'vulnerable', she said, described her son to a T. The police sat her down and took details. She'd brought a couple of recent photos, just in case, and they said they'd make copies and send the originals back. They never did but it was a comfort to know there were thousands of cops out there, keeping an eye open. But nothing happened. No sightings. No drunken midnight phone calls. Not even a postcard. Jason had decamped to outer space. One day, if he really needed her, she told herself he would make his way home. He knew the address. He had a key. He knew he'd always be welcome. In the meantime, she'd do her best with a twenty-year-old telly and her precious cat.

In the weeks following Jason's disappearance, she'd lay awake at nights, desperate to hear the turn of the key in the door, and his footsteps on the stairs, but as time went by even this memento of his passing disappeared. She slept like a baby, and when she thought about Jason at all, she persuaded herself he was happy.

What I couldn't tease from Karen's account were the basics. Was Jason OK with the small print of being out there? Could he read a timetable? Feed and clothe himself? Avoid the attentions of unwanted strangers? Handle himself in difficult situations? To all these questions, Karen said yes. Jason, she said, was a survivor. Naïve? Yes. Full of fantasy shit? Often. Kind? Sometimes. Gullible? Alas, yes. 'He's easily impressed,' she told me, 'especially by certain kinds of men. That's why he worshipped Brad.' Even when Karen presented him with the evidence – all those fucking bills – he refused to believe that his precious dad might be responsible.

Then, only days ago, she'd answered the door to find the manager from the betting shop standing there. This was the man who'd sorted out the room for her. He had a copy of the *Daily Mail* and he showed her a photo on one of the inside pages.

'That's Jason,' he'd said. 'I swear it is.'

She'd taken a look and agreed. 'My son. Definitely.'

She'd gone to the police that morning. It turned out they didn't even have his right name. She didn't know Exmouth, or a woman called Carrie Tollman, and when the policewoman described what had happened, she'd just shaken her head. 'Not my boy,' she'd told them. 'Never Jason. He'd never do a thing like that. He'd never harm a fly. There has to be some mistake. Try looking elsewhere.'

The police had given her a special number. Should Jason get in touch, she was to try and find out where he was calling from, and then phone them at once. She'd told them she couldn't imagine Jason making the effort to lift the phone, but she'd do her best. At this point in our conversation, she'd reached out and tugged me closer.

'Imagine him phoning,' she'd said. 'Do you really think I'd grass him up?'

I thought not. No mother would.

'That's right. No mum would. I'd make him tell me where he is, then I'd go and meet him. No police, nothing. Just him and me. Like the old days.'

Now, sitting in the sunshine in the pub garden, I flick through the notes I've made. When I get back to the apartment, I'll type up a long letter to Karen, promising every kind of support I can. That way, at the very least, she might not feel entirely alone. Then, my coffee drained, I add a final thought to my notes. Karen already has my mobile number. If her son does, by any chance, get in touch, might she let me know?

TWENTY-EIGHT

When I get to Exeter, I detour to the hospital. Pavel is asleep when I make it up to the Stroke Unit but I know at once that he's on the mend. 'Mend', of course, is wildly optimistic but the fact that I can see him breathing, the sheet visibly rising and falling over his chest, and that a faint pink tinge has reappeared in his face, is the reassurance I've been praying for. He's deeply asleep, and he resists all my attempts to rouse him, but he's very definitely back with us.

The nurse I talked to earlier has gone off shift, but he's left me a note with the unit's secretary.

Delivered your message verbatim, the note reads. *Might have raised a smile.*

Sweet. I fold the note, a despatch from the front line in this strange war, and I'm on the point of leaving when I have another thought. Something is still troubling me and I suspect only Pavel has the answer. So maybe now is the time to leave him a message of my own.

I return to his bedside and bend to his ear. 'Carrie had a phone number for Moonie's mother,' I whisper. 'How did that ever happen?'

*   *   *

I'm back in the apartment by half past six. Felip has returned from his friend's place and is very happy for me to use his printer. He also wants to know where he stands. This is Felip's way of asking whether he's still employed, still has a room of his own in the apartment, and I tell him yes. I'm making this up, doubtless for my benefit as well as Felip's, but I tell him that Pavel is beginning to surface, that all his vital signs are good, and that the staff can't wait to get rid of him. Felip, who knows a thing or two about the raw physical business of looking after Pavel, is delighted.

I type my letter to Karen and print it out. Felip has noticed a movie showing in the local cinema and is nice enough to ask whether I'd like to come with him. The movie is American. A mother loses her son to the world of drugs and violence in a mid-western city and sets out to avenge his death. I decline.

'It's got great reviews,' Felip insists. 'It's supposed to be really good.'

I say I'm grateful for the offer but the answer's still no. A girl, I tell him, can bear just so much excitement in her life.

With Pavel gone, I'm settling in for a catch-up evening on iPlayer when the phone begins to ring.

'Long time . . .' It's Deko.

'A day or so,' I say at once. 'Who's counting?'

'Me, if that's a straight question. I've been having a think about our little trip. Drink?'

Our little trip? To my shame, I've forgotten about Douarnenez, and even the memory of our soiree aboard *Amen* has begun to fade.

'A drink would be perfect,' I tell him.

'A pub or *chez moi*? Your call.'

'*Chez toi*.' I reach for the remote and turn the TV off. 'Give me an hour.'

I go to Deko's front door this time. It's huge and very old and has just been repainted a glossy shade of black. He answers my knock and we hold each other for a moment before I step inside. Already, I can smell the oriental sweetness of coconut, ginger, garlic, and – I fancy – a million other delights.

'I thought you might be hungry.' He shepherds me inside. 'Body and soul? Keeping them together? Isn't that the phrase?'

'My body, your soul.' It's the best I can manage. Once again, this man has swept me off my feet. His hair is wet, I assume from a recent shower, and he smells divine.

'I'd have brought wine,' I say, following him towards the stairs, 'if only I'd known.'

'We've got beer. Tiger or Chang. Jenever for starters. We start in Amsterdam and head east. How are you?'

I start to tell him the good news about Pavel, but his phone begins to ring and he grunts an apology as he takes the call. By the time he's finished the conversation, we're at the top of the house. The weather, like Pavel, is definitely on the mend. White battlements of fluffy cloud hang over the hills beyond the river but otherwise there's every prospect of a perfect sunset.

'He's going to make it – Pavel.' I'm still lingering at the window. 'I saw him a couple of hours ago.'

Deko is standing behind me. His sheer physical presence is overwhelming. I want him to touch me again. Badly. And I suspect he knows this.

'So, shall we celebrate?'

'Here?'

'Wherever.'

I turn around and nod at the long crescent of sofa. Moments later, our clothes are an untidy heap on the floor. Aroused already, he leads me to the sofa. I tell him to lie down, close his eyes. Then I ask him what in the world would please him most.

'You know. I know you know. Ask any man.'

He's right. Berndt was exactly the same. I kneel beside the sofa, kiss him softly on his ear, take the tiny diamond stud in my mouth, explore the hardness of the gem with my tongue.

'You said Antwerp.'

'I did. Never speak with your mouth full.'

'That's later.' I pause a moment, struck by another thought. 'You were cooking.'

'I was.'

'Nothing on the stove?'

'It's done. Take your time.'

'I will. So, tell me about the diamond district. Tell me about those days. You're an infant. You've run away to sea. What's the most romantic cargo you delivered? Back then?'

'Cat litter. To Le Havre. The Scandinavians pulp everything. Never be a tree in Finland or you'll end up getting shat on.'

'You know about French cats?' I'm laughing. 'They're ruthless, totally unforgiving, and you're talking to someone who knows.'

'Even the females?'

'Especially the females. You told me you fell in love, Mr Deko, with a woman from Shelly Beach. Pavel told me about Shelly Beach. He went there as a kid. He told me it reminded me of the *barrios* in São Paulo.'

'He's been to Brazil? Seen all that stuff?'

'Probably not, but it doesn't matter. Was it the truth? Something he'd made up? Who's asking? Who cares?' My busy tongue has found one of Deko's nipples now. 'Was she good in bed? This woman from the *barrio*?'

'She was very good.'

'As good as me?'

'Never.'

'Right answer, Mr Deko. You want the main course now? Just say no.'

'No.'

My knees are beginning to hurt. I get up and climb on to the sofa. Deko opens his knees, making a space for me between his legs.

'*En pleine forme.*' I'm gazing down at him. 'How do you manage to stay so trim?'

'I used to climb a lot,' he says. 'I was good at it but there was always something missing.'

'So what do you do now?'

'I box.'

'Box? You mean you fight? You're serious?'

'I am,' he says. 'You want the full conversation?'

'Yes, please.' I've got to his rib cage now and when I lay my ear flat on his chest, I can hear the beating of his heart – thump, thump, low, steady, regular, irrepressible.

'Boxing's the best because it's full of incentive,' he says. 'Unless you want to get seriously hurt, you have to stay fit. And to stay fit, you have to exercise. Your friend might call that a virtuous circle, and he'd be right.'

'My friend?'

'Pavel.'

'Ah . . . so where do you exercise?'

'Mainly the gym. Early mornings, I run.'

'Where?'

'Sandy Bay. Miles of beach and not a soul anywhere. If you get running right, it becomes hallucinogenic. Running back, you meet yourself. Maybe it's the endorphins, I dunno . . .'

I'm exploring the tight little whorls of hair on his belly now. I can feel him stirring beneath my chin. *Running back, you meet yourself.* Interesting.

'This boxing,' I murmur. 'Do you like hurting people?'

'I like beating them. I like winning. I like ending up on top. Hurting them? Not unless I have to.'

'It's a control thing, then. Alpha male? Top dog? Am I getting warm here?'

'Whatever.' He shrugs. 'You're a clever woman. But I knew that from the start.'

'In the pub, you mean?'

'Of course. A single look tells you everything in life. The rest is conversation.'

'So, what did you see?' The question is shameless, but I don't care.

'I saw someone who excited me.'

'I'm flattered.'

'And who made me want to know more.'

'Excellent. And what have you found out?'

'Lots. All of it good.'

I try and press him further. I want details. I want to know what 'good' means. But he simply smiles and says nothing. Then I change the subject.

'You have proper fights? A ring? A referee? The crowd yelling for blood? All that?'

'Of course.' He nods. 'That's all part of it. It's a turn-on. You're in the arena. It's primitive.'

'And you love it?'

'I do.'

'And you always win?'

'God, no.'

'So, does losing hurt?'

'Yes, but not in the way you might think. Physically, you're knackered, but you're still full of adrenalin so you can't feel a thing. The place it really hurts is up here . . .' His big hands cup my head. 'And that's probably worse.'

'You stay friends with these people? Win or lose?'

'Sometimes. Some of them are arseholes and boxing won't change that. Others?' He shrugs. 'They're OK.'

'Does Boysie box?'

'He tried once. My fault. He got hammered.'

'By you?'

'Of course. That's what he wanted and that's what he got.'

'You're ruthless, Mr Deko.' I glance briefly up at him. 'But that can be a turn-on sometimes. A favour?'

'Name it.'

'Do you ever fuck Boysie? Just a nod will do.'

He looks at me for a long moment, and then he nods.

'Good?' I ask.

'Different.'

'Good answer.'

I take him in my mouth and hear a little groan of pleasure. Delight? Definitely. Surprise? I doubt it. An invitation not to stop? Of course.

I explore every part of him, very slowly, very gently, nearly teasing but not quite. In the ring, I'm guessing this might qualify as a round or two of playful sparring. I'm beginning to admire his stamina, his ability to hang on, when he reaches out and eases me towards him.

'A favour?'

'What?'

'Sit on my face?'

'A pleasure.'

I abandon his erection and straddle his big face, making myself comfortable. I'm wet within seconds under his busy tongue, and as I settle a little lower, moving my hips very slowly, back and forth, then a little sideways, then back and forth again, trying to marry myself to his lapping tongue, but I needn't worry because he's found my sweet spot already. He starts making little sucking noises, the lightest pressure, and the sensation is beyond delicious.

'Good?' he wants to know.

I choose not to ruin the moment with anything as banal as an answer. Moments later, to my huge surprise, I come, a deep jolt of hotness that floods every part of me. I gasp, groan, hang my head over the cushion at the end of the sofa, and somewhere fathomless, way down inside me where there's no such thing as a lie, I know that this has been the best. Seriously. The best ever.

He's smiling up at me, his face wet. He knows, I think.

'Again?'

'Yes, please. Just give me a minute or two. Blame my mum. She hated greed.'

We lie together, side by side. There's just room on the sofa. After a while, he stirs and I know he's ready for another round. Ding, ding, I think. Seconds out.

'You're very generous.' I kiss him lightly on the end of his nose. 'And you're a lovely man, but I think it's my turn.'

'We need to fuck.'

'I know. But there's something on my mind and I need to share it with you.'

His face is very close and for a split-second I glimpse, or I think I glimpse, something close to alarm in those deep-set eyes.

'Don't worry,' I tell him, 'it won't hurt.'

He's frowning now. I very badly don't want to wreck this moment. A fuck – slow, intense, much-anticipated – is exactly what we're ready for. But there's a single question I have to ask him before this movie reaches the final reel.

'I've been interviewed by the police again,' I say. 'They've been going through her phone billing, her emails, checking out the people she's been talking to. One of them appears to be you.'

'We're talking about Carrie?' He's staring at me.

'Yes.'

'That can't be true. I don't know any Carrie. Otherwise I'd have told you.'

'That's what I thought.'

'Then what's the problem?'

'It turns out she had another name. Amy.'

'Amy Phelps?'

'Yes.'

'That's different. Of course I know Amy.'

'Knew.'

'Knew. Amy was the matron of the home I bought.'

'So why did she change her name?'

'I've no idea. We had a business relationship. I'd taken a look at the property when it was still up and running. I needed someone to mark my card, explain one or two things. Amy knew the place inside out. She was happy to help.'

I nod. I'm trying to put a name – an adjective – to the way I'm feeling. Relieved is too small a word.

Deko reads me like the proverbial book.

'You think we were close? Me and Amy? Some kind of relationship?'

'I was wondering why you never mentioned her.'

'So now you know. Was she a looker, Amy? Yes, she was. Was she any man's wet dream? Again, yes. Was she the goddess windsurfer who turned every fucking head on the beach? Yes, yes, yes. And would this woman, this vision, have room in her life for a fifty-something Dutchman with no manners and no money? Alas, no.'

We're very close. I can touch him, smell him, taste him. I've asked my question, sought an answer, listened very hard, and I've believed every word. This man, I tell myself, has brought me nothing but pleasure. Please God, spare me losing yet another person in my life.

'Fuck me?' I run a finger over his lips. 'Please?'

TWENTY-NINE

I stay the night with Deko. The gado-gado is a marvel of precision, perfectly balanced, not too sweet. The peanut sauce – fittingly enough – is to die for, and when Deko asks for the verdict I tell him he's a genius. Afterwards, we drink far too much Spanish brandy. We fall into bed and I sleep like a baby, waking up after dawn with a mouth like a sewer and a thumping head. Throwing up in a downstairs loo, currently without a door, turns out to be a good idea. Deko fills the resulting hole with bacon and eggs, plus a side order of beans on toast, and by nine o'clock I'm back at the apartment, ready for anything. Which is just as well.

My relationship with the media over the years has been a bit like the curate's egg, good in parts and rubbish in others. When my movies were playing to full houses, I held court to the usual circus of showbiz interviewers. Some were acute, funny, and knew how to turn a phrase or two. The ones who liked me suppressed their reservations about a particular scene or the director's heavy hand and did my budding career nothing but good. Others weren't shy in naming their price for a good review. I remember one woman, not young, who claimed she could put me in the running for an Oscar. 'Sleep with me,' she promised, 'and the world will be yours.'

It never happened, of course, and more recently – with my name no longer in lights and my career flat-lining – I attracted a journalist of a very different kind. His name was Mitch Culligan and he stepped into my life at the very moment my tumour upped its game and threatened to kill me. Most journalists have an agenda and for Mitch that involved changing the world. The scale of this ambition was matched only by his work rate and his sheer dedication, both of which I admired greatly. He was an easy person to like, less easy to work with. When it mattered, he could be kindness itself and I was very grateful for that, but as I quickly learned, all good journos have the writer's chip of ice in their hearts. When needs must, they can stitch you up and a longish association with Mitch, to be frank, turned into a bit of a nightmare. I liked him to the end and very occasionally, even now, we still share the odd coffee.

All of this should have prepared me for Seb O'Leary, but it didn't. A message is waiting for me on Pavel's landline at the apartment. O'Leary sounds way past middle age. His voice carries just a hint of an American accent. He works, he says, for a leading broadsheet and he's been tasked by his editor to put pen to paper and come up with something nutritious on the mental health crisis. In this context, he's noticed rum goings-on down in leafy Exmouth. His understanding is that I, thesp extraordinaire, may have something to say about a vagrant youth everyone appears to call Moonie. Might I have the time and disposition for a chat?

This message is on the long side and there are a number of key words, all of them – I suspect – deliberately planted. One is 'nutritious'. Does that mean 'meaty', as in sensational? Or life-sustaining, which is what you might expect of a snack? 'Rum goings-on' is another marker, slightly louche, the work of a metropolitan eye cast regally in our direction. 'Thesp extraordinaire' suggests he's been on Google, which is what any journo would do, but the real clue is the word 'vagrant'. Just the sound of it, the weight it so carelessly carries, its brief dalliance with everyone's lazy expectations, makes my blood boil. Karen's boy may technically be a vagrant, but the truth is far, far more complex.

'I was rather hoping I might come to your place,' he says when I call. 'The coffee here is crap.'

'Where's here?'

'The Premier Inn.'

I tell him there's no question of meeting *chez moi*. It's the Premier Inn or nothing.

'So be it,' he says. 'The restaurant's empty by ten o'clock.'

I turn up at quarter past. He's sitting sideways at a table by the window, reading a copy of *Le Monde*. I wasn't wrong about his age. He wears half-moon glasses and the scabby damage around his hairline tells me that, over the years, he's spent far too long in the sun. The denim jacket might suit a much younger man but it's impossible not to admire the scuffed leather of his cowboy boots. As he looks up, he reaches for the tall glass of Pernod on the table.

'You speak French?' Uninvited, I take a seat.

'*Oui*. I also have a flat in Paris. Nineteenth arrondissement, Quai de Jemmapes, but that's another story. I've been in the States a while. Montana. Know it at all? If I'd ever had an ounce of common fucking sense, back in the day, I should have been a wrangler out there, run cattle, maybe ranched. Instead . . .' He gestures at the pad open on the table. 'This shit. Iraq? Afghanistan? Fucking *Syria*? Give me a break. I've done time in them all, and I mean *time*, but one crushed infant too many and you get a little jaded. Not that here is any better. I've been back from the States for less than a fortnight and already this poxy little country depresses me, and so does France now that they've let Le Pen and her tribe into the dress fucking circle. Yep,' he nods, 'Montana, for sure. You want to buy a flat in the Nineteenth? Third floor? Decent resto next door? Three hundred grand and it's yours. I'll phone my lawyer. We'll sort something out.'

I tell him not to bother. If this man is trying to impress me, it hasn't worked. Am I supposed to have heard of Seb O'Leary? Have I been missing something all these years?

'So why Exmouth?' I ask him. 'And why me?'

He folds the paper and reaches for his pad. It's quickly evident that he's already picked up most of this story's threads. He knows, in some detail, what happened to Carrie. Like everyone else in the world, he seems to regard Moonie as the prime suspect. Much to my surprise, he even knows about Pavel's stroke.

'You've been talking to the police,' I say. 'That's where you got Pavel's number.'

'Of course. Our friends in blue can't do without us. The wrong kind of publicity and they're twisting in the wind. The right kind, they're smelling of fucking roses. You want a peek at those files of theirs? Easy. You find their sweet spot, work out what's bugging them, and they're all over you.'

'You're talking about the mental health thing?'

'Exactly. They're richly fucked, and they know it. The percentage of time they're wasting on the loonies out there goes up by the day. Last week it was forty per cent. This week? Forty-five. I don't disbelieve them for a second. And I'm very happy to help.'

'So what else did they tell you? Am I allowed to ask?'

'Ask what you like.' He gestures at the pad. 'You can write the fucking story if you want. Sad is the way I see it; sad and probably inevitable. This country's on the skids. The only way is down and believe me it's going to hurt. Big, big car crash. Blood everywhere.' He leans forward and beckons me closer. I can smell the Pernod on his breath. 'You heard it here first, right? Except that everyone else in Europe, in the States, even in fucking Moscow, maybe *especially* in fucking Moscow, anyone with even half a brain, they're gonna be warming their hands at the fire.'

'Fire?' I'm lost.

'Sure. The wreckers are in for the kill. They've kicked over the furniture and helped themselves to what's left, and when it suits them they'll torch the place and claim on the fucking insurance. You want to talk about the real lunatics? Look no further.'

He sits back again, turning to stare out of the window. This, I belatedly realize, is about our current political situation. In O'Leary's eyes, we're evidently at the mercy of a bunch of ultras determined to clean up. This reminds me of Mitch Culligan at full throttle: the same disbelief that things have gone so far, the same despair that they may yet go a whole lot further. Mitch was obsessed about the skeletons he claimed to have discovered in UKIP's cupboard. O'Leary, on the other hand, has settled on mental health.

'In my game it's all down to focus,' he says, toying with his pen. 'Anything to do with the NHS is a fucking boneyard. It's too big, too complicated, even for the kind of punters who keep our rag going. No, when it comes to the loonies we need a name, a face, a story, and this one sounds perfect.'

'You mean Moonie?'

'Of course. Our Mr Moonie. He of the golden locks and bedside manner. You were there with the victim. She told you everything, right? After he'd paid her a visit?'

'Her name's Carrie,' I point out. 'But you know that already.'

'Sure. Carrie. So, what exactly did she say?'

I don't like this man. I don't like his manner, his easy assumptions, the way he's chosen to kid himself that we're somehow comrades-in-arms in this struggle for the nation's soul. He thinks he's doing me some kind of favour. He thinks I'm an easy sell.

His pen is poised. I say nothing.

'Well?' he says at last.

'I don't know what you want.'

'You don't? But I've just told you. I want to know about Carrie. I want to know what she was like. I want to know about going round to see if she was OK that afternoon. The way I see it, you have a dog in this fight, a guy called Pavel, a guy Carrie likes, trusts, looks after. She's the carer of your dreams and without her you're probably fucked so it's your job to listen very hard when she tells you that story of hers. Does that make sense? Or am I wasting my time?'

'You're wasting your time.'

'Why? Is it money you're after? Let's cut to the chase here. Be honest. Papers like mine are flat broke but there might be ways and means. Name it. How much?'

I'm gazing at him. In truth he disgusts me, and moments later I tell him so. He physically recoils at the table and then reaches for the last of the Pernod, a slightly stagey piece of theatre that confirms my growing belief that the man is a twat.

'Disgust?' He whistles softly and looks round as if I might have someone else in mind. 'That's a big word. Did I hear you properly? *Disgust?*'

'You heard perfectly. I don't need your money and I certainly don't need any of this crap.' I nod down at his empty pad.

'You don't?'

'No.'

'You think I'm talking bollocks?'

'Yes.'

'You're wrong. You ever read any of my pieces from Aleppo?'
'No.'
'Shame. I'll send you a selection. Just give me an email address.'
'Why should I?'
'Because they might interest you. Because they might be relevant. Because they might persuade you that I have a listening ear, and a certain talent with language, and – dare I say it – the best of intentions. That war was evil. Pick the right victims, do their stories justice, and you've touched the conscience of half the fucking world. You want this mental health thing sorted? You want to do something for the memory of that poor bloody woman? Then trust me. Talk to me. Tell me the way it was.'

At this point, I'm tempted to laugh. I know nothing about Seb O'Leary, about the war zones he's reported from, about the awards he's doubtless won, about his book deals and his appearances on *Newsnight*. Every conversation like this, I tell myself, is an audition. And Seb O'Leary has failed to land the part.

He's studying me across the table. He's smiling. Any moment now, he's going to order another Pernod. Because he thinks he's won.

'You're ready?' He pulls the waiting pad towards him. 'We can talk now? Be nice to each other? Behave like decent human beings?'

'In your dreams,' I say. And leave.

DS Williams calls me less than an hour later. I'm on the clifftop path that leads to a village called Budleigh Salterton, trying to purge the anger from my soul.

Williams is apologizing in advance for what she suspects might be an awkward conversation and I know at once that she's been talking to the man I left at the Premier Inn.

'This is about O'Leary,' I tell her. 'It has to be.'
'You're right.'
'He phoned you.'
'Half an hour ago. I think you upset him.'
'Good. At least he was listening.'

There's a brief silence. I haven't finished with O'Leary, nor – for that matter – with DS Williams.

'Someone gave him Pavel's phone number,' I say. 'Someone told him where to find me. Was that you?'
'No.'

'Someone else in your organization?'

'Very possibly.'

'Why? Why did you do that? And how come this man knows so much about Carrie? And about what she told me that afternoon I went round to find her?'

'Not me, Ms Andressen.'

'But someone else? Some other officer? Did I hear you properly? Was that what you just said?'

Williams doesn't need a conversation like this, and it shows. She begins to deny it could be anyone in uniform or CID. She quotes some code of practice or other. Witness rights are sacrosanct, she says. Big fucking deal.

'It must have been a civilian, then? You have a press office? People who deal with the media?'

'We do, yes.'

'And?'

Nothing. No admission. No corroboration. Just a faint whistling noise which may be the wind funnelling up the nearby cliff face. For a moment, I think she's thrown in the towel and ended the conversation. Far from it.

'This is difficult,' she says for the second time. 'I think you know what we all feel about the MH issue. It's a question of public awareness. People out there need to know how bad things have got on the mental health front. Something has to be done.'

'So, you sent O'Leary? Briefed him? Told him what I'd told you?'

'We had no choice in the matter, Ms Andressen. He carries weight. So does that paper of his. I'm told he has a huge personal following, people of influence, people who can change things, people who read what he writes and believe it.'

'You had every choice in the matter.' I'm angry again. 'Have you met this man?'

'No.'

'You should. It's a word I rarely use but the man's a dickhead. I'm used to being patronized but he needs more practice.'

I think I hear a laugh, or at least a chuckle, at the other end. For one brief moment, DS Williams and I are allies.

'I'm serious,' I say. 'Take a look at the man. Sit him down and listen to him. In my trade, he wouldn't even get a walk-on part.'

'You think we can do better than him? Be frank.'

'I do. That's exactly what I think.'

'But you agree with the cause? What we're trying to achieve here?'

'About mental health? Of course I do. It's a scandal, a disgrace. But there are people you shouldn't even consider and in my book O'Leary is one of them.'

Williams seems to agree. She tells me that all this is way beyond her pay grade. She knows very little about the media and if I want the truth, she's never heard of Seb O'Leary.

'What about someone else?' she suggests. 'What if we come up with another name?'

I shake my head and tell her again that I'm as shocked as she is about the lack of provision for people like Moonie but I'm shocked, as well, by the way Operation *Mandolin* has shared stuff I assumed to be confidential.

Another silence. Then she's back on the line.

'Why don't *you* find someone?' she suggests. 'How might that work?'

The conversation ends shortly afterwards. I tell her it's an interesting thought, but I'd need a guarantee that O'Leary will stay well clear. No more phone calls. No more boasts. No more bullshit. The latter makes her laugh again. She's honest enough to admit that what she calls her clout in this affair is strictly limited, but I think we part as friends.

Moments before I hang up, I enquire whether *Mandolin* has a name for Moonie yet. I have one from Karen, of course, but I need to be sure.

'Why do you ask?' Williams says at once.

'Because I have a stake in this game. Someone I liked very much got killed.' I pause. 'Well . . . you have a name?'

'Yes, we do. This is in confidence?'

Confidence? I resist the temptation to laugh.

'Yes,' I tell her, 'of course.'

'His name is Jason Macreadie. His mother came forward after the photos were published. He also turns out to be on the MP list.'

'MP?'

'Missing persons. We looked there, of course, but somehow we never bottomed it out. Is that all, Ms Andressen? If so, I'd like to thank you for your patience.'

I tell her she's welcome and the conversation comes to an end.

I've taken her call on the highest point of the cliff path. Ahead lies the sprawl of a holiday camp, acre after acre of mobile homes, and when I venture as far as the cliff edge, I realize that I'm looking down at what must be Sandy Bay. The sun is out but the bite of the wind has kept the huge expanse of sand virtually empty.

I peer down. I count maybe a dozen stick figures, most of them with dogs. Then my attention is caught by someone else. He's wearing scarlet shorts and a trackie top and he's jogging into the sun, short steps, the balls of his feet just metres away from the lapping tide. Then, as I watch, he spins round, running backwards now, swinging punch after punch at his own shadow, short jabs, heavy uppercuts, his upper body swaying left and right. It's a mesmerizing image and I know with absolute certainty that it will stay with me forever. My man. My Deko. *En pleine forme.* Fighting himself.

THIRTY

I have Mitch Culligan's number on my directory and I wait until I'm back at the apartment before I make the call. The last time we met, more than a year ago, he was still living in Hither Green, in a characterful semi I remember well.

He's checked his caller ID and answers at once. Happily, he seems pleased to hear from me. I ask him if everything's going OK.

'Everything's fine. The world is madder than ever, but you don't need me to tell you that. And you? All well?'

This is code for the tumour. I tell him it's behaving itself. For now.

'And Sayid?' I ask him. 'You're still together?'

Sayid, last time I checked, was Mitch's live-in lover, a Syrian asylum-seeker who fled an assortment of warlords and ended up in the back of a lorry, heading for Calais. In his native Aleppo, he worked as a consultant in a hospital Assad bombed to pieces, but now, according to Mitch, he's appeared before some Home Office tribunal or other, argued his case, and won.

'Permanent right to remain,' Mitch confirms. 'Can you imagine the difference that makes?'

As it happens, I can. I got to know Sayid a couple of years back and – like everyone else who's ever met him – I found his company enchanting. Wonderful eyes, too, and a cake-maker of serious talent.

'Tell him I'm thrilled,' I say, 'and give him a big hug from me.'

Mitch grunts something I don't catch and asks me what I want. This abrupt change of conversational gear stirs a number of memories, not all of them pleasant, but I've made a decision and I've no intention of backing off.

'You're still freelancing?'

'Of course. It's the only game left in town if you want to rattle a few cages.'

I tell him about Carrie, about Moonie, and about my own involvement. It turns out he's kept track of the story, sort of, but I can tell from his voice that I've caught his interest.

'This is about the mental health thing, yeah?'

'No.' I shake my head. 'This is about the kid you saw in the papers, on the telly. That's where it begins and ends, at least in my little head.'

I realize I've lifted this verbatim from Seb O'Leary, but I don't feel the slightest twinge of guilt. Getting one thing right doesn't excuse the rest of our brief conversation.

'You're a material witness?' Mitch asks.

'Yes.'

'You're plugged in to the investigation? Have the ear of the SIO, maybe?'

'I have a contact or two.'

'Have they found this Moonie yet?'

'Not to my knowledge.'

'So, what do you want me to do?'

I explain as briefly as I can about police efforts to raise media interest in the wider implications of the case. Mention of Seb O'Leary draws a bark of laughter from Mitch.

'I thought he was dead.'

'I think he might be.'

'You've *met* him?'

'This morning. It wasn't a long conversation.'

Another grunt from Mitch. Then he says he's in.

'Just one condition.'

'What?'

'You don't talk to O'Leary again. Or anyone else.'

As soon as I put the phone down, I'm wondering what I've done. I like to think I know Mitch Culligan well. I don't trust him completely because certain situations force journalists like him to put loyalty to a larger cause ahead of any personal commitments. Moonie may well turn out to be a case in point but those hideous moments in Carrie's bedroom have convinced me that something has to be done about mental health. In my heart, I know that Moonie – Jason – killed Carrie. The fact that it wasn't his fault, the fact that society – all of us – should have realized just how volatile and dangerous he could be, is the real point. Jason Macreadie should never have been walking the streets in the first place. For his sake, as well as ours, he needed looking after.

When I phone Karen, she picks up at once. She seems eager to talk. She tells me she enjoyed yesterday. No way would she ever have agreed to meet me but now it's happened, and we're mates, and she'd be very happy to get together again.

Mates. I take this as a compliment. I mention Mitch Culligan. I tell her he's a good friend and a decent journalist. He doesn't write rubbish, I assure her, and when something matters to him he works hard to get it right. There's a letter from me in the post to her but in the meantime something else has happened.

'Like what?'

'Like Mitch. He wants to take your story on.'

'What does that mean?'

'He'd need to come and see you. For a chat.'

'Would you be there?'

'If that's what you want, of course.'

'Then yes. The answer's yes.'

'When?'

'Whenever you like. I don't go out much.'

I'm back on the phone to Mitch within minutes, suggesting a meet in Weston with Moonie's mother. Nice woman, I tell him. Interesting flat.

'You're telling me you've met her? His mum?'

'We're mates,' I tell him. 'We had a long conversation yesterday. I made some notes. I'll mail them over. How about tomorrow?'

There's a brief silence. I think I can hear Sayid's voice in the background. Then Mitch is back on the line.

'Tomorrow's fine.' He's laughing. 'Send me the notes. You're in the wrong fucking business.'

THIRTY-ONE

M itch has taken the train from Paddington and I agree to pick him up at Taunton. He emerges from the station in his trademark grey anorak and baggy jeans. He's still bearded, still flat-footed, still a plodder, but he's lost a bit of weight and it suits him.

'Blame Sayid,' he grunts, climbing into the car. 'He promised me jogging for beginners and we've ended up doing five milers, three times a week. I've never been so bored in my life.'

This has to be hyperbole, most journalists' stock-in-trade. Secretly, I suspect Mitch approves of his new self. He says he's cutting down on the booze, as well.

'Sayid, again?'

'Of course. That man was born a saint.'

En route, Mitch tells me about one or two of his current projects. He's acquired a new friend at the northernmost settlement on earth, a Canadian weather station called Alert just five hundred miles from the North Pole, and he says some of the latest temperature readings are seriously scary. Global warming has been a passion of his for years.

Mitch has never been to Weston before but what he sees on the way in doesn't surprise him. Scruffy industrial estates. Boarded-up units. Heavy security outside supermarkets. Kids on their bikes pulling wheelies in the middle of the road, eager for their day in court.

'Karen says they're after minor injuries,' I tell him. 'Something they can blame on careless drivers.'

'Karen's right.' Mitch has seen the same thing in towns and cities in the north. 'A minor break? Abrasions and PTSD? Get the right lawyer and you're talking serious money. One day, litigation will be all we have left.'

I park around the corner from the betting shop. I've tried to get hold of Karen but she's not picking up. On the point of ringing her doorbell, I hear voices coming down her stairs. Karen's I recognize. The other one is also familiar. *Shit*, I think.

I'm right. The door opens, and there he is, Seb O'Leary, tote bag on his shoulder, a wide smile on his face. He and Mitch exchange nods. Karen is looking uncertain.

'Enora?' she says.

O'Leary has turned to say goodbye. He plants a kiss on her pale cheek and holds her briefly at arm's length. 'Fascinating talk, my precious. Real pleasure. Take care of yourself. I'll be in touch.'

Moments later, before either of us can react, he's striding across the road in those leather cowboy boots. He's driving what looks like a hire car and he gives us a little wave as he floors the throttle and accelerates away.

Upstairs, in the fuggy chaos of her room, Karen does her best to explain. She hadn't really followed me on the phone last night, her fault, and when she opened the door to O'Leary first thing this morning, she assumed he was the bloke she'd been expecting.

'But I'd have been there, too,' I point out.

'Yeah, but I thought you must have been caught out by the traffic or something. I'm sorry, I'm really sorry. You must think I'm losing it, and you're right.'

Mitch presses her further. He wants to know exactly what she's told O'Leary. She starts to ramble, but the short answer is more or less everything. He'd brought her fresh bread, hot from the bakery at Sainsbury's. He'd stayed a couple of hours. He'd put up with the bloody cat. He'd been really nice to her, and afterwards she'd been more than happy to go through the photos with him.

'Photos?' This is going from bad to worse. Shots of Jason as a kid, she says. Snaps of him and his dad the day they'd all taken the bus to Bristol Zoo. Plus a photo she especially cherished.

'Brad took it on his birthday years ago. Jason was sitting on my lap with that stuffed bunny he'd never let out of his sight. He looked really happy.' She's smiling at the memory. 'Mr O'Leary said he'd make copies and send them all back. Next week, he said. "Phone me if they don't turn up."'

I ask to see the number. She's written it down on the back of a utilities bill.

'Did he offer you money?' I ask.

'Never. And I wouldn't have taken it, neither.'

'Cheap date, then.' This from Mitch. 'What's he going to do with it all? Did he say?'

'Yeah. He said he'd go away and put it all together. He thought next week for the spread in the paper.'

'Spread?'

'Yes.' She seems to have brightened. 'He thinks this might be the breakthrough. That's the word he used. Breakthrough. He said there was no way other papers wouldn't pick it up. TV, too. Once Jason read it, he was bound to come forward because he wouldn't be frightened any more. All people had to do was understand.'

'Understand what?'

'What it's like to be Jason. To be inside that head of his. That's what you said, too.' Karen's looking at me. 'Last night on the phone.'

It's true. That's exactly what I said, except that Mitch would have made a far better job of it.

'Damage limitation,' Mitch mumbles. We've taken Karen to lunch in a pub on the seafront and he's trying to get O'Leary on the phone. Karen drinks fizzy cider sweetened with cherry juice, and I've persuaded her to have something to eat. The pub is advertising a mid-week OAP offer, coley and chips for under a fiver, and the place is packed. Karen peels back the thick layer of soggy batter and picks at the grey flesh underneath while Mitch keeps stabbing at his mobile. He thinks that O'Leary might be up for a deal, and he doesn't appear to be listening when I tell him that's unlikely.

As it happens, I'm wrong. Legally, Mitch says, it would be suicidal for O'Leary's paper to publish anything ahead of a possible trial. Which leaves him only one option.

'The internet?'

'Of course. He needs a platform, ideally abroad. *Libération* might carry it. *Charlie Hebdo,* for sure.'

'But O'Leary knows Paris. He speaks French. He's got an apartment there. He tried to sell it to me.'

'O'Leary's full of shit. Even assuming it's true, he still needs the contacts. I know these people. They trust me. There's a deal in there somewhere, I know there is.'

'So, who gets to write the piece?'

'Me. That's the whole point.'

'And O'Leary? He'd go with that?'

'He'd jump at it. The man's bone idle. He's lost his appetite, his mojo. For a shared credit, he'd be happy to stand aside and let me do the heavy lifting.'

I somehow doubt this. At the Premier Inn, O'Leary did his best to bully me into a proper interview and this morning he couldn't wait to get to Karen before anyone else knocked on her door.

'So how did he know how to find her?' Mitch has given up on O'Leary.

'The police, of course.' I'm thinking of my conversation with Williams.

Mitch nods. He's had plenty of dealings with the Met, and discreet conversations with senior journalists in the margins of major enquiries don't surprise him in the least.

We finish up in the pub and walk Karen home. A third glass of cider and red has made her slightly unsteady, and when we link arms I can feel her leaning into me. On her doorstep, I ask her where she thinks O'Leary might live but she says she hasn't a clue. London somewhere? No idea.

As we drive away, Mitch tells me not to worry. He has a wealth of contacts. Give him an hour, maybe two. By the time I drop him back at Taunton station, he's been on his mobile non-stop.

'Edmonton,' he says. 'North London.'

'Where, exactly?'

He tears a sheet from his notepad and scribbles an address. 34b Lilac Avenue.

'This place belongs to him?'

'An old girlfriend. He kips there when he's in London. She's working in Brussels at the moment.'

'Very wise. He's there alone?'

'As far as I know, yes.' Mitch's door is half-open. He nods down at the address. 'So, what next?'

I shrug, reaching for the ignition key. 'I'll be in touch, 'I say. 'And thanks for coming down.'

'You're telling me this is over?'

'No.' I'm checking the rear-view mirror. 'Far from it.'

THIRTY-TWO

It's an hour's drive from Taunton to Flixcombe Manor. I haven't been in West Dorset for a while, and spring has settled on these rolling hills. This is a landscape you could almost eat: hedgerows already frothy with cow parsley, trees in village gardens heavy with cherry blossom, lambs in the fields doing their April thing while their mums try and get a moment's peace.

I pause for a moment at the bend in the drive that offers the best view of the house through the trees. Newly repainted, perfectly proportioned, it's a wonderful example of how the Georgians could make a landscape like this even more irresistible. H once told me what a wrench it was leaving his beloved Pompey. Portsmouth undoubtedly has its charms, especially if – like H – you were making a fortune in the drugs biz, but I suspect the move to Flixcombe has done wonders for his blood pressure.

As if. Jessie, the ex-Pompey woman who makes his life run on time, lets me into the house. We share a brief hug and then she says I'll find H upstairs in the room he uses as an office.

'Shit day, so far,' she warns. 'See what you can do.'

H is sitting at his desk. Balls of paper litter the floor. I stoop to retrieve them and find an empty can of Stella in the wastepaper bin. Bad sign. H rarely drinks before six o'clock.

'Can you fucking believe this?' No hello.

He shows me a piece of paper covered in comments and exclamation marks he must have scribbled earlier. It seems to be some kind of official notification and I'm still trying to make sense of it when H spares me the effort.

'Planners,' he says. 'Scum of the fucking earth. Waste our money and make life miserable.' He nods towards the window. 'And the tosser over the way, you know what he's done?'

I shake my head. I don't. Is this the neighbour who won't sell H the extra fields he wants?

'Yeah. Him. And you know why? I should have guessed, should

have sussed it. He's trying to get planning permission for a housing estate and he thinks he's on to a winner. A housing estate.' He nods towards the window. 'Right in the middle of my fucking view. It can't happen. It won't happen. The tosser doesn't know what he's getting into.'

I resist the temptation to enquire further. In these moods, H can rant for hours and time is precious. I tell him I'm planning a visit to the Stroke Unit on the way home. Any chance of a brief chat?

He has the grace to ask how Pavel is getting on. We had a very brief phone conversation yesterday on his prospects but I'm not sure how much H took in. I tell him Pavel is on the mend.

'Can he remember anything about it?'

'I've no idea. One day he may tell me but so far he's still not talking.'

'Because he can't?'

'Because he's still unconscious. Breathing is a major triumph. We live in hope.'

H nods, pushes the pile of paperwork to one side. 'So, what's this about?' he asks. 'How can I help?'

I tell him about finding Moonie's mum, and about Seb O'Leary. I don't bother mentioning Mitch because he and H had a major run-in a couple of years ago, and H has never understood the concept of forgiveness. Mitch tried to stitch H up over his links to UKIP, and Mitch was lucky not to end up on crutches.

'Journalists are scum,' H grunts. 'Worse than planners. No fucking respect. Never know when to stop poking their nose into other people's business.'

This sounds promising. I explain how O'Leary talked his way into Karen's bed-sit, and made off with a lengthy interview and a bunch of photos.

'You're telling me he helped himself?'

'Yes.'

'Why would he do that?'

I do my best to explain about O'Leary's interest in highlighting the woeful state of mental health provision.

'But that's good, isn't it? These Moonie guys should be tucked up somewhere safe. Then our Carrie might still be alive.'

'Of course, that's the whole point. But we don't trust the man. He's sitting on a big story. He's got that boy's life in his hands. He could do anything with it.'

'You want the stuff back?'

'We do.'

'Who's this "we"?'

'Me. I want it back.'

'And then what?'

'And then I'll find someone I trust to do a better job.'

'Like who?'

'I don't know yet. There'll be someone.' I'm staring at him. 'Are you trusting me here? Only it doesn't feel like it.'

H holds my gaze all too briefly, then reaches for a pen. When I give him O'Leary's address, he pauses.

'That's North London. You're sure he's there?'

'No, but he might be.'

'You want the stuff back? His notes? The photos?'

'I do.'

'You want him hurt, as well?'

'I want him away from the story. And I want him away from me.'

'He's been at you?' H has tuned in properly now, and it shows.

'He's tried. It's nothing physical. Nothing I couldn't cope with. He's way past his sell-by date but he'll never admit it and that's rather the point. The boy Moonie is damaged enough already. The last thing he needs is O'Leary.'

'But the boy killed Carrie, didn't he?'

'That's true.'

'So, what are we talking about? Am I missing something here? He rips the poor woman's guts out, he's madness on fucking legs, and he'll probably do it again. Why should we be bothered?'

It's a very good question and it deserves a proper answer. I pull up a chair, determined to keep H's attention.

'Everyone has a story,' I tell him. 'Even people like Moonie. Things just don't happen by accident. There are reasons why people do things to each other, to themselves, why people just lose it. It isn't enough to turn our backs. We need to *understand*.' I can hear Pavel in this little speech, and so can H.

'That's nonce talk. You do what that boy did, you pay a price. But that's another fucking conversation.' He's looking at the address again. 'I'll get it sorted. Leave it to me.'

'When?'

'Soon.'

'Like tonight?' H gets to his feet and has a stretch. He's not a tall man, by any means, but I've always been fascinated by the way his sheer physical presence can fill a room. 'Well . . .?'

He won't give me an answer. Instead, he wants to talk about Malo.

'He was here a couple of days,' he says, 'before he pushed off back to London.'

'Good. I'm glad for both of you.'

'And we talked, like you do.'

'Excellent. I could have done with some of that myself, if you're asking. It was hard, losing Carrie.'

'Yeah? Well, the boy seems to think you might have found someone down there to do the biz.'

The biz. H has always been pathologically jealous, or perhaps territorial. He has no rights as far as I'm concerned, apart from being the father of my only son. We've made love once, just once, and that was twenty years ago. And yet he still seems to think he owns me.

'Big guy? Bit of a voice on him? Looks like he can handle himself?'

I nod. I know exactly where this has come from. Open-mic night in downtown Exmouth, I think, and Malo playing barman.

'His name's Deko,' I say lightly.

'Deko? What kind of name is that?'

'He's Dutch.'

'Anything else?'

'He's been very kind. Very supportive. Just now, that feels important. Am I on a leash, here? Should I ask your permission?'

'To do what?'

This, of course, is the crux. H has already assumed that Deko and I are shagging each other to death. He's not far wrong but that's not the point.

I give him a brief hug and tell him there's nothing to be worried about.

'Mr O'Leary,' I murmur, 'I'd be truly grateful.'

H studies me for a long moment. In some ways he's like the weather. The storms that fuel him come and go, blowing quickly through, volatile, occasionally violent, but never around for long. Just now, he seems to have forgiven me for Deko and there's a smile on his face.

'Edmonton's full of blacks,' he says. 'This could be one for Wes.'

*　　*　　*

I'm on my way home, exploring the maze of country lanes favoured by my sat nav. Wesley Kane is H's enforcer-in-chief. He still lives in Pompey and he probably always will. He's tall, keeps himself fit, and has hung on to his looks. When I was much younger, I'd have given anything for having Wes's hair. H has shown me photos from the old days. Wes was always cool, never smiling for the camera, and his hair, an explosion of natural curls, looked like someone had just lit a fuse and run away. Nowadays, worn longer, plaited, beaded, and threaded with grey, it makes him look even sexier. Last year, when I was trying to disentangle my son from some deeply scary people in the cocaine trade, Wes was very helpful. Despite his reputation for being a bit of a psycho, I like to think we became friends.

Wes, I suspect, will be on the train within the hour. His favourite party piece calls for an electric kettle and someone else's steaming groin but before I left Flixcombe, I made H promise he'd leave Seb O'Leary intact. Just get the Moonie stuff back.

At the Stroke Unit, to my disappointment, there's very little news. They're feeding Pavel via a tube down his throat. Everything below his head is behaving the way it should and he needs no mechanical help with his breathing. He's on a daily dosage of blood thinners and – in the words of one of the nurses – there's no reason why he should still be so deeply unconscious. The workings of the brain, she says, often remain a complete mystery. Too right.

Back at the apartment I find a note from Felip. He hopes I don't mind but he's taken a couple of days off. He has a Spanish friend who's working at a hotel in St Ives. Felip should be back by the end of the week and if I need him before then, all I have to do is phone.

It feels strange having the apartment to myself. What's happened – first to Carrie, and now to Pavel – has left me in limbo. I'm determined to be at Pavel's bedside for the moment when he truly begins to surface, but in the meantime I'm in the hands of the gods of unconsciousness.

I begin to put some music on – Ravel, another Pavel favourite – but then change my mind, and drift from room to room, enjoying the space and the silence. I've no idea what life was like in this apartment before we moved Pavel in, but I suspect you'd never tire of the view, and the low keening of the wind, and the faint chorus of oystercatchers on the roost across the water. I'm thinking of H, and another perfect view, when a text arrives on my mobile.

It's from Boysie. He's due to make a presentation to his backers and he's wondering whether I've managed to come up with a name or two for the Hotel Zuma showbiz weekend he has in mind.

I stare at the tiny screen for a moment. The answer, alas, is no but it's worse than that because my contacts book is very old and if Boysie is relying on little me to come up with any current A-listers, then I'm afraid he's going to be disappointed. It was Deko who told me only days ago that things are tight out there in the world of business. Bits of the economy are falling apart, and Brexit doesn't help. The average punter, he said, has a keen instinct for impending disaster and no one wants to part with their money. So maybe the Hotel Zuma isn't quite as buoyant as I'd thought. Maybe even the casino is feeling the pinch.

I make myself comfortable on the sofa and begin to list one or two thespy friends who might just fancy a weekend in Devon. Then, a far more interesting challenge, I start scribbling random thoughts about the places filming has taken me, and how the business of being paid to be someone else can be surprisingly liberating, not just on set or on location, but in the theatre or the recording studio. I've always treasured those moments when the character I'm playing takes over completely, and I cease to be Enora Andressen, and by the time I've run out of paper, it's dark outside.

Putting the notes aside, I wander into the kitchen and pour myself a glass of wine. Tomorrow, I think, I'll drive up to the hotel and try out some of these ideas on Boysie. If he likes them, if we stay friends, then I might invite him and Deko back here to the apartment for a meal. I ponder the thought for a moment or two, thinking about possible menus, then I change my mind. I want only one face at my dining table, and it isn't Boysie's.

THIRTY-THREE

ext morning, my sat nav takes me back to the Hotel Zuma. It's still early, barely half past nine, and I'm having a companionable little fantasy about fresh coffee with Boysie on the terrace at the front of the property, when the woman at reception tells me he's up in the woods taking yet another look at his pigs. She's recognized me from the evening Boysie gave me the tour. The pigs, she seems to be implying, have become a bit of an obsession. Lately he's been spending more and more time up there. Organic free-range pork is one thing, but there's also the small matter of a hotel to run.

'Shall I wait for him to get back?'

'Don't bother. He may be hours. I'll draw you a map. There are two gates in the fenced area. I'll mark the one you need.' She stands up to check what I'm wearing on my feet. 'Runners? Just as well.'

The path I need to follow begins beyond a wicket gate at the top of the hotel's veggie patch. The path has been well-trodden and is easy to follow. Almost immediately, I'm swallowed up by the darkness of the trees. The wind has dropped overnight, and the heat of the sun seems to have released the scent of pine resin. I pause to savour it. The breath of the forest, I think. Songbirds flutter from branch to branch, shadows in the gloom, wholly welcome after the chorus of squawky seagulls which seems to have become the soundtrack of my life. Then I'm aware of a tiny movement, barely metres away, and I look round to find myself looking a deer in the eye. It must be young. It stands there, waiting for something to happen, then I slowly extend a hand and it bounds away. I watch it disappearing into the trees below me. Magic, I think. No wonder Boysie loves this place.

Further up the hill, the path becomes boggier, thanks to a tiny stream that's appeared from nowhere. I step sideways on to the knobbly bed of fallen pine cones and keep going, avoiding the path. Ahead, emerging from the trees, is a newish-looking fence with a gate. Beside the gate is a warning, in red capital letters. NO ADMITTANCE, it says. DANGER – WILD BOAR.

No one has mentioned wild boar. At the restaurant table the other night, the talk was of free-range pigs, which I took to be regular porkers, sausages on four legs. Wild boars, about which I know nothing, sound altogether more exotic. At first sight the gate appears to be padlocked, but then I realize that the chain is hanging loose, unsecured. I slide the latch back and when I give the gate a little push, it swings open. I stand stock still for a second or two, wondering whether to go any further. The word 'wild' is the clue. A domestic pig isn't small. This version might be a hooligan. If it's having a bad day, it might hurt me. In extremis, say in a Pavel movie, it might eat me alive.

I shut the gate and decide to follow the line of the fence through the trees and see where it leads. The other gate must surely be nearby. Maybe there are two enclosures, one for the wild boar, the other for the domestic version. I consult my map. No clues. If I was sensible, of course, I'd phone the hotel, or even Boysie, for directions but there's something about the busy silence in these woods that appeals immensely. We all need an adventure from time to time, I tell myself, and this is mine.

The fence has turned a corner and is climbing the hill again. I stop occasionally and peer into the enclosure, but there's no sign of anything moving. What do wild boars look like? Are they pink, and fat, and rather endearing, like normal pigs? Or should I be looking for something altogether more feral? I'm still debating the difference when I spot the other gate. Had I followed the path, as instructed, it would bring me here.

This gate is closed but there's no chain, no padlock, nothing to tell me to turn around and go back down the hill. I step inside the enclosure and pull the gate shut behind me. The track continues up through the trees. I can see no sign of pigs, though there are plenty of footprints in the dampness of the flattened soil. Another minute or so and I've lost sight of the fence. When I stop and turn around to look for it, it's gone. Then, through the trees, comes a squeal, almost human. How close? I simply don't know. Rooted to the spot, I'm wondering whether to retrace my footsteps, but then comes a hoot of laughter, definitely human, and I tell myself it must be Boysie.

On I go, following the track. In maybe a hundred metres, the trees part to reveal a small clearing. This space has been levelled and is flat enough for someone to have built what looks, at first sight, to be a makeshift bungalow. The property is single storey, brick-built, with a pitched roof and a chimney. The windowsills are green with moss and one of the two windows has been boarded up. Paving slabs, crudely laid, lead to the front door which must, once, have been a deep shade of blue. Now, like the windowsills, it's an act of surrender to years – maybe decades – of neglect.

The door stands ajar. I'm still looking at it when I hear the squealing again, much louder. It comes from inside this wreck of a building. Has to. This time, there's no laughter.

I'm tempted to call Boysie's name, but I don't. Instead, I begin to move towards the open door. A footstep away, I pause. I can hear movement from inside. An animal? A pig? Boysie? A feral boar? I've no idea. I push the door fully open. Inside, what appears to be a hall is in darkness. As my eyes get accustomed to the gloom, I make out a bucket and a heavy-duty plastic sack. The wooden floorboards are bare, and one or two are missing. I step inside. The place smells fetid, and damp, and there's something else, too, a scent of something I can't quite put a name to. It's coppery, almost metallic, underscored with a strange sweetness.

Halfway down the hall, on the right, is another door. Five steps, and I'm there. Time to declare my presence, I think. Time to own up.

'Boysie?'

The door has no handle. I push it open. Thin daylight from the window washes over the bareness of the room inside. This is a scene that nature has painted. Except for the deep scarlet spill of blood from the piglet on the floor, it's scored for blacks and whites and various shades of grey. Boysie is kneeling over the body of the dead piglet. The animal's throat hangs open and the huge knife in Boysie's hand is covered in blood. Propped against the far wall is a chainsaw.

Boysie doesn't seem the least surprised to see me. He gets to his feet and extends a bloodied hand, which I ignore.

'Reception told me you were on your way.' He wipes his hand on his jeans. 'Welcome to Dunsnorting.'

'What on earth are you doing?' The joke is in very poor taste and I tell him so.

He dismisses my qualms. The piglet, he says, will be delivered to the abattoir. He'll bag it up and carry it down the hill. By close of play, it should have been gutted and returned, barbecue-ready, to the hotel cold store. This weekend, the Zuma is already advertising a feast for a select clientele of lovers of organic pork.

'Cochinillo asado. Suckling pig. Spanish recipe. So tender you can cut it with a plate. Join us and see for yourself. Fill your boots. Enjoy.'

I'm still gazing down at this little tableau. The limp piglet, doubtless still warm, is dripping blood on to the bare boards. If I ever had any taste for suckling pork, it's gone.

'I came up to discuss that showbiz weekend idea of yours,' I tell him. 'Maybe now's not the time.'

'Now's perfect.' Boysie shakes his head. 'Just give me a hand with this little chap.'

With the dead piglet in the black plastic bag, Boysie and I leave the bungalow. I've held the bag open while Boysie dropped it in and it's much heavier than I'd expected. Boysie leaves it on one of the paving slabs while he secures the bungalow door with a heavy chain and a padlock. After he's pocketed the key, I ask him about the wild boar.

'You know about them?' He looks briefly surprised.

I nod and explain about the other gate.

'Them?' I enquire.

'We've got two,' he says. 'He and she, George and Willow. We were lucky. We got them from a bloke who traps them in the Forest of Dean. Getting them down here was a bit of a performance because they don't travel well, but we managed it in the end.'

'We?'

'Me and Deko. The dream team. Don't you just love that man? There's a road up to the back of the cottage. Place where I just did the biz.' He nods back uphill to the bungalow. 'You have to be nifty on the transfer. George especially will have you on the ground before you know it and then you've got a real problem. Deko knows no fear and they sense that. Good as gold, George was, and Willow just followed. Meek doesn't begin to cover it. With Deko around, she might have been born a lamb. Into the enclosure they went, and we've left them to it ever since.'

'You feed them?'

'Big time. They'll eat anything. Just like normal pigs. Kitchen waste? Rotten veggies? Meat that's seriously out of date? Woof. Squeal. Gone. Recycling on legs. We're blessed.'

'They're vicious?'

'They're wild. Never been domesticated. Lawless creatures, the pair of them, unless Deko happens to be around.'

'But they'd hurt you?'

'Of course. That's what happens in the wild.'

The wild. I can't help thinking of Moonie. He, too, has ended up in the wild.

Back at the hotel, Boysie disappears to get washed and changed while I settle in the lounge with a copy of *Devon Life*. It's a back issue, and by the time he returns, I'm up to speed on last year's County Show. Wild boar, by chance, has featured in a piece on game preparation. The meat, it seems, can be tough, and I show the article to Boysie when he returns to the lounge.

'They're right.' He's scanned it in seconds. 'But it's nothing a day in the slow cooker can't solve.'

'You'll be eating George and Willow? In the end?'

'Maybe. Maybe not. Just now, to be frank, we need more punters through the door.' With a flick of his fingers, he summons the waitress and orders afternoon tea. 'That little showbiz idea of mine . . .' The smile is tense. 'Any ideas?'

THIRTY-FOUR

Deko turns up at the apartment nearly an hour late. I've scoured the internet for sea bass recipes – anything but pork – and settled on a Thai offering which involves ginger, garlic, bird's eye chillies, and thinly shredded scallions. By the time he announces his arrival outside the door at the block's front entrance, I've drunk most of the first of my two bottles of Chablis.

I meet him as the lift door opens. My attempts to play sober don't fool him for a moment.

'I've brought champagne,' he says. 'But I'm guessing it may be a bit late.'

'Guess what you like, Mr Deko.' I've already seized the bottle. 'It needs five minutes in the chiller.'

'How about fifteen?' He's smiling.

'Later,' I say. 'All in good time.'

We go through to the kitchen. On reflection, I decide that the champagne is cold enough already and Deko pops the cork.

The bits and pieces for the sea bass are on a chopping board beside the cooker and Deko inspects them with interest.

'Sea bass?'

'Of course.'

'Brave woman. A delicate flavour like that? Be careful . . .'

'Have you been a control freak all your life?' I ask. 'Or is this something new?'

Deko ignores the question. He's been here before, of course, but now he's taking a serious interest in the small print.

'All those books next door? They're yours?'

'Pavel's. And there are loads more in his bedroom.'

'You used to read them to him?'

'I did. And I will again once he's back with us. Carrie did, too. Another reason why we miss her so much.' I raise my glass. 'To Carrie. Or would you prefer Amy?'

'Either. Makes no difference to me.'

'But you never knew Carrie,' I point out.

'I never knew Amy, either. Not properly.'

I've been thinking about this for more than a day now, and I'm still not sure that Deko's given me the full story.

'Properly?' I'm trying to be playful.

'Whatever,' he shrugs. He doesn't get it. 'We had a couple of conversations. It was a business thing. I thought I told you.'

'You did. Am I allowed just a tiny scintilla of doubt? Take this as a compliment, Mr Deko. You're a gorgeous man. Any woman can see that. So, what makes Carrie – sorry, Amy – so different? Was she involved with someone else? Did the thing with Jean-Paul start rather earlier than anyone thought? What was her story?'

These are questions I can sense at once that Deko doesn't need. Mention of Jean-Paul offers him a change of subject.

'He's left town. Did you know that?'

'I didn't.'

'His wife threw him out. At least that's what I've been told. He's on police bail so he can't have gone far.'

'They think he did it? Killed Carrie?'

'I expect they need to keep tabs on him. They can't have any evidence, otherwise they'd have charged him and banged him up. Motive isn't enough.'

'Motive? You mean the baby she was carrying?'

'Baby?' This appears to come as a surprise.

'Yes.' I explain about the pair of them being together since Christmas.

'And she told you about a baby? She said she was pregnant?'

'She told Pavel. And then Pavel told me.'

'You talked to her about it?'

'She was dead by then. Pavel respects a confidence. He always used to say it was in his contract.'

'Between?'

'Himself and himself. And if you think that's surreal, Mr Deko, think again. That man was seriously clever.'

'Was?'

'Is. He'll come back from the dead because that's what he does. And not only that, he'll bring news, dispatches, from the other side.' I raise my glass again. 'To Pavel.'

We work our way through the bottle while I put the new potatoes on. Champagne, as my mother used to say, is all too easy to drink. With the potatoes drained and done, I flash fry the garlic and ginger, add the chillies and the scallions, and then slip the fish on top. Five minutes, I tell myself, and we're ready.

Deko is next door, setting the table. When I appear with the meal pre-plated, he finds a couple of mats and fetches the surviving bottle of Chablis from the fridge. I'm starting to lose track of time by now, but it seems that barely minutes pass before we're talking about Carrie again.

'How close were they?' Deko is gazing at me. 'Amy and your friend Pavel?'

'Very close. That was the whole point. I think I told you. She was everything to him. She fed him, watered him, poured him gin or whisky in the evening when she stayed late, read to him, emptied him, kept him clean, kept him amused, everything you'd need if you were Pavel.'

'And him? To her?'

'Father confessor. Maybe more confessor than father but you'll get the point. I think she told him everything and I'm sure she'd have done that because she trusted him. The other bit, the father bit, was the key. Amy, Carrie, they were troubled women. He helped the pair of them, the one of them . . . Christ, I'm drunk . . .'

I try and get up but it isn't as easy as I've always assumed. On my feet, beyond unsteady, I'm trying to keep Deko in focus. He's circling the table, trying to catch me before I fall, but it's far too late. A huge bang, and then everything cuts to black before the world slips away into silence.

'You hit your head on the edge of the table. Here.'

The face above me belongs to Deko. I'm sure it does. He's looking concerned and he's holding something in his right hand. I try and reach for it but nothing happens. I watch my hand moving limply in front of my face, as if it had nothing to do with me. I feel completely helpless. Much like Pavel.

'Dear God,' I manage.

I can smell the vomit now, and I understand at once that it must be mine. I shut my eyes, try and make an effort, try and draw all these threads together, but the sheer effort is stupefying. Then comes a sensation of intense cold on a corner of my forehead and I open my eyes again to find Deko's face an inch above mine. He's found the ice tray, I tell myself. My lovely man, as capable as ever, is playing nurse, swabbing my wounds, saving my worthless life.

'You sorted out George and Willow,' I manage. 'And now you're sorting out me.'

I feel Deko's hand pause in mid-swab. Icy water is dripping down my face. My left hand, crabbing sideways, has found the pool of vomit. Not nice.

'You've been up to the hotel?' I'm watching Deko's mouth move. Remarkable.

'I have.'

'Talked to Boysie?'

'Of course. He tells me everything, that man. Does suckling pig turn you on, Mr Deko? Or is it just middle-aged women?'

'You mean you?'

'I might.' I try to swallow. I can feel particles of vomit behind my teeth. Horrible. 'Sorry about the meal,' I mutter. 'And everything else, really.' I make a brief attempt to sit up, but I know it's beyond me. 'Bed? Does that make any sense?'

Deko lifts me bodily and carries me through to the bathroom. When I tell him that Pavel's en suite might suit me better, a wet room with shower nozzles on every wall, he ignores me. Off comes my dress, my underwear, everything. Then I'm conscious of a sponge on my naked flesh, my face, my poor ruined forehead, everywhere. He's using the cold tap and that's probably sensible because I'm beginning to suspect that I'm not, after all, dying.

The bath was built for someone Deko's size, not little me. I'm lying in an inch or so of cold water and I'm starting to shiver. From time to time, Deko, my saviour, takes a tiny step back, looking down at me. I'm a work in progress, I think. What a picture.

'And what a fucking disgrace,' I murmur.

'You?'

'Me.'

He nods. He's not disagreeing, as I half want him to, but there's something else in his face, way beyond disapproval, and I'm making a big, big effort to recognize what it might be.

'Do I frighten you?' I manage at last. This is close, very close.

'You do, yes.'

'Why would that be, Mr Deko? After everything you've done? All the places you've been? All that stuff you must have seen? Why me? Why would I ever frighten you?'

'You want the truth?'

'Of course, I want the truth, but don't worry. Say what you like because I'll never remember.'

At last, a smile. He fetches a towel from the rail. Happily, the rail is switched on and the towel is warm against my flesh. Moments later, in a trick he must have learned in some circus or other, he's hauled me out of the bath and sat me on his lap.

'You're sitting on the loo?'

'I am.'

'That makes you King.' I start to giggle. 'King for the night. King for tomorrow. King forever, Mr Deko.'

He's towelling me dry. He takes a good look at my forehead and tells me it's not as bad as he'd thought.

'No stitches?'

'No.'

'But you'd have done it, wouldn't you? Needle and thread? Zig zag? Overlock? You'd have put me back together again? Made me whole? Forgiven me?'

He puts his lips close to my ear. I love the warmth of his breath on my goosebumps. Cause or effect? I don't know, don't much care.

'You'll have a huge bruise in the morning,' he whispers. 'Maybe I should keep you locked up for a day or two.'

'Why would you do that?'

'In case they think I've been beating you up.'

'They?'

'Whoever.'

'Would you like to beat me up? Would that be a turn-on? Be honest.'

He doesn't answer, just shakes his head the way you might treat a child. That's me, I think vaguely. A child. I've given my poor head, inside and out, nothing but grief. And now this lovely man is making me feel better. Pop round for a meal. And then clear up the wreckage. How much more generous can a girl be?

'Grief,' I whisper. 'If a tumour comes knocking at that lovely door of yours, say no.'

'Not today, thank you?'

'Exactly. More fucking trouble than they're worth.'

He pats me down with the towel one final time, and then carries me through to my bedroom, laying me carefully on the carpet while he turns down the bed. Moments later, I can feel the cool of the sheets beneath me and the loom of the ceiling overhead. I'm still very drunk, I know I am, but there's something I still need to rescue from this evening, and I don't want to let that precious moment pass.

'Pavel's room,' I say. 'A book. Black and white cover. Man in a Nazi uniform. Thin face.'

Deko nods, or I think he does. He returns with Jünger's diaries.

'In Paris,' I tell him. 'The man was in Paris. Up to all kinds of stuff. Deep thoughts. Pavel loved them. So did Carrie. Amy. Whoever she was.'

'You want me to read to you?'

'I do, I do. King Deko . . . reader *extraordinaire*, probably reader to a whole generation of drunks. What a pleasure. What a privilege.'

'Anything in particular?'

I close my eyes. I'm doing my best to remember. Morning time in the forest, I think. The avenue of waiting soldiers. The playing card over the heart. The volley of shots. The sagging body. 1941? 1942? I shake my head. It's hopeless. Champagne and Chablis, I think, are no fun when it comes to dates, or page numbers, or even the name of the fucking month.

'Unfair,' I murmur.

I open one eye. Deko is leafing slowly through the book, pausing from time to time, and I suddenly picture Carrie's pencilled markings beside the text, key passages preserved for Pavel's special delectation.

'She spoiled him,' I mutter. 'She spoiled that man to death.' I shake my head. What a terrible thing to say. 'I'm sorry. I'm so, so sorry.'

'What for?' Deko has looked up.

'Everything. The meal. Killing the poor fish with all those flavours. Throwing up. Everything.'

Deko shakes his head. 'No apology required,' he says.

'Just say accepted. Apologies accepted. Give me the right to be in the wrong.' I turn my head away and start to laugh. I can't help it. I can feel the cool of the pillow against my forehead, a nice feeling. And then I move my head again, looking up at Deko beside the bed. He's got to the end of the book, I can tell from the way the pages are lying, and he's got that special frown on his face that means he's concentrating.

My memory is letting me down again. What's so special about that final page? Then I get it.

'That's Moonie's mum,' I tell him. 'Carrie must have had her number.'

Deko nods. He seems to have lost interest in reading aloud to me which comes as a relief because there's no way I can direct him to the right entry.

'It's about a firing squad,' I tell him. 'They shoot a deserter and Jünger has to be there.'

'Why?'

'I can't remember. Maybe he has to bear witness. Isn't that what all history is about?' I swallow a tiny gust of nausea. 'Witness?'

Deko gazes down at me a moment, and then starts to undress. I do my best to follow this tiny piece of theatre, but my eyes keep giving up on me and the result is a series of jump cuts, faintly comic. One moment Deko is fully dressed. Then he's half naked. Then he's standing beside me in his Lonsdale Y-fronts, telling me he won't be long.

'Why?' I whisper. 'Where are you going?'

He mutters something I don't quite follow about clearing up the mess next door, then leaves the room. When I look vaguely for the book, it seems to have gone. I lie back on the pillow and pull the duvet up to my chin. I love the warmth it brings, the sense of being safe again. Fuck the mess, I think. Just leave it for tomorrow.

Sometime later, I've no idea when, Deko slips into bed beside me, arranging his long body around mine. The last thing I remember is the feel of his lips against my ear once again.

'We'll sail tomorrow,' he says. 'The tides are perfect.'

THIRTY-FIVE

The tides may be perfect but the weather – inside my head and outside the window – is anything but. I awake to a note on the pillow. Deko has departed to lay in supplies for the voyage. He's anticipating a departure around noon, and he'll call by and pick me up. He has loads of wet-weather gear aboard, plenty to keep me dry, but I might like to sort out warm clothing and something to wear ashore at Douarnenez. We'll be in company, he's written, with a French guy. Choose something tasty. We need to make an impression.

'We', I know, means me. An impression? I'm gazing at myself in the bathroom mirror. As promised, the bruise on my forehead is spectacular, a whirl of purples and blues already beginning to turn a liverish yellow. The edge of the table broke the skin, but the wound isn't deep and the blood has scabbed. Tender, yes, but nothing serious.

The pounding headache, and the certainty that I can no longer trust my stomach, are more pressing. I kneel in front of the loo, stick a finger down my throat, and throw up. I barely touched the fish last night and my stomach is virtually empty. I spend another ten minutes or so retching. A thin dribble of something green and viscous attaches itself to the back of the pan and slips slowly into the tiny puddle of vomit. It tastes of bile, which rhymes – appropriately enough – with vile. My fault, I keep telling myself. Why can I never keep the cork in the bottle?

Outside, I can hear the wind. Howling would be the wrong word, far too dramatic. The windows have yet to rattle, and the building has yet to shake, but when I return to the bedroom, I catch the dance of the halyards against the metal masts in the dinghy park, and it's started to rain. I throw on a pair of jeans and an anorak, lace my boots, and make for the door. I feel better already. Time for a brisk walk.

The promenade skirts the marina on the seaward side and the

moment I leave the shelter of the apartment block, the full force of the wind stops me in my tracks. The incoming tide is racing through the harbour narrows. Boats are straining at their moorings, tossed this way and that while the sheer force of the water, itself tormented, does its best to tear them loose. I can see the curl of the beach beyond the harbour. Wind and tide are driving a succession of waves from way out to sea. The big grey waves roll in, ever higher, and the surf rears up before thundering on to the sand. In the hands of a decent artist, or photographer, this would be a scene you might hang on your wall but just now the only word I can muster is *Amen*. I've no doubts that Deko and his sturdy Thonier will survive the hours to come. The only weak link is me.

Back in the apartment, I try out an assortment of head scarves. The best, a treasured print in subtle blues and reds I bought years ago in Marseille, hides the worst of the bruising. I fold it carefully, wind it round my head, tuck in the loose ends, and then add a large pair of sunglasses. For the first time this morning, I manage a smile. Ageing thesp prepares to rob a bank. Beyond chic.

Deko appears just after midday. He tells me the tide has turned and the front is moving nicely through. This appears to be good news. My last attempt to cross the Channel ended in a shipwreck on the Isle of Wight. A half-submerged shipping container put a hole in our boat and threatened to sink us, but as we walk down to the marina basin and climb into Boysie's RIB, I'm determined to put those terrifying hours behind me. Lightning, I tell myself, never strikes twice. Believe in this man, because it's his life on the line as well as yours.

I make myself comfortable beside Deko in the RIB, eyeing the provisions he's already brought on board. Five Tesco bags, one of them full of beer and wine bottles. He fires up the outboard and we slip carefully out through the narrow dock entrance. He's right about the tide. Someone's had a word and the churn I saw earlier has gone. The wind, too, has had second thoughts and is now blowing across the river. It feels much colder, but the rain has stopped and there's even a glimpse of blue through the rags of racing cloud.

Amen looks as beautiful as ever, untroubled, a thing of infinite grace, and I touch her lightly with my fingertips as we come along-side. Deko makes fast, and I pass up the Tesco goodies, and my own bag. The latter has seen me through countless foreign locations, and I've come to regard it as an amulet, a talisman, as well as something deeply practical. It will look after me. It will keep me safe.

'What's in here?' Its weight has taken Deko by surprise.

'A million aspirins,' I tell him, 'and the remains of the kitchen roll. You did a great job on the carpet. I never said thank you.'

Within half an hour, we're ready to leave. Deko checks the weather forecast one last time – NW wind easing to Force 5, showers and sunny intervals – and I slip the mooring rope at the bow while he holds *Amen* steady in the outgoing tide. We ease into the main channel and thread our way between the red and green buoys. We're passing the penthouse apartment block when I realize that I haven't been in touch with the hospital.

Deko is at the wheel in anorak, jeans, battered life jacket. When I ask him when we might be back, he says Tuesday, latest.

'You're sure?'

'I am. Ajax and Spurs. Champions League semi-final. We have a date at the Arms. Eight o'clock kick-off.'

'Who?'

'You and me.'

The Exmouth Arms is where the hard-core football supporters gather, a noisy mix of builders, chippies, plasterers, plumbers, and anyone else you might need to construct the house of your dreams. I went there once with H, expecting anything but football, and found theatre in the raw. I loved it but H was unimpressed. We'd abandoned the game for a curry by half time.

On the phone to the Stroke Unit, I talk to the male nurse who's been so helpful. I explain that I'm away for a couple of days, back early next week. I confirm my mobile number. Any problems, I say, and I can always take a plane back.

'Where are you off to?'

'France.'

'Pleasure? Business?'

'Both, I suspect.' I'm looking at Deko.

Another brief exchange about Pavel and the call ends. Deko wants to know how he is.

'Still out,' I say. 'But showing signs of life.'

'He's talking?'

'No.'

'He can hear OK?'

'Maybe. Maybe not.'

'But soon?'

'*Inshallah* . . . yes.'

Deko nods, says nothing. We're out in the deep-water channel now, still following the line of red and green buoys, the engine throbbing beneath our feet. The channel ends with a single red and white buoy, and maybe ten minutes later Deko hauls the boat into the wind, throttling back the engine until we're stationary in the tide.

'Sails?' He gestures up at the bare masts. 'You're happy to help?'

I haven't done any of this since my week on *Persephone*, but Deko talks me through it, and together we haul on the ropes and raise the big gaff sail. Two others follow. Deko peers up, ever the perfectionist, and we make an adjustment or two before he kills the engine, spins the big steering wheel, and *Amen* begins to shiver as the sails belly and fill. Then comes the moment when the old Thonier shakes her feathers and begins to move, and all I can hear is the lapping of the waves, and a low groan as the sails and rigging get the feel of the wind.

'Magic.' I'm looking at Deko. 'Didn't we do well?'

By nightfall, with the wind still blowing from the north-west, we're nearly fifteen miles south of the Devon coast. I'm huddled on deck in waterproofs and several layers of clothing, watching the sweep of the light from what Deko tells me is the lighthouse on Start Point. He secures the wheel and takes me down below to check our progress on the GPS readout. He says we're making seven knots against a neap tide, which appears to be good news, and suggests I get something together for supper. He's brought tins of soup and fresh bread. Nothing fancy.

I'm very happy to do his bidding, but *Amen* is wallowing in a big swell, with waves breaking over the bow from time to time, and the motion does nothing for my peace of mind. It was much, much worse than this on *Persephone*, but the way the hull shudders under the impact of the bigger waves stirs some uncomfortable memories. After I've found a saucepan in one of the cupboards in the little galley, and warmed the soup, I'm glad to be out in the fresh air again.

'Nothing for you?' Deko is cupping his big hands around the mug.

I shake my head. 'Best not to tempt fate,' I tell him. 'Eating can wait until dry land.'

I spend the entire night on deck. Mid-Channel, the swell is much heavier, and the boat begins to corkscrew, *Amen* rolling sideways off the bigger waves and burying her nose in the trough that follows. Shipping comes and goes, distant lights – red and green – in the darkness. At Deko's insistence, I'm wearing a safety harness clipped into lines laid on the deck, and from time to time water sluices over the rubber boots he's given me to wear. I'm sitting on the bare deck, using the main mast as support. By dawn, I'm exhausted. Deko must have done this passage countless times because nothing seems to trouble him, but when he tells me again to go below and get my head down, I simply nod.

My bunk lies forward of the saloon. I peel off the waterproofs but don't bother to undress. The pillow feels damp beneath my cheek and the motion of the boat is much worse. Up here, closer to the bow, it rears and plunges like some demented horse. I've taken sea sickness tablets earlier, and thankfully they seem to work, but my body – or maybe my mind – refuses to switch off, and so I lie in the half-darkness, braced against the next wave, and the wave after that, wondering what might await us when we get to Douarnenez. As playful and opaque as ever, Deko has refused to tell me what to expect. 'Pretend we're here to enjoy ourselves,' was the most he would say.

I must have gone to sleep in the end because suddenly it's much lighter in the cabin, and *Amen* seems to have made her peace with the wind and the swell. I force myself back into the waterproofs and clamber up on deck. Deko is still at the wheel. He's smoking a thin cheroot and he looks like the captain of my dreams, imperturbable, solid, a giant of a man. *Amen*, he says, has been making six knots for most of the night. He gestures forward. Way off to the left I can make out a low, grey smudge that appears to be France.

'That's Brittany?'

'Yeah. We'll raise Ushant in a couple of hours.'

Brittany, I think. I check my watch. Nearly seven. The last time I was with my mum in Perros-Guirec, it was Christmas and I woke to drifts of snow beyond the bedroom window.

Just the sight of land is a tonic. I go below and spoon instant coffee into a couple of mugs. *Amen* is still rolling but I've learned how to brace myself and the motion feels gentler, kinder. Back on deck with the coffees, I find Deko with a phone to his ear. His French is much better than I'd expected.

'Douarnenez?' I hand him the mug.

'Early afternoon.' He's returned the phone to a pocket in his anorak. 'The guy's called Dominique. You'll love him.'

THIRTY-SIX

We make better time to Douarnenez than Deko had expected. On the radio, he's requested a deep-water berth inside the jetty in the old harbour, which he appears to know well. The berth is available, and we motor slowly in while I use Deko's binoculars to look for the house across the bay that used to belong to my aunt. We round the end of the jetty and I'm ready to clamber up the rusty old ladder and take the first of the mooring lines that Deko throws up.

It's a beautiful day. The wind has dropped and the old town is bathed in sunshine. As a child, I used to think that Brittany was built entirely of granite, which can give the towns and villages a slightly forbidding look, but in a light like this the little houses climbing up from the water are definitely in the mood for summer. If Farrow & Ball want a new shade on their colour chart, I think, they could do worse than Breton Grey, lightly seamed with yellow lichen.

Deko joins me on the quayside in time to exchange a handshake and kisses on both cheeks from a portly official who seems to be in charge. I watch this courtly little piece of French theatre, aware that Deko is no stranger here. He introduces me as his deckhand, a job description that draws a roar of approval from the Harbour Master, and I, too, get the treatment.

'Vous êtes française?' He's looking me up and down.

'Oui.'

'Il vous a tabassé?' He touches his own forehead.

Has Deko beaten me up? I nod. Does our new friend have a number for the Commissariat, by any chance?

Mention of the police station produces more laughter, then Deko taps his watch. Work to do, he murmurs. A pleasure to be back in Douarnenez.

We return to the boat. Deko checks the mooring lines and then leads the way below deck. Beyond the bunk spaces forward of the saloon is a wooden partition. Deko unlocks the door, reaches in to find a light switch and suddenly I'm staring at a scatter of what looks like scrap iron: old anchor chain, engine bits, metal fence posts. Deko stirs it with his foot. Underneath is a plywood floor. This, he says, has to come up. But first we need to shift what he calls the pig iron.

'Why? Why are we doing this?'

He looks down at me. For some reason he's smiling.

'Because tomorrow night,' he says, 'we'll be picking up a consignment of stuff out at sea. You'll ask what and I guess now's the time to tell you. We're talking a hundred and fifty kilos of cocaine, uncut. If you don't want me to go on, you have a choice. You can leave now and pretend nothing's happened. Or you can leave and call the police for real. Your mobile's still charged?'

'Yes.' I'm staring at him. I should be amazed by his boldness, by how reckless he can be, but somehow I'm not. 'There's a third choice?'

'Of course. You can stay aboard. Help me out. That weight of cocaine, cut on the street, is worth four and a half million quid. That's not what will be coming to us but it's quite close.'

'Us?'

'Yeah. If it all goes to rat shit, we'd be looking at ten years at least. Probably more. That's something else to think about.'

'Fuck.'

'Exactly.' Half a day in the sunshine has given him the beginnings of a tan. 'Your call, *ma chérie*. Time waits for no man.'

I'm looking down at the tangle of scrap iron. Cocaine, I think. So simple. So obvious. Four and a half million pounds for a single trip. That sort of windfall, and Deko's money worries will be well and truly over.

'So, the stuff goes where?'

'On top of the ballast. There's a special cavity. We move all this crap, get the floor up. Underneath there's plenty of room. We do the prep now, get everything ready, and sail tomorrow night. We'll make a rendezvous offshore where no one will see us. The weather gods are on our side. High pressure for at least a couple of days. A hundred and fifty kilos? Say one hour, max. A couple of minutes to settle up and we're on our way.' He nods down at the scrap iron. 'Afterwards, you con us north while I get everything sorted down here.'

'You've done this before?'

'Twice.' He's laughing. 'How do you think a Dutchman with no money comes to buy all that property? Nursing homes? Houses on the Beacon? A Breton Thonier? How does he put food in his mouth? Have money for the pub? Have time to meet a gorgeous woman and whisk her off to France? I could try for a bank loan, but I'd never get past the door. Cocaine is money without the paperwork. Call it investment. Call it what you like. *Ça marche.*'

It works. I nod. H, and Flixcombe Manor, and now Pavel's penthouse, are the living proof. Despite numerous invitations to sample what H always calls 'the marching powder', I've steered clear of cocaine all my life. How strange it should finally catch up with me in the bowels of a Breton Thonier in a little harbour I know so well.

Deko is beginning to get impatient. I recognize the signs.

'Well . . .?' he says.

I mumble something about all this being a bit sudden. 'Do I get a moment here? Can I take a proper look at the script? Or is this strictly improvisation?'

The latter thought delights him. He gives me a hug and then bends to haul the first length of chain towards the door.

'I'll take that as a yes,' he grunts. 'We'll sell the film rights later.'

We work in the forepeak for the rest of the afternoon. By six o'clock, the scrap iron is stored in the bunk space and Deko has removed the false floor and its supporting timbers. I've no idea what 150 kilos of cocaine look like, but there's plenty of space on top of the concrete ballast and Deko is meticulous when it comes to calculations.

Afterwards, we treat ourselves to a beer on deck. We're both filthy, caked in salt from the crossing, but Deko – to my relief – has booked a room in a nearby hotel. We have a date, he says, with a Creole friend of his.

'Dominique? The guy you were talking to on the phone?'

'Yes. Half seven. Pipi's place. Another mate. *Moules* to die for.'

Deko locks up, and we go ashore. The hotel is tiny, three rooms at the most, and the woman who owns it greets Deko like a son. She has a very French interest in yours truly, looking me over with a frankness I always find oddly refreshing, and despite the state of my forehead I sense she must approve because she sends us upstairs with a bottle of champagne and a couple of glasses. We open the champagne and drink the first glass under the shower. Deko soaps me all over and I return the favour before we retire to bed. We finish the bottle, make love, and sleep a little. After more than twenty-four hours at sea, I couldn't be happier. Would my Aunt Beatrice approve? Should I be sitting in an interview room in the Commissariat, telling some *flic* what a bad man I've fallen for? *Tant pis.* I don't care.

Pipi runs a restaurant tucked into one of the narrow side streets on the hill that climbs up from the harbour. More kisses and tall glasses of *kir* while Deko catches up with the local news. The more of these people I'm meeting, the more I get the impression that half the town are in on the cocaine biz. Once, I think, this prosperous little town got rich on sardines, a hard living wrestled from the sea, processed and tinned in factories along the waterfront, and then dispatched to the far corners of the motherland. Now it's become a magnet for tourists, and – I suspect – regular consignments of the white powder ghosting in after dark.

Dominique, according to Deko, is the key link in the chain. He appears from nowhere in jeans, T-shirt, and flip-flops. He's very black, very slight, with beautiful hands and the face of an angel. Despite his looks, his bushy Afro is threaded with grey and he carries himself with a sense of something I can only call gravity. Deko calls him the Thin Controller. The nickname doesn't translate well into French but watching him and Deko put their heads together, I understand at once who's in charge. Dominique talks in a whisper, never raising his voice, but his eyes never leave Deko's face.

We eat fresh fish – *loup de mer* – and drink sparingly. Deko scribbles a long sequence of digits on a piece of paper and gives it to Dom. Dom studies it a moment before leaving the restaurant to make a call. When I ask Deko what's going on he says it has to do with the deal on the cocaine. Funds are waiting in an account in Gibraltar. A coded message tomorrow night will release them.

'This is your account?'

'No.' He shakes his head. 'It's third party but I control it. Everyone plays the same game. You don't need to know the details.'

'And afterwards? Once you've sold on?'

'The money gets washed. It goes in dirty and comes out clean. That's trickier but we're getting better at it.'

'We?'

He smiles at me, his big hand over mine, and changes the subject. Dom, he says, is in touch with a yacht offshore, confirming tomorrow night's meet. The money will only be released once we've taken delivery.

'We get tomorrow off? During the day?'

'We do.'

'A girl can go shopping?'

'She can.'

We say *au revoir* to Dom in a car park down by the harbour. We take it in turns to shake hands – no kisses this time – before the Thin Controller climbs stiffly into a sleek Mercedes and purrs away.

'Paris tonight, and Lyon tomorrow.' Deko is still watching the car. 'When does that little man ever sleep?'

THIRTY-SEVEN

I wake up late, gone nine. My mobile is ringing and a glance at caller ID tells me it's the male nurse at the Stroke Unit. I get out of bed, leaving Deko still asleep, and take the call in the tiny bathroom. Pavel, says the nurse, is now fully conscious. The night staff checked him at dawn and found him able to move his head.

'Anything else?'

'Not yet. But it's a start. And we wanted you to be the first to know. Holiday going OK?'

'Perfect.' I feel strangely deflated. 'He can't speak?'

'No. But he responds when we talk to him, tiny facial movements, so we think his hearing's OK. Fingers crossed, eh?'

The call ends and I slip back into the bedroom to find Deko up on one elbow, rubbing the sleep from his eyes. The news about Pavel seems to please him. Like me, he wants to know whether he can speak or not.

'Alas, no,' I say. 'At least not yet.'

'And his hands? Can he use his hands?'

'No, but that's been the case since the accident. He can hear, though, and it seems he can nod or shake his head. I'm not sure that qualifies as conversation but at least he's still in there somewhere.'

We spend the morning wandering the streets of Douarnenez. Deko wants to show me the museum and we spend a couple of hours surrounded by sepia photographs, exploring the history of this little port. To my shame I never knew that Douarnenez was the first town to elect a communist *maire*. We emerge into the sunshine, hand in hand. In truth, I'm only half taking all this in because I'm still trying to process the consequences of yesterday's little bombshell.

As an actress, I'm used to the challenge of new personas. For my entire working life, it's been literally my business to become someone else, but this latest role, I suspect, may be forever. Has Deko turned me into a drug dealer? A low life? A criminal? *Une femme au milieu?* And does that put me in the same league as H? This latter thought has a pleasing irony but events last year, when Malo got himself entangled with the cocaine biz, tell me that the marching powder can lead to somewhere very dark indeed. And so in the end I settle for 'smuggler', because it feels more honourable. This is denial, of course, but it definitely helps me cope. I've become a character in a period movie, I tell myself, the dashing blonde with her handsome beau, always one step ahead of the Revenue Men.

At lunchtime, I persuade Deko to take the walk through the pine trees to the nearby beach. *La plage du Ris* is truly spectacular, a deep crescent of startling white sand that seems to stretch for ever. Just the first glimpse of it through the trees conjures all kind of memories. We take off our sandals and splash through the shallows while I tell Deko about long-ago picnics, and rockpool expeditions, and the afternoon when I got into trouble in an offshore current and nearly drowned. The latter story briefly gets his attention, but I know his mind's elsewhere. Time and again, his gaze drifts back towards the distant harbour, and by four o'clock, we're back on board.

We leave Douarnenez within the hour. Deko takes on more fuel at a pontoon in the *Port de Plaisance* and we motor west, no sails, following the line of the coast. Mercifully, the sea is calm, not a whisper of wind. Out beyond the headland at Plogoff is a little island, *l'Ile de Sein*. Local boats use the channel in between, while the bigger ships – wary of the Breton coast – are way offshore. This leaves a discreet little area west of the lighthouse where, in Deko's phrase, we can park up and relax. No snoopers. No watching eyes. No Revenue Men.

Perfect? Safe? *Une bonne idée?* To be honest, I've no idea. The fact that Deko has done this before, not once but twice, is deeply comforting. I know he's no stranger to risk, but I trust his competence because I've seen him in action, and I sense he wouldn't be doing this without weighing the odds. H always tells me that you've got to be stupid, as well as unlucky, to get caught out in the drugs biz and that, too, is a comfort. What little I know about French prisons fills me with dread.

We're passing the lighthouse as dusk shrouds the low line of the coast. Every French child, and every English tourist, knows this landmark. It features on a million calendars, normally the very centre of a huge white explosion of spume and surf, and it's become a kind of watermark that badges everything Breton. Deko, at the wheel, points out the heavy black letters on the grey stonework, *Ar Men,* Breton for *The Rock.* This, of course, is the name Deko has adopted for his beloved Thonier. In its adapted form – *Amen* – it's taken on a slightly religious overtone and in view of the hours to come, I'm wondering whether now might be the moment for a prayer or two, but then I tell myself that trust is a much simpler proposition.

'That's you.' I'm pointing to the lighthouse. '*Ar Men.* My rock.'

An hour or so later, dark now, Deko consults his GPS and then throttles the engine back until we're drifting, almost motionless. For minutes on end, we stand together in the darkness, waiting for the next fierce stab of light from *Ar Men*, watching the beam sweep towards us, briefly turn everything bone white, and then move on.

Deko has lit another cheroot. The yacht we're due to meet, he says, has just sailed across the Atlantic. Three weeks ago, it left a Caribbean island called Aruba. On board are a mixed bunch of Colombians and Antillaises under a maverick American skipper called Noah. After us, she'll probably be heading south again to another island called Groix for a second drop-off.

'And then?'

'They go ashore. Probably La Rochelle. And party.'

The yacht appears three hours later. It's much bigger than I'd expected, the long hull a shape in the darkness, then tall masts caught for a moment in the beam from the lighthouse. Deko is talking to the skipper on his phone. The skipper has an American accent and laughs a lot. Very slowly, the yacht approaches and I glimpse sallow faces on deck. In a rough sea, a rendezvous like this would be very difficult, but tonight the conditions are perfect.

Deko has already hung fenders from the rail and I feel a gentle bump as the big yacht comes alongside. Hands reach up for mooring lines. Then Deko is swinging the long wooden boom out towards the yacht. A big blue net I've seen earlier below is now dangling from the end of the boom. Crew on the yacht reach up to secure it and moments later they're filling it with plastic-wrapped blocks the size of a hardback book. Deko calls them 'bricks'.

'How ya doing?' This has to be Noah.

Deko reaches down and shakes his hand. Noah says they've had the dream crossing, the westerly trades much kinder than usual, nothing to speak of in the way of weather. When Deko asks about rumours of early retirement, Noah says they're true.

'Got myself a little island.' He's laughing again. 'And three women to go with it. I'd invite you over, but I don't want no fox in the fucking coop. Good luck, buddy. I'll be over in a minute.'

Deko swings the boom back in and we unpack the first net full of bricks. Earlier, I'd cleared a space in the saloon. Deko has produced a pair of electronic scales and it's my job to weigh each brick and keep a tally as they come in. We carry them down the narrow stairs. I can just manage three bricks at a time. Each of these, according to Deko, is worth thirty thousand pounds. An armful, therefore, is ninety thousand pounds. That's a lifetime's supply of Chanel No 5, I tell myself. Truly weird.

Quicker than I ever expected, the transfer is over. I count the bricks twice. Each weighs exactly one kilo and in all there are 150. Some of them are marked *Diamante*, others *Brillante*. Deko checks one more time, just to make sure, and then we're joined by Noah, who's clambered aboard with a couple of bottles of bourbon. I rustle up three glasses and we crack the first bottle open. Noah is scruffy-handsome, slighter than Deko, but carries himself with the same sense of something I can only call entitlement. These guys, I think, are truly the Masters of the Universe. They play for the highest stakes, and they rarely lose. They also have a lot of fun in the process and it shows. Fuck the odds. Death to the Revenue Men.

Just do it. Do I feel guilt? A little. Am I impressed by the sheer smoothness of this operation? Alas, yes.

Deko offers the piece of paper I saw in the restaurant last night. Noah scans it quickly and then makes a call on his mobile. He spells out the line of digits, listens for confirmation, then keeps the line open while Deko gives him the shot of bourbon. We all clink glasses and toss the scorching liquid back.

'Another, buddy?'

Noah shakes his head. He's listening to a voice at the other end. '*Gracias*,' he mutters, then looks up at us. 'Done.'

Done. The two men are back on deck. I hear their footsteps overhead as Noah heads for the ladder and leaves. Then comes the cough of an engine, and I imagine the big yacht vanishing into the darkness, pursued by the restless beam of the lighthouse.

Done. Four and a half million pounds' worth of cocaine. It occupies all of the table and most of the floor beneath, a neatly organized spread of 100 per cent pure cocaine, a market guaranteed, eager takers in every city on earth, money for virtually nothing. I start transferring the bricks to the space Deko has made on top of the ballast, picking my way between the bunks, trying to avoid the pile of scrap metal. In the forepeak, I kneel, arranging the bricks carefully side by side, exactly the way Deko has showed me. One layer takes thirty bricks. I start another, and then a third, stooping back and forth in the half darkness. By now Deko has started the engine and we're underway, *Amen* moving sweetly north, away from the lighthouse.

Finally, I've finished. The door is still open behind me and the plastic jigsaw of wrapped and taped bricks gleam in the spill of light from the saloon. A couple of days ago, before we set out on this voyage, I'd never have dreamed of an image like this and I'm tempted to take a photo on my phone but already I'm wary of what might end up as evidence in court. Be careful, I tell myself. No footprints in the snow.

Back up on deck, Deko stands at the wheel. Behind us, I can still see the regular sweep from the *Ar Men* lighthouse, and when I look up the blackness of the night sky is pricked by a trillion tiny stars. There's also the hint of a new moon, no more than a creamy yellow shaving, hanging above the horizon.

'Three hundred and fifty-six.' Deko nods down at the compass in the binnacle. 'Almost due north. We're making four knots. No need to hurry. Off Ushant in time for an early lunch.'

He stands aside, letting me take control. My eyes are accustomed to the darkness by now and I play with the big wooden wheel, the spokes between my fingers, moving it left and right, trying to get a feel for the boat. Deko has warned me that she's slow to respond and he's right. Take her to port, feel her gently heel, and the temptation – at once – is to over-correct. Take her to starboard too soon, and exactly the same thing happens. Deko watches me for a minute or two as we zig-zag slowly north. At last, the compass needle settles on 356 degrees, and he lights another cheroot.

'Everything stowed?'

'Yes.'

'Enjoying yourself?'

'Yes.'

'No regrets?'

'None.' I shoot him a look. 'Am I being naïve, here? Or is it always this easy?'

He chuckles. It's a lovely sound, utterly in keeping with the velvet peace we seem to have found, everything behaving itself, everything on our side. Down below, I think, four and a half million pounds are waiting for their master to tuck them up and kiss them goodnight.

'What will you do when we get to Exmouth?' I ask.

'Go to the Arms and watch the football.'

'That's not my question.'

'I know it's not.'

'So, what's the answer? We arrive with all this stuff. You've put the floor back, put down a layer of whatever, piled the scrap iron on top. What then?'

Deko is standing by the rail, staring into the darkness, the tip of the cheroot glowing between his fingers, and I'm starting to wonder whether he heard my last question.

'You forgot the oil,' he says.

'Oil?'

'Old engine oil. That goes on last, just a sprinkle. It smells foul. No dog would ever get a sniff of the coke through that.'

I smile, checking the compass again. Deko breaks the law the way he cooks, I think, with minute attention to every last detail. I'm wondering whether to ask him again about what happens next but then decide it can wait. Back in Douarnenez, I bought fillets of sea bass for this morning's celebratory lunch. As soon as he's finished down below, I'll surrender the wheel and set to in the galley. No wine this time.

'Look.' Deko is pointing back towards the coast. There's the faintest hint of dawn in the east, the day rekindled, and even as we watch the darkness seems to be vanishing.

'Time for you to clock on, Mr Deko,' I tell him. 'And a cup of coffee for the helmsman might be nice.'

The coffee never happens. I stand at the wheel for the next couple of hours, listening to the sound of hammering from down below as the sky lightens and the sun comes up. Tiny ropes of cloud plait and re-plait over the distant coastline. From time to time, far out to sea, I catch a smudge of what might be smoke from one of the bigger ships but otherwise – apart from a lone trawler heading back towards Douarnenez – we're completely alone. It's a strange feeling but under the circumstances I'm more than grateful.

Last night, back in the hotel, I asked Deko why he hadn't chosen to make a UK landfall somewhere more remote than Exmouth. Some little creek in Cornwall, say, or even west Wales. Wouldn't that be safer? Rather than a busy estuary like the Exe? He said he understood my thinking but I was wrong. Turn up somewhere as a complete stranger and you immediately attract attention. Return to a mooring where everyone knows you, and no one turns a hair. Deko's back. Big deal.

By nine o'clock I think I can make out a low smudge to the north that might be Ushant. Minutes later, Deko emerges on deck to confirm my suspicion. The goodies, as he quaintly terms our cargo, are now beyond the reach of the most conscientious rummage crew. He's laid a thin coat of cement over the false floor and as soon as it's dried, he'll re-stow the scrap iron and add a splash or two of engine oil. Only if you physically take the boat apart will anyone find the cocaine.

He takes the wheel, checks the heading, and invites me to inspect the results of his efforts in the forepeak. When I suggest we eat in an hour or so, he nods.

'Whenever,' he says. 'You'll find garlic, ginger and chillies in one of those bags. The fish is in the fridge. *Bonne cuisine, quoi?*'

Good luck in the kitchen. I go below and make my way for'ard. I can smell wet cement and a glance through the still-open door reveals a floor that might never have been lifted. Clever.

Back in the galley, I boil water for coffee and add two spoons of sugar to Deko's mug. When I take it back up to the deck, he's standing at the wheel, whistling a tune I faintly recognize. 'Over the Rainbow', I think. Very appropriate.

'Hungry?'

'Starving.'

I return to the galley. The light isn't good down here. I find new potatoes and a head of broccoli in one of the Tesco bags. I put the potatoes on the stove to boil, chop the broccoli into florets, and put them aside to be steamed. I peel and chop the garlic and ginger, and slide a knife the length of the chillies. The fillets of sea bass, as promised, are still in the fridge. I fetch them out. Unwrapped, they lie on the tiny work surface.

I have a problem with rogue pin bones in my fish, and when I test the flesh with my fingertips I can tell they haven't been filleted properly. Pin bones are a pain. To get them out in one go you need a pair of fish tweezers. I have a pair at home in London, a present from Pavel when he was still mobile and loved my cooking, and they're perfect for the job.

I'm looking around the cluttered space that is the galley. Deko, I know, also adores fish. Given his attention to detail, he might have a pair of tweezers on board. There are just three drawers where I might find them, and they're secured by a vertical bungee cord to keep them shut during rough weather. The first is full of knives, forks, spoons and anything else you might need for the table. The second, more promising, contains a selection of cooking implements. I rummage among the peelers, garlic crushers, draining spoons, and sundry other items. No tweezers. The third drawer is at floor level and is difficult to open.

I get down on my knees, remove the bungee cord, and wrestle with the drawer until it begins to give. One final yank, and I pull it open. At first it seems to contain nothing but an assortment of drying-up cloths. Then I spot a wooden box at the back. Curious, I fetch it out. The box once contained Belgian chocolates and is secured with a little swively thing in black metal. I hook it back and open the box. Inside is one of those waterproof pouches with a neck lanyard that dinghy sailors and kitesurfers use. I recognize it at once because Carrie had one. Inside the pouch is a mobile phone.

I gaze at it for a long moment. It's an iPhone, an old model, and when I switch it on there's plenty of battery left. I've learned in my life that the quickest way to find out who owns a phone is to go to the Gallery icon. Photos are always the giveaway.

The drawer is still open. *Amen*, untroubled, is puttering along, the steady beat of the engine beneath my feet. I can picture Deko at the wheel, enjoying the sunshine. Should he decide to leave the wheel and pay me a visit, I'll hear him coming.

Just now, I've forgotten all about the fish tweezers and the pin bones. What interests me far more is this phone. Why the box? Why the bottom drawer? Has Deko had some reason to hide it?

I access the Gallery and seconds later I find myself staring at a grid of photos. There's no mistaking the set of the face, those perfect lips, the deep-green eyes. Carrie. Or Amy. Or whoever she really was. She features in most of them, smiling at the camera in a variety of settings, as gorgeous as ever. But then I realize that no one takes so many selfies, and that this phone must belong to someone else.

I swipe to a new grid of shots, and this time it's more than obvious that she's not alone. Neither is she clothed. I've never seen Carrie naked but here she is, more beautiful than ever, offering herself to the camera. Some of the poses are explicit, a present you'd only offer someone you loved. Then, on the bottom row, my finger hesitates over another shot.

I gently touch the screen. Milliseconds later I'm looking at a naked Carrie pleasuring an erection I recognize only too well. Deko, I think. With his Amy.

THIRTY-EIGHT

For the second time in twenty-four hours, I'm thanking God I'm an actress. The photos on the phone, no matter who they belong to, tell a story I've never wanted to believe. The man I'm sharing this boat with, the man whom I've bedded, the man who's just turned me into a cocaine smuggler, the man who can put me in a prison cell for a very long time, was Carrie's lover. The implications are beyond troubling. When did this affair of theirs really end? The more explicit photos are date-stamped November last year. Does that make the baby Carrie was carrying Deko's? If so, what happened to bring it all to an end?

Beyond this, of course, are a series of other questions. I've absolutely no doubt that Deko has sought to control every last detail of his colourful life. He's that kind of man. Nothing, and no one, would ever be permitted to stand in his way. That's why, in certain lights, he's so commanding, so attractive. He has total self-belief. And unlike the rest of us, that makes him indomitable.

So, what really happened to Carrie that night she died? Was it really Moonie who found his way back to her basement flat? Or is there some other explanation? I shake my head. Playing detective means keeping your head and just now, to be frank, I'm scared witless. I've got this plot hopelessly wrong, and the implications – should Deko find out about the phone – don't bear contemplation. Somehow, I have to busk my way through the next day or so before we make landfall. Only then might I have the presence of mind to work out what to do next.

'Up here or below?' I say brightly.

I'm standing on the top ladder, playing the mistress who knows a thing or two about cooking sea bass. The phone is safely back in its wooden box, and all the drawers are firmly closed and secured with the bungee cord. Everything is ready except the fish itself. Five minutes, I tell Deko, is all I need to serve the meal of his dreams.

'Down below.' He gestures forward. 'Ushant's still five K away. It's low tide. We can drift for half an hour at least.'

'Fine.' My heart sinks. The last thing I want to share just now is the half-darkness of the saloon. Intimacy is one thing. Menace is quite another. 'Are you sure you don't want it up here? I can steer. The sun's lovely. We can take turns to eat.'

Unlike me, Deko would make a great detective. Something in my voice has caught his attention. Maybe I've overdone the brightness. Schoolgirl error. Unforgiveable.

'You OK?'

'I'm fine. Just a little queasy.'

'In this sea? When you've done so well so far?'

'Yeah.' I shrug. 'I dunno. Maybe it's the smell down there. Wet cement was never my thing.'

'Sure.' I can tell he's far from convinced. 'Up here, then. *En pleine air.*'

Out in the open. I retreat to my cave, relieved to be spared his presence across the table. The frying pan is still on the stove, the dash of olive oil still hot. When I turn up the heat and drop the fish in I realize my hands are shaking. I close my eyes for a moment, then swallow hard. To my knowledge, there's only one other person on this boat. The footsteps thump-thumping down the stairs from the deck have to be his. The missing knife, I think. The missing knife in his kitchen. Japanese. A Kamikoto. The biggest in the set. Razor sharp. And Carrie, poor Carrie, her belly ripped open in the darkness of her bedroom.

I'm still standing at the stove. There's just enough room for Deko to squeeze in behind me. I can feel him pressing against me. Then those big hands close over my breasts.

'Something I said?' he whispers.

'Nothing. Absolutely nothing.'

'You're sure? Just say. I'm a big boy. I can take it.'

Big boy? Oh, yes. One tiny little part of me wants to shake him free, wants to throw hot oil in his face, wants to know the truth behind those hideous photos. Why the lies? Why the denials? Why the careful pretence? Instead, all too predictably, I try and confect a pleasurable squirm or two under his touch and tell him I've got to turn the fish fillets over before they burn.

'Maybe later,' I say. 'Yeah?'

He doesn't answer me. I feel his lips settling briefly on the nape of my neck in a parting kiss. Then he's gone.

I'm really shaking now, both inside and out. I steady myself, turning the gas off, moving the pan aside to let the fillets cool. Just the sight of them, after what's just happened, makes me nauseous. Maybe I should give in. Maybe I should deliver his plate of precious sea bass and throw up over the side. Then, at least, he might leave me alone.

I briefly warm the plates over the pan, then dish up. Steady, I tell myself. Stay in control. You can survive this, and you must. For Pavel's sake, for your own sake, maybe even for Moonie's sake. I make it up to the deck, the plate in one hand, the stair rail in the other. Deko's smile at the sight of the sea bass is unfeigned.

'Wonderful,' he says as he takes the plate. 'Any chance of a knife and fork?'

'Shit.' I make a big thing of playing the idiot. 'You want wine?'

'No.' He shakes his head. 'This is perfect.'

I fetch him a knife and fork and take over at the wheel while he stands at the rail, inspecting Ushant from afar, forking the food into his mouth. After a while, almost absently, he shakes the remains into the sea and returns to the wheel.

'Have I told you I love you?' he says.

'No. Never.'

'Do you believe me?'

'I'd like to.'

'Then you should,' he kisses me lightly on my sorry bruise, 'because it's true.'

We push on through the afternoon, clearing Ushant and setting course for the Devon coast. In the end, I passed on the sea bass, blaming some treacherous tummy bug, an excuse Deko seemed happy to accept. The sun is still out and the deck beneath my bare feet is warm. I fetch a couple of blankets from down below and sit on them with my back against the mast once again. I've noticed over the course of our brief relationship that Deko is very comfortable with silence, and this is another blessing. Just now, I'm not sure I could handle any kind of conversation.

Towards six o'clock, Deko announces that he needs to see whether the cement has dried. If so, he'll drag the scrap metal back into the forepeak, and after that, he'd rather like a brief kip.

'You OK, up here?'

I get to my feet, fighting a wave of dizziness, and say yes. We're on the edge of the Channel shipping lanes now but I can see nothing in either direction, and once I've taken the wheel Deko checks on the GPS down below. I do my best to steady the needle on the compass heading he's given me, thankful that I have the deck to myself. Then his head appears in the hatch.

'We're bang on,' he says. 'Any problems, give me a shout.'

As if. Minutes later, I hear him dragging the heavy chain into the forepeak. Then comes the clang-clang of assorted metal before silence once again descends. He's covered it all up, I think. Just like he's hidden everything else in his life.

For the next couple of hours, we push ever deeper into the English Channel. I'm tempted to reach for the throttle and go faster but I know there's no point. Already, Deko has told me that we'll be lying off the Devon coast until daybreak. Fishermen are laying more and more lobster and crab pots on the seabed, tethered by a rope to a buoy above. The buoys are impossible to spot in the dark and it's all too easy to end up with the rope fouling the propeller, a situation that would leave us requesting a tow. The last thing *Amen* needs is this kind of attention, and so we'll park up again, and make ourselves comfortable, and wait for daylight. Only hours ago, I could think of nothing more delicious. Now, the prospect fills me with dread.

THIRTY-NINE

According to Deko, the beam from the lighthouse on Start Point is visible from twenty miles away. The first clue is a flicker of light on the horizon, coming and going, but as we get closer, I can see the beam reaching towards us. Closer still, it washes Deko's face with a rich yellow light. He hasn't shaved for days and if I wasn't so preoccupied, I'd say it suited him. Even now, knowing what I know, I feel just the faintest stir when his face briefly emerges from the darkness. I fucked that man, I tell myself, because he was irresistible. And now I must cope with the consequences.

It's gone three in the morning when Deko finally kills the engine and we drift to a halt. We're safely outside the crab-pot zone but there's a four-knot tide running beneath us and Deko says he has no choice but to lower the anchor. I give him a hand with the big winch up for'ard. He slips the brake on the chain and lets the anchor drop to the seabed. We're both peering into the darkness over the bow. Deko has a torch. He pools the light on the anchor chain and says he thinks we're fast. Fast appears to be good news. *Amen* is shivering in the tide now, held by the anchor. I know exactly how she feels.

'Cold?' He has his arm round me.

I want to say no. I want to tell him I need to stay out here on deck for as long as it takes for the sun to come up and chase the darkness away because then we can be on the move again. I want the feel of dry land beneath my feet, the comfort of my own bed, the knowledge that the apartment door is treble-locked, and that this nightmare has come to an end.

'I'm fine,' I tell him.

'You're not. You're shivering. Come below.'

I tell myself I have no choice. What would be truly unthinkable is Deko finding out that I've seen the photos. Should that happen, I tell myself, then I might not get home at all.

I follow him down to the saloon.

'Coffee?' I suggest.

'No.' He shakes his head. 'We should get our heads down. There's room now up for'ard. Yeah?'

I'm not quite sure what this innocent little invitation really means. The last time I got my head down as far as Deko is concerned was on his sofa on the Beacon. And the last time Carrie did something similar, he took a bloody photo.

'You're right.' I manage a stagey yawn. 'I'm knackered.'

We clamber into adjoining bunks, an arm's length between us. For a minute or two, hoping against hope, I think he may have gone to sleep. Wrong.

'It'll be better when we get back,' he murmurs, 'I promise.'

'Better how?'

'You're tired. You've never been a drug dealer before. Never rehearsed.'

In any other context this could be funny. Being a drug dealer, I can cope with. Sleeping within touching distance of someone I thought I knew is very different.

'I'm a smuggler,' I say. 'It's more romantic.'

'Sure. But tell me it wasn't a shock.'

'Finding out?'

'Yes.'

'About you?'

'About the cocaine. What it's funded. Why I do all this stuff.'

'Of course.' I nod in the darkness, not knowing what else to say.

There's a brief silence. Listen hard and I can hear the murmur of the tide against the wooden hull.

'Should I have told you earlier?' he asks at last. 'Would that have made a difference?'

'How?'

'Would you still have come?'

It's a good question. When I tell him I sort of knew already, he laughs.

'I don't believe you,' he says.

'It's true. I know it's hindsight but there had to be a way you paid for all the stuff you do. To be honest I never thought too hard about it because there was no need. You never settled your bills and you owed the taxman a fortune but that didn't seem to matter so I just assumed you'd got it all in hand.'

'You're right, I had. Give me a week or two and I'll be square with everyone. And even after that, we'll still be rich.'

I roll over, telling myself this might be interesting if I need it later.

'So how do you sell all that stuff? You have a buyer? Someone you know?'

'Of course.'

'Someone local?'

'Christ, no. Exmouth's a lovely place but it doesn't have that kind of money.'

'London, then?'

'Bristol. One phone call and the man is on the motorway. We meet at a farm a friend of his owns. We do the biz. He won't buy the lot, not straight off, but I'd be surprised if he doesn't want at least half, maybe more. That's going to be a couple of million.'

'In cash?'

'Euros or dollars. The pound's sick. You have to think ahead.'

'And he can lay hands on money like that?'

'Of course.' A chuckle this time. 'This is cocaine. It sells itself.'

I nod, struck once again by how simple these transactions are. If you're selling the marching powder and you have the bollocks, as H once told me, you have no option but to get very, very rich.

'And will this little consignment be enough?'

'You want the honest answer?'

'Yes.'

'Then that depends.'

'On what? Am I allowed to ask?'

'Of course.'

'Then tell me.'

There's another silence, much longer. Then I hear him stirring in the bunk. For a moment I think he may be coming over to join me but I'm wrong. He's turned over, and when I risk a look, I can see the pale disk of his face staring at me.

'It depends on us,' he says quietly. 'It depends on what you want.'

'Why me?'

'Because what I have in mind might need another trip or two. But only if you say yes.'

'To what?'

'To you coming with me.'

'Where?'

'The States, first. There are places along the New England coast I've never been, up near the Canadian border, Kennebunkport, Bar Harbor. I've read about them, heard stories from other people, and they all say the same thing. Take a look. Hunker down. Stay awhile. Then we could head north again, up towards the Saint Lawrence, maybe as far as Quebec. Nova Scotia is another place I've always dreamed about.'

I nod. Twenty-four hours ago I'd have jumped at a proposition like this, even with Pavel as sick as he is.

'It sounds amazing,' I tell him. 'You're telling me *Amen* would be our home?'

'Sure. For as long as you could cope.'

'With what?'

'Me.'

'Me?' It's my turn to laugh. If this was a movie, I think, Pavel would have written the dialogue. Irony is too small a word.

'Why are you laughing?'

'Because it sounds so . . .' I shrug. 'Plausible.'

'Like it won't happen?'

'Oh no, on the contrary, like it can.'

'Does that mean will? *Will* happen?'

This, I realize, is very close to a formal proposal. A hundred years ago Deko would have been on one knee, asking for my hand in marriage. Now, he's suggesting we sail away and see how it all works out. Very 2019.

'Tell me about the woman you fell in love with on Shelly Beach,' I say.

'You're changing the subject.'

'No, I'm not. Just tell me. Did you love her?'

'Yes, that's what I thought.'

'How much did you love her?'

'A lot. But I was so young, for Christ's sake. I knew nothing. I loved her enough to write. I've told you already, I'm not a great writer. It never came easy. But I did it, because she'd got to me.'

'Because you wanted to keep her?'

'Of course.'

'Own her?'

'Yes. In a way, yes.'

'And is that why you bought her the diamond ear stud? The one you bought in Antwerp?'

'Yes.'

'Because you thought that would do the trick?'

'Because she'd become part of me. Being at sea as a deckhand isn't the best place if you want a relationship. At first I thought she might ask me to give it all up and live with her and the kiddie.'

'And did she?'

'No, never. Looking back, that should have marked my card, but it didn't.'

'And would you have done it? Would you have left the sea? Stopped being a wanderer? Put all those eggs of yours in her basket?'

'You want the truth? I don't know.'

'But you might?'

'Yes.'

'And you might not?'

'I didn't. It's probably the same thing.'

'And when you finally got back, whenever that was, she'd gone. Have I got that right?'

'You have.'

'So how did that make you feel?'

He doesn't answer. Not immediately. Then he sighs and tells me again that he loves me.

'That's not an answer, Mr Deko. I want to know how you felt when you knocked on that door and there was no one at home. She'd moved away. Have I got that bit right?'

'You have. She'd gone to Birmingham and taken her daughter with her.'

'So how did you feel? Just tell me.'

'Why?'

'Because I want to know.'

'OK. The truth is that it broke my heart. But that's not all. It also taught me a lesson. When the voice in your head tells you you're in love, ignore it.'

'And now? Me? You're telling me that's different?'

'Yes.'

'How come?'

'Because all my life I've wanted to meet someone I know I could never truly control.'

'And that's me?'

'That's you.'

'Why couldn't you control me? What makes you think I'm so strong?'

'Not strong. Mysterious. Your own person. Out of reach. Just. I told you I was crap with language. If I put all this in a letter, you'd laugh in my face and I'd never see you again. I'm clumsy. I know I am. I'm sorry. Here . . .'

I can see his hand outstretched in the darkness. He seems to want to touch me and instinctively I recoil.

'Please,' he says. 'Just take it.'

'Take what?'

'This.'

With extreme reluctance I extend a hand and open it. Something light drops on to my palm. I touch it with my other hand, feeling its hardness, picturing what already I know it must be.

'This is the other ear stud?' I ask him.

'It was mine once,' he says. 'And now it's yours.'

FORTY

We haul up the anchor on the winch engine shortly after dawn. Deko says he's slept a little but looking at him I think that's a lie. Under the deep tan, his face is drawn, and he seems to have no interest in conversation. This is definitely a relief but he's never been this way before and I know he's aware of me watching him as he fires up the main engine and hauls *Amen* across the tidal stream to pick up the heading for Exmouth.

We close the buoy that marks the entrance to the approach channel shortly after nine o'clock. We've avoided the scatter of offshore pot buoys, and as we putter past the marina and the dock entrance, I gaze up at the penthouse apartment. With luck, I think, Pavel may be back here within days. The thought comforts me, and daylight is definitely another blessing. There are people around on the foreshore, most of them walking their dogs, and the water is busy as well. For the first time since we left France, I don't feel quite so alone.

Together, we secure *Amen* to her mooring buoy. Boysie's RIB is still made fast but when I tell Deko I need to get ashore, he uses his mobile to summon a water taxi. He says he still has a couple of hours' work to do down below. Whether this means he'll start work on the forepeak, liberating four and a half million pounds worth of cocaine, I've no idea. Neither, at this point, do I much care. I need to get to the hospital to plan Pavel's discharge. After that, there's the small matter of Deko and Carrie. Everything else can wait.

When the water taxi appears, nudging alongside, Deko barely acknowledges its presence. I'm on deck with my bag. He emerges from below, wiping engine oil from his hands on a rag. He wants to know whether the trip was worth it.

It's a strange question, and I don't know what to make of it.

'Worth it? Of course, it was. We scored, didn't we? Or at least you did.'

'That's not what I meant.'

He steps a little closer. He's never been this uncertain before. The old Deko, confident, utterly sure of himself, seems to have vanished. He holds my gaze for a long moment.

'You're not wearing it.' He taps his ear. He means the diamond stud.

'I'm not. You're right.'

'But you've still got it?'

'Of course.'

'Good. Talk later, yeah?'

Before I have a chance to answer, he's turned on his heel and disappeared down below. The skipper of the water taxi is getting impatient. Time to go.

The apartment is empty, no sign of Felip. I shower and change and within the hour I'm on the road north to Exeter. The thought of being with Pavel again, of maybe stirring a hint of recognition, has given me exactly the lift I need. By the time I've found a parking space at the hospital, I'm kidding myself that I'm back in control. Pavel, I think. Concentrate on who needs you most.

I take the stairs to the Stroke Unit. Mid-morning, the nursing staff are busy, moving from bed to bed, and nobody notices my arrival. I'm fine with this. I don't want to bother anyone. I know exactly where to go.

Pavel's side room is at the far end of the ward. The door, unusually, is closed. I knock softly, not wanting to wake him if he's asleep, and raising no response I open it. The bed is empty, the sheets folded neatly down, no sign of the flowers I'd brought before we left for France. I'm still assuming he's been moved elsewhere when I feel the lightest pressure on my arm. It's the consultant.

He shepherds me into the room and the moment he closes the door behind him I know this is the worst of news.

'He's gone?'

'I'm afraid so. He had another stroke last night. We did what we could but . . .' He shakes his head. 'I'm afraid it was probably inevitable. I'm glad you're here. We were about to phone you.'

I'm still looking at the bed. Oddly enough, despite everything, it's never entered my head that Pavel wouldn't make it. I've always assumed a brain that big would never shut down, ever, and the fact that he's turned out to be as mortal as the rest of us has come as a huge shock. Dead? Impossible.

'How?'

'How what?'

'How did he die?'

The consultant can't hide his confusion. It's an idiotic question, and we both know it. My role here is to accept that these people did their best but failed. No blame. No recriminations.

'Here.' The consultant has extracted a tissue from the box at the bedside. 'Would you prefer to be alone for a moment or two?'

I nod. I realize I'm crying. I hear the door close as he steps out of the room. That bed again. So empty. And my poor, dear Pavel. Gone.

A little later, the male nurse walks me to the hospital mortuary where I need to formally identify Pavel's body. I also want to say goodbye and once again the staff have the tact to ghost away and leave me alone. A phone call from the Stroke Unit has already fetched Pavel from one of the big fridges where they store the dead. Now, he lies on a metal gurney, a single sheet tucked up around his neck. His eyes are closed, and he looks more peaceful than I can ever remember.

I bend over him. When I kiss his forehead, his flesh feels cold against my lips. It may sound strange, but I know with absolute certainty that he's still listening, still tuned in, and that he always will be.

'Not the end,' I whisper, 'just the beginning. Think about that second act. Work on the dialogue. We'll talk again later, I promise. I love you, Pavel. Take care in there.'

I don't remember the drive back, not a single detail. Did I pay for the parking ticket? Did I jump that traffic light on the Topsham Road? Were there children I never noticed and ran over? I have absolutely no idea. Back at the apartment, which still belongs to Pavel in my head, I collapse on the sofa and gaze numbly at the wall. The small print of what has to happen next has begun to dawn on me. Pavel has never discussed his family and I've never asked. Does he have a mother and a father? Did he ever bother with being born at all? Or did he arrive on earth fully formed, a dreamweaver of genius? Who do I contact? Who do I tell? To all these questions I have absolutely no answer, but I do remember, months back, having a conversation about funerals. Pavel hated them. He claimed never to have attended a single one and when we fell to discussing what my mum would call *les arrangements*, he said he'd be more than happy to leave them to me. Burial? Cremation? A NASA ride to the moon? Or the black hole? My call.

I shake my head, more confused than I can ever remember, and this feeling of lostness darkens when I realize there's absolutely no one I can turn to. H wouldn't understand. Malo would be too busy to listen. Which leaves Deko. A week ago, I'd already have phoned him, found him, sat him down, had a good cry. Now? I shake my head. He, like Pavel, has gone.

Mid-afternoon, my phone starts to ring. It's Felip. He's still in St Ives, still tucked up with his Spanish friend. When I tell him there's absolutely no need to hurry back, he sounds relieved.

'They look after him OK?'

'I'm afraid he's dead, Felip. He died last night.'

There's a long silence and I know exactly what's coming next, so I hang up. Grief, after a while, is like any other burden. When it gets too heavy you simply have to put it down. Otherwise you'd never walk another step.

By early evening, apart from a single visit to the kitchen, I haven't moved from the sofa. I know I ought to be thinking about Carrie, about those photos, about what I ought to be saying to DS Williams, but somehow it's beyond me. Already, as Pavel might have put it, my brief affair with Deko belongs in another script, another life. I believed him utterly, every word he said, because he had the knack of making me so happy. Now I feel like a child told that Santa Claus never existed, that he was a fantasy. First comes bewilderment. Then disbelief. And soon, maybe, anger. You helped yourself to the best of me, Mr Deko, and now you'll steal away.

Very soon, it's getting dark. They gave me Pavel's only possession in the Stroke Unit, his glasses. I find them in my bag and carry them through to his bedroom. This, I know, is another farewell, maybe more personal. It takes nothing to imagine his long, skinny frame under those sheets, his head on the whiteness of the pillow, his sunken cheeks, his thinning hair, and those lovely hands, forever lifeless. Carrie used to soap his nails in hot water, and then give him a manicure. He couldn't feel a thing, and he could never see the results, but he knew that she loved doing it, and that – in turn – made him very happy.

Pavel? I shake my head, circle the room very slowly, adjusting this, tidying that. Then, gazing out at the last of the sunset, I open his balcony doors wide, feeling the chill of the wind on my face, knowing that at last Pavel's spirit will be free. Before I leave the room, I put Pavel's tinted glasses gently on his pillow.

Will he ever need these again? Who knows.

By half past nine, I've drunk half a bottle of wine and toyed with a bowl of olives from the fridge. I haven't eaten all day, and the wine has gone straight to my head, but that's fine because I've loosened my moorings and cast myself adrift. Today has shut a great many doors in my life, I tell myself, and now is the time to sleep.

In the bathroom, for the first time in nearly a year, I pop a diazepam and retire to bed. In seconds, I'm fast asleep.

FORTY-ONE

I awake in what feels like the middle of the night. The diazepam has made me groggy and for a moment I'm at sea again, in the belly of *Amen*, trying to get my bearings. Then I remember Pavel, and the empty bed at the Stroke Unit, and his glasses on the pillow next door, and I groan and roll over.

Very slowly, I sense a presence beside the bed, a physical shape in the darkness, someone tall, staring down at me. Frightened now, I reach for the light beside my bed. My heart skips a beat, then I feel my blood turn to ice in my veins.

Deko is dressed entirely in black: black jeans, tight-fitting black polo-neck, black runners. He's swaying slightly and at first I think he's drunk. Anything but.

'I'm sorry,' he says, 'I shouldn't be doing this.'

'Too right.' All I can think of is Carrie. Same situation. Same time of night. To my relief I can see no signs of a knife, Japanese or otherwise. 'So how did you get in?'

He says he climbed up the outside of the building, storey by storey, until he found the balcony with the open doors. He'd checked earlier and there were no lights in the apartments below. I nod. This makes sense. Both apartments are second homes, the owners normally elsewhere.

'You've been watching me?' I pull the duvet tightly to my neck.

'I've been watching the block.'

'Why?'

'I didn't want to disturb anyone.'

'But why didn't you phone? Press the bell at the front door?'

'Because you'd never have let me in.'

'Why not?'

'Because you found the phone in the drawer on board. There's a bungee cord. You probably remember it. The hook on one end's dodgy and I always put it at the bottom end. You did the reverse.'

I nod. *Fuck*, I think. 'You're telling me you didn't see the photos?'

'Of course, I saw the photos. You and Carrie? How could I not?'

'You were checking up?'

'Yes.'

'Why?'

'Because I wanted to know who the phone belonged to. And because I wanted to be sure of you.'

'Sure of me how?'

'Sure that I'd got you right. Sure that I wasn't fooling myself.'

'And?'

'I was fooling myself. You lied about Carrie, Mr Deko.'

'Amy. I lied about Amy.'

'Did she matter to you?'

'Yes.'

'As much as the woman on Shelly Beach?'

'Yes.'

'As much as me?'

'No. And that's the truth.' He sounds, if anything, distressed. 'You believe me?'

I shake my head. I'm not frightened any more, because I don't think this man is going to hurt me.

'Tell me about Carrie,' I say. 'Tell me what really happened.'

'We had an affair. I was besotted. She was an amazing woman. I also wanted her to come to the Beacon when everything was ready.'

'To live with you?'

'To run the place. To look after the clients.'

'And?'

'She said no. She was already looking after your friend by that time and she wouldn't leave.'

'Pavel's dead. He died last night.'

'I'm sorry.'

I nod, say nothing.

'What about Moonie?' I mutter at last. 'Where does he come into all this?'

'That boy was crazy.'

'Was?'

'Is.'

'You know him?'

'Yes. He wandered into the nursing home when I was working there. He wanted a job and somewhere to get his head down in the evenings. I gave him one of the rooms upstairs in exchange for navvying. I paid him, too.'

'You got to know him?'

'We talked. He had a problem with his father.'

'He committed suicide. Did he tell you that?'

'He did, yes.'

'And I expect you could relate to that? Your own father?'

'Of course. I felt for the boy. Anyone would.'

'So, what happened to him? After Carrie died?'

'I've no idea. He just disappeared. I never saw him again.'

'You think he did it?'

'I don't know. In certain moods he might have done.'

'You mean he was violent? Or suggestible?'

Deko won't answer. Carrie, I think. In love with Jean-Paul. In love with another man.

'Did you kill her? Carrie? Because she was pregnant? Because she was carrying another man's child? Because she was once yours?'

'No.'

'You're telling me the truth?'

'Yes.'

I nod. I have absolutely no means of testing any of this story, but I badly want him out of my life and I think he knows that.

'Why did you come here tonight?' I ask him. 'Be honest.'

'Because I wanted to be straight with you. That matters to me, believe it or not.'

'Why? Do you think it will make any difference?'

'Probably not.' For the first time he's smiling. 'But I always live in hope.'

'Hope's not enough. You should have been straight with me earlier.'

'And?'

'Now's too late. Have you told me the whole story? I doubt it. Did you kill Carrie? You say you didn't. Have you come here to kill me? Christ, I hope not. We've had good times, Mr Deko, and that's what hurts most of all. Good times, the best times, and then you blew it because you thought you could fool me about Carrie. That would never have happened, not in the long run, because stuff like this always comes out. You could have had me for keeps, Mr Deko, if you want the truth. But like I say, now's too late.'

He nods. I've never been so blunt in my life, even with Berndt, and I'm hoping to God I haven't pushed him too far.

It seems not. I ask him to go next door and leave me in peace for a moment or two.

'You want me to go?'

'Not yet.'

He frowns, uncertain again, then steps next door. My dressing gown is hanging on the back of the door. I get out of bed and put it on. My bag is on the sofa in the lounge. Deko watches me empty the contents on the table and pick through all the rubbish until I find the little twist of paper.

'Yours, I think.' I give it to him.

He feels the shape of the ear stud between his fingertips, staring down at it.

'You'll never see me again,' he says, avoiding my gaze. 'I'll let myself out.'

FORTY-TWO

I wait for Deko to leave. I hear the lift descending and from the balcony outside Pavel's bedroom, moments later, I watch him disappear along the walkway that skirts the water. He has a small day sack on his back and, much to my relief, he doesn't once look back.

I lock the balcony doors. DS Williams's card is among the debris I've emptied from my bag. My mobile tells me it's 04.47. When she finally answers, I explain what's happened. For a moment, she seems to think I've woken up to find a stranger beside my bed.

'Not at all,' I say. 'His name's Deko. You've met him.'

'Mr Miedema? Your friend? The guy who came to the station?'

'Yes.'

'So, what's the problem?'

I'm tempted to laugh. Problem? Does she want a list?

'I think he may have killed Carrie,' I say. 'And I think it might be my turn next.'

Williams sends a night-shift patrol car. It has to come from Exeter, and I'm showered and dressed by the time the driver appears at the main entrance downstairs. I've been checking the view from every window but there's no sign of Deko.

Williams is waiting for me at the police station in Exmouth. Apart from the driver, whom she asks to stay, there appears to be no one else in the building. She's obviously dressed in a hurry because her hair is a mess and I sense that *Mandolin* hasn't been going well.

We're talking in her office. I start to describe in detail what's been happening, but she shakes her head.

'Give me the headlines,' she says.

Headlines? I tell her that Deko and I became lovers. I tell her that I trusted every word he said. I explain about the nursing home he's doing up, and about his place on the Beacon. And finally I tell her about *Amen*.

'This is a boat?'

'A Breton Thonier. We sailed to France last week and picked up a hundred and fifty kilos of cocaine. That's how he funds all these projects. He's a drug smuggler.'

At last I have Williams's full attention. She sits back in her chair, her arms crossed.

'That's a lot of money,' she says. 'You were part of this?'

'I was part of him, part of his life. I didn't know about the cocaine until we got to France.'

'You didn't think of going to the French authorities? The police? The Harbour Master? Maybe put a phone call through to us?'

'No.'

'Why not?'

'Because I was in love with the man.'

'Was? And now?'

I explain about finding the photos of Carrie on the phone. I'd challenged him about his name cropping up in her call records, but he'd told me there was nothing to worry about. Strictly business, he'd said. Nothing more. Then came the photos.

'You challenged him again?'

'God, no. We were alone. We were in the middle of nowhere. If he'd lied to me once, what else was he hiding? No, I put the phone back, kept my head down, hoped I'd get back in one piece. He's a big man, he's strong, he works out, he's a boxer. Maybe that was all part of the attraction. But he's sick, too. Obsessive. Whatever he wants, whatever he needs, he helps himself. Nothing stops him. Nothing gets in his way. That can be a turn-on, believe me, until you realize where it might lead. It's odd. I thought Moonie was the crazy one. Now I'm not so sure.'

'And Carrie?'

'He was mad about her. Literally.'

'Mad enough to kill her? Once she'd found another man?'

'Yes. Or mad enough to have her killed. Either way, I'm guessing she wouldn't be dead had she never met Deko.'

'And you? What about you?'

'He's mad about me, too.' I shrug. 'He climbed three storeys to prove it. Might there be a pattern here?'

Williams is checking her watch. I give her an address for the nursing home, and for Deko's place on the Beacon. She wants to know where *Amen* is moored, and where the cocaine has been stashed. Most important of all, she wants to know where Deko might have gone.

'I've no idea,' I tell her. 'He's told me he'll leave me alone now but that's another lie. He'll be back, I know he will. The man can't help himself.'

'And that's why you phoned me?'

'Of course. I'm unfinished business. He'll come looking because that's what he does. I'm an itch in his life. He can't leave me alone.'

Williams nods. The faintest smile has warmed her face.

'You're a lucky girl,' she says.

'For meeting him?'

'For surviving.'

She asks me to leave her office. The uniformed driver is downstairs. He'll keep an eye on me while she makes some calls. I get up and head for the door, then pause.

'Am I under arrest?'

'Not yet.' Williams is already reaching for her phone. 'That'll be down to my SIO.'

The Senior Investigating Officer is a lean, balding forty-something with a Zapata moustache and the faintest suggestion of a limp. Williams's phone call has roused him from his bed, and he's occupying an office in the Major Incident Room by the time we get to police headquarters in Exeter. Williams has clearly briefed him in some detail on the phone but he makes me go through the whole story again. The fact that he doesn't make notes or record my account is oddly reassuring. A man with a memory, I think.

Once I'm done, he gets to his feet. He's looking at the remains of the bruise on my forehead.

'Did Miedema do that?'

'No. I fell over.'

'Really?' I know he doesn't believe me, but it doesn't seem to matter. He and Williams leave the office to confer. More of *Mandolin*'s team are arriving by the minute, most of them nursing cups of coffee. I've found myself a seat in the corner of the big open-plan office, content to feel safe, and none of them even spare me a glance.

The SIO returns and beckons me into his office. I'm not under arrest, he says, but it will be helpful if I remain in the MIR for the time being. At some point this morning, a detective will need to take a full statement. In the meantime, *Mandolin* will be putting forensic teams into Deko's nursing home, and the house on the Beacon, while a rummage crew board the boat on the estuary. Is there anything else, he asks, that I might want to tell him?

I nod.

'There's a man called Boysie,' I say. 'He's a friend of Deko's. He runs a hotel up in the woods on the edge of the Common.'

I tell him about the Hotel Zuma, and the hints from both Boysie and Deko that the business might be in trouble. When I mention the casino, the SIO nods.

'You say your friend has done the cocaine run before?'

'Twice.'

'Similar weights?'

'I think so.'

'Then he'd need to wash that money. A casino would be perfect. They're friends, you say?'

'Bosom pals. Buddies. Birds of a feather.'

'Chancers?'

'Definitely.' The word makes me smile. 'But talented, too.'

I tell him a little about the efforts Boysie has made to brighten the hotel: the décor, the cuisine, the pigs running wild in the adjoining woods, even a couple of wild boar.

The SIO nods, and I watch him make a note of the hotel's name. Then his head comes up again.

'So, will I be free to go?' I enquire. 'After I've made my statement?'

'No, I'm afraid not. For one thing you might be a flight risk. You might decide to bale out. And for another, to be frank, you're currently our biggest asset. We think you're probably right about Miedema. We think he'll come back for you. We'll make every effort to find him today, but if we don't we'd like you to go back to that penthouse and spend the night there.'

'Alone?' I'm appalled.

'No. There's a DC I'll be briefing. His name's Brett. He's a good lad. I think you'll like him. He'll be in the flat with you tonight and we'll have other assets in the vicinity. It's very hard to disappear in this country of ours, especially when you've every reason to hang around.'

'For what?'

'For the cocaine, Ms Andressen.' He offers me a thin smile. 'And for you.'

I nod. A clearing in the jungle, I think. And the tethered goat that will tempt Mr Deko out of cover.

'What if I say no?'

'That would be disappointing. To be frank, we've yet to take a view about you and the cocaine, but I'm a policeman, and policemen are born suspicious. Don't get me wrong. This story of yours is persuasive. But did you really know nothing about what that man of yours was up to? Were you really expecting nothing more than a jolly? A couple of nights in France? A stroll on the prom? A meal or two?'

I hold his gaze. The deal doesn't need spelling out. If I do *Mandolin*'s bidding, then all will be well. Otherwise, I'm probably doomed.

'Can you keep me here against my will?'

'Only if we arrest you.'

'And would you do that?'

'Of course. If needs must. In the meantime, you might fancy a spot of breakfast. Brett will take you to the canteen.'

Brett turns out to be a slightly older version of Malo. The same hint of attitude in his slow half-smile. The same hint of mischief in his light blue eyes. Whether or not this is deliberate I can't say, but I'm beginning to develop a healthy respect for Operation *Mandolin*. A major enquiry like this, I've concluded, is a bit like an iceberg. Everything happens out of sight.

According to the badge on his lanyard, Brett's surname is Atkinson. When I ask him whether he enjoys his job, he nods.

'I love it,' he says. 'Just like my dad used to.'

We sort of bond over scrambled eggs and brown toast. He's been reading the interview transcripts and he wants to know about my career in the movies. I assume at first that this is simply conversation, a courtesy you'd extend to any stranger, but the harder I listen to him, the more I realize that this is simply another way of getting to find out about me. Brett has a talent for subtle changes of direction, for skating lightly over the thinnest ice in my private life, for establishing that I became a divorcee with no fixed emotional abode, and that – in my own phrase – bringing up a stroppy adolescent in today's culture can be a nightmare.

'I'm sure you're right,' he says. 'Me and Shaz only talk about having kids when we're pissed. Am I right in thinking that must tell you something? Odds on, we'll end up with a Labrador. Less bother.'

Back in the incident room, I settle down with a copy of the *Daily Mail*. Brett reappears at midday, but I turn down the offer of lunch.

'You like music?'

'I do. Very much.'

He crosses the office and rummages in a drawer in his desk. Then he's back with a Walkman and a pair of headphones. He's on Spotify and he can stream any music I want.

'Berlioz,' I say, thinking at once of Pavel. 'Romeo and Juliet.'

I spell Berlioz for him. He taps the letters in and moments later I'm listening to the opening bars of the piece that always reduced Pavel to tears. Brett is watching me. His concern for my well-being is touching.

'You want somewhere more comfortable?'

I do. There's a smallish room attached to the MIR where detectives working late can snatch an hour or two's kip. I choose the smaller of the two sofas but there's still room to lie full-length. Brett finds a blanket and a couple of pillows in a cupboard and within seconds, regardless of Berlioz, I'm asleep.

FORTY-THREE

By the time I awake, the MIR is beginning to empty. It's nearly six, and the *Mandolin* SIO has just brought the daily wash-up meeting to an end. In the car going back to Exmouth, Brett brings me up to speed. Forensic teams, he says, are still at work in both of Miedema's properties. One room at the nursing home has definitely been slept in recently, and DNA samples have been submitted in the hope that they match material gathered from Carrie's bedroom. This, he says, would confirm Miedema's claim that he fed and watered Moonie in return for services rendered.

'And the boat?' I ask. '*Amen*?'

'The floor was already up in the forepeak. Miedema must have started to ship the stuff out, but there's plenty left.'

'Like how much?'

'Eighty-eight kilos so far and counting. The customs guys are there, too. They think it's Christmas.'

He says a warrant is now out for Miedema's arrest on suspicion of class A drug trafficking. I've been happy to supply one of my own photos of Deko to *Mandolin* and this has been circulated nationwide. I took the shot the day we walked the cliff path to *la plage du Ris* at Douarnenez. It shows Deko among the pine trees with the vast expanse of the beach behind him. He has his leather jacket hooked on one finger over his shoulder and the smile is completely unforced. Another person, I think, in another life. Not Miedema at all, but Deko.

At the apartment, I tell Brett to make himself comfortable. When I say he can have Felip's bedroom for the night, he shakes his head. His job is to keep me safe. When I ask him about supper, he says he'll be happy with pasta. When I offer him a drink, he shakes his head.

'If only,' he says.

I turn the TV on. The news ends with a preview of tonight's big game. Brett, it turns out, is a big Tottenham fan.

'You've got BT Sport here?'

'I'm afraid not.'

He pulls a face. Tonight's game, he says, is absolutely key for Spurs. Slot a couple of goals against Ajax, keep a clean sheet, and the return leg in Amsterdam should be in the bag.

'Ajax was Deko's team.'

'Deko?'

'Miedema.'

'He's into football?'

'He is. That's why we came back when we did. He needed to catch the game.'

I retire to the kitchen and put a saucepan of water on for the pasta. I normally make my own topping but tonight I can't be bothered. A jar of the gloop I keep for Malo will have to do.

The thought of having to spend the evening in the apartment depresses me. The place is full of ghosts: first Pavel, now Deko. I drain the pasta and spoon on the topping. Back in the lounge, Brett is on the phone. I put the tray on a table beside the sofa and wait for the call to end. The DI I've met has a nickname.

'That was Spud.' Brett pockets his phone. 'He's on the boat. They've got it all out. A hundred and sixteen bricks.'

'That's millions.' I'm trying to do the sums.

'Yeah. Harry Kane's kind of money. Silly, isn't it?'

I nod at the pasta. 'I've had a thought,' I tell Brett. 'Why don't we go to the pub tonight? Watch the game?'

His first instinct is to shake his head. No way. Then he looks brighter. 'You want to? You're serious?'

'I am. Anything's better than here.' Brett begins to fork at the pasta. Then he produces his phone again. 'I'll see what Spud says. No harm in trying, eh?'

The DI refers the decision to the SIO. By the time the Guvnor finally phones back, it's gone half past seven and Brett's given up.

'Sir?' He bends to the phone. Moments later, he's on his feet. 'Result!' He sounds just like Malo. 'As long as we're back by ten.'

We drive to the middle of town. Brett knows the Exmouth Arms well. The pub is already bursting, smokers huddled on the pavement, more fans arriving by the second. Inside, it takes an age to get anywhere near the bar. The pub is L-shaped, with room for a couple of pool tables at the far end, and we're spoiled for screens. I spot a table in the far corner only half-occupied. Brett, who knows the barmaid, mimes a raised glass. What am I drinking?

'Red wine,' I shout. 'Preferably Merlot.'

'Big? Small?'

'Silly question.'

I nod at the table and fight my way through the scrum of drinkers. The teams have just emerged on to the pitch and the crowd in the stadium has erupted. Cameras pan slowly across a sea of waving scarves. The stadium, according to the commentator, is brand new.

'That's right.' Brett has arrived with the drinks. 'Nearly a billion quid. Life's all money, isn't it?' He hands me a brimming glass of red and settles in the pub's one remaining chair. 'Top work, Ms A.'

'Enora.'

'Enora.'

'My pleasure. Here's to Spurs.'

We clink glasses. Brett is drinking orange juice, his gaze anchored on the screen above our heads. The two captains are shaking hands with the match officials. Then comes another roar from the crowd as the game kicks off.

I know very little about football but Brett's news that Ajax are the team in black seems richly appropriate. Deko, I think. The figure at my bedside in the middle of the night. Clad entirely in black.

Spurs appear to be favourites for this first home leg but it's clear within minutes that the Dutch haven't read the script. They're a young team, quick, fearless, full of ideas, and they stroke the ball around, mounting attack after attack. Time and again, an Ajax player with the ball at his feet does the matador thing, goading the men in white to commit, and then pulling the Spurs defence out of shape. The pub has gone very quiet and even Brett is beginning to look thoughtful. Then comes the moment when the star Dutch attacker, a child called Van de Beek, finds himself in front of the Spurs goal. He takes a tiny step to the left, balancing himself for the shot, and then slots the ball neatly past the Spurs keeper.

From the pub's collective groan emerges a single raised arm. It's a gesture of triumph, of celebration. The arm is leather clad, and even across the crowded bar I recognize the shape of the head, the fuzz of once-ginger hair, the sense of sheer physical presence. Then he turns his face up to the screen again and there's no mistaking the grin on the broad face. Deep inside, I'm starting to shake again.

Deko.

I say nothing. He hasn't seen me. I know he hasn't. Neither does Brett have a clue that he's here. The game has resumed. Spurs, eager to level the score, mount attack after attack. The pub, like the crowd in the stadium, is urging them on. Wave after wave of white shirts curl and break over the Dutch defence but the attacks come to nothing. The Dutch, I think, must have nerves of steel. Much like my ex-lover.

I can't take my eyes off him. There are three other men at his table. They all look like builders, and he doesn't appear to know any of them. From time to time, he sips at his beer and then wipes his mouth on the back of his hand, a gesture I know only too well. Him and me, I think. Together one final time. The thought is all the sweeter because for once in my life I have total control. At a moment of my choice I can bring this whole sorry episode, the passion, the glee, the betrayal, the fear, to an end. And I will.

Five minutes before half time, the thirstier drinkers are already heading for the bar. Both our glasses are empty.

'Same again?' Brett, too, is on his feet.

'I'll come with you,' I tell him.

'Why?'

'I need the loo.'

He nods. We join the press of bodies at the bar, of outstretched arms, of empty glasses. Every step we take brings us closer to Deko's table. The game is still in progress, but the ref is checking his watch. Deko's hand feels for his glass and he lifts it towards his mouth. He's almost within touching distance. Almost.

The ref finally blows for half-time and Deko's big face turns towards me. For a moment, I'm not sure he's recognized me, but I'm wrong. A single nod, just the faintest tip of his head, acknowledges my presence. I hold his gaze, aware of Brett checking me out over his shoulder.

'You OK?'

'I'm fine,' I tell him. 'Kiss me.'

'What?' He's looking confused.

'Kiss me. Properly. Pretend I'm Shaz. Just do it.'

'Why?'

'Please? Like you mean it?'

'You're serious? *Here?*'

'Yes.'

Brett shrugs, manages to turn around, and ducks his head towards my face. He must have been sucking mints because I can smell them on his breath. The kiss is perfunctory, a peck, like I might be his maiden aunt.

'Again,' I tell him. 'Full-on.'

This time, he puts some effort in, cupping my face between his hands. When I slip my tongue between his lips, he grunts and puts his arms around me, and all the time I'm looking at Deko.

He's staring at us, totally impassive, his big hand still wrapped around his empty glass. Then he seems to physically flinch, the way you might react to a wasp sting, and heads at the bar turn as his glass comes crashing down against the edge of the nearest table. Deko in a bar in Algiers, I think. Deko in a thousand of life's tighter corners. Deko totally out of control. Deko the killer.

Brett, too late, has recognized the face in the photo. He raises an arm to try and protect me as Deko lunges forward, but the first jabbing blow is for Brett, not me. I hear the faintest groan, part surprise, part alarm, as the young cop clutches at his throat. The jagged mouth of the broken glass has torn through the flesh and nicked the big artery on the side of his neck, and blood – the deepest red – is seeping through his fingers.

A woman two tables away begins to scream. Deko is very close now. I'm looking into his eyes, knowing that it's my turn next, knowing that nothing on earth can save my face, but nothing happens. He just looks at me, his eyes expressionless, blank, terrifying. This is a frozen moment in time, one of those single frames, no soundtrack, that Pavel – when sighted – would have adored. The man is a shark, pitiless, always on the move, possessed by his own needs, his own appetites. I, far too late, at last understand that. There is nothing, no single life, no single individual, that will stand in Deko's way. Then, with a roar, the pub is suddenly alive again, as he submerges beneath a blizzard of flailing arms, half a dozen men forcing him to the floor.

These guys, too, are no strangers to pub brawls, but I know Deko will never give up, and I'm right. Fights like these are clumsy, no space, no scope for real violence, and as the kicks and punches go in, he shrugs them off. One of the barmaids, her face the colour of chalk, has a phone pressed to her ear. Another throws me a bar towel. I wind the scrap of wet cloth around the gaping wound in Brett's neck, trying to stem the blood loss.

Then, suddenly, it's all over, and the fight has gone out of Deko.

As the men on top of him slowly disentangle themselves, he's lying on his back, his own throat slashed, blood pumping on to the whiteness of his T-shirt, the glass still in his hand. Something else arrives from the bar, a towel this time, but no one lifts a finger.

'Let the bastard bleed,' one man grunts, rubbing his arm.

'Too fucking right,' says another.

The crowd have backed away now, leaving Deko on his back. His eyes flicker briefly open, gazing up at me, and I swear there's the hint of a smile on his face.

'What's his name?' someone asks. 'Anyone know?'

'Miedema,' I say.

Brett survives, just. A paramedic transfuses him in the ambulance while I squat beside the stretcher, keeping pressure on the wound. This, I know, is my fault and under the circumstances it's the least I can do. At A&E, staff fast-track him to the operating theatre where surgeons suture the torn artery in his neck and give him yet more blood.

I stay at the hospital all night, curled up in the waiting room, and at dawn comes the news from one of the *Mandolin* team that Deko never made it. His choice, I suspect, and his doing. Interviews with the men who took him down are inconclusive, but the consensus seems to be that he slashed his own throat. The Deko I once loved. In charge until the very end.

FORTY-FOUR

Over the days that follow, Operation *Mandolin* winds down. There are still no sightings of Moonie, despite all the publicity, and I'm too busy making arrangements for Pavel to pay much attention to anything else. That Deko is dead is all I need to know.

Then comes a call from DS Williams. She's in her office at Exmouth police station and she wants to pay me a visit.

'Is this official?'

'Yes, in a way.'

'Should I phone a lawyer?'

'That won't be necessary.'

This comes as something of a relief. *Mandolin*'s SIO has given me the impression that I won't be facing any charges over the cocaine, but so far there's nothing in writing. Williams arrives ten minutes later. The moment she walks out of the lift, I realize I've never seen her looking so well. My mum has a phrase for it. *Plein d'entrain*. Spry.

I brew a fresh pot of coffee and ask her about Brett. She says he's out of hospital now, recovering at home, but he should be back at work within weeks. Already she's browsing Carrie's collection of recipe books. This morning, she's a woman, almost a friend, not a cop at all.

'Well . . .?' I say.

She's looking at a Rick Stein take on poached halibut. She glances up.

'Boysie? You remember him? That Hotel Zuma?'

'Of course I do. Deko's mate.'

'We arrested him yesterday. I thought you might like to know.'

A *Mandolin* forensic team, she explains, had been crawling over the hotel room by room, finding nothing. Only when they took a proper look at the derelict bungalow in the woods did they hit pay dirt.

'What did they find?'

'Blood. Most of it turned out to be animal, we're assuming pigs' blood, but there were tiny traces on the teeth of a chainsaw that were human.'

'And?'

'They got a match to DNA from the room in Miedema's nursing home.'

'You mean Moonie?'

'Yes. And I'm afraid it doesn't end there. You're aware of the wild boar enclosure?'

'Yes.'

'We went through that, too. Proper POLSA search, hands and knees, a dozen officers.'

'And?'

'Human bones. From here . . . and here . . .' She touches her thigh, and then her upper arm.

'Moonie?'

'Yes.'

'They chopped him up and fed him to the pigs?'

'To the boars. Apparently, they eat anything.'

I nod. There's no way I can avoid the next question, no matter how hard I try.

'They?' I ask.

'Boysie. And your Dutch friend, Miedema. Boysie coughed it last night, first interview, open account. Full confession. We didn't even have to try. He's up before the magistrates first thing tomorrow. We're thinking Crown Court by the autumn, latest. He'll be away for a long time.'

'He was in love with Deko. Did he tell you that?'

'He did. He told us he's heartbroken and I believe him.'

'Heartbroken about what?'

'About the man killing himself. The word he used in his interview was "immortal". Does that make any sense?'

'It does. Deko was a god. A man like that, you stop asking the awkward questions. He fooled me, too.' I'm frowning at the memory. 'What else did Boysie tell you?'

'You really want to know?'

'I do. Of course I do.'

'The boy Moonie stayed at that home Miedema was doing up, just like you told us. According to Boysie, Miedema took him under his wing, listened to the boy, talked to him. Apparently, he was obsessed by the Paras and what happened at Goose Green.'

I nod, remembering Karen describing her son's passion for books about the Falklands War.

'Did he ever make contact with his mother?'

'No, but the boy gave Miedema a number, asked him to call. Apparently, the boy did the same thing to Carrie, that night he paid her a visit. He never wanted to talk to his mum himself. He wanted strangers to do it, just to let her know he was OK.'

'OK?' I'm staring at her. 'You've just terrified a woman out of her skin, and you leave your mum's number at her *bedside*? That's crazy.'

'Indeed. Completely insane.'

'But why didn't Carrie make the call?'

'Good question. Our best guess is she wanted nothing more to do with either Moonie or his mum. She made a note of the number and left it at that.'

I nod, remembering how hard it was to get any kind of account from Carrie when I went round after Moonie's visit. Williams is right. She was in denial.

'So who killed her?'

'Miedema.'

'You're sure? Not Moonie?'

'No. The boy died the previous night. Killed at that place up above the hotel. They'd had him chained to the radiator. Miedema again. He needed a prime suspect. Someone who'd obviously done it, but someone who'd simply disappear. Clever. And totally psychotic.'

'And Boysie saw all this?'

'He did. Miedema cut his throat. Then they sawed him up and fed him to the wild boars. After that, Miedema took care of Carrie. Job done.'

'But why? Why did he do it?'

'Because she blew him out. Because she wouldn't do his bidding. Carrying someone else's baby was the final straw. According to Boysie, your friend took that personally.'

'He knew?'

'Yes. There was an old lady at the home. She was very close to Carrie.'

'Peggy,' I say at once. 'She drank red vermouth by the bottle.'

'That may be right. I've no idea. But Miedema knew where she'd been transferred and went to see her. What he really wanted to know was whether Carrie was missing him. Instead he found out she was pregnant by the Frenchman. Carrie had shared the news with Peggy, and Peggy told Miedema.'

I turn away, shaking my head. I'd mentioned the pregnancy to Deko after Carrie had died, and the news appeared to have come as a surprise. More games, I think. Another sleight of hand.

'Something else.' Williams hasn't finished. 'Miedema sent Moonie round to Carrie's place the night after he'd seen the old lady. He told the boy to frighten Carrie and that's exactly what he did. Your friend was canny. All he had to do, according to Boysie, was feed him a line or two. Swear her to silence, he'd said, on pain of death. It worked a treat.'

'This was some kind of punishment?'

'Exactly. She'd stepped out of line. She deserved to be frightened. It wasn't enough, of course, but Carrie wouldn't have known that.

Moonie was Moonie. As far as she was concerned, he had nothing to do with your friend.'

My friend. I nod. Thanks to Williams, the order of the killings at last tells me everything I need to know about Deko. Most killers sort out an alibi afterwards. A rush of blood to the head, a squeeze of the trigger, or a thrust of the knife, or a volley of blows, followed by a hasty covering of tracks. Not Deko. Everything pre-planned. Everything under control. Should I be surprised? Probably not.

'So how did Moonie get into Carrie's flat?'

'Miedema gave him a key. He'd bought the flat for Carrie when they were still together, and she'd never changed the locks. The damage to the door frame was a bluff.'

'To take you to Moonie?'

'Of course. And it worked beautifully.'

Psychotic indeed, I think. I shake my head, imagining Moonie chained to the radiator in that tomb of a bungalow. This is a scene that belongs in the Third World, I tell myself, the infant Moonie taken hostage by a sequence of events beyond his comprehension. Then poor Carrie, sprawled in the darkness of that hideous bedroom, bleeding to death.

'They never had a prayer,' I mutter. 'Meet someone like Deko and the rest writes itself.'

This realization is deeply shocking, and it takes me several days to come to terms with how fortunate I've been. I wander round Pavel's empty apartment, only too aware that – for whatever reason – I've been spared. Sitting on my bed, the front door treble-locked, I replay those moments when I awoke to find Deko in the darkness. I'd denied him what he needed. I'd told him he was no longer welcome in my life. So why didn't he kill me, too? There and then, in my bedroom? Or later in the pub? This is a question to which I have no answer and it's no comfort to realize I probably never will. Luck? Fate? The black hole? God knows . . .

The weekend's *Observer* carries Seb O'Leary's piece on mental health. To my surprise, it's beautifully written, a *tour de force*. It's obvious that O'Leary still has the inside track on the *Mandolin* investigation, and he's cleverly interwoven the brutal facts of Carrie's death, and Moonie's disappearance, with the limbo that passes for mental health provision. No beds, no assessments, no places of safety. Just three more bodies in the mortuary and a government without the grace to hang its head in shame. Mindful of the Coroner's Court, O'Leary's piece stops short of a full account, but he's done Moonie's story more than justice.

Chastened, I hunt out O'Leary's phone number and give him a ring. He claims to be surprised to hear from me, but I don't think it's true.

'I just wanted to say well done. I got you wrong. I'm sorry.'

'No problem. Occupational hazard.'

'One other thing. Do you mind?'

'Not at all.'

'Did you get a visit from a black guy? Tall? Fit-looking?'

'No.'

'You're sure?'

'Absolutely. I'd have noticed something like that.'

This comes as a relief. As an afterthought, I ask him whether he still lives in Edmonton.

'Christ, no. That was the woman before the woman before last. It's Muswell Hill just now, my dear. And her name's Rhona.'

We say our goodbyes to Pavel at Exeter Crematorium the following week. A couple of obituaries in the *Guardian* and *The Times* have paid tribute to his screenwriting talents, and I know from Pavel's agent that a number of actors and producers want to say their goodbyes in person, but Pavel has always insisted on just a handful of true unbelievers – his phrase – at his funeral, and so barely half a dozen of us are awaiting the arrival of his coffin: H, myself, Felip, Pavel's agent, Ndeye, and the male nurse from the Stroke Unit.

Pavel's determination to leave God out of his passing extends to the event itself: no hymns, no prayers, not a single mention of the Almighty. Instead, as I hope he would have wished, I've scored this brief little celebration for a Schubert impromptu, played on the recording by Paul Lewis, and the *largo* from Pavel's favourite Dvořák string quartet. I say a few words about what an inspiration he was, and read a poem, *Musée des Beaux Arts*, which Pavel always regarded as the best thing Auden ever wrote. The poem reminds us how the world goes on regardless, despite our hunt for significance and meaning, and we bow our heads as the curtain closes on Pavel's coffin.

Afterwards, H insists on treating us to lunch at a floating café on the Exe, upriver from Exmouth. We eat mussels and fresh bread and drink far too much Chablis. Twice, H catches me gazing across the water at the mooring where *Amen* used to be. Thanks to DS Williams, I know the boat has been towed away for further investigation, but the drunker I get, the greater the temptation to indulge in a memory or two.

'You're seeing things,' H grunts. And he's right.

The following week, I return to the crematorium and collect Pavel's ashes. The one place that meant more to him than anywhere else on earth was Prague, and one day, I tell myself, I will take a flight, and stand on the Charles Bridge, and scatter his ashes over the river below. In the meantime, while I wrestle with the complications of his estate, they will occupy one corner of my wardrobe at home in Holland Park.

In June, H and I have a brief conversation on the phone about the penthouse apartment. We agree that it's served its purpose and neither of us want to hang on to it. I audition a selection of estate agents and later that month, when Exmouth is at its best, it goes on the market for £850,000. H has priced it for a quick sale because he needs to fund his fight with his neighbour about the housing development and we get an offer within days.

I make one final visit to Exmouth before the new owners move in. All the equipment that kept Pavel alive has already gone, donated to the Spinal Unit outside Salisbury, and I wander from room to room saying a private goodbye to an apartment which – thanks to H's largesse – served us so well.

The best of the place was undoubtedly the view, and I linger on Pavel's balcony, watching a stately procession of yachts leaving the estuary for some race or other. Malo's love affair with kitesurfing appears to have cooled for the time being and he's recently put his rig on eBay, but I tell myself that one day – when the memories are less raw – I'll come back here. Pavel, bless him, once fell in love with the place. And, much, much older, so have I.

The hottest summer I can remember finally expires, and in London we all start breathing again. It's early autumn now, and I'm at home in my apartment in Holland Park when the buzzer goes. The video entry screen is in the hall. I'm looking at a tall man, probably young. He's wearing a nice coat, maybe cashmere, and he's obviously aware of the camera because he's looking up at the lens. Something about his face is familiar but at first glance I can't quite place it.

'Ms Andressen?'

'Yes.'

'My name's Stukeley. Ivan Stukeley. I think you might have known my dad.'

I'm staring at the face on the screen. Ivan Stukeley has an Australian accent but there's no mistaking the smile. Did Pavel really have a son? And if so, why didn't he tell me?

'Come in.' I press the entry release. 'Fourth floor. The door will be open.'

By the time he steps out of the lift, I've managed to compose myself. I invite him in, put his lovely coat on a hanger, make coffee. Like most Australians I've ever met, he doesn't waste time in small talk. He read news of his father's passing in a back issue of *The Times*, sent from the UK by a friend. He teaches World Literature at the University of Western Australia, in Perth, and he's here in London for an academic conference.

'How did you get my name? My address?'

'I asked around. I knew nothing about my dad until I read the obituaries. Dad's agent mentioned your name. I'm surprised she hasn't been in touch.'

'So am I.'

'You mind me being here?'

'Not at all. I'm delighted. Your dad was beyond special. I know I'll never meet anyone like him again.'

We spend the rest of the day talking. Pavel, it appears, was married to an Aussie woman he met in Edinburgh. She was a student at the university. After graduation, he followed her back to Perth, where they married. Ivan's mother was already heavily pregnant, and she gave birth two months later.

'Any brothers? Sisters?'

'None. I can't remember anything about Dad. It was like I never laid eyes on him. He'd gone, fled, before I even got to my first birthday. Maybe it was my fault. Mum had remarried by the time I got to school, and my stepdad brought me up. That was fine. I was very lucky.'

I nod. Moonie, I think, losing his dad. Deko's father killing himself under a train. And now this stranger, all that's left of Pavel, turning up on my doorstep, eager to know who brought him into the world.

I help as best I can. I tell him about our time together, about Pavel's blindness, and about the accident that broke his neck and put him in a wheelchair.

'And you nursed him through all that?'

'The paralysis, yes.'

'That makes him very lucky.'

'No.' I shake my head. 'It makes *me* very lucky.'

The conversation drifts to money. Pavel, as it turns out, was a rich man. There was no mortgage left on his Chiswick house, and his film and TV work are still producing a flood of royalties.

'We're talking at least two million,' I say, 'with more to come. If you're sole next-of-kin, you might like to have a think about that.'

'But who knows?' He's smiling. 'Who knows how many other wives he might have had?'

He's right, of course, and if I ever needed proof that this delightful academic was carrying Pavel's genes, then here it is. Because the truth is that none of us could really separate Pavel from his more baroque fantasies, and I – for one – had given up trying.

'He was a mystery,' I murmur. 'He re-wrote the script day by day, and I loved him for it.'

Ivan seems to understand that, and when I tell him that *A Day in the Life of Ivan Denisovich* was always one of Pavel's favorite reads, he seems more than pleased. Just now, he says, he's teaching a module in Twentieth Century Russian Literature, and Solzhenitsyn lies at the heart of the syllabus.

'Strange,' he says, following me into the kitchen.

I pour large gin and tonics for both of us. A cartoon is Blu-tacked to my fridge and has caught his attention. I tore it out of the *Guardian* the day they discovered the black hole in space, and it's been with me ever since, a reminder of the times we live in.

Two angels are fishing on the edge of the cosmic hole, their feet dangling over the inky darkness below. It's obviously been a slow day.

'Nothing?' asks one angel.

'Nothing,' the other confirms, 'but that's the whole point.'

Ivan, like his father would, gets it at once.

'Very funny.' He's laughing. 'But insane.'

'Exactly,' I say. 'Totally mad.'